Requiem for a Gypsy

ALSO BY THE AUTHOR

Siren of the Waters
Dark Dreams
The Magician's Accomplice

Requiem for a Gypsy

Michael Genelin

Published by
Soho Press, Inc.
853 Broadway
New York, NY 10003

Library of Congress Cataloging-in-Publication Data

Genelin, Michael.
Requiem for a gypsy / Michael Genelin.
p. cm.
HC ISBN 978-1-56947-957-5
PB ISBN 978-1-61695-160-3
eISBN 978-1-56947-958-2
1. Matinova, Jana (Fictitious character)—Fiction.
2. Police—Slovakia—Fiction. 3. Women police chiefs—Fiction.
4. Murder—Investigation—Fiction. 5. Assassination—Fiction.
6. Slovakia—Fiction. I. Title.
PS3607.E53R47 2011
813'.6—dc22
2011005709

Printed in the United States of America

10 9 8 7 6 5 4 3 2 1

To Susy, who gave me courage

Requiem for a Gypsy

The old man in the Dodgers cap walked down one of the center aisles of the Saturday outdoor market on Boulevard Richard Lenoir. It was early enough in the morning to avoid the crowd that would be there in the next hour. As always when in Paris, he visited the huge market to reexperience the sights, sounds, and smells of the city he'd first enjoyed so many years ago. It took him, for the moments he was there, out of the modern Paris that was losing so much of its character. Too much clogging motor traffic, too many fast-food chains, supermarkets, and girls in gym shoes and baggy, stained khakis—and, of course, there was the array of beggars. Outside the market, he saw the very essence of what he thought of as French coming under attack.

Here, the old Paris was still present: the merchants in their separate stalls under the canvas, the vegetable-stand staffers shouting their specials, the fishmongers extolling fresh cod and bream, the pastry and bread stands wafting their scent over the neighboring rows, competing with the bouquets of the olive stands, which boasted dozens of differently colored, sized, and seasoned olives. These, in turn, complemented and contrasted with the smell of the chickens turning on spits and sausages being stewed, fried, or roasted in the stands farther down the aisle.

The booths went on for blocks, and Pascal, as he was known in Paris, made sure to traverse the whole market, picking up tidbits from here and there to keep him in edibles for the next several days. The scene was like an old movie that had been colorized, so vividly chromatic that it made him feel as if he were inhabiting a rainbow dream made of food.

When the main body of the Saturday shoppers arrived to crowd the aisles, Pascal sighed, disappointed that his comfort time was over but ready to leave, his purchases stored in the two-wheeled shopping cart he'd bought a few days earlier. Once you get on in years, the prospect of carrying bundles in your arms, even just for the few blocks he had to walk to his apartment, becomes onerous; so he'd brought the cart, even though it was not regarded as the masculine thing to do.

Pascal crossed over to the other side of the boulevard, glancing up at the golden winged figure at the top of the monument on the former site of the Bastille, then walked the short distance around the traffic circle to Saint-Antoine, making his way from the monument toward the tourist-friendly Saint-Paul area where he had his apartment. He walked a few blocks, and then, like so many Parisians do, perceiving that it was safe to ignore the traffic light, he cut across Saint-Antoine. The old man never saw the truck that hit him. Almost the exact center of the front bumper struck Pascal, the blow scattering his cart and groceries and sending Pascal himself flying through the air, slamming through the plate glass of a bus stop, its shards raining all over the street.

Pascal was killed on impact, so many of his bones broken that he looked like a jelly-filled scarecrow when he was put into a body bag and lifted onto the coroner's gurney. The truck driver had driven on as if he hadn't just killed a pedestrian, abandoning the truck several blocks from the collision. The truck proved to be stolen, so the police could not find anyone to hold responsible, which always angers police officers. And Pascal had three separate sets of ID on his person, which made things even more troubling for them. After all, how can you notify the decedent's next of kin, or even inform his landlord, if you don't know who he was or where he lived? The problem was passed on to the detective bureau.

The detective assigned to the case sent queries out to both Europol and Interpol, transmitting photographs of the dead man, shots of several tattoos found on his body, prints taken from him in the morgue, and all the names on his IDs. Let them do their job for a change, the detective reasoned. While he waited for identification on the victim, he moved forward to his next pending case. They were all piling up, and he only had so much time to spare on any one of them.

Pascal, or what was left of him in writing, stayed on the detective's caseload for the next six months without anything being done about him. If he had still been alive, he would have approved and encouraged the lack of action. Pascal had been a man who prized anonymity; and besides, as he'd always reasoned, being dead was a plus. Nobody ever bothered you when you were gone. "Gone" was a wonderful euphemism. You were just somewhere else. So, he was not there.

Chapter 2

The discussion, if that was the word for it, had now lasted for close to two hours. The relatives of the decedent—his mother and father, an aunt, a grandmother, and two sisters, all of them gypsies—were demanding action against the killers and were not listening to Commander Jana Matinova. Their dusky skin, dark hair, deep-set eyes, and volatile hand gestures were a whirl of frustration. They had come to criticize the police for their lack of action in the teenager's death, and they were pouring out a continuous flow of angry despair. The boy had been hunting and had stumbled when climbing through a fence, shooting himself in the neck, which had abruptly ended his hunting and his life. The family members had convinced themselves that the teenager had not shot himself, but that his two companions had engaged in a conspiracy to kill him.

Jana had gone over the facts very carefully, had read the statements, the coroner's reports, and the investigator's findings. Everyone who had touched the investigation had come to the same conclusion: accidental death. The youths had had one shotgun between them, using it for alternate shots at rabbits, squirrels, and any other rodent, bird, or large insect that came their way. They had been larking around and become careless, which is always a mistake when dealing with firearms. It was not a conspiracy but certainly a tragedy, which was why Jana continued to listen attentively to everything the family said. She interrupted only to correct misstatements of fact or gross exaggerations, hoping that the family would slow their anguished outbursts to the point where they would listen to her, even for a few seconds.

Jana eventually sensed them winding down, their sighs coming less frequently, their voices becoming lackluster and falling into a lower register, their eyes growing duller. She took advantage of the moment, conveying to the family that she would consider everything they had told her, reexamine all the facts objectively, and make a judgment. She singled out the father, the head of the clan, and told him that she would call within the next few days to let him know her conclusion. The family thanked her for listening, and Jana gave the mother, the grandmother, the aunt, and the two girls individual hugs. The father vigorously shook Jana's hand, tarrying for a moment to whisper to "Madam Commander" that his son had been a good boy. Then they all filed out, trailing a small wake of tears behind them.

Jana sighed as she closed the door. It was always like that when people abruptly lost a loved one, particularly when it involved a violent ending. There was never enough satisfaction for victims in any investigation or prosecution. There was no way that any police officer could bring the dead back to life or give the relatives of the deceased anything approaching what they really wanted: to see, to hold, to kiss their loved one one more time. In that way, every case was unwinnable; the relatives always continued to mourn, and too many police officers became depressed at what they perceived as their ultimate failure: that they could not make anyone whole again.

Jana did what every cop tried to do for themselves in these situations: put the family, and the emotions that they had generated, behind her. She had just sat down at her desk, ready to leaf through the reports one last time, when Seges, her warrant officer, knocked at the door and came inside. He was carrying a small parcel in his hands.

"For you, Commander."

Jana took the parcel, noting that it had been opened. "Did you enjoy reading the material, Seges?"

"We've been told to always check for bombs in parcels, Commander Matinova."

"You thought this might be a bomb?"

"Just doing my duty, Commander."

"Was it interesting, Seges? Anything salacious inside?"

"A request from another agency, Commander. More work."

Jana slipped the materials out of the mailer box. "More work? My goodness, we may have to earn our pay." Seges was notorious for trying to avoid anything that suggested labor. "It's required on occasion, even for warrant officers, Seges."

There was a series of reports inside the package, all written in French, a number of photographs, and a cover letter in Slovak. Jana read the letter, a query from their liaison in Europol trying to determine whether a man who was the subject of a French police investigation as a victim in a crime might be identified by the Slovak police. Europol had concluded that he was a Slovak on the basis of one of the tattoos on his body. Jana examined the photographs as she talked to Seges.

"You checked the materials. Is he a Slovak?"

"The tattoo is in Slovak."

"Not the thing he would do if he were not a Slovak," Jana agreed. She looked closely at the photographs of the tattoo. It was an image with two lines of text. The inked drawing was a black ensign with a large white circle in the middle, the circle containing a single vertical stripe crossed by two parallel stripes. The stripes were vaguely similar to the double cross on the Slovak flag. The two lines of text, one above and one below the ensign, read *Nas Boj* and *Na Straz.*

These mottos, "Our Struggle" and "On Guard," had no resonance for Jana. The tattoo was different from the tattoos on the other parts of the man's body: it was quite faded and stretched out of shape. An older tattoo, Jana thought, one that had been put on his left bicep when he was very young, perhaps even when he was a small child.

She rotated the photo of the tattoo on the desk so that it faced Seges. "Recognize the symbol?"

"I've never seen it."

She rotated the photo back. Something tugged at the back of her mind as she studied it. "'On Guard.' I've heard that before."

"A fencing match?" Seges sniggered.

Jana looked up at him, sighing internally. The man would never change. "Thank you for delivering the package. I'll take care of it now."

Seges stayed where he was, his face expectant.

"Yes?" Jana began putting the papers back in their box. "You want more?" She paused, remembering what he was anticipating. "Ah, yes. Did I ask Colonel Trokan if he had approved your request for a transfer? I not only asked him, I practically begged him to approve it. He sneered at me, and then berated me for my cover letter suggesting that the request be granted. The colonel seemed to feel that I was trying to slough you off onto another supervisor. I assured him that I was." She shrugged. "I had to tell the truth. A commander does not lie to a colonel. Colonel

Trokan laughed and laughed and laughed, then told me no. 'No!' with an exclamation point. He said maybe at the end of the year. Then he laughed again. The colonel is a very cruel man."

"Yes . . ."

Jana favored Seges with a dour look. "Are you taking it upon yourself to claim that the colonel is a very cruel man? I'm entitled to say that, because I've known him so long. You, however, are not."

Seges looked like a rat caught in a trap of its own making.

"I . . . agree, Commander."

"Good." She put the package from Europol on top of the reports about the dead boy. "Have a good day, Seges."

"Thank you, Commander."

He did an about-face and left the room, leaving the door open.

"You're supposed to close the door behind you, Seges," Jana muttered to herself.

She checked her watch. She had to go home, freshen up, and get dressed to go to a party being given by one of the new breed of businessmen that the country was hell-bent on developing: high-profile figures who wanted to be international players and were determined that everybody should love and admire them for their ruthless corporate plundering. So far, at least, tonight's businessman, the larger-than-life Oto Bogan, had miraculously avoided criminal prosecution and so was still on the "we can associate with him" list for police officers.

Colonel Trokan had been pressed into going to the party by the president of police. Bogan had been a generous supporter of the minister of the interior since the time when the minister had first become a member of parliament; and because the minister was currently out of the country, the president of police had pushed Trokan to go to Bogan's party as the minister's representative.

Trokan, having long experienced men like Bogan, wanted someone to go with him so there would be a witness to everything Bogan said or did in his interactions with the colonel. It was not beyond a man like Bogan to later make ridiculous claims about having been given police promises by Trokan at the party. It would be Jana's job to refute any and all claims of special favors, or whatever problematic inventions the serpentine mind of a Bogan could come up with.

On the positive side, Colonel Trokan might be able to get in a few words with the financier about the need for police budget increments for the new community policing program, and it was possible that he could get Bogan to put in a good word with the minister about it. The man might even be persuaded, as unlikely as it seemed, to sponsor a part of the program himself. After all, he was a budding politician, and wouldn't it look good to the electorate if he contributed to a law-enforcement program?

Jana got up and stepped to the coatrack, putting on her winter jacket, and then stopped herself. She went back to her desk and pulled the photographs sent by Europol out of their box, looked at one of the multiple-angle photographs of the tattoo with the Slovak writing, then tucked the photo into a pocket. Jana thought she knew where she could get an answer to the meaning of the tattoo. While she was at it, she also decided to take the file on the youth who had shot himself. She'd promised the family to assess it. Maybe she could get out of the party early, go back home, and finish her reappraisal. The family needed closure, and it would be torture for them if she delayed her conclusions.

First, she went down to the holding cell area to look for Smid. Smid was a retired police officer who was allowed to work for part-time wages as a cellblock guard. The man's pension was miserable, so he was glad to have the job. He was old, perhaps too old for this kind of work, but even the prisoners liked him. The man was thickset and given to rolling his eyes whenever he ran into a problem, but he was also easygoing and—surprisingly for a jailer—cheerful and polite to the inmates. He was also the unofficial institutional historian for the police department. He remembered, in minute detail, everything that had happened—good, bad, and indifferent—within and to the agency over the last fifty years.

Jana found Smid in the anteroom to the cells, where he'd just sat down to eat a late meal with a prisoner.

The two men looked up, and Smid stood as Jana came in. He nudged the prisoner. "Get up. Show respect to a senior officer."

The prisoner jumped to his feet.

"Sit, both of you." Jana pushed down slightly on Smid's shoulder as both a gesture of affection and an added impetus for the man to sit. Both men sat.

"This is Yuri, Commander. He's one of the prisoners." Smid gestured at the man. "Very good with a mop. So I got him an extra meal today," he said, by way of explanation for his eating with the prisoner. "Besides, we've known each other for years."

Jana eyed the prisoner. "Too much to drink too often?" she asked.

Yuri nodded, spooning in a mouthful of food.

Smid smiled at the man's obvious enjoyment of his meal. "He doesn't say much, but he's a long-time acquaintance, and I'm so old that I'm running out of them."

Jana gave a slight assenting nod to Smid's breaking of the rules. "Sorry to interrupt your meal, Smid, but I want you to look at a photo and then tell me what you can about it."

"Sure, Commander." He wiped his hands on a napkin, pushed his nearly finished meal to one side, and gingerly took the photograph she handed him by its corners, laying it in front of himself.

"A tattoo that I think may have started out in Slovakia but that wound up on a dead man in France," Jana explained.

"One of our exports that went bad?"

Jana smiled at the joke. "Possibly."

Smid studied the photo of the tattoo for a few moments and then nodded, looking up. "I recognize it." Smid's tone carried a sense of pride. "I always come through."

"Tell me."

"The Hlinka Guard. Second World War, under Tiso. Their salute was the same as the Nazis', only the Hlinkas said *Na Straz* instead of *Heil*. The Nas Boj faction of the Guard was the worst of the worst. Ugly men. They operated under the SS and murdered anyone they could, given half an excuse. The Nas Boj led the roundups of the partisans and Jews and gypsies, all the while stealing everything they could get their hands on for themselves. Criminals; all of them murderers and thieves. Estates, jewels, money, gold . . . and women."

He looked more closely at the photograph. "I didn't know any were still around. Most of them were killed by the Russians. Some of them on the Eastern Front. More at the time of the occupation. Others fled with the Nazis when they retreated. They didn't survive either. Well, a couple of them here and there." He looked up at Jana. "He also could have been one of their children. A number of the creatures were so proud of their nastiness that they had their own babies tattooed. As the old saying goes, 'Like father, like son.'"

He handed the photo of the tattoo back to Jana. "Did you get this man's name?"

"They didn't know it."

"When I said they were thieves, I wasn't joking. The few that did survive were known to continue practicing their criminal professions after the war. I had some of them in here. Check the records in the old files. We logged them."

"You and your son want to earn a few euros?"

Smid knew the old records like no one else. He'd even trained his son, now the proprietor of an old and rare stamp shop. Lawyers, prosecutors, private counsel, or the department itself would occasionally pay the duo to go through the voluminous non-computerized portion of the police records to find the odd bit of information that was needed in a case.

"My son can use it more than I can, but what the hell? It's fun working together with him, so why not?"

"I'll approve it."

"Three days' work," Smid suggested.

"I know the two of you. No extra day; no extra money. All you get is one day."

"Two days."

"A day and a half," Jana countered.

"Done."

She dropped the photograph in front of him.

"Thank you, Smid."

Jana turned to go.

"If anything's there, I'll find it," he called after her.

"I know you will."

She walked out.

Chapter 3

The financier Oto Bogan's party was a high-profile affair for Slovakia, ostensibly put on to celebrate Bogan's name day; but its real purpose was to flaunt his most recent acquisition, a small bank in Vienna, as well as to show off his growing international celebrity status. All the invitations for the gala carried the logo of the bank.

The party was also about Bogan's own flirtation with a political life. He had been floating the idea of a future run for a parliamentary seat. The coverage of the social event would keep the potential voters enthralled and bring into his ambit people who might consider involving themselves with him politically.

His wife owned the only movie studio in Slovakia, a gift to her from Bogan, a rather dilapidated facility with two small soundstages on the edge of Bratislava. It was used, on rare occasions, by foreign film companies; but for the last year it had lain dormant, somewhat to the chagrin of Mrs. Bogan, who thought she'd be getting additional cash flow to make her husband an even larger force in national politics.

The party was taking place in the smaller of the soundstages. The front of the building had been painted, but that hadn't done much to make the building look like anything but what it was: a vaguely forbidding cracked-stucco box enclosing an uninviting interior. To try to cover up the drabness, balloons and ribbons had been strung inside the barn-like structure. A band was playing at one end. A dance floor, especially laid down for the party, was filled with couples; tables laden with food and bottles of cheap champagne occupied the other end of the stage.

The one thing Slovaks cannot resist is a free meal with wine and music, so they had come in droves. Jana had arrived as late as she could without risking getting anyone angry at her tardiness.

She had, as Trokan insisted, come in her dress uniform, to "wave the flag" of the police, entering the soundstage with a great deal of misgiving. Jana disliked this kind of event and knew she was going to be both bored and angry with herself by the end of the evening. She didn't like being a functionary with no substantial purpose except as a spear-carrier in a soap opera.

Jana put on her best face, the pleasant, nonthreatening "how can I help you" civil servant face, and consoled herself with the thought that the colonel was going to be suffering along with her. She looked for Trokan, hoping he was already with Bogan so that they could get on with their business and then leave the event as quickly and gracefully as possible. She pushed through the crowd, people moving out of her way as soon as they saw her uniform. She greeted the people she recognized, all the while hoping to spot the colonel. Ahead, she saw Bogan dressed in a tuxedo, surrounded by well-wishers, everyone trying to get their few seconds with him, all of them faithful followers or wannabes.

Trokan was not in the group. Jana began to rove through the crowd in increasingly wider circles, trying to find him. She saw a former friend who was now a legislator, and the two of them nodded as they passed, neither of them wanting to pick up a conversation—or the friendship. She noticed a short man, rather garishly dressed, whom she'd put in prison a few years before, apparently now released and sufficiently rehabilitated to be invited to a political hopeful's party. The man saw her, fear distorting his mouth before he quickly looked away. It aroused her police instincts. Perhaps the man had obtained entry with a stolen invitation? No, she told herself. He wouldn't be stupid enough to advertise his presence in such attention-grabbing clothes if that were the case. Besides, she thought, rejecting her impulse to confront him, she was present tonight merely for show, rather than as a police officer on duty. She moved on.

Jana continued to recognize others, but still no Trokan. She decided to have a glass of champagne. She eased her way over to the drinks table, where a bartender was pouring plastic flutes of champagne and setting them on the table for the guests to help themselves. She took one of the flutes, then turned and surveyed the room. It was rapidly becoming more crowded, to the point that there was very little room for people to move without treading on some other guest's toes. She caught a glimpse of someone across the room, a slender man with an erect, alert posture. She saw him only for an instant before he was concealed by the shifting groups of people between them. Seeing the man gave her a shock. If he was who she thought he was, she had a right to be shocked.

Jana began shouldering her way through the intervening crowd. People reluctantly moved aside, giving her withering stares for ignoring party etiquette by being so aggressive, the most aggrieved throwing out angry comments behind her. After skirting the dance floor, she could no longer see the man. Jana grabbed a chair that had just been vacated by a woman going to the dance floor and stood on it, peering over the crowd. She spotted the man's head wedging through the swell of people, moving toward the large front doors. Even though she could not see his face, she was more convinced than ever that it was him. Jana jumped off the chair and began weaving through the crowd more aggressively than before, angling toward the front doors. The man was now clearly in sight as he went through them. Thirty seconds later, Jana cut through the same exit.

She glimpsed his head inside the right rear of a black sedan as it drove off. It had to be him. Jana started to run after the vehicle, but there was no way she could have caught up with it. She stopped just as Trokan drove up, parking in a spot reserved for him near the door. He got out, looking smart in his dress uniform, and stood still, watching her. Jana tried to cover her frustration at not being able to stop the man in the sedan and confirm his identity. Taking a deep breath, she walked over to Trokan, pasted a genial expression on her face, and gestured at the façade of the soundstage.

"Bogan's had the front painted and left the other sides drab, peeling and ugly."

Trokan grimaced, checking out the building.

"A Potemkin palace. Just the façade prettied up. Very Slavic. And still drab." The colonel looked back at Jana. "You seemed about to chase after that car. Remember, you're a commander. Commanders don't give out traffic citations." He laughed uproariously at his own joke, taking off his greatcoat and folding it over his arm. "You think you can catch the car, just go right ahead."

"I believe it was Makine. He was at the party."

Trokan was visibly jolted by the news.

"Are we talking about the Makine who is also called Koba? The criminal Makine? The murderer Makine?"

He reflected on the possibility. "I find it difficult to conceive of Makine coming to this party. Wanted men generally like to keep low profiles."

"I know what Makine looks like."

"You're absolutely sure that it was him?"

"I only caught a glimpse of his face, but for me it was enough."

"So we think it was him, but there's a doubt."

Jana hesitated. ". . . Yes."

"Brief looks and questionable identifications aren't enough to start a general manhunt." He eyed her. "You really believe you saw the man in the flesh?"

"I do."

"Okay." He paused, looking uneasy. "When was the last time one police agency or another reported him dead?"

"A year and a half ago. In Belarus. He was reported cornered in a building. There was a shoot-out. They hit the structure with a pair of shoulder rockets. It started a fire. Afterward, there was half a body found. Nothing really positive on the ID of the corpse, only the word of an informant who led them to the location. He collected a reward."

"How many times has our friend Makine/Koba been pronounced deceased?"

"Eight or nine times, maybe more. But, he always turns up alive. We should act on this."

Trokan considered what to do. He knew that Matinova was rarely wrong. However, starting a massive search on the basis of split-second recognition was not practical. He decided to compromise.

"Put out a bulletin on the man. Say he is *reported* to be in Slovakia, possibly in Bratislava. It will at least alert the street cops."

"Koba has to be after something that's worth the risk of

showing his face at a gala in Bratislava. He's obviously into something important."

"If he's here," Trokan reminded her.

"He's a risk-taker. It's the kind of thing he'd do for a sufficient payoff."

"Maybe." Trokan shrugged. "Who knows what goes on in this crazy world, particularly in his mind?" He walked toward the entrance, Jana falling into step with him. "Everything *we* do has a touch of insanity in it, and he's even more insane than we are." They went inside, the sound of the party hitting them suddenly. "Lots of people. It must have cost a treasure chest full of money."

"Bogan has enough."

"Never. Rich people always want more. Where is he?"

"The man is holding court on the other side of the room."

They began their effort to get through the crowd.

"I want to check with my sources on what they have on Koba being in Slovakia," Jana said. "Any problems with that?"

Trokan shrugged again. "If you want to make more work for yourself, that's your business. As usual, keep me apprised."

He glanced at Jana, noting her sober expression. "When we meet Bogan, for God's sake, put a smile on your face. Hang on his every word. Use the feminine wiles that all you sisters are so famous for. I want him to talk to the minister about how much he likes our community policing concept. Perhaps we can even suggest that Bogan supply the department with a small gift of capital that we need for opening that community storefront as a real program. Right now it's just a proposal on a piece of paper. So, show your pearly white teeth."

"I'm a police officer. Police officers aren't supposed to smile, and I'm certainly not good at seducing businessmen."

"Try, Matinova!"

"Yes, Colonel."

They got to the edge of the group clustered around Bogan. The colonel, as politely as possible, edged his way through with Jana following until the two of them finally reached Bogan. As soon as he saw them, his face lit up. He took a step toward them and shook the colonel's hand.

"Congratulations on your name day," Trokan told him.

The financier swung to Jana, shaking her hand as well.

"Best wishes, Mr. Bogan," Jana got out.

"Did you know that my name day is the same as . . . ?" He tried to think of the man and failed. "Too much to drink," he apologized. "I'm doubly celebrating, for both him and me." He cackled at his joke. "My wife, who is somewhere back there . . ." Bogan waved toward the rear of the room. "She says that I'm doubly lucky, not only because the name days coincided, but because I also have her." He pointed to an area up in the rafters. A banner hanging from a large crossbeam read: KLARA IS MY DOUBLE LUCK.

The financier laughed again. "She loved seeing her name hanging in the rafters." He took both Jana and the colonel by the arm, excusing himself from the group around him by citing the need to talk about police business, and walked them some distance away to a small space behind one of the food tables so they could talk with a degree of privacy. The colonel had barely started in on his speech about the virtues of the new community policing program when Bogan's wife, an extravagantly dressed full-figured woman with an air of aggressive sexuality, came bustling up.

"Oto." She kissed Bogan on the cheek. "I think everything is going splendidly, don't you?" She was wearing a flowing evening gown with a large rope of semiprecious stones plunging into extreme décolletage. "It's time for the cake, and then we'll all sing, and everyone will be very happy for you, particularly me, and we will have started you on your way to becoming the newest member of parliament," she said in a single breath. Hardly pausing to inhale, she patted Trokan on the shoulder, deliberately ignoring Jana, and then continued talking. "I'm so glad to see you, Colonel Trokan. I trust you're here to respond to the death threat against my husband."

Trokan looked from Klara to her husband, then back again. "I haven't heard about any death threat against your husband, Mrs. Bogan."

"I was just going to tell him, Klara." Bogan put a hand on his wife's shoulder in reassurance, turning to Trokan. "I was informed a short time ago that a story is circulating that I'm about to be assassinated. Why would anyone want to assassinate me, you ask? I haven't the vaguest idea."

"Some people just don't like famous and powerful men, darling," Klara said. "So, Colonel Trokan, what are you going to do about protecting my husband?"

"This was not a joke, Mr. Bogan?" the colonel asked.

"I didn't think so," said Klara, a slight tone of offense in her voice as she answered for her husband. "My husband and I were shocked."

"I am a little concerned," Bogan admitted.

"Of course you are, darling." Klara stroked her husband's arm. "*I* certainly am."

"Who told you that you were being targeted, Mr. Bogan?" the colonel asked.

When Bogan hesitated, Jana chimed in. "Were you given any specifics, Mr. Bogan?"

There was a sudden fanfare from the band, then a long drumroll. The lights in the massive room blinked on and off. Finally, a spotlight swept over the guests and came to rest on a huge multitiered birthday cake being towed into the room by a small tractor. A second spotlight found Bogan and his wife. The guests applauded, and Bogan waved to the darkened audience. Klara pulled him by the sleeve, laughingly towing him through the crowd toward the cake. People clapped him on the back, and both husband and wife shook hands with friends and acquaintances as they passed, the spotlight staying on them the whole time.

"For a man who has been told that he may be assassinated, he doesn't seem to mind walking under a spotlight," Jana ventured.

Trokan grimaced. "The wife will blame it on us if it happens. So will everyone else."

"Of course."

They exchanged glances, knowing what they had to do, and they began moving after the Bogans, gaining ground on them thanks to all the well-wishers slowing the Bogans down.

"They're not going to like it if we pull the name-day boy out of his dream life," Trokan muttered.

"It'll be worse if we have to cart his body out of here."

"Go easy when we get to him."

"They won't go easy."

"We act like we're his bodyguards, the prow of a ship moving them through this sea of people," Trokan said.

"Very poetic, but not very effective. It won't work."

They caught up with Bogan and his wife. The colonel leaned toward Bogan. "If you're the target of an assassination attempt, putting yourself in the spotlight is very brave, but not very smart."

Bogan shrugged. "I'm trying not to believe it. Who comes to a man's celebration to murder him?"

"If I were going to kill you, this would be a perfect place to do it," the colonel snapped.

Jana edged closer to Bogan. "All that we ask is that you

keep a low profile until we find out what's happening."
She waved around them at the intense luminescence.
"And get out of this spotlight."

"This isn't the night for me to keep a low profile,"
Bogan muttered between smiles to his guests.

"This is Oto's night," his wife said. "You can protect
him later."

They neared the cake, the spotlight they were moving
in about to merge with the floodlight around the huge
iced confection.

"You're one very large target when you stop moving.
You'll be lit up like a supernova, perfect game for a
shooter," Trokan warned, his tone becoming more urgent.

"Oto *is* a supernova," said Klara.

"I always listen to my wife." Bogan leaned over to kiss
her as they continued, leading to cheers and more applause
from the onlookers. "You see how they love her?"

Jana's instincts were on full alert, roaring at her to take
action, telling her that despite the lack of concrete evidence,
there was going to be an attempt on Bogan's life any minute
now. She looked just ahead of them. If there was going to
be an assassination try, it would be made shortly after the
two circles of light joined when Bogan presented himself in
all his vulnerable glory. She leaned toward Trokan.

"We have to keep him out of there, Colonel."

"The name-day boy is not going to be dissuaded."

"A little force might discourage him."

"I love the fact that you're directing your colonel to
get on the bad side of one of the chief supporters of his
minister by making a stupid move."

"We're saving a life."

"Maybe . . ."

"Given time, he'll thank us."

"Never. People like that don't ever thank anybody. They're chosen by God."

"We didn't join the police to be liked."

"Thank you for the reminder, Jana."

Everyone in the huge room was now moving toward the joining spotlights, both officers fighting to maintain their position, forced to push through the throng of people getting in their way.

Just as Bogan reached the center of the merged spotlights, Trokan and Jana lunged into him, the force of their weight pressing him down and to one side. Bogan let out a bellow of protest, but it was submerged almost immediately by a series of shots. Trokan was bludgeoned to one side by the force of two bullets striking him; Klara, also shot, was dead before she hit the floor. Jana climbed on top of Bogan, trying to shield him with her body. Pulling out her automatic, she tried to determine where the shooter was so she could get a shot off at him and stop him from targeting Bogan again.

The crowd erupted in fear, people screaming, trying to get away, clambering over each other in the dark, fighting to clear a path for themselves, clawing at anyone who got in their way. Men and women fell to the floor, trampled in the rush. There was a moment of additional shock when the lights came back on and the general carnage became visible. The crowd froze for a second, and then the panicked exodus began again, this time with more purpose.

Within minutes, the huge soundstage floor had emptied, leaving just the people who had been trampled and those who had been shot. The stage floor looked like a film set arranged as the aftermath of a battle in which the combat had been one-sided, the wounded and dead littering the ground, the sound of sobbing heard somewhere offscreen.

Chapter 4

Trokan was out of the hospital after a week, conva-
lesced at home for another two weeks while slowly
going crazy, then decided that his "recuperation" had
gone on long enough—despite the doctor's orders—and
went to work. His wife was glad to see him go, and he
was even happier to see her disappear behind his front
door as he was driven to the office. They made each other
angry and anxious when they were together and less angry
and less anxious when they were apart, so they welcomed
separation. It was as if a burden had been lifted.

The colonel's office had been decorated with a large
welcome sign, and the heads of various divisions were
waiting for him when he arrived. The welcome-back celebration ended when Trokan growled that all of them still
had the business of crime to attend to. Everyone quickly
evacuated the room. Trokan eased his sling around to
one side so he could sit without bumping his arm and
shoulder, then immediately telephoned Jana Matinova.
Jana had been conspicuously absent during the brief celebration of his survival. She was in his office five minutes
later, laying a small pastry container on his desk before
sitting down. He gave her a jaundiced look. "Bullets aren't
enough? You're trying to kill me with sweets."

He undid the small ribbon around the box and opened

the top. There were two pastries inside, along with a distorted bullet round sitting on top of one of them. He laid the spent slug next to the box, then handed her one of the pastries, taking the second one for himself. They both took bites of their confections, quietly chewing as they enjoyed a peaceful moment together.

Trokan's voice was slightly accusing. "You didn't come to the welcome-back party."

"I decided not to show up. You can't have personal moments at parties."

"True."

"How are you feeling?"

"Better."

"The shoulder?"

"Getting there. The X-rays showed that the doctors lined up the bone properly. The bone ends are together, giving it the right length, so I'm fine. Except the pins give me aches and pains when it's going to rain."

"You can hire yourself out to the weather people. Extra income."

"I don't need the money that badly." He smiled. "The metal comes out in maybe a month and a half."

"And your side?"

"That aches without pins." He picked up the spent bullet and rolled it around in his hand. "They told me they gave you the slug they dug out of the bone cavity. I take it this is the little beast?"

"I thought you might want to put it on a key chain. Perhaps have it mounted?"

"Did you do ballistics on it?"

"Too distorted. Nothing except the probable caliber. We couldn't find the other bullet that went in your side. It was a through-and-through wound, so we figured the stampeding crowd must have swept it somewhere along with them."

He nodded, looking the slug over once again. "Thank you for the memento." He opened a drawer in his desk and put the bullet inside. "The next time you suggest we do something impetuous, I'll open the drawer, look at the bullet, and be able to tell you no."

They each took another bite out of their pastries. Trokan talked while slowly chewing on the small piece he'd bitten off. "The minister put you up for a medal. It was the photograph in the newspaper of you protecting Bogan with your body that did it. You are now the Saint Joan of Arc of Slovakia."

"I don't quite picture myself as a saint."

"Neither do I."

"Good."

"Update me on the case."

"You'll have to ask the special investigations group that's looking into the shooting." Jana made sure that her tone conveyed her displeasure. "I'm a victim and a witness, so they've left me out of the loop."

"Bad decision." He thought about it. "I haven't seen anything about Bogan in the news since his wife's funeral. The media had their fun with it. Then they moved the event to the second page; then smaller and smaller follow-up stories." His voice took on a quizzical resonance. "I expected more noise and fury from the man."

"Bogan's gone to ground. He's in a burrow somewhere."

"Do we have anything at all on the killers?"

"I told you, I'm not in the loop."

"Then get in the loop. Find out."

"Everybody's informed me, not so very kindly, that I'm to stay away from the investigation. Maybe they think I'm angry because the shooting took place right under my nose. Maybe they think I was careless. Perhaps they think I'm going to be raging around, stepping on people's toes?"

He considered what she'd said. "Maybe nobody wants to associate with Saint Joan of Arc." He drummed his fingers on his desk in irritation. "We both realize that you and I couldn't stay away from this investigation if our lives depended on it. And for all we know, they may. We *think* the target was Bogan. We *think* our actions in pulling him out of the line of fire saved his life. We *think* I was shot—twice, mind you—because I stepped into the line of fire. But I want to *know*. And I've decided it's your job to find out."

"I have my division to supervise."

"Handle it."

"I'm to ignore what the president of police has ordered? And the minister?"

Trokan hesitated. "Yes."

Jana smiled. "If I disobey them, I may not get my medal."

"Is the medal that important?"

"No."

"Did you get a bulletin out on the possible sighting of Koba?"

"Yes."

"You think he was involved in the shootings?"

"I find it hard to believe that—if he was there—he had nothing to do with the events of the evening."

"Maybe you didn't really see him."

"You said that before."

"So I did."

They munched on their confections for a while longer. Finally, Jana took the remainder of her pastry and dropped it into a trash can.

"Too much butter and fat in that thing," she pronounced.

Trokan's face took on a slightly mocking look. "Exert yourself more. It will take off the extra ounces."

"Sweets are for colonels. Time for me to pay attention to business."

"Good."

"Watch my back if I step on anyone's toes."

"And you be circumspect and subtle, and try not to offend the wrong people."

"Impossible."

"I know." He finished his pastry. "Thanks for the special welcome."

"Glad you're back, Colonel."

"So am I."

Jana walked out of the office. Trokan waited a moment, then opened the desk drawer containing the bullet and pulled it out.

"You are a miserable little shit," he said, examining the slug. Then he held it by two fingers, as if it were a dead bug, and dropped it back in the drawer. "I hope you're afraid of the dark."

He closed the drawer with a satisfying thump.

Chapter 5

J ana went to the soundstage. She had called ahead, so the watchman was at the main entrance to let her in. He unlocked the two built-in locks and a padlock that was on the door, hustling in ahead of her to turn on the lights. They came on with an audible thunk, revealing the remnants of the party still in place in the huge room. The trays of food and the unopened bottles had been removed, but the tables were still set, covered with dirty linen, empty and overturned glasses and bottles strewn around. The bunting and signs hadn't been removed, although the one praising Mrs. Bogan was now hanging from one end. Scraps of various kinds littered the unswept floor, and chairs and service tables were askew all over the room. Prominent in the middle of it all was Bogan's huge ruined name-day cake.

The watchman waited by the entrance as Jana walked around the room, first studying the small catwalks above. The gunmen had to have been up there, their line of fire unobstructed by the crowd of people. It would have been a clear, relatively easy shot to get Bogan. Jana turned back to the watchman.

"How do you get up to the catwalk?"

He pointed to a curtained alcove highlighted by a NO EXIT sign in the corner of the soundstage. "There."

Jana strode to the exit and went through the curtain. A metal stairway led upstairs to the rafters. Jana took the stairs two at a time, quickly reaching the catwalk above. From there, the whole soundstage could be seen without obstruction. She began walking around the catwalk, circling the room, studying the floor below as well as the catwalk itself.

Then she stopped, the glint of a metal object in one of the braces that supported the catwalk catching her eye. Jana reached into the brace and pulled out a shell casing. She checked it, noted the caliber, and then smelled the front of the casing. It still carried the acrid smell of expended gunpowder. Jana put the shell casing in her pocket and continued her catwalk trip around the interior of the building, eventually returning to the area near the stairs where she had begun.

She surveyed the huge room again, remembering the mass of people that had occupied it, all of them gathered to celebrate the hubris of Bogan and his wife. It reminded her of *Richard III*, the play she'd seen the week before at the National Theater. It was all about people's ambition, pride, jealousy, greed, lust, willingness to do anything and everything to achieve their goals—all universal sins no matter what language they're in. And the title characters who display those attributes in both fiction and real life usually wind up dead. Mr. Bogan had just survived his brush with the grim reaper; his wife Klara had not.

"A horse! A horse! My kingdom for a horse!" King Richard had screamed, trying to save himself while locked in combat. The line echoed in Jana's mind as she looked over the "battlefield" below her, but the words were transmuted to "A gun! A gun! My kingdom for a gun!" Where was the gun that had been used in the shootings?

Jana put herself in the killer's place. Any competent

would-be murderer had to know that a pistol would not have done the job, given the distance between assassin and victim. It was a long shot from the catwalk down and across the room. The murder weapon of choice in this building, and with that crowd, would be a semiautomatic rifle with a telescopic sight. Jana was off the case; but given her position in the police department, she would assuredly have known if the murder weapon had been found and sent to the forensics laboratory for analysis.

A rifle could have been broken down and hidden under an overcoat, or perhaps in a carryall, when the shooter had completed his attack. Except that there would have been very little time for a murderer to break his rifle down into its component parts after the shooting, particularly in the dark. And all the assassin would have been thinking about immediately after the shooting was how vulnerable he was up here on the exposed catwalk. He'd want to flee as quickly as possible. The killer had to have done something else with the gun.

A short distance from where Jana now stood was a door leading off the catwalk and out of the building. There was obviously a stairway on the outside of the structure. She went over to the door and examined the lock. It was a standard built-in key lock that bolted inside to the surrounding door frame. Jana tried to open it. It was solidly fitted and secured.

Jana ran through the scenario of the shooter's escape. Rifles are bulky. They're not an item you want to carry when you're running. In this case, no matter which way the gunman had fled, he wouldn't have escaped unnoticed if he'd been carrying a rifle. As a hypothetical, Jana first tried assuming that the man had run down the stairs from the catwalk and into the crowd below, mixing with the people streaming through the exits. Jana took a deep breath and rejected the hypothesis. If he'd been carrying a rifle, the man would have been apprehended. That night, after the shooting, when Jana had been there with the other police who had come to the scene after the killing, there were no reports by anyone of men seen fleeing with guns. No question: the man had fled down the outside stairs leading from the catwalk. A point of evidence against that hypothesis, however, was the fact that the door leading directly to the outside—and to the ground below—was locked.

Did that mean the gunman had used a key? And where was the rifle?

Jana went downstairs and walked to the area where Mrs. Bogan had been shot. The vague chalk outline where her body had fallen was still there. Blood had stained the floor both where she had been killed and where Colonel Trokan had dropped to the ground after being shot. Jana looked back at the catwalk where she'd found the shell casing. The positioning of the bodies in relation to the angle of fire bothered her.

Jana eyed the ruined cake. She could use that as a fixed position to orient herself in relation to the events that had occurred on the night of the killing. She measured the distance from the cake to the area where she had pulled Bogan down. In her mind, Jana saw the colonel being hit. Two bullets in him; two in Mrs. Bogan. Jana mentally marked off the distance between the spot where they must have pulled Bogan down and the chalk outline that showed where Klara had fallen. She looked at the position of the cake again to be sure of her estimate of the other positions.

It was impossible for Klara Boganova and Colonel Trokan to have been hit by the same shooter at the same time.

Even allowing a second or two between the shots, one man would have to have been a magician to have hit them both. But had there even been that much time between them? Jana thought back to the moment of the shootings, focusing on the sound itself. The sound of the shots had of course been distorted by the size of the room, the noise created by the mass of people, the playing of the orchestra, and her own focus on saving Bogan. But even taking these things into account, she remembered that the shots had almost overlapped each other. That reconfirmed her prior conclusion: there had to have been at least two shooters.

Jana checked the distance between the bodies again and noticed something even odder: Klara had clearly been several feet in front of her husband when the shots were fired. The newspapers had implied that Klara had been hit by shots intended for her husband. Jana had thought the same thing. But the physical evidence refuted that conclusion.

The colonel had taken the bullets probably intended for Bogan when they pulled him down. But, given the victims' positions, the shots that killed Klara could not have been aimed at Bogan. It looked very much like the shooters had been trying to get two people and had succeeded in getting one of them: Klara. She had been a primary target for the shooters—perhaps even *the* primary target.

Jana walked to the exit, turning to take a last look at the soundstage. A stray frivolous thought went through her mind: the case involving the Bogans was now unquestionably more interesting than any movie that had ever been filmed on this soundstage.

Jana exited the building, the watchman trailing after her, leaving the lights on in case she wanted to come back inside. Jana walked to the side of the building that the door from the catwalk led to. A metal staircase ran up to the door. Jana climbed it. It was locked from the outside as well. She examined the lock for any marks that would indicate it had ever been forced open. There were none.

She went back down the stairs, the watchman staring at her from below. Near him, attached to the building at ground level, was a large fuse-and-switch box for the high-intensity lights used in the soundstage. There was no lock on it. Jana opened both of its doors. There was a board inside containing the electrical gauges, switches, and fuses that one would expect in this type of container. There were no guns.

Jana started to close the fuse box, but then noticed an oddity about the gauges: they weren't reflecting even the slightest movement. The needles on the dials were absolutely still. Not even a flicker. The watchman had left the lights on inside: that should have been registering on the gauges. If the gauges were not connected, the board was not functioning.

Jana examined the board and then pushed on it. It gave slightly. She pushed harder, and the whole panel shifted. Jana gripped its upper edge and pulled as hard as she could. The panel suddenly gave way and fell to the ground.

It was a false front.

Tucked neatly inside were two rifles.

Chapter 6

J ana drove to the attorney general's office on Kapunska. The SID unit investigating the Bogan shooting had been moved over to offices near the prosecutors, so they could work together on developing a thorough investigation leading to a successful prosecution. Unfortunately, no perpetrators had been charged as yet. Worse, as far as Jana knew, there were not even any suspects.

She walked into the building carrying the rifles wrapped in heavy brown paper slung over her shoulder in carriers, flashed her credentials at the guards, then turned toward the east wing of the building and went up the stairs to the floor that housed the special investigations group. The secretary immediately recognized Jana when she entered the office, and a worried expression washed over her face. Her expression got even more worried when she noticed the rifles that Jana was carrying.

"Commander," the woman greeted her. She immediately called the inner office and announced, "The commander is here," without indicating which commander it was, assuming the call's recipient would know. The inner door opened, and Investigator Jakus came out.

"Good afternoon, Commander," he said, his voice naturally raspy.

"Hello, Jakus."

Jana had never been fond of Jakus, who had worked with her for a while. He'd transferred out of her division a year ago. The man had a web of influential relatives who were always pushing the administration to give him better jobs and to promote him. That was probably the reason he had been placed in charge of the police investigation of the Bogan shooting. He was a decent investigator, although uninspired in his approach to cases, taking them from one precise step to the next, never making the evidence-based leaps of imagination that so often propelled difficult cases to successful conclusions.

Jakus looked nervous, unsure of what he should make of her visit. Or of the guns she was carrying.

"I'd invite you inside, Commander, but I've got strict orders to maintain confidentiality in the investigation, and I have all kinds of exhibits exposed on the boards, so . . ." He brightened slightly. "If you'd like to talk, we can talk out here. What was it you wanted?" He eyed the rifles but was too insecure to ask about them.

"An update on the case, Jakus."

"Since you're a witness, Commander, I've been instructed to keep you away from the investigation. Your testimony might be distorted by seeing the other evidence we've found."

Jana stared at him, not liking what she had just heard. "Have you found something? A piece of evidence that has led you to the shooters? Perhaps a motive? Or, even more startling, you've found that Bogan's wife arranged the whole thing to exploit the movie-studio setting and leave behind her a legacy of one of the most dramatic events ever to have taken place in Slovakia?"

Jakus stared at her, his mouth slightly open, wondering how he should respond.

"I went to the soundstage where the shootings took

place," Jana told him. She reached into her pocket and pulled out the shell casing she'd discovered. "I found this on the balcony where our shooters fired. It was in one of the support braces. Do you want me to mark the location on the scene schematic you've done?"

She tossed the shell to Jakus. He looked at it for a moment, agonizing over what to do, then finally nodded. "I suppose it would be better if you indicated the exact position of the casing on the chart." He opened the door of his office wide enough for her to go inside.

The office had two desks and a long side table. There were corkboards on three of the four walls and a movable chalkboard in front of the other wall. The chalkboard had the names of the guests at Bogan's party written on it. They were arranged alphabetically, and most of them were crossed out. Two of the corkboards were covered with photographs of the crime scene; the deceased woman, both in life and from various angles in death; the colonel lying on the floor with the EMT response team working on him; victims of the stampede following the shooting; even several of Jana, her arm around a shaken and crying Bogan as he tried to come to terms with the events.

The last corkboard held a massive graphic of the entire floor of the soundstage, along with an auxiliary inset of the catwalk running around it. There were all kinds of notations on the graphic, indicating the positions of the bodies, including both Bogans, the colonel, and Jana; the celebration cake; the places where the victims of the human stampede had fallen; the possible locations of the shooters; and the possible trajectories of the shots.

Pinned to the upper right-hand corner of the board was a smaller schematic of the locations where the shell casings ejected from the rifles that had targeted the Bogans had been found. Jana took her time looking over the items in the room, then walked to the corkboard containing the shell-casing schematic and quickly x-ed the location where she had found the casing, initialing it.

"Two guns, right?" she asked, turning to Jakus.

He hesitated, staring at the rifles she was carrying, then nodded.

"Professional assassins." She slowly walked around the office, looking at the items posted on the other boards. "Lots of work to do here."

"Yes."

She stopped, and looked directly at Jakus.

"You have nothing, right?"

He managed a reluctant head bob to indicate that Jana was correct in her assessment.

"Sorry to hear that. If I can be of any help, feel free to call on me." She started out of the office, and then momentarily turned back. "The prosecutor who has been assigned to the case: what office is she in?"

"Prosecutor Truchanova is two doors down," he managed after a pause.

"Thank you. Nothing for you to worry over. I simply want to talk to her." Jana half turned as if to leave again, then stopped. Jakus was staring at the wrapped rifles. Time to ease the man's misery, Jana thought, even if just a little. "Yes, *the* rifles, Jakus. I'll leave them with the prosecutor after I'm through."

Jana stepped out of the inner office, nodded at the secretary as she passed, went down the corridor to the prosecutor's office, and entered. The door to the inner office was open, the woman's secretary inside, poised to take dictation, waiting for the prosecutor to get off the phone. The prosecutor glanced up to see Jana walking into her office.

"She's just come in," Truchanova nodded as she spoke

into the phone. "Yes, I'll take possession of the guns." She hung up, waved the secretary out of the office, and motioned at one of the chairs to indicate that Jana should sit. She watched as Jana set the guns gently down on the floor, and then waited for her to get comfortable. Truchanova was older than Jana, evidently reaching that age when women start using a little too much makeup to conceal the aging process and often dress slightly too youthfully for their unwanted maturity. However, that didn't affect her competence. Truchanova was still very ambitious and bright enough to do her job well.

"Thank you for the visit, Commander Matinova. That was Jakus on the line. A little excited. You've found the guns in the Bogan killing?"

"More than likely. Ballistics will have to confirm it." Jana flicked a plastic bag she had attached to one of the rifle carriers. "I also found two pairs of surgical gloves in the same hidey-hole as the rifles. Thin plastic so the shooters could still feel the trigger and get off accurate shots without leaving prints on the weapons. Leaving the gloves may have been a mistake: there could be prints inside the glove fingers, although they're probably smeared from the finger movement. Even so, we might get enough of a print to match it."

"I'll see to it." Truchanova eyed Jana, wondering why she had chosen to turn the guns over to her rather than just giving them to Jakus. "You have more?"

"I want something in return for my good deed." Jana's voice was quiet, but assured. "I need access to the ongoing investigation."

"You've been barred from the probe because you're already a major witness on the case. It's not good to have a major witness investigating a case."

"Every police officer on every case becomes, at some

point, a material witness. That doesn't stop them from going forward with the investigation."

Truchanova winced at the truth of the observation. To justify her position, she tried a slightly different approach.

"We're doing it because of the high-profile aspects of the case. We keep you free of any suggestion that you're compromised in any way by exposure to any evidence we subsequently find. This way, there can't be any subsequent charges that you've distorted the rest of the investigation. Or the prosecution."

Jana waved this argument away. "Madam Truchanova, let's face it: you need another pair of eyes on the case. The way the investigation has been proceeding isn't working. There isn't criticism coming your way yet; but soon, we both know, there will be. No results, no case; no glory, no job. I simply want to save the rest of your professional life. My first effort toward that end is my gift of the rifles."

The two women stared at each other, Jana smiling at Truchanova, trying to give her additional assurance. "I'm not looking to be in front of the cameras. I take a bad picture." She waited for the other woman to say something, then went on when the prosecutor remained silent. "My promise is that I'll take no overt part in the investigation. I'll pass on everything to you; then you go forward as any prosecutor would in constructing a case. If I discover evidence, you get it, along with the right to do with it what you feel is strategically necessary. I'll stay out of the picture. No one has to know, until I testify, of my new involvement." Jana tapped the guns with a finger. "My second contribution to this agreement: the guns will be clean, but there are two bullets in the clip on one of them. I've left them there. Shooters sometimes forget when they're loading guns that the bullets also take prints."

Truchanova's face had taken on a slightly avid look. She liked the evidence she'd been given. "Where were the guns?"

"In an outside fake electrical box, down the stairs that led from the catwalk, where the shooters went to ground on the side of the building. They fled, stashing the guns so they wouldn't be seen with them. The box was obviously set up to hide the weapons, so they knew the layout well before they did their killing."

Truchanova mulled over the windfall she had just been given, looking for a way to be grateful without seeming indebted. She came out with a weak "Thank you for finding the guns."

"Are we agreed on the terms of our bargain?"

The prosecutor sat, not moving for another minute as she thought her position over, then nodded reluctantly. "Agreed."

"Good." Jana stood, placing the weapons on the woman's desk. "I'll need a copy of the murder book."

The prosecutor reached into a lower drawer of her desk, and with both hands, pulled out a binder thick with reports. The name Bogan was inked on the outside cover in black letters. Truchanova handed it to Jana.

"Everything is there."

"Thank you, Madam Prosecutor."

"I hope our silent cooperation will be a fruitful one, Commander Matinova."

"So do I, Madam Prosecutor." She hefted the murder book in her hands. "Very heavy. Have you noticed that all murder books become weightier in proportion to the media's interest in the case?"

"Always."

"I trust you'll give me the results of the fingerprint evaluation and the tracking on the ownership of the guns."

"I will."

"Good-bye, Madam Prosecutor."

Jana walked out of the room. Truchanova waited until she heard the outer door close, then closed her own office door. She went back to her desk and dialed the number for Jakus.

"I have the rifles. They will need to be fingerprinted; manufacture, sale, and ownership tracked. Also the interior of the gloves the shooters wore. And bullets in one of the clips. I've agreed that Matinova can, without *official* authorization, silently assist us in the investigation." She listened for a moment, her lips pursing in irritation. "Don't be an idiot, Jakus. The Rostov Report was not included in the murder book, and I didn't give it to her." She listened for another few seconds, getting even more irritated. "I will remind you that these are guns that *you* failed to find. Now, get in here and pick them up."

She slammed the phone down in its cradle. "Fool!"

Chapter 7

Jana decided to take a walk through Old Town. She could relax in the old city center. The leisurely pace of the pedestrian milieu where few cars were allowed, and the disheveled grace of the old buildings, encouraged the rambler to enjoy the calm of seeming to inhabit another century. Today, although there was a nip in the air, the sunlight added to the peacefulness of the walk as Jana traced a wide arc through Kapitulska, then angled past creaky old St. Martin's Cathedral toward Panska, eventually reaching the mall-like Hviezdoslavovo Namestie. Jana's objective came in sight: the Verne, a small café decorated with illustrations of Jules Verne stories.

It was a good day for Jana to visit the Verne. The café, furnished with antiques and decorated with a pastiche of objects related to Verne's books, lent itself to casually eating *palacinky* or simply zoning out over a paperback. Jana took a seat in an easy chair near a small wall mural depicting Captain Nemo in diving gear staring at an octopus. She plunked the murder book down on a side table next to the chair and pulled the table closer so she could read easily.

Before she began, Jana looked around at the other occupants of the café: a few college students; a waitress leaning over a handsome young man, trying to make a favorable impression; and, close by, a pair of Polish tourists attempting to figure out a map. Jana understood enough of the Polish to gather that they were flying back to Kraków in the early evening and trying to decide over a cup of coffee what to do with the last few hours of their vacation.

The waitress eventually gave up on the handsome young man and came over. Jana ordered a hot chocolate, then settled in to read the murder book cover to cover. It took her two hours and two hot chocolates to get through it. As she had expected, there was very little of real note. But, as always, there were little pieces that were interesting—not only from what was contained in the reports, but from what was missing.

The interviewing of the guests at the party had to have been a nightmare. There had also been an evidently painstaking series of follow-up interviews based on the guest list. Almost none of the interviews had produced even the smallest bit of new information on the shootings. It was as if the guests at the party had been blind to anything beyond their immediate fear when the shooting began. There was one outstanding exception: a Mr. and Mrs. Jozel had arrived late, reaching the outside of the building just as the other guests began streaming out of the doors, escaping from the shooting inside. The pair was walking past the alley at the side of the building, moving toward the entrance, when two men bolted out from the alley, one of them colliding with Mr. Jozel, knocking him to the ground. The man had screamed at Mr. Jozel in a rage, even though the collision had been the man's fault. Mrs. Jozel had seen the man from a distance of no more than two feet and had remembered his face in a very detailed way.

Odd how human nature betrays us, Jana thought. A man, while committing a dreadful criminal act, a situation in which he could not have wanted to call attention to himself, makes a foolish mistake while fleeing, then compounds the mistake by inviting even more attention. His description was now contained in an investigation report, a result anyone committing a murder would want to avoid. Stupid. But, then again, committing a murder is an intrinsically stupid act.

Jana read the description of the man: medium height, barrel-chested, hair covered with a watch cap, thick-featured with a large, full mouth. Mrs. Jozel had noted one other salient feature that would be enormously helpful in identifying the man: he had a very recognizable face because of a large chestnut birthmark on his right cheek. The man was marked. The murder book indicated that a query had been put out to Europol to try to locate him. There was no response logged in. The witnessing couple had not focused on the other man and could not describe him. Jana folded down the corner of the page so she could come back to it.

When she finished the book, she closed the covers, spooning up the last of her hot chocolate, thinking about what she'd read. There was the one item of substantial relevance: the fleeing men. There were also other things that should have been included but weren't. The missing pieces created very serious holes in the investigation, holes that should have been closed by then. Oto Bogan was one of the keys to the resolution of the case, but there was only an absolutely minimal statement by him. He was described in the preliminary report as semi-hysterical, crying, and not able to say anything more than a few words over and over about his wife being killed for no reason.

There had been no follow-up: investigators hadn't spoken to Bogan again. There was a small report indicating that an attempt had been made to question him, but Bogan had not been found either at home or at work, and there had been no significant effort to locate him after that. It was getting very late in the game. Not to have the man brought in for questioning was absurd. Slipshod. The only known witness who might be able to shed some light on why this had happened was a missing person in the case.

Jana ran through the physical evidence in her mind: the timing of the shots, the position of the people at the time of the shooting, the two guns she'd found. Both Bogan and his wife had been targets.

Why the wife?

There was nothing in the murder book about her background. Friends had not been questioned. Relatives had not been tracked down. A son living in Berlin had only briefly been questioned by telephone. No one on the Slovak police force had taken the time to go to Berlin to interrogate him in person. Why? In a case of this importance, intimate questioning of the son was an obvious necessity.

Jana began to get angry at the careless way the investigation had failed to expand and examine all aspects of possible motive. There had been no attempt to look into the couple's finances; and with a financier as one of the targets, it was imperative to see if he had made any serious, intractable enemies or been involved in any fractious transactions that might have left people looking for ways to get even. Money was truly the root of most evil, particularly in a case involving dual assassins in a planned killing like this.

Jana tried to reason out why the investigation had moved so slowly. The only immediate explanation she could come up with was that Bogan and his wife had moved in the rarefied circles that law enforcement personnel always approached gingerly. Police were careful to avoid the kinds of repercussions that only the rich and powerful can bring down on them. That thought did not make Jana's conclusion any less damning: so far, the investigation had been mired in glue. At this point, it was a complete botch.

The chief investigator, Jakus, was not the best man for this type of case. Not imaginative enough. But it was more than just that: much of what had not yet been done was basic, and any experienced investigator should have gone much further than the murder book indicated. The prosecutor assigned to the case was not stupid. She had to see the holes that still needed to be filled. Why was this investigation being allowed to simply creep forward? There was something more here, something that had not been documented in the murder book, an item of proof or process that had not been included.

And Jana had to find out what it was.

Chapter 8

There were large, loose flakes of snow drifting through the air, melting when they hit the ground. It was the precursor to the larger snowfall that was expected when the evening's colder air swept through the area. The icy gusts coming off the Danube pushed at Jana as she walked to her car. She drove back to her office thinking she would try to leave early so she could get home before the full fury of the storm hit.

In the police building, few of her investigators were around, most of them out in the field working on their cases or heading home early to beat the heavy snow. Even the office felt colder, as if in anticipation of the night winds. Jana took off her coat, slinging it onto one of the office chairs, turned her portable office heater on, and set the murder book on the corner of her desk. Juggling multiple cases is the norm for investigators. Unfortunately, as with all supervisors, Jana had to deal with personnel matters as well as her cases. She hated the personnel issues, since they took time away from the investigative process, but they had to be attended to.

She unlocked her desk drawer, pulled out a number of the personnel folders, and began going through them, taking notes on each one, preparing to write up evaluations of the people in her division who were up for promotions.

She focused on the task for the next few hours, finally finishing, only then realizing that her pen hand was sore from writing and her back ached from sitting for so long. She noticed the hour and made up her mind to go home.

She thought about what work she would take home with her, something she could comfortably ease into on her living-room couch. Jana had promised the relatives of the young gypsy man who had accidentally killed himself that she would go over the evidence in his case one final time. It was a small enough file, so she put it in her carrying case. As she did so, she realized that she'd thought of the death of the young man as accidental. Preconceived notions about cases were the bane of good investigations. She had to try, once more, to consider the file with an open mind. Promises had been made to the young man's relatives that she would be objective, and she was determined to keep it.

Jana momentarily listened to the absence of sound from the other offices. Most of the lights were out. Everyone in her division had gone home, and here she was, still working. Empty offices are lonely, distant places. It was hard for Jana to tolerate even herself in this type of atmosphere. The cold outside had come inside. Jana's eyes went to the picture of her granddaughter on the desk. They hadn't talked in a month. The girl lived with her father's parents in the United States. Time to make a phone call.

Jana began to dial the number, then stopped. As much as she wanted to make the call, she was not allowed to dial long-distance numbers from the police lines unless the call was work-related, and all long-distance calls were automatically recorded, logged, and sent to the accounting division. She set the telephone back in its cradle. Her cell phone did not have international service, so she would have to make the call from home.

Jana put the personnel files back in her desk drawer and locked it. Then she put on her coat, took the carrying case with the file on the dead youth in it, and walked out of her office. She was home in thirty minutes. The first thing she did, before she even took off her greatcoat, was call her granddaughter. She got a recorded message. The family would be away for a few days. Jana hung up, angry at herself for needing to hear her grandchild's voice so much. Police officers weren't supposed to be so needy.

It was just that it was hard to be alone on a cold evening.

Chapter 9

The wind was keening outside Jana's house, icy snow-flakes peppering the windows, rapidly creating a white coating, blocking most of the outside view. She made herself some hot tea, then spread sheep cheese on a number of crackers. She set her tea and crackers next to her couch in the living room, then wrapped herself in a blanket, getting ready to read the file on the young man who had been killed with a shotgun, when there was a knock at her front door. The knock was so light that she almost ignored it, thinking she was mistaken. Then she heard it again, this time slightly louder.

Jana went to the door, opening it with the chain still on. Outside stood a girl who looked no more than thirteen. Her hair and clothes were caked with snow, her teeth were chattering, her face was blue with the cold. With the snow swirling around her, she was rapidly turning into an ice sculpture. Jana quickly unlocked the door chain and, without asking the girl why she was there, pulled her inside and closed the door.

The girl stood shivering in the middle of the room, holding out two small metal objects to Jana.

"Earrings," chattered the girl. "Earrings for sale."

Jana took the earrings, a pair of bare-metal crescents,

then grabbed the blanket that she had left on the couch and wrapped it around the girl, who clutched it tight to herself.

"Sit down," Jana said. The girl stared at her as if she didn't quite comprehend what had been said. The girl was frozen, ready to go into hypothermia. Jana pulled one of her easy chairs over to the girl, then half pushed, half lifted her into it. "I'll be right back. Stay there."

Jana went to her bathroom and pulled a large bath towel from a cabinet above the tub, then darted into her kitchen, poured a can of soup into a pot, and put it on the stove to heat. When she went back into the living room, the girl was standing by the crackers and cheese that Jana had made, stuffing them in her mouth. She saw Jana watching her but didn't demonstrate any concern that she had been caught eating someone else's crackers. The girl was consumed with the need to fill her stomach.

"You're welcome to the crackers." Jana spoke softly so as not to frighten the girl. "I have soup on the stove. Bread. I'll make eggs as well."

The girl nodded, going into the box of crackers, stuffing more in her mouth. She soon finished the box, regarding it somewhat regretfully now that it was empty. The blanket Jana had wrapped around her had fallen around her ankles. The girl put down the empty box and wrapped the blanket tightly around herself again. Jana walked over to her and toweled off her head, the girl continuing to chew all the while, her cheeks fat with the remnants of the crackers she'd stuffed in her mouth.

"You're not dressed warmly enough," Jana said.

"I have two sweaters on," the girl mumbled through her full mouth. "That's enough."

"If it's enough, why did you get so cold?"

"I'm not so cold."

"I could have sworn your teeth were chattering," Jana countered.

"So, they were chattering." There was a tone of belligerence in the girl's voice, as if she resented that Jana had pointed out a weakness in her.

"Your mother should have given you a coat."

"I think she's maybe living in Moldova."

"Then why aren't *you* living in Moldova?"

"Even the hot water is cold in Moldova." The girl rubbed a hand over her body, then slapped it on her thigh several times, trying to restore some feeling. "My mother had other things on her mind, so she left me. I think she found another man. He took her somewhere. I don't know where."

"Your father, then."

"He's somewhere else."

"Where?"

"He didn't tell me where he was going when he left. My mother left before he did. Actually, I'm not sure she was my mother."

"Why aren't you sure?"

"She never said she was. At least my father said he was my father."

Jana stood back several feet from the girl to look at her. Her hair tousled, she looked like an irritated, wet monkey.

"The soup should be ready." She took several steps toward the kitchen. The girl remained rooted to her spot, not following her. "We eat soup in the kitchen!" Jana pressed. She continued into the kitchen, and the girl, after a brief hesitation, followed, her stomach overcoming her intransigence. Jana pointed to a chair at the small kitchen table, and the girl sat down. Her shivering was now only spasmodic, her teeth less like castanets. The girl was becoming more alert to her surroundings, visually examining everything in the kitchen as if she were a wary animal, checking where the easy exits were.

Jana watched her. She was a young girl who had seen a little too much, had been exposed to too much, had been disappointed and hurt a little too much. She also had a defensive anger about her, her searching eyes reflecting a pressing need to control her environment, always expecting and preparing for the worst.

Jana stirred the soup, decided it was ready, and fixed a bowl for the girl, pouring a small part of the soup into a juice glass for herself. She put the bowl, along with a spoon, in front of the girl, then stood leaning against the kitchen counter, sipping at her own soup. The girl didn't bother with the spoon, gulping directly from the bowl.

"You'll burn your tongue," Jana warned her.

The girl slowed down, taking smaller sips.

"What's your name?" Jana asked.

There was no answer.

"If you eat my crackers and drink my soup, you have to give me your name," Jana insisted.

"Call me Em. My last name is Mrvova." The words came reluctantly out of her mouth between sips. "That's my Slovak name."

"You have more names?"

"When we move, we always take a different name."

She might be a Rom, Jana thought, but the girl's coloration did not look typically gypsy. But perhaps it was in the eyes.

"Rom?" Jana asked.

"No." The girl thought about it. "Well, maybe my father was. Part, maybe, but I don't know. My 'mother' never said. She called me Em. So she knew my name. That's all I asked."

"How did you get into Slovakia if your mother and father aren't in the country?"

"My mother brought me here. Then she left."

Em used her finger to clean the last remnants of soup from the bowl, then licked the finger.

"Are you going to buy the earrings?" Em asked, finished with her finger.

Jana had forgotten about the earrings. She picked them up from the counter where she'd laid them when making the soup. They were crudely made, but not badly shaped.

"I make them from scrap aluminum," Em said. "They're light. Cheap, so I can sell them cheap. They still look good enough to wear." Her chin jutted out defiantly, as if she expected criticism; then she went on quickly. "Each one is a different design. People can afford to buy two pairs. You want two pairs? Three euros for one, five euros for two pairs." Em focused her gaze on the refrigerator. "You have any milk?"

Jana took a carton of milk out. "It will be cold."

"Warm it," demanded the girl.

"Please?" Jana suggested.

"Okay, I don't need the milk," Em concluded, stiffening up, challenging Jana.

Jana opened the refrigerator, ready to put the milk carton back.

"Please," Em said through gritted teeth, wanting the milk more than getting her own way.

Jana closed the refrigerator, rummaged around until she found another small pot, then poured milk into it, setting it on a lit burner.

"You have no money?" Jana guessed. "No place to go?"

"I have a place," Em asserted. "They just want money for staying. Maybe I can borrow some from you?"

"You would never pay me back."

Em thought about it. "That's true. I need all I can get, so there's no way I can pay you back."

Jana eyed the girl. "Your clothes are wet. You need to take them off."

"Why?"

"To get more comfortable. So you don't die of pneumonia."

"I don't know you well enough to take my clothes off."

Jana thought about it, then made a decision. "I have clothes that belonged to my daughter. In the small bedroom." She pointed toward the bedroom door. "Go into the closet. They're there. Pick what you want that fits and put them on."

The girl hesitated, not sure what to do. "They're your daughter's."

"She died." Jana generally hated to say those words, and she wondered as she said them why they came so easily this time. "The clothes that you put on will be much better than the ones you're wearing. It's a good trade."

Em thought about it, then nodded her agreement. "Okay."

"Take a hot bath first."

"You saying I'm dirty?"

"Wet. And dirty."

Em glared at her, her mouth tight. Jana shrugged, sipping the last of her soup. "You're selling earrings. This means you're a businessperson. It'd be good business to take the bath. Remember, you get new, dry clothes afterward." Jana pointed firmly in the direction of the bathroom.

Still looking as if she'd been insulted, Em got out of her chair and stalked down the hall to the bathroom. Jana waited another minute for the milk to warm, then poured it into a large glass, took a box of cookies out of a cabinet, opened it, and carried the cookies and milk to the bathroom. The door was open; there was no bath running. Jana felt a small surge of annoyance. The girl had not listened, had obviously headed straight for the new clothes. Jana stalked into the small bedroom. Em was on the bed, still wrapped in the blanket, breathing evenly, dead to the world. The girl suddenly seemed strikingly vulnerable, looking very much like the at-risk child she was.

Jana pulled the feather comforter from its place at the foot of the bed and slid it over Em. She took a last look at the girl, then turned off the light, leaving the room. Em could take her bath in the morning.

Jana sat back down on the couch in the living room and picked up the file on the young gypsy man.

The file was not very thick. Most police files sum up people's lives quickly, giving individuality short shrift. Only things related to the crime are put in the report; everything else is incidental. The dead youth had been seventeen, recently enrolled in a trade school hoping to become a computer technician. Everyone wants to work on computers now, Jana thought, even the gypsies. His mother and father reported that he would have a drink every so often, but just with his friends, on special occasions, and he never drank heavily. Jana went to the coroner's report briefly. The young man had been drinking at the time of death, and according to the toxicology report his blood alcohol indicated that he would have been very drunk. Not good when you're carrying a loaded shotgun.

If his mother and father were wrong about him never drinking heavily, what else were they wrong about? Listed among the items found on his person was a small aspirin tin containing five acetaminophen/codeine tablets. Jana went back to the toxicology report. The coroner's office had not run a test for any toxins other than alcohol. One of the technicians, or perhaps the autopsy surgeon himself, had decided to save time and money on an investigation that looked run-of-the-mill by ignoring the possibility that more testing needed to be done. Why had the young man been using painkillers? Jana went over the medical report again. This time she focused on the full-body diagram, on which the coroner had made notes.

Other than the death wound to the neck, the young man had one other remarkable injury: both knees had been surgically repaired, both of them requiring implants. The coroner noted that the area around one of the implants showed inflammation, indicating that there had been a problem with that artificial joint. Jana assumed that the knee that had shown inflammation had still been giving him pain, requiring the medications he'd been carrying. Which raised a question: why had a young man, who had at least one knee that was still impaired enough that he was taking painkillers, gone on a slog through the woods in winter? The walk would have had to aggravate his condition. Then again, he had been young, and young men do stupid things.

Jana made a mental note to find out how the teenager had hurt his knees. Her second question was what the synergistic effect of the painkillers and the alcohol would have been on the young man. If he had dosed himself with the medication at the same time he had ingested the alcohol, the effect would have been significant, particularly given the high blood-alcohol content. How impaired had his physical coordination been? What degree of awareness of his physical surroundings would he have had? Cognitive functions? Would he have even been conscious at the time of death?

Suddenly the failure of the toxicologist to go further

with the blood analysis became critical. Jana made another mental note to ask the coroner's office to do further analysis in the morning.

She decided to postpone further assessment of the case until that analysis was done. She put the file aside, took a quick shower, and went to bed. Tomorrow would be a busy day. Her "unofficial" work on the Bogan investigation would begin in earnest.

When Jana roused herself in the morning, it was dark outside, snow still falling, although it had let up slightly. She dressed very quietly to avoid waking Em, making sure, a few moments later, when she made herself tea and toast, that the glass didn't bang against the kitchen counter or the pot against the stove. After she had finished her breakfast, she went to leave; but when she opened the front door, she immediately noticed a note pinned to the outside of it. Scrawled on the note were the words "See you soon." She walked back to the room where Em had slept. The girl was gone.

All through the drive to work, which was slow because of the slippery conditions, Jana could not stop thinking about Em. What an odd event to have Em appear at her house; what an odd event to have her disappear again. Jana felt an unexpected sense of loss now that the girl was gone, then chided herself for feeling that way. She had no real connection to the child. Em was not her granddaughter; her granddaughter was seven thousand miles away. Jana and Em were not linked through any birth-related bond. Jana was merely being protective of a vulnerable and threatened young person.

No! The reason she felt a sense of loss over the girl having left, Jana told herself, was because she herself was lonely. That was not acceptable. Not at all. Jana ordered herself to stifle the emotion.

But as she drove, thoughts of the girl popped up again. There was another reason, a more acceptable reason, for her emotional response to Em. Jana had admiration for the girl. The teenager, as beaten-up by the weather, as hungry and tired as she had been the night before, still had had the determination and discipline to wake up before Jana, leave the warmth of the house, and, in the pitch black of early morning, with the snow still coming down, go about her life. She'd even left a good-bye note.

Yes, thought Jana, a very unusual little girl.

Chapter 10

Jana wasted no time when she arrived at the office. She ordered the additional toxicology analysis on the young gypsy who had been shot to death. Then she called Oto Bogan's office to set up an appointment with him, only to be told that he was out of town and would not be returning for several weeks. Jana asked if Bogan was in Berlin. There was a long silence, and then Bogan's secretary said she had no idea where Bogan was at the moment, an obvious lie. Jana told the secretary to have Bogan call her immediately when she next heard from him and then terminated the conversation. She was left with the conviction that Bogan would not call her. He was staying as far away from the investigation as possible, deliberately avoiding the police.

Jana called Seges and informed him that they were going into the field, cutting off all his excuses for not going by giving him the order to "dress warm." She hung up to avoid any further complaints. Jana didn't like partnering with Seges, but she tried to follow the rule that you should have another officer with you in the field at all times on an investigation. It meant that there was another witness to what happened, and it provided immediate assistance in case of danger. Since all of her other officers were already overburdened with their own caseloads, Jana had to make do with Seges.

Jana obtained the address of Bogan's residence from the murder book, noting that there was a second address listed as an alternate residence, which was across the border, on the way to Sopron, Hungary, a relatively short distance from Bratislava. The area had recently been built up, with a number of well-off Slovaks, Austrians, and other expatriate Europeans buying land cheaply and building houses that were larger than they could have afforded if they'd tried to live in or around Bratislava.

Seges continued to complain as they drove, until Jana couldn't stand it any longer and told him to shut up. Seges shut up, but he pouted for the rest of the drive until they reached Bogan's house in the hillside area rising above Bratislava near the huge Slavin World War II Memorial to the Russian dead.

As Jana expected, it was one of the bigger houses in the area, two stories, newer than most, showing a mixture of styles, as if the architect hadn't been able to decide what type of house he wanted to erect. Certainly, the Roman colonnade of the building front did not go with the ultramodern wings, nor did the wings go with the blue-tiled, Japanese pagoda-style roof. However, the house did convey one thing: the man who had built it had money.

They went up to the front door. Jana knocked, then rang the bell. She waited and, when there was no response, knocked and rang again.

"No one home," Seges brightly surmised, happy that their visit was going to be a short one.

"Nobody has *answered*," Jana corrected him. "We'll go around to the back." She started toward the side of the house, Seges lagging behind. "Are you still determined to get an answer to our first knock every time we try to get inside a house?"

"If we go around to the back, we should have a warrant," Seges counseled, his tone sanctimonious.

"I know the rules, Seges. Unfortunately, no one reports having heard from Mr. Bogan since shortly after the attempt on his life. He has not been going to work, and his secretary told me that she had no idea where he was. As a police officer, I must therefore conclude that he may require assistance. Perhaps he's even lying wounded or dead inside his house." She smiled at Seges, watching him unsuccessfully try to come up with another excuse.

Jana trudged through the snow, Seges reluctantly following her. The backyard was spacious, laid out in a formal fashion; two wrought-iron, glass-topped tables with matching wrought-iron chairs sat in the garden looking incongruous beneath their covering snow, as if they were waiting for tea-party celebrants who had long ago abandoned them. The rear door to the house was wide open.

"Someone's forced the door," Seges volunteered.

"I can see, Seges."

Jana walked to the door, Seges slipping his gun out of its holster and following behind her. The snow had drifted into the house, and there were no footprints visible to indicate that anyone had gone in or out since the snow had fallen. Jana walked through the door, then listened. Not a sound. She didn't have to search the house to know that it was vacant. The house was telling her that no one was inside.

"Take the downstairs, Seges."

"What are we looking for?"

"Ghosts."

Jana walked deeper into the house, noting the occasional knocked-over chair, bureau drawers that had been rummaged through and left open, a broken vase on the floor. Someone had searched the house looking for something specific. It was not a petty burglary: too many items that could have been sold at a local pawnshop were in plain sight, left behind because they weren't what the thief had been looking for. Jana went upstairs and looked through the bedrooms, minor signs of dislocation visible in all the rooms. Within a few moments, she reached the master bedroom suite. Unlike the rest of the house, which had been gone through thoroughly but not trashed, the bedroom was an absolute mess, mattress slashed open, chaise longue cut apart, chairs mutilated. The door of the walk-in closet was open, clothes haphazardly dumped on the floor. An oil painting had been taken off the wall, the safe behind it open. Jana checked the safe. There was expensive jewelry and cash left in it.

Jana examined the door of the safe. It was not a cheaply made safe, but it had been opened without the use of force. Whoever had done it either had had the combination or was a consummate professional, able to open safes with relative ease. Jana opted to believe he was a professional. But why leave the jewelry and the money? The thief or thieves must have been looking for something so important to them, with such a driving imperative behind their search, that the valuables inside the safe had no interest to them. And the condition of the rest of the room, the almost uncontrolled slashing and ripping of the furniture, the clothes dumped on the floor, suggested to Jana that the men who had come looking for that *thing* had gone away without finding what they wanted. Whatever it was, it was still out there for someone to find.

She hurried back downstairs and collected Seges, who was startled at being rushed out of the house. The two of them climbed back into their vehicle, and Jana instructed

Seges to drive to Hungary and to the second house that had been listed in the murder book. On the way, she called their own forensics people, directing them to the Bratislava house. Then she telephoned the Hungarian police. The captain she talked to was very cooperative when she told him she needed help on a murder case, and he agreed to meet her at the second house. Jana urged Seges to drive faster, hoping that whoever had searched the first house was not aware of the second one.

Her hope was in vain.

When they got to the second house, the Hungarian police were already inside, and upset. Jana quickly explained, in case the Hungarians misread the circumstances, that she and Seges had not been the ones to rape the location. As soon as Jana walked into the house, she could understand why the Hungarians were distressed. The place had been completely trashed. The Hungarian forensics people were scurrying through the chaos trying to lift fingerprints, or hoping to find any signature item that the burglars had left behind. Jana doubted they would find anything.

She didn't stay long. There was no reason to. The conclusion was obvious: the ransacking of the houses was related to the shootings on the soundstage. Building on that belief, Jana had to suppose that the people who had done the soundstage shootings, and the people who had done the house burglaries, were still looking for Bogan, and for some object that Bogan was in possession of. And they wanted them both very badly.

For Bogan's sake, Jana hoped she could find him before they did.

Chapter 11

The drive back to Bratislava was fairly quick. When they arrived at the police building, Jana directed a reluctant Seges to return to the Bogan home in Bratislava to oversee the Slovak forensics crew, then took the elevator up to her floor. As soon as she walked into the offices occupied by her division, she realized that things were a trifle askew. Grzner, a generally glum and caustic man who took work very seriously, was cheerfully hanging strings of mistletoe over his desk. Other desks already had strings of it hanging over them. Jonas, another one of her detectives, was hanging small blinking Christmas lights along the wall. Several secretaries were putting paper figures of Father Frost and other imaginary Christmas creatures along the edges of the desks, with another one of her secretaries taping candy canes along the edge of one of their large standing corkboards normally used for pinning up exhibits.

"What's going on?" Jana asked.

"Your niece said you wanted us to make the place more cheerful," one of the secretaries responded. "She said you wanted us to put up the Christmas decorations early."

"My niece?"

"She's in your office."

"It's not time for Christmas lights," Jana informed Jonas.

"She said you thought it would be nice if our witnesses were cheered up when they came into the offices."

"My niece again?"

"Yes."

Jana stared at Grzner hanging the mistletoe. The overweight and brutish Grzner looked absurd, Jana noticing for the first time that he was wearing a Christmas tie with a big American Santa Claus painted on it. "Grzner, you're not the type of man who wants to be wearing a tie like that."

"Your niece said—"

"I've already heard. She's in my office?"

"Yes, Commander."

Jana walked into her office, already having a good idea whom she would find. Em was sitting behind her desk, reading the murder book on the Bogan shootings.

"Good afternoon, Em."

"Afternoon," Em replied, not looking up from the book.

"Em, you're in my chair."

"Sorry." The girl got up, holding on to the murder book, still reading as she slowly walked around the desk to sit in a chair against the wall. Jana took off her coat, hung it up, then walked over to Em and took the murder book out of her hands.

"I haven't finished," Em protested.

"It's confidential, not meant to be read by anyone who's not in some branch of law enforcement. You're not, so you're out." Jana sat behind her desk, slapping the book down. "And you are not my niece."

"Your officers are very nice. When they found out that we were related, we had a long conversation, and they agreed to make the place more cheerful. It's really ugly in here. Just because you mix with dead people is no reason to be dead yourselves."

"How did you know where I worked, Em?"

"You had papers. Letters addressed to you. There was stationery from here in your place." Em shifted in the chair, making herself more comfortable. "Wooden chairs are hard to sit on." She held out her hands, palms forward, showing them to Jana. "Scrubbed now. You said I was dirty. I needed a place to clean up. I went back to your house." Em frowned. "You leave your front door unlocked when you're out of the house. You shouldn't do that, you know. It's not safe."

"If a thief wants to get in, he's going to get in. It's very easy to open a locked door."

"That's true."

"Did you expect that you would have to break in when you went back to my house?"

"You told me to take a bath and put on the other clothes. I was only doing what you said. The door being open made it easy." She slipped off the chair and did a quick pirouette, showing the clothes she was wearing. "You see, I put on the clothing you said to put on." Satisfied that she had made her point, Em settled back into the chair.

Jana stared at Em, realizing that she was seeing the girl in her daughter's clothes. They were a perfect fit. For the first time, Jana realized that Em even looked slightly like her granddaughter. Or was it her daughter at that age? Or maybe, she told herself, all children of a certain age resembled each other.

"Did you eat?" The question came out of Jana's mouth before she had even thought about it. She mentally kicked herself, telling her conscience to stop acting like she was responsible for Em. The girl was not related to her. Jana had no responsibility for her well-being.

"I ate soup. And there was *halusky*, which I warmed up, and *udeniny*. So there was enough."

"Good. Now I think we have to get you someplace where you'll be warm and can sleep out of the snow."

"You mean like a home for children?"

"We have places that keep children warm and safe and fed."

"I've been there before. Once, in Belarus."

"I thought you came from Moldova."

"There too. Ugly places. They're not for me."

"We have to find a place for you to stay."

"I called my father. He's coming for me in three days. So I'm fine."

"You told me that your father had left you. And your mother too, for that matter."

"They did. I went to see a friend of my father's when I left you this morning. Jacob, a Jew who used to be my father's boss. A nice man. He's in the electrical supply and repair business. He works for a French company out of Prague. I knew he was in town, so I got up early to make sure I'd catch him before he left Bratislava for the day. He said my father has been working with him again. My dad's due back in town, and Jacob's agreed to take me in."

The story that Em had related was amazingly glib, told in what sounded like all innocence. Jana found it somewhat astounding that the girl could lie through her teeth so well.

"I've just heard a little girl tell me a cock-and-bull story," Jana said.

"Of course," Em admitted with a cheery smile on her face, showing no embarrassment at being called on the lie. "My father doesn't work in electrical supplies. He's a criminal. So I can't tell you what he really does, or where he's going to meet me, because you're a police officer, and you might try to arrest him, and that wouldn't be good."

"Your father is a criminal? How do you know he's a criminal?"

"I heard them arguing. The woman who's been acting as my mother called him a criminal. He admitted it. He's okay to me, but he is a criminal."

"Criminals don't make good fathers."

"I agree," Em affirmed. "But he has a sister, my aunt, and she's not a criminal. She's going to take me in. So I'll be staying with her."

Jana stared at Em. Either the girl was an incredibly adroit prevaricator, or she was telling Jana an outlandish truth that sounded like a lie.

"What's your aunt's name?" Jana asked.

"Em. I'm named after her. She doesn't want her name-sake wandering the streets, so she's going to be my foster mother."

"If that's true, which I have my doubts about, you'll have to stay with the welfare people until you're picked up by your father."

"Oh, no, I couldn't do that. I told you, my father's a criminal, and he couldn't pick me up there. You'd be waiting to arrest him. Besides, once you get into the hands of the welfare people, they don't let you go very easily. They'd take weeks or months just deciding to let me go. If you put me in, I'd have to do what I did before: escape. Then I'd be on the streets again until I could get in touch with my father."

"If I don't put you with the welfare people, where are you going to stay until you meet your father?"

"Your place, of course."

Jana was taken aback. "You can't room at my place."

"'Course I can. It's only for a short time."

"A police commander doesn't take in stray waifs."

"Why not?"

"It's against departmental rules."

"That's an untruth. I'll bet the department's rules don't even discuss it." Em frowned disapprovingly at Jana. "Police commanders are not supposed to tell stories."

"Even police commanders have to tell 'stories' on occasion."

"Why on this occasion?"

Jana couldn't think of a reason.

"Good. Then it's all settled," Em declared when Jana didn't answer.

"No, it's not!"

"I think we should both think about this," Em announced.

Jana gaped at the girl. The way that she talked reminded Jana eerily of her granddaughter, her daughter, and herself.

"And I'd like to finish reading your murder book," Em continued. "I just have a short way to go, and it's very interesting."

"No!"

"Too bad. I could have helped you."

Em's tone and the set of her features had changed. They now had the look and the sound of honesty.

"You can't read any more of the book." Jana thought about what the girl had said. "However, I'd like to know what you mean by 'I could have helped you.'"

Em's voice took on a triumphant tone. "Okay! Let's make a bargain, then: I tell you what I can help you with, you let me stay in your house. How about it?"

"Not okay."

"It sounds like a good bargain to me."

"First we see what you have to tell me. Then I decide."

"If it's good information, then I stay." She waited for Jana to agree. When Jana said nothing, the girl sat up very erect in her chair. "Unless I hear you say it's a bargain, then no words come past my lips." She made a zipping motion in front of her mouth, then waited, getting impatient. "Say it, or that's it!"

Inwardly, Jana groaned, not liking what she was probably getting into. However, the offer was irresistible, particularly coming from this girl. Jana wanted to find out just what she would come up with. "Okay. If it's good information, you stay."

Jana waited.

"What?" Em asked.

"The information," Jana reminded her.

"Oh," said Em.

Then she began to talk.

Chapter 12

Jana, her officers, and Em sat outside Sipo's soup and sandwich shop for two hours before Sipo arrived. A female employee had come an hour earlier and done all the setup so that by the time Sipo got there, the place was ready to open. As soon as Sipo went inside, he hauled out a sign advertising the day's specials. Setting it up in front of the shop, he spotted Jana and Seges walking toward the place. The man instantly darted in through the door, running through the shop and out the back door—into the huge arms of Grzner, who slapped handcuffs on him and marched him back into the store. The female employee huddled in fear in a rear corner of the shop, probably convinced that both she and Sipo were going to be murdered by the ugly-looking thug who was manhandling her employer.

Seges, almost by reflex, helped himself to a sandwich as soon as they got into the shop, much to the disapproval of Jana, who immediately told him to throw it away and pay the listed price. Seges reluctantly placed the money on the counter, and Jana turned her attention to Sipo. The man kept his head bowed, refusing to look her in the face, knowing that nothing good was going to come of this confrontation.

"Wouldn't you like it if the handcuffs were removed?"

Jana asked, smiling at him. "They're painful; uncomfortable at best." She nodded to Grzner, who removed the cuffs. "Next time you see us," she suggested to Sipo, "don't run. It makes things much easier, particularly for you, if you simply stand still."

She took a seat at the counter. "Mr. Sipo, we saw each other at the Bogan party. I had no idea we would see each other again so soon. Did you enjoy the soirée?" Jana looked him over. He was wearing a jacket edged in red piping, and yellow pants with black stripes. "Still the same dandy that you've always been, I see. It must have been nice for you to get out of those drab prison clothes." She waited for him to respond. The man stood dumb, as if in shock. "I asked you a question about the party, Sipo. Did you enjoy it, at least before the shots were fired?"

The man remained mute.

Jana nodded at Grzner. Not too gently, he slipped the handcuffs back on Sipo, whose body jerked as if he were a steer being branded. For a moment he strained against the cuffs. Then his shoulder slumped as he realized there was no way to escape.

"You see, we agree, Sipo. It's much better to be free of those things than to be in them. So, once more, how did you like the festivities before the gunmen started shooting?"

"I didn't have anything to do with the shooting." His words came out in a hoarse murmur.

"Louder, please. I can't hear you."

"I wasn't involved in the killing." His voice was louder, his posture jerking erect. "I was frightened, just like everyone else. It's not good to be in a shooting gallery."

Jana again nodded at Grzner, and the investigator unlocked the cuffs, removing them once more. Sipo rubbed his wrists and hands as if he were washing them.

"Nicer, isn't it, without the manacles? I'm sure you felt that way when you were released from prison: surpassingly better to be out than in. I would think you wouldn't want to see the inside of that grim place for a second time. Or is it a third time? I also have to believe you'd never want handcuffs on again. Besides, the color of the metal doesn't exactly go with the clothes you like to wear, and you are obviously a man who cares about how he looks. I think it all comes down to self-esteem, don't you? Chains and prison do bad things for one's self-esteem?"

"Yes."

"So, tell me: who sent you the invitation to the party?"

"I wasn't sent an invitation. I knew it was happening, so I went."

"You *crashed* the party?"

"You could call it that."

"You did, or didn't, arrive uninvited?"

Sipo hesitated. "Uninvited."

"How'd you get in without an invitation?"

"I mixed with a group of people walking in. Everybody around me flashed their invitations at the doormen and just kept walking. I went with them. Easy." He gave Jana a self-satisfied look. "Anyone can get into large parties. The bigger they are, the easier it is to get in."

"Did you say hello to Mr. and Mrs. Bogan?"

He thought about the question for a full minute. Grzner grew impatient.

"Manacles back on?" he asked Jana.

Grzner was good at the game, perhaps because he liked it too much. This was also Jana's cue to up the threat level.

"Sipo, the investigator holding on to you wants to put you back in handcuffs. If he puts them on again, I'm going to suggest that Investigator Grzner make them one notch tighter this time. I think they were too loose before. If they're loose, it's an incentive for you to attempt an escape, and we would be dreadfully ashamed to face our fellow officers if you got away. Even more important, Investigator Grzner won't take the cuffs off again if he puts them on this time. Too much work. He has to keep up his strength. So, once more, did you say hello to Mr. and Mrs. Bogan that night?" Jana waited for a moment. "Perhaps you wished him a joyful name day, clapped him on the back? Told him that you hoped he'd have many more of the same? Answer me!"

Sipo was breathing heavily, shuffling his feet, wishing he were anyplace but there. He tried to lie, but the lie was scrawled all over his face.

"I thought, as a guest at his party, the least I should do was to wish him well."

"Even as a guest without an invitation?"

"Yes."

"And what did he say in reply?"

Sipo shuffled his feet. "'Thank you.'"

"And his wife, did she also thank you?"

". . . Yes."

Jana leaned close to Sipo. "Not exactly the words that you exchanged with Mr. and Mrs. Bogan, were they?" she said sarcastically. She gave him an artificial, disappointed sigh. "You went to either ask him something specific or tell him something specific, right?"

"Yes," Sipo admitted.

"Good man, Sipo." Jana patted him on the shoulder for encouragement. "See what we're doing here? Just a simple, straightforward conversation that can only benefit both of us. So, what did you two say to each other?"

"I had nothing to ask him."

"I know, Sipo. You had information you wanted to *give* him."

He stared at her, wondering how she knew. Jana stared back, letting him think about it.

"Handcuffs?" asked Grzner.

"No, thank you, Grzner." Jana kept up her friendly attitude, once more patting Sipo on the shoulder, urging him on. "Tell me what you told Mr. Bogan, Sipo."

"This and that. We just chatted."

"Chatted?" There was a limit to Jana's patience, and getting Sipo in the right frame of mind to talk was beginning to wear on her. She raised the volume of her voice a notch. "We are not talking about chitchat, Sipo! What did you tell him?"

"I was trying to sell him a small item."

"Goods?"

"Not goods."

"I'm losing patience, Sipo. If not goods, then what? Now, Sipo! I want it now! No more time!"

Grzner loudly opened and closed the cuffs, adding incentive for Sipo to talk. The words began to come out of Sipo's mouth in a jerky fashion, seeming to stagger through the air.

"I heard . . . well, you know how you hear . . . that the man . . . Bogan, that is . . . was marked. . . . Yeah, marked. He was going . . . to be . . . you know, stabbed or shot, I don't know what. . . . Why, I don't know. . . . Anyway, I told him."

"Did you tell him when this was going to happen?"

"Soon, soon, soon. That's all."

"That's all?"

"I told him, you know. . . . Well, business is slow here in my shop. Business is business. He wanted to know more. I didn't know any more. I asked for a fee, you understand. I'm saving the man's life. You figure, well, you'd figure he . . . he should give me a few euros. I . . .

I even told him I'd try, try hard, to find out more. The son of a bitch wouldn't give me a cent. Nothing." Sipo reflected on his not being given any money for his effort. "I'm glad he got shot."

"And Klara, his missus?"

"She told me to get away from her husband. That's all. She didn't even thank me."

"Who gave you the information?"

"It was all street talk."

"It didn't come with the wind, Sipo. There were people out there. Name just one person who told you. Names, Sipo."

"There was a guy named Akso. He's also got a friend, Balder. Balder's a German. It was just a normal conversation between us."

"Balder, first name Kabil. One-point-eight or so meters tall, kind of a narrow face?" Grzner asked.

"Yeah, him." Sipo said. "He does cars. Expensive ones. From Germany to Albania or Croatia."

"I know the man," Grzner told Jana. "Stolen autos. He specializes in top of the line—Mercedes, BMWs—running them to the Balkans where their numbers are altered and the cars are fixed up with clean papers. He's rumored to be a good safe man, too."

Jana immediately thought about the safe that had been opened in the Bogan home in Bratislava. They'd have to talk to Balder if they could find him.

Jana got on her cell and called Jonas. "Bring her to the window and have her look inside. The man is here." Jana hung up and turned back to Sipo. "Look straight ahead, at the wall behind the counter. If you move your head or try to see who's standing outside the front window, Investigator Grzner will snap your head off. Do you understand?"

Sipo nodded, facing the wall. Grzner ran a heavy hand over the man's hair and kissed him lightly on the neck, signaling that if he even so much as moved, Grzner would take great pleasure in using force on him.

Jana watched Jonas bring Em to the window and point out Sipo inside. Em stared at him through the window, then nodded to Jana, indicating that she knew him. Jana waved to Jonas, and the detective led Em away from the window and out of sight.

"All right, Sipo. You can relax."

Grzner stepped away from Sipo, looking somewhat disappointed that he hadn't been allowed to hammer him into the ground. As soon as Grzner moved back, Sipo became visibly less tense.

"The witness identified you, Sipo. The witness told us that you were at a meeting where you were given the information. I'm happy that you've been honest about receiving the information. Unfortunately, the witness also said there were two other men at the meeting whom you failed to tell me about. Who were the other men, Sipo?"

"I don't know any other men." There was suddenly a dry, hoarse quality to Sipo's voice, and he began to shake. "Just the two of them and me. I swear, just them."

"A lie, Sipo."

The change that had come over Sipo was dramatic. He had the look of sheer fear in him. "I'd give them up. You know me. I want to avoid trouble. Everyone knows that."

In mounting waves, the shakes overtook Sipo, his body swaying, his legs looking like they were about to give way. "No one else. Just us. No one else."

The man was convulsing so violently that he was losing his balance.

"Okay . . . there was another . . . the Turk."

"Help him, Grzner," Jana said.

Grzner put a hand to Sipo's arm, steadying him.

"Where can we find this man, Sipo?"

Even Seges could see that Sipo was collapsing, and he moved in to help Grzner hold him up.

"Tell us the man's real name, Sipo," Jana pressed.

"That's all I know. 'The Turk.'"

"Good, Sipo." She patted him on the shoulder, trying to calm him. "So, what were they all talking about?"

"They argued."

"A falling-out?"

"It seemed to be."

"About what, Sipo?"

"The others were going to do something, and he opposed it."

Sipo suddenly looked stricken, as if he had said too much.

"Maybe they were just trying to patch up their grievances? Is that right, Sipo?"

Sipo had taken on the look of a pet dog that had eaten the family dinner and was now awaiting punishment. "Everyone fights once in a while."

"What were they fighting about, Sipo?"

"I stayed outside the door. I couldn't make out the words. I didn't want to know."

"They were shouting?"

"A couple of them. The Turk was real loud. Insulting."

"Good, Sipo."

"He was stupid to get insulting. You don't get insulting to him."

"To whom, Sipo? Whom did he get insulting to?"

He had slipped again. Sipo tried to focus on anything but Jana. Jana started to close the circle that she'd been building around him.

"In those kinds of meetings, it's stupid to get angry. Except, once in a while, everybody gets angry." She smiled encouragingly. "These men were very angry at each other, eh? They couldn't reach an agreement. There was a big falling-out. They were now enemies. That's why you were sent to warn Bogan. Right, Sipo?" She snapped her fingers as if she had just understood something. "So, one of the men sent you to warn Bogan. Right, Sipo? After the meeting failed. And it did fail, right?" Jana didn't wait for an answer. "Let's see, who could that person have been, the one who sent you to warn Bogan? Not the Turk, or Akso, or Balder?" She checked Sipo's face. It was none of the men she had just named. "Obviously, the men you've named were on the same side. Otherwise one of them would have warned Bogan. That's why you said 'they,' meaning the three of them, were on the same side and were going to do something, and *he* opposed it. So, it had to be this other man who sent you to Bogan, the one you haven't named. Correct, Sipo?"

Sipo's fear had become all-consuming, an earthquake of tremors racking his body.

"The last man, Sipo?" Jana asked. "The final man at the meeting. Give me his name, Sipo."

Sipo managed to shake his head no. His mouth was trying to make sounds, but he was unable to get any words out. Abruptly, the man's bladder gave way, urine staining his pants. All three of the police officers took an involuntary step back from the frightened man, not wanting to be splattered.

Sipo looked down at his pants, aghast at what had happened.

As far as Sipo was concerned, the fifth man who had been there when he got the information on Bogan was much more terrifying than Jana or her officers could ever be. Jana was sure of one thing: just thinking of the man was so terrifying to Sipo that he would surely never name him.

Jana didn't like what she had just done. It might have been necessary, but it was ugly. There was an inhumanity to the process. She was embarrassed for Sipo and angry with herself. It all came down to how far you could go as a police officer. There is always a point in an interrogation when a police officer can take a step too far over the line; and although they had not beaten the man or used other, more draconian, coercive techniques, Jana felt that she had taken that step. Sipo was the kind of man who wouldn't know much more anyway, because he wouldn't have wanted to hear it. He would know that becoming aware of the wrong kind of information would be very dangerous to him.

And they didn't even really need to get the information from Sipo. They already had the information. The girl had supplied it. The girl was something of a liar, so Jana had simply needed to confirm her story.

Time to leave Sipo alone.

"Stand him up against the counter," Jana ordered. Grzner and Seges propped him up against it as a support and stepped back quickly, afraid the man might fall and grab for them, getting urine on them in the process.

"Let's go." Jana motioned toward the front door. She trailed behind the other two officers as they left, to check out Sipo one last time. Acutely conscious about what he had done, and how he looked, he turned away, vainly hoping to conceal his urine-stained trousers.

Feeling sorry for him, Jana decided to give Sipo a parting message.

"Any man who leaves you this frightened isn't one you want to hang around with, Sipo. Men like that kill folks, or worse. Who knows, Sipo? You might be next on his list. If you need help from me, call." That possibility, given the circumstances, was very real. "Do you understand, Sipo?"

Sipo nodded.

Jana walked out, finding herself surprisingly discomfited.

Jana went over the names of the men, besides Sipo, at the meeting. The Turk? Was Sipo afraid of the Turk? It wasn't the Turk that Sipo was afraid of. Nor was it Akso or Balder. No. He'd given all their names up to get the officers off his back. Sipo was afraid of someone else.

The other man at the meeting.

Chapter 13

Years ago, when Jana was a young teenager, the Young Communist League group that her mother led had gone to see the Slavin War Memorial. It was a trip that they took at least once a year, to show the world how much they appreciated the help their brother Slavs had given Slovakia when the Nazis had occupied their country. On this outing, as on the other outings that her mother led, Jana and Sofia, her best friend, stayed as far away from Jana's mother as possible. Past experience had shown Jana that it was best to avoid her mother at events like this, because her party fanaticism always got the better of her.

That day, Jana's mother kept up an active verbal exchange with the Communist youths throughout the bus ride. She kept up a barrage of commentary, simultaneously questioning members of the consomol group on what she had been "teaching." This trip had already proved hard enough for Jana. Her mother had a favorite target to focus on when she was teaching: Jana. It had been impossible, on the bus, with her mother patrolling up and down the aisle, to avoid the question-and-answer game her mother was playing.

"And why are we glad to be allied to the Soviet Union?" Jana's mother pointed to her. It was Jana's signal to give the answer she had learned by rote from her mother.

"Because they are the leaders of the progressive forces

in the world. We are in conflict with the reactionary groupings that seek to subvert our homeland, and we can rely on the leadership, protection, and partnership of the Soviet Socialist Republics. We are one!" At her mother's urging, all of the other kids on the bus would begin to chant, "We are one! We are one! We are one!" Her mother beamed at the group, the young Communists validating her own "patriotism" and her local Communist Party work, which were driving forces in her life. She was happy because she was influencing the next generation of party faithful.

Everything was fine until Jana's mother started on her next round of proselytizing, popping questions and prompting other young Communists, preparing to focus on Jana again. "And what happened yesterday in Prague is an example of the anti-democratic forces still at work in our country. The attempt to hold a demonstration in our capital city, a disturbance which attempted to vilify the beneficial presence of our Soviet brothers, is a forceful example of the continuing attempts to undermine our unity of purpose and collective strength. Why do you think these people would do such a thing?"

Jana's mother looked around, hoping to find a volunteer. Finding none, she turned to Jana. "We all know that these hooligans are troublemakers. Why were they intent on doing the damage they did in Wenceslas Square?"

Jana had heard that there was a demonstration in Prague, but she knew nothing about the particulars. "I don't know much about it, Mother."

"I am called 'Comrade' here, Jana," her mother reminded her.

"Comrade Mother," Jana corrected herself.

"Then let me tell you all about it," her mother said, her voice going up a notch in volume so she could be sure it would reach all the children. "Unauthorized, non-per-mitted, lackey elements of the Fascists in Western Europe and America gathered and marched up Vaclavske Namesti to the great statue of Wenceslas near the National Museum. They carried signs and chanted terrible slogans. Warmongers shrieked for action against our government and our allies, even calling for us to withdraw from the Warsaw Pact, a symbol of the union between brother nations. They lit a bonfire and fought our police when they were quietly asked to leave the square in peace. Why would they do that, Jana?"

"Fight the police?"

"That, and everything else they did."

"I heard a student burned himself to death the other day."

The children made sounds of recognition. Everyone had heard about that.

Jana's mother was angry at the student who had delib-erately burned himself to death to protest the Communist regime, not because he had chosen to martyr himself but because he'd attacked the government she had invested so much of her time, energy, and hope in. "And who here thinks that burning yourself to death in some bizarre and deranged protest is the way to help our country?"

There was silence as the kids stared at each other, shaking their heads. None of them could conceive of burning themselves to death, no matter what the issue was.

"Part of the fanatic behavior that the enemies of the state all exhibit. It shows how misguided they are and why the police have to take action against them. We cannot let our country descend into chaos or let criminal elements corrode people's minds."

There was a general murmur of approval.

"Do you agree, Jana?" her mother asked her pointedly.

"Of course, Comrade Mother."

"And the police were correct in clearing the streets of that trash when they marched?"

"I believe so, Comrade Mother."

Jana's mother looked her over, thinking that she had heard a doubt in her daughter's statement.

"Are you sure, Jana?"

Jana thought about her answer, aware that she had better say something that her mother would approve of. She made her voice as firm and assured as she could. "Whenever the public does an act that threatens the general well-being of the nation, then it is the responsibility of the police to discharge their duty."

"Good," said her mother, satisfied.

When the bus stopped and the Young Communist League group went outside, Jana retreated to the back of the crowd with her friend Sofia.

"Your mother is very strong," said Sofia.

"She's a caring person," Jana affirmed, deliberately misreading Sofia's meaning.

"Does she always talk about Communism at home?" Sofia wanted to know.

"She talks about the things that all mothers talk about," Jana assured her.

"And socialism too?" Sofia probed. "Perhaps most of the time?"

"Of course," Jana said, not quite liking what her friend was suggesting. "But she loves our family."

"Not like she acts here?"

"She's my mother," Jana insisted, "and she acts like all mothers do with their families."

"Good," Sofia mouthed, not quite believing it.

They reached the monument to the Russian dead who had fallen in their assault on the Nazis defending Bratislava. The first thing the group saw was the central memorial hall, its high obelisk topped with a statue of a Soviet soldier looming over everything; then the mass graves with the six thousand Russian soldiers interred in them. Then they saw the people carrying placards marching in front of the monument.

It was an unexpected shock. The placards read: RUSSIANS GET OUT, FREE CZECHOSLOVAKIA, and END THE OPPRESSION, and the eight or ten demonstrators were all young, enthusiastically shouting anti-Communist slogans. They were all of college age, looking like everyone's older brother or sister, so it was easy for the group of young Communists to relate to them.

Suddenly, a group of twenty or thirty police officers appeared. Without any provocation or any apparent order being given, they charged the group of demonstrators, clubbing them, pulling them to the ground, dragging them to waiting vans and slinging them inside, totally ignoring the demonstrators' pleas for the police officers to stop.

Without realizing that she was doing it, Jana began walking to the front of the Young Communist League group, her steps quickening, propelled by some inner drive to stop the beatings. She screamed at the police to stop, her pace increasing to a trot, when she was abruptly grabbed from behind. Her mother held her by the hair and then twisted her around by her arm, pushing her back toward their group.

"What are you doing?" she half screamed in Jana's ear. "Those are police. They are doing their job. Stay away from them."

"They're hurting those people," Jana managed to get out.

"That's the fault of the demonstrators," her mother growled, her anger at Jana's action driving her to twist her daughter's arm even more.

"They shouldn't be clubbing them, Mother." Jana began crying, not sure if she was crying because her mother was hurting her or because she was upset at what was being done to the protestors.

When they got back to the Young Communist League group, Jana's mother released her just as one of the protestors, attempting to escape from the police, dashed past them, only to be caught by the pursuing officers. The officers systematically began to beat him. The group of young people in Jana's group started screaming in terror, crying and hugging each other for protection. Jana tried to pull away from her mother to help her fellow student— as she thought of the young man being pounded by the officers' clubs—only to have her mother tighten her grip.

The young man was beaten to the ground and two of the officers, one holding each leg, dragged him away. The young man's head bumped along the ground from stone to stone, and Jana wondered how his skull could stay in one piece, picturing it fragmenting into shards at any moment, like a dropped egg. The youth's eyes popped open, and for a brief second Jana thought he was conscious enough to exchange a glance with her. "Why has this happened to me?" he seemed to be asking. Jana had no answer for him.

All she knew, despite her mother's arguments, was that the police had savagely maltreated innocent people, particularly this one human being, and there was no excuse for it.

Chapter 14

Jana walked to the car where Jonas was sitting with Em. The girl got out as Jana approached. She was jumping with excitement. "What I said was the truth, wasn't it? Next time you won't doubt me."

"Yes, I will." Jana's voice was firm. "I doubt everything little girls tell me. I was a girl once, and I know they mix lies and facts together when it suits their purpose. And you, Em, have a purpose."

Em stopped dancing around and stared up at Jana. "What purpose could I possibly have in lying to you?"

"Are you saying you would never lie to me?" Jana paused, letting the question sink in. "Never?"

"Everybody lies sometimes," Em reluctantly acknowledged.

"So how would I know you were telling the whole truth unless I checked? To make both of us less uneasy, and to make sure that I don't waste police resources, I'm informing you now that I will always check everything you tell me."

Em caught a hint of mockery in Jana's tone. "You're making fun of me."

"A little bit."

"Why?"

"You didn't tell me the whole truth about one of the men who talked to Sipo."

Em frowned, her nose and mouth wrinkling up as if she had just been placed in close proximity to something distasteful.

"Am I right, Em?" Jana inquired, watching the girl, waiting to see how she would react.

Em shrugged, neither afraid nor embarrassed that she'd been caught for having presented a slightly distorted version of the facts. "Okay, so he wasn't a Jew; he was a Turk. Everybody blames the Jews, so what's the harm?"

"You harmed yourself. You have to understand that now, at this moment, I can't completely trust you. To give me back that confidence that I've lost in you, you'll have to tell me who the other man was as well."

Em looked up at the police officers now surrounding her, then waved her hand in a gesture of agreement. Then she began to nod enthusiastically as if she'd come up with an idea. "First we have to make another bargain." She giggled. "It's only fair." Em pointed to one of Jana's ears. "Besides, you're wearing my earrings, and I need to be paid."

Jana had put the earrings on that morning. The three other officers stared at her as if the earrings were alien bugs that had just hopped out of nowhere to nest on her earlobes. Jana was somewhat unnerved at the scrutiny.

"You gave me the earrings because I rescued you from the snowstorm," Jana reminded Em.

"I paid you back with the information I gave you."

"You gave me the information because you wanted to stay out of the state welfare home. That was the payment."

Both of them were raising their voices, arguing.

"You don't seem to be grateful at all that I gave you the information," Em said.

"I've told you I'm grateful; grateful for the *correct* information."

"You're certainly not showing it."

Before she really started shouting, Jana realized that she was quarreling with a teenager. It was not an appropriate thing for a commander of police to be doing. It was also not very adult. Jana lowered her voice and made a conscious effort to take the edge off, trying to sound reasonable.

"We have to be candid with each other, Em. Belief is based on trust. I trusted you. And you trusted me. To keep that mutual trust, you have to complete the rest of your agreement: identify the other man."

Em didn't like the idea. She turned and stalked back to the police vehicle, climbed into the rear seat, and, looking straight ahead, ignored everyone. Jana waited a moment to let the girl cool down, then went over to the car, got in the front seat, and turned around to face Em. She wanted information; Em had it. A little compromise was in order.

"You wanted to make another bargain?" Jana said. "Tell me what it is. I'll decide if I want to accept the terms."

Em remained stiff in her seat, her lips tightly closed. Jana lowered her voice even more, trying to soothe whatever raw feelings the girl had suffered in their brief tiff. "I'm giving us another chance to make a bargain. Both of us lose if we don't. If, however, you want to make a contract between the two of us, you'll have to decide to keep all the terms. No leaving anything out. We tell each other everything. Agreed?"

Em didn't move for another few seconds; then she flashed a smile. "Agreed."

"Good."

"All I want is for you to take me to the clothing stores on Obchodna."

"Clothing stores?"

"I have a list of places, up here." She pointed to her head. "I'm not having much success selling door to door. Besides, it's freezing at this time of year. So I've been scouting which places might take my earrings. The jewelry stores don't like my kind of stuff; the ladies' clothing stores should. Women always want the little things that go with their purchases, but nothing too expensive. The earrings I make are perfect. Cheap, but nice. Except the store owners won't buy from me because of my age. They don't think I'll come through with their orders. If you come along to reassure them, they'll buy."

Jana shook her head in disagreement. "Not good. I'm in uniform. I'd be using my official position to help you. I can't do that."

"I didn't ask you to help me: I only asked you to come with me. You don't even have to stand next to me, and I'll never mention you."

"They'll know I'm with you."

"So what?" Em shifted impatiently in her seat. "You get what you want; I get what I want. I'm not doing anything illegal; you're not doing anything illegal. And, at the end of it, I take you to the man you want."

Jana reconsidered her reluctance to go with Em. Say she went into the stores with the child. It wasn't as if she'd be asking for graft. Besides, the greater good would be served by getting the girl to truthfully identify the fifth man included in the talk with Sipo. It was just a tradeoff. Still, it was irritating for Jana to be bargaining with a young teenager and, worse, to feel like she had in some way come out second-best in the bargaining process.

"An agreement, then," Jana consented.

The two of them sealed their bargain with a handshake.

They went to six locations in the Obchodna business

district, the other police officers waiting in their cars as Jana and Em both went into the stores together. As soon as they entered, Jana would wander off to look at the clothes, the clerks and the managers all eyeing her, knowing she was there with Em, all of them giving the girl orders for her earrings. It was a cheap price for them to pay for the future goodwill of the police. Jana had to tell herself that the businesspeople were suffering no loss, and in fact they would eventually make a profit for themselves by reselling the earrings at retail prices.

When they had finished with the last of the stores on her list, Em said she could now tell Jana where to find the Turk. But Jana and Em had not talked about Em telling Jana where the Turk was: the bargain had been for Em to identify the fifth man at the meeting. Jana felt her annoyance rising, and she was on the verge of insisting that Em follow through on her promise, when her instincts kicked in and told her not to argue with the girl again. A major investigative rule is to follow up on the information at hand, and Jana would go with that for the moment. She would confront Em with the issue of the fifth man later.

Em had them drive to a small courtyard store advertising electrical repairs. The door was locked, the place apparently closed—except that the lights were on inside the establishment.

Jana eyed Em. "You're sure he works out of here?"

"Positive."

Jana peered through the window, past the counter to the rear of the store, but couldn't see anyone. She considered leaving, but she kept coming back to the fact that the lights were on. She could see the items on the shelves. There were a number of old appliances with tags indicating that they were in there for repair.

A few "new" appliances still in their boxes could be seen,

closer to the windows, but the boxes were smudged and dusty, their edges blunted or torn, indicating that they had been on the shelves for some time. It suggested to Jana that nobody was really interested in keeping the sales items pristine enough to sell to a potential customer. The establishment could not possibly be making enough money to cover its rent, much less to turn a profit selling those beat-up old goods. The shop was for another purpose, the pieces of junk spread around it used as a cover.

Jana looked the door and window over. There was nothing on either of them to indicate that the store was closed. Jana checked her watch. According to the sign on the door listing the business hours, the store should have been open. She signaled to Grzner, and within seconds he had forced the door.

The Turk was in the back of the store, crumpled up behind the counter.

There was an ice pick in his eye.

Perhaps Em was frightened out of her bargain with Jana by seeing the dead man, or perhaps she had simply changed her mind, but she rebuffed all of Jana's attempts to make her talk about the fifth man at the meeting.

Chapter 15

Colonel Trokan slouched at his desk, his face showing no expression as he went over the file copy they had on Makine/Koba. Jana sat across from him, waiting for him to finish. He'd already read the material Jana had put together on the Turk. She unconsciously tapped her forefinger on the chair's armrest, impatient, wanting to get to his observations. In due course, he let out a grunt, then slapped the large file box closed, staring at its cover while he absorbed what he'd read. Then he looked up at her with a mordant smile.

"You might at least have the courtesy not to tap, tap, tap when I'm reading."

"The finger has a mind of its own."

"*You* have a mind of your own," he emended.

"You're upset because we found another body?"

"It's our job to find the bodies that other people leave haphazardly around the country."

"You're upset because I've concluded that Makine is at work in Slovakia."

The colonel scowled, looking unhappy. "I always maintain my composure."

"Not true."

"Stop correcting your superior officer."

"I never correct him when he's right."

"I thought I was always right." He smiled again. "My mother used to say I was always right. She babied me. Of course, she was my mother." He decided to stop joking. "Unfortunately, this time I think you're the one who is correct. I emphasize the word *unfortunately*. The man is in Slovakia." He ran his fingers through his hair in frustration. "Why is our friend Makine, Koba the murderer, the shit who makes every law enforcement agency in Europe wish they were practicing another profession, in Slovakia?" He took a deep breath, then sighed, his voice taking on a slightly wistful tone. "We still don't know for sure that he's here."

"Wishful thinking."

"Anyone might have put an ice pick in the Turk's eye."

"Not *anyone*."

"If it was him, maybe we should thank the man. The Turk was a very ugly human being. A bad man who should have been killed years ago. He was the one we thought was behind the killing of that diplomat involved in selling passports out of the Bulgarian embassy."

"We *thought* he was behind that."

"Now we don't even have to think about the Bulgarian affair, or about the Turk." Trokan pulled a tissue from a box on his desk, blew into it noisily, then crumpled it and dropped it into his wastebasket with a flourish. "He's gone, just like that, from my mind." He snapped his fingers. "No more Turk."

"Wrong," Jana corrected.

"I choose to look on the bright side of this problem."

"What part of it is the bright side?"

"The side that I'm not required to look at." He shifted in his seat, adjusting his injured shoulder to make himself more comfortable. He grimaced from a twinge of pain. "The world is going to shit."

"Only parts of it."

"I only worry about our parts of it."

"How's your shoulder?"

"Becoming even more proficient at predicting the weather."

"You now have a secondary profession to fall back on."

Trokan grunted, not amused. "If I can't do my job, I deserve to be reduced to predicting the weather. So . . . save my job, Jana. Your suggestions are in order."

"We have to find out what the Turk was currently into that got him killed. It's the best way I can think of to get Makine."

"I don't want to think it's Makine," the colonel snapped, trying to retreat from confronting the man's presence in Bratislava. "We've gotten no response to the bulletin we sent out to our people; there are no other reports about Makine being in this country. The only reason we believe it's Makine is because of the weapon he used on the Turk."

"And where he *placed* the weapon. That's been a signature for him."

"And where he placed the ice pick in the man," Trokan reluctantly agreed.

"And his presence at Bogan's party," Jana reminded him.

"It might not have been him."

"You said that on the night of the party."

"I don't want to think of the night of the party."

"Too late. You're already thinking about it."

The colonel let out another grunt. "I keep coming back to it in my mind. What else am I thinking?"

"If Makine was at the party and you're thinking that he was involved in the Turk's murder, then you're putting together the Turk's murder with the Bogan killing and deciding that they're both related."

"I am not," he insisted.

"It's what we're both thinking."

"Okay," he grudgingly allowed. "We're both thinking it."

"The other immediate question is, why did Makine let us know he did it? He has to be aware that ice pick killing is a signature of his that we'd pick up on."

"He always lets everyone know. The man wants his competition to grasp that he's a monster. He tells them what he is, and it frightens them all. Nobody fools with him. Hell, the man frightens *me*."

"I think it's something else."

The colonel moaned. "Why am I so worried about what you're going to reveal?"

"I think he may have led us from the Bogan killing to the Turk intentionally. Why would he want us to connect the two?" She reflected on her supposition. "Maybe to let us know that there's a war on and to expect more deaths. More of the fear game he plays."

Trokan winced at the suggestion of more deaths. "Why would he want us to come into his game at all?"

"Maybe he doesn't want us to come in. Perhaps it's a warning to stay out?"

"I'd love to stay out. Unfortunately, considering what we do for a living, we can't." Trokan began massaging his temples. "I'm tired of the man. You'd think he would have gone away by now."

"Kobas don't go away. We have to make them disappear."

"A good thought. Make him disappear, Jana."

"I'm not a magician."

"Yes, you are. I've come to depend on the magic."

He sat up and pulled a new file in front of him, making a show of organizing the papers inside to demonstrate that he had other work to do; then he looked up, his face telling her that he was relying on her. "Help me on this, Jana."

"I'll try, Colonel."

"And the little girl?

"In my office with Seges."

"The girl took you to the man who told you about the Turk. Then to the Turk. Too much to believe it was chance when she first came to you."

"Yes."

"Ask her."

"I will."

"Commander, my head will be on the butcher's table over this thing. Do your best."

"Of course, Colonel."

"Commander, just because she's a young girl doesn't make her your grandchild. If it interferes too much, you have to take yourself off the case. You're a police officer. Get the information, no matter what you have to do."

"Thank you for reminding me of my duty, Colonel." There was an edge to her voice. "I'm always forgetting it. Right, Colonel?"

"Never, Jana." He smiled at her. "Don't take offense. I'm just doing what colonels always do: pass the worry down the line."

He blew his nose again as Jana left the room.

Jana's ration of worry quickly got even worse.

As soon as she passed some of her men in the hall, she knew things were not right. They were uneasy, watching her out of the corners of their eyes, waiting for an expected reaction. She walked into her office, where Seges was supposedly keeping an eye on Em. Em was not in the room.

Seges's face was easy to read, the worry lines around his eyes and mouth apparent, his shoulders hunched.

"She escaped, Commander."

"Escaped, Seges?"

"Gone, Commander."

"How?"

"She went to the bathroom. Then, just like that, she was gone."

"Just like that?"

He hesitated. "Yes."

"Seges, I will refrain from pistol-whipping you only because of my enormous willpower. However, unless you are out of sight within the next twenty seconds, I will lose my self-control. So I advise you to leave."

Seges scurried out of the office.

Jana took stock, wondering how she was going to sugar-coat the news that the girl had successfully run away from police custody. The colonel was definitely not going to like hearing this. It was not the kind of "help" he'd had in mind when he'd spoken to her just a minute ago.

Chapter 16

Jana sent Jonas, Grzner, and Seges out to the studio to speak to the manager and staff of the soundstage. There were a number of questions that were still unanswered after her earlier visit. Despite the generally rundown nature of the studio, and despite its inactivity, it *was* a fenced and locked location and there had to be people overseeing and safeguarding the area. They would have some of the answers Jana needed. Seges didn't want to go, as usual. Jana, for her own peace of mind, needed him anywhere but around her, so she insisted that he go. She gave instructions on what was to be done.

There was a message for Jana from Smid. He and his son had the information on the tattooed Slovak who'd been run down in Paris, and he wanted to see her when she had the chance. More to get herself away from the office and the nagging question of where Em had gone than because she was eager to get the information, Jana drove over to Heydukova near the small area post office where Smid's son, Jiri, had his stamp shop. The tiny store was sandwiched between a locksmith shop and an even tinier day-old, marked-down baked goods place. It was obviously a minimal rental area for businesses.

The son's shop was empty of customers but filled with shelves of stamps, most of them multi-stamp packages meant for low-level collectors who wanted to fill out their collections, the more valuable single-issue stamps in locked glass cabinets. Despite the cleanliness of the place, there was, as in all establishments of that character, an air of mustiness that no amount of air freshener could erase. Jana found Jiri and his father sitting at a pair of small back-to-back half-desks in the rear of the shop. They both stood when she came in. Smid, a big smile on his face, trotted over to Jana.

"I told you we'd come through, Commander."

Jiri, slower than his father, his shoulders sloped from perpetually looking down at his stamps, pulled a loupe from his eye, picked up a small file, and followed his father. He laid the file on the counter in front of Jana.

"Good day, Commander."

"How have you been, Jiri?"

"Good, thank you." He opened the file, pulling out copies of a number of documents. He went through them with Jana, pointing out the salient facts for her.

"Here is the reproduction of the tattoo that you gave us. Then the make sheet on the person with the tattoo. Even several old police reports. They're all difficult to see. These are from old fiche, reproductions of reproductions. The man's photo is very blurred, but you can make enough of it out to use it for identification. You can see the arm." He looked around the counter for a magnifying glass, then handed it to Jana, indicating the spot for her to focus on. "Blurred, but the tattoo is in the right place, with the same stretching. There's also a fingerprint set in the documents, but the lout who generated the fiche didn't do the best job. There's one partial I can make out. I matched it with the print on the same finger of the subject the French are tweaking you about. There are five points of comparison I can make out, none different, but not enough points for a match according to the rules of the print game."

Jana examined the photograph, then checked the report that came with it. The man's physical characteristics matched the dead man's when you took into account the changes that age had made: same eye color, height, and approximate age as the French police subject. And the one fingerprint that they could compare appeared to be close enough to suggest a match.

There was another set of reports detailing the man's background in Slovakia. Jana scanned them. He had been the son of one of the leaders of the Hlinka Guard and had become a member of a fascist adjunct youth group that they had formed shortly before the war ended. The Communists had suppressed the group, as they had done with all dissenting groups. No loss on this, Jana thought.

Shortly after that, while still very young, the subject had begun a criminal career: home burglaries, arson, armed assault. He had done time in a youth facility, in local jails, then one stint in prison. Eventually, in what was by then a full-blown criminal career, he had faced multiple charges for forgery, counterfeiting, and fraud. There was even an arrest on suspicion of murder. The boy had become a man; the man had become a more sophisticated and dangerous thief.

Then it had all ended. The man had dropped off the face of the earth thirty-five years ago, and there were no other entries in his criminal history after that point. Jana made a mental note to run a recent criminal history request to Interpol before sending the file to the French police. That would make it a more complete, professional job.

"Satisfied?" Smid asked.

"Very satisfied," Jana answered.

Smid held up a finger, indicating he would be just a

second, then ran to his desk, picked up a sheet of paper and a pen, then trotted back to Jana.

"Our payment authorization." He laid it in front of her. "Notice I only charged for one day rather than the day and a half authorized." Smid handed her the pen.

Jana quickly scanned the page, then inked in a correction. "I'm giving you payment for the extra half day. You've earned it." She signed her name, handing the paper and pen back to Smid. "Thank you both."

"Thank you, Commander," they chorused.

Jana took the file, nodded to the two men, and then left the store. As she emerged, Jana realized something that she hadn't registered before: the name of the man in the documents. It was Jindrich Bogan.

Bogan.

Jana immediately became very interested in the French police case.

Chapter 17

Some winters are cold; others are colder. But there is always one that stays in memory as the worst. The winter of 1946 was very, very cold in southeastern Czechoslovakia, with extremely heavy snowfall, even in the low-lying areas. It had been a bad time for the Bogan family, with Jindrich's father being hunted by the Soviets. They had moved from location to location, trying to stay away from the old family cabin outside of Levoca until they no longer had any alternatives. Their last move from Orava had been a forced march, with Jindrich's father warned just in time that the hunters were coming for him. The family had thrown their things into an old horse-drawn wagon, Jindrich and his mother hitching up the horses and picking his father up on the outskirts of the town. They'd headed east along the rough roads leading through the western Tatra Mountains, finally reaching the area near Spis Castle where the cabin was located.

The Soviets had consolidated their hold on the area, rooting out everything they perceived as potentially anti-Communist. They were still setting up their own home-grown Communists in power; to make sure that the young trees took hold, anything that smacked of the old Tiso regime was being extirpated. And Jindrich's father had very much been a part of that old fascist regime. Everyone had known of him. His picture, in full uniform, had been published a number of times in the newspapers. His men, when he was in power, had done their jobs with, perhaps, too much enthusiasm.

He told his son that people had lied about him. They'd claimed that he'd assisted the Germans in suppressing the national uprising against them, that they'd seen him actually killing people whom his group had rounded up. They'd made up falsehoods built on other fabrications, his father assured Jindrich and his mother, making him out to be a terrible man, which was simply not true. And, like most wives, Jindrich's mother, through both good and bad times, supported her husband, and now they were all running and hiding for their lives.

The cabin had been in the family for many years, but they'd only come here on a few occasions since Jindrich's father had become involved in the cause. As he'd patiently explained to his son, dedication to one's country, under trying circumstances, was the mark of a man, and he had done his part. The fact that times had changed for the worse did not mean that his father had made the wrong decision. People simply had not understood the position he'd taken and how Czechoslovakia, and the Slovaks in particular, had benefited from his activities until the war had turned against their allies, the Nazis. History would redeem his beliefs and the actions he had taken on them.

Now they were back in their family cabin, pretending that they were on a vacation. His father assured them, in the warmth of the cabin fire, that when the Soviets left and their country came back to its senses, the family would prosper again—but, for the moment, survival was the basic rule governing their lives.

One morning, Jindrich and his mother had gone into Roznava to get supplies. It was some distance from where they were staying, but Jindrich's mother came from Roznava and a few of her relatives were still there. It would be safer for them to make their purchases in the small town where his mother could use her maiden name and depend upon the close-knit townspeople to protect one of their own than to go into Levoca. It was a hard trek for the horses through the snow, with the trip to Roznava and back taking most of the day. It was not until they were getting near the cabin that Jindrich's mother sensed that something was wrong.

It was not the quiet that seemed to envelop them on the road, because winter always makes for quiet on mountain roads. It was the birds that told her, suddenly emerging to fly in a high circle over the hills to the west. The birds were so far away that they could barely hear them. It was their activity that concerned her, much more activity than even a marauding predator would have created.

Jindrich's mother pushed the horses harder, their already-depleted stamina reflected in their continued plod through the snow. Finally, the wagon reached the top of the hill overlooking their cabin. His mother, even more worried by the continued unusual activity of the birds, insisted on driving the horses into a surround of trees and demanded that Jindrich stay hidden with them while she warned his father. Jindrich watched her slog through the deep snow, down the hill into the little glen that housed the cabin. Nothing seemed out of place as she went through the door; but at the moment she entered, Jindrich heard the roar of engines.

The birds truly had warned them. Two trucks with Russian markings came from the direction of where the birds were circling, steaming over the hill much faster than

Jindrich would have thought possible given the depth of the snow, heading directly for the cabin. Someone had informed on them.

Jindrich could only watch, his mouth agape, as the trucks pulled up to the house and soldiers jumped off of them, kicking the door of the cabin open and storming in. Jindrich could not hear any sounds from inside the cabin over the noise of the engines, which the drivers revved continually to make sure they would not freeze up in the cold. Every few seconds, soldiers would come out of the cabin, some of them laughing and gesturing for others to go inside. Pieces of furniture occasionally flew out of the door. Jindrich grew detached, watching a scene that seemed like a bizarre, slow-motion happening. As time passed, Jindrich fell into a semi-stupor from the bitter cold, and from the fear.

Eventually, they brought his father out.

The soldiers carried him, his arms and legs dangling at abnormal angles. His face was bloody, seemingly even redder than blood, edged in dark crimson against the contrasting background of white snow. The soldiers dumped him in the back of one of the trucks and piled into the vehicles. The trucks roared off. Jindrich waited until they were out of sight before he began his slog down to the cabin, his legs stiff with cold, not obeying his commands very well. He slipped and fell, then willed his arms to push him erect, only to walk a few more meters and fall again. When he got to the cabin door, Jindrich hesitated, afraid of what he would find inside. There was no alternative: he had to go in, because he knew he'd freeze to death if he stayed out in the cold.

Inside, the cabin had been savaged, the furniture all broken, his mother just another piece of the broken furniture on the floor. She was half-dressed, her legs splayed apart, blood on her thighs. Jindrich, even as young as he was, recognized what had happened. His mother had been raped by the soldiers and, somewhere along the way, angry and perhaps ashamed, they'd killed her.

Jindrich didn't quite know what to do. His mother was dead in the corner; his father had been taken away to be killed, if he wasn't dead already. The boy stayed frozen, as aloof and detached as the hills around the cabin, until instinct, the final resort of all wounded animals, pulled him out of his stupor.

He prepared to leave.

There was nothing much that he could salvage from the house: a little money that the soldiers had overlooked in his mother's discarded purse, a keepsake photograph of himself and his friends from the youth group he'd been in, an old blanket to wrap himself in for further insulation against the cold.

The last item Jindrich took with him had been hidden under a loose floorboard. Jindrich was forced to move his mother's leg to get to it. He told himself not to mind too much, because she was dead and couldn't feel it anyway. The item he pulled from its refuge was his father's prized possession, one that he'd taken out and gloated over from time to time, telling both his wife and son that it would be their saving grace one day when the times and events were right to make use of it. Jindrich carefully wrapped it in some of the clothes strewn on the floor of the cabin, then tore a strip from one of his father's shirts to use to tie the bundle together.

The next question he faced was what to do with his mother's body.

Jindrich knew he was supposed to bury her in the ground. That was what people did with the dead. But the ground was so frozen that he couldn't possibly dig out a space big enough to hold her. He finally decided that the easiest course of action was to burn the cabin. He pulled his mother's body to the middle of the room, then piled everything in the cabin that could be burned on top of her. There was still a small amount of kerosene left in the fuel container of the overturned stove. Jindrich poured it over the pile. He then scrabbled through the debris on the floor to find a match. He carefully lit it, then ignited the funeral pyre.

Jindrich watched it flame into life, standing near the pyre, warming himself with the accelerating flames. It was nice to be warm, even for a little while. When the roof of the cabin caught fire, Jindrich knew it was time to leave. Clutching the items he'd retrieved, he slogged up the hill to the horses. There were provisions in the wagon that would feed him for a while.

Jindrich couldn't think of any friends who cared for him, or for his mother or father. This didn't bother him much. He'd never really cared about anyone, not his relatives—or, when it came down to it, even his mother and father. He hoped, despite that, that one of his relatives in Roznava would take him in. After all, Slovaks took care of their families, no matter who they were or what they'd done.

He turned the horses around, starting back to Roznava. He never looked back at the burning cabin. It was unimportant. That part of his life was over.

What had happened had taught him that survival was all that mattered. The means that he used to survive did not.

Chapter 18

The primary targeting of Klara Bogan during the shooting intrigued Jana. Unless they were political figures, women weren't usually the targets of assassinations. However, in this case, killing both Oto and Klara Bogan, husband and wife, had clearly been the objective of the shooters. Investigating the death of one of them required attention to both. Jana decided to focus on the financial assets of the Bogans. With a murder carried out by hired killers, there was invariably money involved, so Jana commandeered the best accountant from their major fraud unit, Lubos Papanek, and put him on the task of ferreting out the Bogans' finances.

Papanek started the "follow the money" game with the small bank in Vienna that Bogan had recently acquired. Unfortunately, as with most tracking procedures involving finances, it would take time for the accountant to complete his inquiry, so Jana focused her own investigative efforts on the Bogan family itself.

The Bogans' son, Zdenko, was at the top of her list, but he was in Berlin and she hadn't yet managed to contact him. That meant her initial approach would be to deal with the family members who were still in Slovakia. She dug into every record she could think of: births, deaths, phone accounts, land records, tax returns, military files, corporate listings, media coverage, even simple census name registries. Odd. From what Jana could find, neither of the Bogans had any living relatives in Slovakia, although both listed themselves as having been born in the country. Klara's maiden name was Zuzulova; but Bogan or Zuzulova, there was still no family. Also odd, although the birth records in some rural areas were occasionally listed only in church registries, neither of the Bogans was accounted for in any municipal birth registries.

Government records that both Bogans had filled out as adults indicated that their parents were dead and that they had been born near each other in central Slovakia. The two listed no siblings. They'd moved to Bratislava, although in different years, as young adults, apparently meeting again in the capital. The one indication that they had anything like another living relative was that Klara had been briefly married to another man just before she came to the capital. He was listed as the prior spouse on the Bogans' civil marriage application. The man's name was Radomir Kralik.

On an impulse, Jana checked for Kralik's name on the list of people invited to the studio party. It was there. She then checked for it on the list of the actual partygoers that the police had compiled. He was not on that one. The man had still been on good enough terms with his ex-wife to be invited to the party, but had apparently chosen not to come. Jana ran Kralik through government records. He was now a resident of Vienna.

It was a simple matter for Jana to then have the Austrian police run Kralik's name through their system. They quickly tracked him, informing her that he was living just outside the Ring limits, on Gumpendorfer, near Alfred Grunwald Park. Jana knew the area. Clean, fairly high rents. Most people who lived in that neighborhood near central Vienna were in the upper income category. The man's recent Austrian job registration was at the Internazionale EuroBank as a vice president in charge of foreign investment.

The IEB was the bank that Bogan had recently bought the majority interest in. It was strange that Bogan would invite Kralik to his party, and even stranger that Bogan had enough confidence in his wife's ex-husband to use him as a bank officer. Then again, as Jana had so often seen, the world was an odd place, and things frequently only seemed abnormal if you didn't know the circumstances that surrounded them. Jana simply had to examine the circumstances. She called Kralik at the bank, getting a secretary who was very Austrian-proper and businesslike on the telephone, and after a brief moment off the phone to get Kralik's approval, the woman made an appointment for Jana to see him that afternoon.

Jana took the train from Petržalka Station, just across the Danube, and in less than an hour she was in the Südbahnhof. She caught a cab and directed the driver to swing by the address that Kralik had listed as his home. He would be at the bank, waiting for Jana to keep their appointment, which was good. You often found out more about people when they were not at home to receive you.

It was older but well kept up and still respectable, a gray stone-and-concrete building that one could easily believe a bank executive might live in. Jana told the taxi driver to park and wait for her, then got out of the vehicle and looked up at the building. According to the government records, Kralik lived on the sixth floor. Jana counted the stories. He lived on the top floor in lofty splendor. After doing a visual check of the area, she walked to the entrance to check the mailboxes just inside the building. There she had a stroke of luck: the building's cleaning woman was mopping the tiled entrance area.

Jana pressed the apartment buzzer listed under Kralik's name, and the cleaning woman checked Jana out as she stood pretending to wait for an answer from the apartment.

"He's at work," the cleaning woman told her in an accent that suggested her German wasn't native, her speech inflections acquired in a classroom across the river in Slovakia. Jana answered in Slovak, and the woman immediately brightened, responding with a *dobry den*. The woman's presence here was not unusual. Slovaks came to Austria to get work, mostly menial jobs like this woman's. The job paid substantially more here than she could have earned in Slovakia.

"I'm here to see Mr. Kralik," Jana said. "He was supposed to supply me with a package."

"No package." The woman spread her arms to take in the surrounding space, showing that there was no package in the area. "He didn't leave anything with me."

"He actually said he'd leave it by the door to the apartment. Do you think I might go up and look for it?"

"I'm not supposed to let anyone in," said the woman.

Jana showed the woman her Slovak police identification. "Police." Jana waited while the cleaning lady took a hasty look at the credential, then smiled reassuringly at her. "I promise not to loot the apartments if you let me inside the building. I do need that package," Jana assured her. "It's vital for an investigation."

"You're not an Austrian officer. This is Austria."

Jana decided to try another tack. She made a big show of going through her purse, eventually finding a pair of two-euro coins. You stayed low if you were going to give a person a gratuity. Offering too much money would suggest that she was very anxious to get inside the building, possibly with an unsavory reason for wanting to gain access.

Jana pressed the coins into the woman's hand. "For your brief inconvenience. I just need a minute upstairs, and I'll come back past you on the way out so you'll know I haven't taken anything."

The woman eyed Jana, ultimately deciding that she was dressed too presentably to be a thief. Besides, she did have a police credential, and she was a Slovak. Most of all, near-poverty makes for greed. The woman opened the inner door for Jana to go inside.

"Five minutes. If you're not down by then, I call the Austrian police. Understood?"

"No problems."

"Five minutes," the woman called after her, tucking the coins away and going back to her work.

Jana took the elevator to the top floor. As soon as she stepped out, she was confronted by a single large, polished wood door leading into the lone apartment on the floor. A single apartment on the top floor! Quite posh. Exclusive. Upmarket. The opportunity to see the interior of the apartment was too much for Jana to resist. She had the lock picked in less than a minute and was inside the apartment a second after that.

It was even bigger and better furnished than Jana had anticipated. The décor was a little more modern than Jana's taste, but everything was polished, the wood gleaming, the couches soft leather, the rooms painted in attractive pastel colors. However, it was the display of photographs in the main room that caught her eye.

The same two people appeared in almost all of them: Klara and a man who could only be Kralik. The photos showed them in a variety of cute poses and relaxing locations. Always smiling, lovingly feeding each other at a restaurant, in bathing suits with their arms around each other at some resort, posing with tennis rackets.

Surprisingly, Oto Bogan was also with them in one of the photographs, the three of them seated on a couch, smiling at the camera, all looking very comfortable with each other. Even more strangely, they all were wearing contemporary clothes in that photo, and Klara had a contemporary hair style. The snapshot had to have been taken in recent years, long after Kralik and Klara had been divorced. And yet there they were—Oto Bogan, Klara, and Kralik—looking like three companionable friends.

Jana made a quick foray into the huge master bedroom and opened a vast wardrobe closet near the bed. Women's clothing filled it. Jana checked the sizes. They would have fit Klara. And in the master bathroom, with its huge step-down bath, women's toiletries were arranged for use next to one of the two sinks, a man's toiletries next to the other. Cozy his-and-hers. Klara and Radomir Kralik had still been a twosome, even though they were divorced and Klara was married to Oto Bogan.

And from the photograph taken of all three of them, it looked like Mr. Bogan was aware of the continuing relationship between his wife and Kralik and was untroubled by it. Sometimes abnormal situations remained astonishing, no matter how much they were explained. This was one of them.

A few minutes later, Jana was on her way to see Kralik at the bank. She wondered how he'd shed light on the situation.

Chapter 19

The Internazionale EuroBank was a block behind St. Stephen's Cathedral on Wollzeile, a street that appeared to specialize in nondescript businesses. The bank had a contemporary storefront, with a multi-angled window facing the street, giving the impression of studied risk without loss of stability. The place, once entered, was quiet, a deep pile rug dampening any footsteps. There was one teller window with a solitary customer, and a small number of working executive desks spread around the floor bearing the names and titles of their occupants, most of whom were on the phone. The bank did not seem to encourage walk-in traffic, rather catering to a select few businesses in the Vienna area and a clientele suggested by its name: people and firms interested in international banking.

Jana walked in, asking the woman acting as a receptionist at the front where she could find Kralik. The nameplate on the desk read: ELKE RILKE. It was the same woman who had taken Jana's call about arranging the appointment with Kralik. Rilke directed Jana to a larger-than-usual desk in the rear of the bank, the desk protected by a surround of tubular chrome railing that declared the importance of the desk and its occupant. As Jana approached, she could make out Radomir Kralik's name and his title, Vice President, in slightly larger type than on the other desk nameplates, another sign of rank for anyone who might notice.

A man came from the rear of the bank and approached the desk at the same time as Jana, taking a seat behind it just before she got there. Kralik, realizing she was the appointment he was expecting, immediately stood back up, extended his hand, and gave her a hearty *Grüss Gott*, the standard Austrian greeting.

Speaking in fluent German, Kralik told the receptionist to hold all calls, then switched to Slovak to talk with Jana.

"Very happy to meet you, Commander. I was shocked, terribly shocked by the death of Mrs. Bogan. She was very important to this bank, and we are all grieving her loss." Kralik had a black armband around his upper left arm to signify mourning. "The way she died was unbelievable."

"My condolences."

"Thank you," Kralik responded, his face and voice taking on the tone of sorrow appropriate for the moment. Within seconds, though, he was back to his standard cordial vice president's mien. "So, you've come to ask questions which have been raised by the murder. Feel free to ask me anything."

"Anything?"

"Of course. We have nothing to hide."

"Good." Jana settled back in her chair. "How long had you known the Bogans, Mr. Kralik?"

Kralik looked surprised. "You haven't come to discuss Mr. Bogan's involvement in the bank? That's what I prepared for."

"Not this visit. At a later time." She watched Kralik. He hadn't anticipated that she might be here to talk about his personal relationship to the Bogans, and he didn't quite like it. "I'm aware that you've known them for a number of years. The 'problem' that generated the attack may have emerged from their past. That's the purpose of my visit."

"I see." Kralik's tone was worried. "I prefer not to get into their personal lives."

"Is there something in their personal lives which you feel should be kept private?"

Kralik looked like a deer who suddenly realizes he's framed in the gunsight of a hunter. Jana made matters worse for him: "I understand you had a relationship with Mrs. Bogan of long standing. Can you describe that relationship?"

It took him a while to get the words out.

"I . . . we were married at one time," he finally said. "However . . . we remained good friends afterward."

"All three of you?"

"Yes."

"You were divorced from Klara?"

"Yes."

"An amicable divorce?"

"We were both reasonable people."

Elke Rilke came up to Kralik and placed a document on a letterhead in front of him to sign. She murmured an apology for interrupting. Kralik signed the paper without even reading what was written on it. Rilke nodded her thanks to Jana for waiting, then walked back to her station.

"An efficient woman," Jana commented.

"Very trustworthy," Kralik acknowledged. Kralik's eyes had taken on a glazed look, not from any of the secretary's actions, but because of the subject that Jana had brought up.

"I see there are lots of items for you to attend to," Jana said. "This shouldn't take too long."

"Good."

Jana was silent for a few seconds, watching Kralik. He

was apprehensive, moving too much in his chair, trying to deal with whatever emotions her questions had generated. "Mr. Kralik, you and Klara were still lovers, weren't you?"

Kralik's eyes snapped back to attention. He was rocking slightly. He started to stutter a denial, then cut himself off, then began again, this time forcing himself to be open.

"I always loved her. Always."

"She's the one who wanted the original divorce?"

"She'd met Bogan. They saw something in each other which they needed. Suddenly, I was a divorced man. It was business for them. I was last year's goods."

Kralik ran his fingers through his hair.

"Then later, you became a couple again," Jana suggested.

"They no longer needed or wanted each other for closeness. He had other women when he wanted one. That was all right with Klara. Klara found me again."

"And that was okay with Bogan?"

He hesitated. "Even better."

"How was it better?"

"He had Klara as a loyal helpmate, a partner who made no demands on him. She had me, so she didn't need Bogan in that way. I had Klara back again, which was good. And Bogan could depend upon me in every way as far as business matters were concerned, since I was involved with Klara."

"Your apartment on Gumpendorfer was purchased by the Bogans?"

Kralik tried to answer the question without embarrassing himself. He couldn't quite do it. "Klara wanted a nice place for us."

"And your bank position here? A happy family?"

"Yes."

"Their son. Is he part of their business?"

"Zdenko." He paused, as if having a problem conjuring up their son in his mind. "I seldom dealt with Zdenko. But, to answer your question, I don't think so." He searched through his memory. "Perhaps the bank dealt with him on one or two things, but not through me."

"Are any other of the Bogans' relatives still alive?"

"Klara never spoke of any. It never came up with Bogan."

"I've been trying unsuccessfully to talk to their son in Berlin. Do you have any phone numbers for him? Perhaps his place of business?"

Kralik went into his desk and came out with a file card. After a period of hesitation, as if he didn't want to part with the card, he handed it to Jana. "Keep it. I have no reason to contact him."

Kralik's voice had grown hoarse, his body shrinking into itself as if he loathed what he had just done.

"Did you get along with Klara's son Zdenko, Mr. Kralik?"

There was no answer. Jana became more insistent.

"Can you answer the question, Mr. Kralik?"

He did not answer Jana's question directly. "He's Klara's son. That's enough for me."

"Do you have any idea why anyone would have wanted to kill Mr. Bogan?"

"None."

"Were you aware of all the business dealings Mr. and Mrs. Bogan had?"

"I came into Bogan's business life quite late, so the answer is no."

"And Klara. Why would anyone want to kill her?"

Kralik looked at Jana as if he couldn't quite understand what she was saying. "I thought she was killed because she got in the way during the shooting."

"The news media surmised that. We have reason to believe otherwise."

Kralik appeared deeply shaken by the information. His lips quivered, and his head wobbled slightly on his neck, as if it had developed loose ball bearings at the base. "I can't think of any reason."

Jana didn't believe him. The man had thought of a reason Klara Boganova might have been killed, but he couldn't get it past his lips so that Jana could hear it.

"You were invited to the party, Mr. Kralik. Why didn't you go?"

He shrugged as if to suggest he didn't know. Everything about the man's demeanor now indicated that he was emotionally, and conversationally, moving further away from Jana.

"What are you thinking, Mr. Kralik?"

Kralik pulled himself together. "My thoughts are mine. Private matters are private."

"Not if they're also police issues."

"I have work to do, Commander. There is nothing more I can add."

"Nothing?"

"Nothing, Commander."

Jana plunged on, but the well had dried up, Kralik answering her questions in a monotone with "I don't know" and "I have no information about that" answers. She needed to find the lever that would pry the man's now-sealed collaboration back open. Perhaps Klara's son, she thought. Whatever it was that Jana had triggered within Kralik, it was eating at him now.

A few minutes later, after a very wet and very slack hand-shake from an extremely nervous Kralik, Jana stepped out of the bank. She walked toward where she knew she could get a taxi, about thirty meters away, planning to catch a ride to the train terminal and head back to Bratislava. The street had become busier, and Jana was nudged aside by a large woman trying to get into the first taxi just before the initial bullet burned through the surface of the dorsal side of her upper arm. It pulled her around slightly so that the second bullet came at her face, nicking her under the chin and leaving a wound that looked like a shaving cut on a man having a very bad razor day.

Jana scrambled to the side of the road, ducking into an open children's furniture shop. The customers, all of them either pregnant women looking to fill out their baby-furniture needs or mothers-in-law trying to ingratiate themselves with their new daughters-in-law, stared at the bleeding woman who had suddenly dropped in on their lives to spoil their innocent pleasures. Someone called the police. A few minutes later, both an ambulance and the Austrian police arrived to take Jana to the hospital.

For the moment, Jana was very glad to have a police escort. Under the circumstances, it provided a certain amount of comfort.

Chapter 20

Trokan was frantic, much more worried than Jana was. He called half a dozen Austrian officials to make sure that she was not only protected in the hospital but that she got absolutely the best doctors. He called her hospital room every two hours, which began to annoy her, but he was her colonel so she tolerated it.

The Austrian police were professional but starchy, as the Austrians always are, and they got even starchier when they realized she was a police officer. Jana tried, unsuccessfully, to explain that she was not in Austria to create problems. The Austrians became even more unhappy when they discovered that she hadn't bothered to clear her presence as a Slovak investigator in their country before interrogating a witness; they weren't even placated by the fact that the witness she had questioned was a Slovak. Her saving moment arrived when a call eventually came in, alerting the Austrian officers that Jana had friends in high places on their own police force. It had to be Trokan at work behind the scenes. Jana silently thanked him.

Unfortunately, when the Austrians tried to question Kralik at the bank, they found that he'd absented himself. He had told his staff he was going to visit his old and sick mother. When they contacted her, she cheerfully informed the police that she wasn't sick and hadn't heard from her son in months. After the Viennese police had finished with their initial shooting-scene examination, they told Jana they had no idea who had shot her, or even where the shots had come from.

Jana's wounds were not serious. There was no severe muscle impairment in the arm, and the bullet had gone straight through. The doctors simply sewed up the wound. The lesion under her chin worried her more because she thought it might leave a significant scar. The plastic surgeon they brought in for a quick consultation assured her it would merely leave a thin scar that would be virtually invisible, unless, he added jokingly, her lover kissed her on the neck. He chuckled at his own humor all the way down the hospital corridor.

Early the next morning, Jana slipped out of the hospital and went to the train depot, taking the first scheduled train of the day to Bratislava. She had parked at Petržalka when she'd gone to Vienna, and she quickly found her car when she arrived. She drove directly to the Obchodna business district and left the vehicle in a no-parking zone, setting her police permit on the dashboard to avoid problems with the parking police. She then walked to a newspaper, magazine, and periodical store across from the women's clothing shop that had placed the largest earring order with Em. There was a large picture window in the front of the magazine store which had just enough space around the advertisements taped to it to allow Jana a clear view across the street.

Snow had started falling again, beginning to cover the grime that coats the streets after a day of normal urban life in a business district. Jana plucked one of the magazines from a wall rack, browsing through it as she waited, watching the pedestrian traffic. It wasn't until the third or fourth tram that Jana saw Em through the increasing snowfall. The girl hopped off the Number 8 tram coming from the direction of Bratislava Castle and went directly to the clothing shop. Jana put her magazine back in the rack, walked out of the shop, and went across the street to the clothing store. The first thing she saw when she went inside was Em arguing with the manager.

Jana used the mat to kick the snow off her shoes, then walked over to the register where the store manager and Em were having their confrontation. Em noticed Jana coming and gave her a brief smile, not surprised to see her. Em turned in triumph to the manager as if Jana's appearance had been planned.

"I told you I wouldn't let you cheat me." She turned back to Jana. "This woman has sold eight pairs of my earrings and refuses to pay me the money she owes me. So pull out your gun and shoot her." She folded her arms across her chest, waiting for Jana to comply.

Jana stared at the girl just long enough for Em to understand that what she was requesting was ridiculous. "I'm not about to shoot anyone to satisfy your business needs," she snapped. Then she addressed the manager. "Did you sell eight pairs of her earrings?"

The manager nodded. "It's just that I need the owner's authorization to pay out what she's owed," she murmured by way of explanation.

"I'm leaving the city," Em announced. "So I can't wait for the owner to say it's okay to pay what's due me. If it's owed, it should be paid."

"I agree. Pay her!" Jana insisted. "Take it out of the register and tell your boss to call me if she has any doubts." She turned back to Em. "And you are not leaving the city."

"I have to go."

"No, you don't. Remember, I'm allowed to shoot fugitives, so I can shoot you if you run. Understood?"

"You wouldn't shoot a child."

"Okay," Jana said, "I won't shoot a child. On the other hand, I can beat you in all the places that won't show. So, I would advise you to quietly come with me to a small snack place four doors down where we can eat and talk." She looked back at the manager. The woman hadn't moved to pay what was owed to Em. "I said pay her," Jana growled.

The manager quickly opened the register and counted out the few bills that the store owed Em, sliding the money over to her. Jana scooped up the money before Em could and started walking toward the front door. Em darted after her.

"That's my money."

"Who says?"

"You told the manager to pay me. You approved it."

"And you agreed to live up to your bargain with me, and you didn't. You left before you completed it."

They reached the front door, the snow outside now coming down as hard as it had been doing when Em had first stumbled into Jana's house.

"Come on," Jana yelled at Em, dashing out into the snow and down the block. After a moment's hesitation, Em ran after her. Jana led them into the small snack shop that she'd mentioned. The old man behind the counter raised a hand in greeting. Without waiting for an order, he poured a large mug of coffee, then set it at the end of the counter. Jana sat on the stool in front of it. Em looked the place over. She continued to stand, not quite sure what to do.

"Sit down, young lady," the old man suggested.

Jana placed the money the store manager had given her on the counter in front of the stool next to hers. She gestured an invitation to Em to sit on the stool. "All you have to do is sit, then eat and drink what the old man gives you. So talk to me and it's yours."

"She looks like the hot chocolate type," the old man said, quickly fixing a mug of hot chocolate and setting it next to the money. "You think she wants a pastry?" he asked Jana.

"All teenagers want pastries."

He looked at his small display of pastries, selected one, plated it, and placed it next to the hot chocolate. "Winter berries. It's fresh. Good with the hot chocolate."

Jana handed him a bill, and the old man pulled change from his pocket to give to her. Another customer came in, stamping the snow from his shoes, slapping at his jacket to get the flakes off before they thawed enough to soak the wool. He took a seat at a small table near the rear. "He's a tea man," the owner mumbled to Jana, preparing a cup of tea.

Em reluctantly reached a decision, sliding onto the stool next to Jana. She stared at the money. "That's mine."

"If you want it that much, take it."

Em made no move for the money. "I'll take it when I want to."

"Do you want to know how I knew where to find you?"

"Not particularly."

"The store owed you money, so I knew you'd come. All I had to do was wait."

The girl pretended she didn't care, looking in every direction but at Jana.

"I want to know what you were doing at the meeting when Sipo got the information about the plan to kill the Bogans." Jana used her best police voice, her tone indicating that she would brook no argument. "Tell me."

"The Turk asked me there."

"The Turk didn't ask you there. Another man did."

Em took a small bite of her pastry, then sipped at the hot chocolate.

Jana watched Em silently mull over what she should say. "You're trying to think up an answer which you hope will fool me rather than tell me the truth. It won't work."

"I'm entitled to eat my food, aren't I?" Em's voice had a querulous note to it. "That's all I'm doing."

"You're just stalling."

"Okay, so I'm stalling."

"Why were you at the meeting?"

"I was asked to come."

"And the reason?"

"To run an errand. I run errands for people. They pay me to bring a thing from here to there." She drew a line on the counter with her finger, then touched one end, then the other. "Maybe they can't go here or there, so they use me."

"You carry things for them?"

"I don't talk about what I do. Ever. I'm not going to now. That's why people use me."

"They use you because you're a pretty girl and won't be suspected by the police. You're a courier for illegal items."

"Business, is all it is."

"You're going to be caught," Jana warned.

"That's why I'm trying a new trade: earrings. Except they don't like to pay me, even when the earrings sell." She bit off another piece of the pastry, this one larger, washing it down with more of the hot chocolate. "How come the old man who runs this place knows what to give people to eat?"

"You just toddle in here and he decides what you eat. It's like a trademark for the place."

"I'd like to be able to do that. Tell people what to do."

"Unfortunately, it's too often the other person who does the choosing and the telling."

"That's true."

"Em, why were you at the meeting?"

"To pick up a thing and deliver it."

"What thing?"

"I don't know."

"From whom?"

"Another man."

"Who is the other man?"

"I don't know. Just a customer. He calls me from time to time. He called; I came. That was it."

"What did he tell you?"

"I went to the location. They were already there. I waited. Then, when he finished his other business with the men, the ones you already know about, he just said he didn't need me after all. So I left."

"You heard them talking together?"

"Just bits and pieces. I've told you about Sipo and the Turk and the others."

"Describe the other man."

"Tall, I guess. He's not fat. Dark hair. And scary."

"Scary?"

"Yeah."

"Why scary?"

"He just is."

Jana thought about the description. Very general; nothing specific that could be used to identify the man.

"What color eyes does he have?"

"Kind of muddy. I never look too close. I don't think he'd like that."

"Em, you said your father was a criminal. Is this man your father? Is his name Makine? Or perhaps he uses the name Koba?"

"He's not my father."

"You're sure he's not your father?"

"He's not any kind of a father. He's a customer. And I never heard of the guys you named."

She stuffed the last of the pastry in her mouth.

"Good pastry. I like this place."

She pointed to the money on the counter. "Can I take my money now?"

If the girl had other useful information, she was doing a good job of concealing it. Jana nodded and watched as Em scooped up her money.

Time would tell if what Em had said was true, and what Jana would do about it if it was not. "Do you still want to stay at my place until your father comes?"

Em gave her a triumphant smile. "I knew you would come around."

"It's only for a brief time," Jana warned her.

"Of course," Em confirmed, the sound of victory still lingering in her voice. She focused on Jana's face. "What happened under your chin?"

"None of your business," Jana replied. Then she laughed. "I cut myself shaving."

She paid the old man, and the two of them walked out of the store together, into the driving snow.

Chapter 21

The investigators tried to relax at the table in the crowded office they called a conference room. It was really only slightly bigger than the other offices on the floor. The Communists had built the building when they still had an army lurking around the outskirts of Bratislava to enforce their whims and their police force hadn't needed to deal with an expanding population. The police force had now increased, but the size of the building hadn't. They had to make do with the limited space. In a way, the closeness encouraged communication.

Grzner, Jonas, and Seges were in their best sprawl, with only Lubos Papanek, the accountant from Frauds who was looking into the Bogans' financial dealings, sitting upright. He looked so neat that it appeared as if he'd been sewn into his clothes. All the men were eating nuts, drinking coffee, talking football, and complaining about politics and their wives while they waited for Jana and Colonel Trokan. When Jana arrived, they stopped complaining about their wives, and they stopped talking about politics when the colonel came into the room. Jana went through her mental checklist, beginning the conference by asking Jonas, Grzner, and Seges for the results of their investigation at the studio. Jonas led off.

"They were very cooperative at the studio. We talked

to the staff manager. It turned out she knew very little about her job."

"She was a friend of Mrs. Bogan," Grzner threw in.

"Just an acquaintance," Seges chimed in.

Jonas continued, ignoring the interruptions. "We went right to the switch box where the rifles had been hidden. The electronics had been switched to another board at the larger soundstage. That way, the lights still functioned on the smaller stage. When they disconnected the old board, it was rebuilt with just enough space to hide the rifles behind the old switches."

"Who authorized the changes?" Jana asked.

"The manager said that Bogan's wife told them what to do. Members of their own crew did the work."

"Bogan's wife? You're sure it was Klara?" The colonel's face reflected how shocking the disclosure was. "It couldn't be. She was the one who was killed."

"Maybe the lady was committing suicide?" Seges snidely suggested.

Nobody paid any attention to him. They were focused on the issue.

"Could the manager be fabricating this story?" Jana asked.

"We checked with the crew who did the changes," Jonas replied. "They verified what the manager told us. There was an authorization on the work sheet. "

"How about the keys to the door at the top of the side stairs?"

"Four sets at the studio, all accounted for. Mrs. Bogan also had a set."

"Have we looked for that set?"

Jonas nodded. "None in her possession. No keys in the Bratislava house. We have no idea where they are."

"If they used her keys, it would explain how the

shooters got in and out so easily." The colonel winced. "This is turning into an even crazier piece of business."

"Not so crazy if Mrs. Bogan participated in the planning, not expecting to be one of the targets," Jana suggested. "In that event, I would assume the lady was merely trying to kill off her husband." She laid out what they knew of the events. "Mr. Bogan is warned by Sipo. Sipo says he merely heard about the plan and decided to take advantage of the knowledge by making money from Bogan by alerting him. But I think Sipo lied about that to cover himself. There were five men at the meeting Em told us about: Sipo, the Turk, Balder, Akso . . . and the unknown fifth man. It's my belief that Sipo must have been told to warn Bogan by the fifth man at the meeting. Except Bogan didn't listen to him, or to us. Why?"

The colonel understood what Jana was getting at. "Because his wife, Klara, wanted Bogan to go forward with the ceremony. She said as much to us, and to him, just before the shooting. She wanted her gentleman in the spotlight."

"Why would she want to be shot at?" Grzner asked.

"She didn't," Jana explained. "The lady thought that only Mr. Bogan was going to be killed."

"And she would walk away from the shooting as the grieving widow," the colonel added.

"Except it all went wrong," Seges suggested.

"Not for whoever added the supplement to the plan," Jana concluded. "I checked with the fingerprint people. Nothing on the gloves we found in the box. Nothing on the rifles or the shells still in the weapon. So there's no help for us there."

"Very practiced." There was the hint of admiration in Seges's voice, as if he approved the professional planning and execution that had gone into the murders.

"Not so very practiced," said Jana reproachfully. "They left too many paths for us to follow."

"The financial tracking," suggested the colonel.

"The two surviving thugs who were at the meeting with Sipo," Jonas added.

"Anything on them from Interpol or Europol yet?" Jana asked.

"Nothing yet," Jonas said.

"They take their own sweet time. That means we make our own telephone calls and do the footwork. We know one of them, the man we think is named Balder. Balder was involved in the stolen-car business with the other thug, Akso. Call around to get additional information on them. Try the surrounding countries, with the Czech Republic as a start. After that, the Balkans. Russia and Germany as well. Then we'll see what we have. Ask if they know of a criminal who has a large chestnut birthmark on his face. If the man exists, we should come up with him if he has a record. Along with them, the dead Turk and the informant Sipo.

"There was also the fifth man," Jana reminded them. "We don't have a line to follow up on him yet, unless he's the man with the birthmark. Keep him in mind during your investigations."

"How about the shooter who tried to get you?" Jonas asked.

"What about him? The Austrians have nothing to go on in the shooting."

"He may try again."

"Protection may be in order," the colonel suggested.

"We're police officers. We take our chances," Jana reminded him.

"You're adamant. No protection?"

"None." Jana turned to Seges. "Check with the Hungarians who are investigating the Bogan house burglary in their jurisdiction. Perhaps they found Klara's set of keys. And find out anything else they came up with. And check with our crew on the Bogans' Bratislava house."

"I've got something," Grzner suddenly piped up. "Maybe."

Everyone stared at him. Grzner generally provided bulk and muscle in investigations, not analysis.

"What?" asked Jana.

"There was some word around that there's evidence on the case that's being withheld from us."

They stared at him for a moment, the room becoming very still. Policemen are a very paranoid group, and when an internal threat materializes, they take it as an ominous event.

"What information, Grzner?" the colonel prompted.

"It's just a rumor," Grzner warned.

"Tell us the rumor," Jana urged.

"We're not being told everything. By our own people. And the prosecutor. The whole other 'official' team that's looking into Klara Boganova's death."

The colonel and Jana exchanged glances.

"Who told you, Grzner?" Jana's voice was very quiet. It was not unreasonable to believe that one team was withholding evidence from the other to make their own investigation appear more successful. "Someone working in the special investigations group?"

"Just a grunt on patrol. I tried to track the rumor down. You know how it is: one person tells another, and pretty soon you find out that it's just a big circle screw with the same people who started it now getting the information as if it were new and no one able to say where it began. So maybe it's crap?"

"Okay, maybe it's crap. Still good to know, just in case." Jana began to sum up what she had concluded. "Everyone, we have a new focus: Bogan's wife being involved in the attempted killing of her husband. Also the trashing of both of their houses. What were they looking for? And don't forget the man with the chestnut birthmark on his face." She looked over to Papanek. "Anything from the financial side yet?"

"Too soon for me to have anything."

Jana had expected that answer. "Okay, everyone. We know what to do. Keep at it." She looked at Trokan. "If I could talk to you for a moment, Colonel."

The colonel and Jana waited as the men filed out of the room, Jana signaling for Seges to close the door as he went out behind the others.

"What did you pick up that you don't want the others to know, Jana?"

"Grzner's *rumor.*"

"For goodness' sake, Jana. In every investigation rumors like that are like the tides in the sea. They come in and out, and where they start, no one knows. It just happens. Petty jealousies, malice, a cop having some fun at another one's expense, a newspaper story that has no foundation in fact. You've seen them before. They mean nothing."

"Colonel, the 'approved' investigation has blanks in it that shouldn't be there. Their investigation is going at a snail's pace, creeping along. Reading the murder book, I had the impression that it was like some anemic, terminal patient being left on the operating table by a surgeon hoping the person would die sooner than later."

The colonel ruminated on what she'd said. "I'll nose around and see what I can pick up."

"Thank you, Colonel."

Back in her office, Jana wondered about the rumor. Well, the colonel would nose around. It was all she could ask. Jana checked her telephone messages. One of them was from Interpol, asking if she'd found anything on the case involving the man killed in Paris. There was also a message from the father of the boy who had been killed with the shotgun. He was asking for Jana's promised answers.

First, Jana called Paris to speak to the French cop, a man named Jobic Masson, who was listed as the investigator on the killing of the old man. Masson turned out to be a cheerful man, and the two of them amiably chatted away in French. When the chitchat died away, Jana informed the investigator that they had identified his victim as Jindrich Bogan. She promised she'd forward the records they'd come up with, but she had a few requests of her own.

Masson was not very eager to go in a direction that he first thought was tangential to his own case; but as he listened, he began to change his attitude, particularly when Jana informed him that his case might be related to the high-profile murder case she had in Bratislava.

Perhaps, Jana suggested, the hit-and-run in Paris was not just an isolated accident. Perhaps the driver of the truck that killed *their* French Bogan was connected to the actual and attempted Bogan killings in Slovakia.

The hypothesis intrigued Masson. There might be an outside chance, he allowed, after Jana itemized the evidence.

Had he done any search of the area in Paris where the old man had been killed? Jana asked. She reminded him that his own reports on the killing indicated that their Bogan had had groceries in his arms when he'd been killed. This suggested that he lived somewhere near where he had died. Since he hadn't come home, wherever home was, perhaps someone—a neighbor, or a landlord, or a woman he lived or went out with—had reported that a man fitting his description was missing.

Yes, that reasoning was sound, the French cop agreed. He'd look into it and get back to her. In the meantime, Jana promised to share whatever else she found that could have any bearing on the French case. When she hung up, Jana thanked the lucky alignment of the stars. It was a good one. Getting a cooperative officer in a foreign jurisdiction to agree to work with them was always a problem. Not that day.

Jana had the records on Jindrich Bogan sent to Paris, then called the forensics unit to find out what the drug tests on the young man who'd been shot to death had determined. The results were startling. There was enough codeine in the young man's system, particularly when combined with the blood-alcohol content, to have put him in a comatose state. Unless he had been a modern-day Hercules, the lab man told her, he was unconscious at the time of his death. And unconscious before he was killed.

How could a man have accidentally killed himself if he was unconscious? There was no way the young man had done himself in as he was climbing through a fence. Someone else had shot him.

Nothing is ever as it seems. Most good police officers found that out early in the game. Jana could remember the first time she had learned that lesson.

It had been before she became a police officer.

Chapter 22

When she was a teenager, Jana had nightmares of the student beatings she'd seen the police administer, particularly the beating of the student who'd tried to get away from them. Her mother was not sympathetic. If anything, she remained angry at Jana for trying to help the dissidents, talking to her in monosyllables or berating her with cutting remarks in the days after the event. Her mother was afraid of being questioned by the police or reprimanded by the Communist Party for her daughter's conduct. She carped at Jana's father about what might happen to the family and to her own position in the party if the police had noticed Jana's actions.

Things changed later that year when there was a school break. Jana spent as much time out of the house as possible in order to escape her mother's constant agonizing. Unfortunately, there was only so much time that she could spend with her friend Sofia, so Jana would often take a book and cross Nový Most bridge to the other side of the river to sit on a bench in Sad Janka Kráľa park and read. When she became tired of the book, she'd watch the lovers, feeling a small stir of envy, or she'd simply watch the young mothers playing with their children, feeling a different type of desire.

Old men and women would walk by, and Jana would

observe the other end of the life span, the elderly enjoying the remainder of their lives amid the greenery of the park. The day she saw the student, Jana was having a hard time getting through a melodramatic Tolstoy novel about a woman who she knew was about to throw herself into the path of an oncoming locomotive. She put the book down, looked up, and there he was.

His head was bandaged, his face still showing bruises from his beating. He was also walking with a cane, his left leg appearing to drag slightly. Jana's breath caught. Even after the beating, with the bruises and his slightly laborious walk, Jana thought he still held himself erect, still proud. She had to talk to him.

She found herself getting off the park bench and walking across the grass to intersect the path he was taking, hesitating for a moment when she caught up with him, wondering what to say. She was thinking of going back to her bench when he turned to her, smiling a wide, crooked smile that was endearing because of its openness.

"Hello. You wanted to see me?" he asked.

Jana stared at him. His smile, if anything, became wider.

"I'm not the man you thought I was, right? Nothing unusual about my features. Although today, I admit, you have to deal with the bandages and ignore the bruises. Except, with or without them, everyone mistakes me for someone else. I'm just an everyman, even in my own mirror."

"More than an everyman," Jana managed, becoming upset with herself as she voiced the words. It wasn't what she'd wanted to say. She hurried ahead with an explanation. "I think that I may have caught sight of you before. No," she corrected herself. "I *know* I've seen you."

"Where?" he asked, an amused lilt in his voice. "You've seen me in the movies, right?" His voice was self-deprecating, his smile reaching his eyes. "You think I had the lead in a film about a hero who comes to the rescue of a damsel threatened by a human beast, a horrid man who wants to steal all her lands and titles for himself. I destroy the beast, and she throws herself in my arms, right?" He tilted his head forward in a mock bow. "One hero, at your service."

"You don't think you're a hero."

"Unfortunately not. I'm far from the man in the movie."

"It wasn't a movie; and you *were* a hero."

He examined her face, trying to figure out what she was talking about. "I don't think I've ever been a hero."

"At the Slavin monument. The police were after you."

His smile washed away, leaving just a touch at the corners of his mouth. "You were there?"

"Yes."

The smile disappeared completely. "It was a horrible event. Not what I thought would happen."

"Horrible," Jana agreed.

He continued walking, Jana keeping pace with him.

"Things simply didn't happen the way they were supposed to," he put forward.

"And you were hurt. Hurt badly." She indicated his bandaged head. "It must be aching."

A faint smile returned. "It's stopped hurting."

"I'm glad. And your leg?"

He looked troubled. "It's not the leg that's hurt. It's what happened up here." He tapped himself on the forehead. "I saw a neurologist. A blood vessel was injured. It leaked. The damaged area controls the leg. I can't seem to walk right just yet." He quickened his pace as if to reassure himself that he was going to overcome his physical problem. "The doctor said time would tell. There's nothing they can do just yet. I'm taking pills. The doctor recommended physical therapy. So, I'm out walking." His expression was worried. "I'm seeing another nerve man tomorrow."

Jana remembered him being dragged along the ground, his head bumping from stone to stone as the police hauled him away. "It's good to have another opinion. My dad says that." Jana tried to keep the dismay from her face. The student had been permanently injured by the police.

"My name is Georg. Georg Repka."

"Jana."

"Will you walk with me?"

"My pleasure to walk with a hero."

His smile came back.

"I can only walk for a short time. I have things to do."

"Me too."

They walked toward the central fountain in the park. Georg read the title on the book Jana was carrying.

"*Anna Karenina*. Tolstoy. Quite tragic."

"Very tragic," Jana agreed.

"Yes. Anna acted without thinking clearly. She didn't realize the consequences of her actions, what her duty was, before she did what she did."

"Passion," Jana explained.

"We all have passions."

He didn't seem to approve of Anna Karenina.

"You had passion at the Slavin Memorial," Jana reminded him.

Georg blushed, ducking his head away. "My passion was appropriate, I hope."

"Oh, it was!" Jana confirmed, the words coming out louder than she intended. She looked away from Georg, momentarily abashed at her own intensity.

"Thank you, Jana."

They walked for a distance in silence until Georg signaled for her to stop, panting slightly.

"That's the other thing that happens. I get tired easily. The doctor said it was natural, considering the injuries. I hope, in the near future, that I'll be over it. Then I can get back to my work."

"Good."

"Work is important."

"I thought you were a student."

"I am. Except botany can't be anyone's life work. It's too isolating. One can slide into becoming disconnected from people if it becomes all-consuming. Essentially, if that were the major force in my life, what use would my life be? We have to interact with people. Don't you agree?"

Jana nodded, although she was not sure exactly what Georg meant. He was older and more mature than she was, and she desperately wanted to seem mature to such a far-sighted man. So she kept on nodding whenever he made a declaration that appeared to warrant an affirmation.

They began walking again.

"What did you say your family name was?" he asked.

"Matin. Judge Matin is my father." Jana was proud that she could tell Georg that she was the daughter of a judge.

"I don't know your father."

"You're not a lawyer. People don't know judges unless they're lawyers. My father laughs about it. He says all judges are anonymous. He likes it that way."

Georg developed a quizzical look. "I know a Matinova. She's in the party. A woman of very substantial convictions. Is your mother in the party?"

For a moment, Jana was not sure she should answer the question, afraid of the consequences. "Yes," she responded after a pause.

The gorgeous smile returned. "A wonderful woman. We've talked at party meetings. The two of us agree on many things. I'm glad to see her daughter is so much like her. Can you say hello to your mother for me when you go home?"

Jana was slightly bewildered. "I don't think my mother recognized you when you were being beaten by the police."

"Everything happened too quickly. Time accelerates. Or it freezes. Nothing looks right in an event like that."

"I guess so." Jana's puzzlement had grown. "You were with the students protesting the Russians being here, weren't you? Protesting the events in Prague?"

"Well, yes and no. I was there as a party representative."

"The party sent a member to a demonstration against them?"

"I found out about the demonstration at school. I told the party; they told me to attend."

Jana was confused. It didn't quite make sense. "Georg, you told the party about the demonstration. Did the party tell the police?"

"Of course. It was only right that they tell the police."

"And then the police came to break up the event."

"Certainly. If police are responsive agents of the proletariat, they function as extensions of the party."

Jana's head was whirling. Everything was askew: the scene of the police beating the students, the attack on Georg.

"Did you talk to the police about the event before you went?"

"Naturally. That was expected of me."

"Then why did the police beat you?"

Georg sighed. "They weren't supposed to. A mistake. You know how it is under those circumstances. It became a great stew, individuals running around, everyone excited, not seeing straight, the stress. I was carrying a protest sign, so they came after me."

"*You* were carrying a protest sign?"

"How could I go to the demonstration not carrying a protest sign?"

"I see."

"No one counted on my getting hurt."

"No."

"Things never go exactly as planned."

All Jana could think of was that the person she'd thought of as a hero, a victim of a vicious attack, had turned out to be a state informant. Even her mother disliked informants. And agent provocateurs were the worst. They were Judas goats, leading people into danger. Georg had led his fellow students, his friends, into the clubs of the police.

Jana's perceptions of Georg, and of the event she'd seen at Slavin, had been completely wrong. The whole thing was wrong, and sinister, and immoral, and frightening. Her impression of Georg Repka had completely changed. Black was now white; white was now black. And neither color could be trusted to remain as it was.

Jana couldn't wait to get away from Repka. She kept the semblance of good will on her face, waiting for the next juncture in the path to break away from him. When they reached it, he said a smiling good-bye, reminded her to say hello to her mother for him, then walked on, his left leg continuing to create an uneven gait.

When she got home, Jana didn't tell her mother she'd met Georg. They would have argued about what he'd done. It would have been too ugly.

It was all so odd.

Jana promised herself she would remember the event, fixing it in her mind.

Nothing is ever as it seems.

Chapter 23

J ana needed to fly to Germany on the Bogan case. Aside from trying to contact Bogan's son, and to determine where his father was in hiding, she had to find out about the German, Balder, and his partner in crime, Akso. Colonel Trokan raised a small fuss about her going, arguing that the German police would do the work needed. It was a weak argument. Neither of them trusted another state's agency to get the job done. They wouldn't have Jana's familiarity with the facts of the case. She and Trokan were really just going through the exercise that they went through every time she needed approval to spend out-of-budget departmental funds.

It was a familiar diversion for them: Jana would argue that her travel was important to the case, as she did now, and Trokan would offer unsatisfactory alternatives. As expected, in that day's argument, the colonel blustered into his standard warning for her not to spend money by eating in expensive restaurants, nor to patronize the infamous clubs of Berlin. Both of them knew she'd never do that anyway. It was just one of the steps in their ballet.

When the "argument" was over, Jana had to deal with another issue: what to do with Em while she was in Berlin.

The easiest thing would have been to turn her over to child welfare, but Jana had promised the girl, at least for the time being, not to do this. Em had urged Jana to help her stay out of the welfare people's clutches until her father came. Two days of freedom, she said, was all she was asking for.

When Jana asked Em how her father would locate her, Em smiled. He would know, was all she would say to Jana.

Em wanted to stay by herself at Jana's house while she was gone; but from her past experience with the girl, Jana knew that that wouldn't be wise. Em would be out on the streets within minutes of Jana leaving her alone, and Jana might have more trouble finding her again. The only other alternative Jana could think of was to get one of her people to house the girl.

One by one, she asked all of her personnel, from clerks and secretaries to her most senior detectives, if they could take Em for a few days. All of them had reasons not to. They ranged from "I can't stand children" to "I have too many children already," climbing up the excuse ladder to "My wife will divorce me." One unmarried officer even told her that his girlfriend would think that he'd lied about his marital status before going out with her. Or, even worse, that Em was an illegitimate child whom he had deliberately not mentioned before, and she'd probably break a bottle over his head.

After Jana had asked almost everyone in her department, the only person she had left who might be remotely satisfactory to care for Em was her warrant officer. When she called Seges into her office, he already had an idea from the other officers of what she was going to ask.

As soon as he walked in, Jana saw from his haunted face and jutting chin that he was going to refuse. That didn't surprise her, but she hadn't expected the immediate attack strategy that he employed. If he took Em to his house, Seges predicted, he would be killed by his wife. She would throw kitchen knives at him—if she didn't shoot him first with his other service weapon, which he kept in a bedroom drawer that she had access to. If she didn't succeed in killing him, she would put him through weeks of torture, which would be even worse than the easy death promised by the gun or the knives.

Jana cajoled, promised favors, offered to give him additional time off, promised she'd strong-arm the colonel into approving his transfer to another unit of his choice. But none of it worked.

Jana had stashed Em in a spare office one floor down; when she went there to confess her failure, the girl proffered a possible solution. She suggested that Jana take her to see Seges's wife and let her talk to the woman. Maybe she would be able to sway her. Jana hesitated; then, telling herself she had nothing to lose, she agreed to try it. The two of them drove over to the Seges residence, a very small house on the outskirts of the Devin Castle area.

Seges's wife was a rather harried-looking woman with frizzy hair, a big bosom, and a look on her face that said "You're not going to fool me, so don't even try." When Jana haltingly explained that she was trying to find a safe place for Em to stay, Seges's wife displayed all the indicia of pre-stroke behavior—until Em stepped in.

"I have a pair of earrings which I made especially for you, Madam Segesova." Em's voice had taken on the tone and mannerisms of a younger child. At some point, Em had gotten hold of some enamel paint. The pair of earrings she gave to Mrs. Seges was not aluminum-colored, but covered in bright yellow and red enamel.

"Can I do them for you?" Em asked, not waiting for an answer, but going straight to Segesova and, with a great deal of deference, putting them on her ears. She then stepped back to take a look.

"Good, but we need to fix the hair a little. And I'm sure that you have a top that matches better. If you don't, we'll have to go shopping. Let's look in the closet."

She led a pleasantly surprised Segesova into her bedroom, and the two of them began to busily go through her clothes. Once they had selected an outfit that matched the earrings, Em insisted on redoing the woman's hair. By the time it was done, the two of them were twittering together like sparrows, Segesova insisting on Em staying at her place.

When Seges came home, he was faced with a fait accompli. There was no way he could stand up to his wife on the issue.

Em gaily waved at Jana as she drove off, Jana awed at what the girl had done. She had, very quickly, found Segesova's weakness and taken advantage of it to woo the woman into letting her stay there. There was no mischief in what the girl had done, but there was certainly feigned innocence. Em had seen what she had to do, and had unhesitatingly courted the woman, getting what she wanted. Unusual for a girl her age, to say the least. Manipulative, at worst. The girl had a skill that could be used, under the wrong circumstances, toward very bad ends.

Jana drove home, made a flight reservation on Czech Airlines with a connection in Prague to a flight going to Berlin, packed an overnight bag, and, an hour later, was on the flight.

On the plane, there was a major surprise. Truchanova, the special prosecutor assigned to the Bogan case, was on the plane, seated just across the aisle from Jana. Sitting next to the prosecutor was Jakus, the primary investigator on the case. Truchanova eyed Jana, both of them realizing that the other must be going to Berlin to explore some aspect of the Bogan case. They exchanged awkward pleasantries, then buckled into their seats as the plane took off, each trying to determine how best to deal with the situation. Jana, as usual, decided to be direct: "We're both going to try and locate Bogan's son, I would think."

"That's a good assumption," Truchanova said.

"You know where to find him?"

"The Berlin police have agreed to help us. They have an address which they've identified. According to them, they've passed by several times and seen no signs of activity. They'll have a magistrate's warrant to search the house ready when we get there. The house is in Charlottenburg. Hopefully we'll turn up something."

"A very nice area to live in."

"And why are you going?"

"Also trying to locate him."

There was a long silence. "You have anything else to go on, Commander?" Truchanova asked. "Other information on where the man can be located?"

"I have a phone number. One that wasn't in the murder book."

"Have you correlated it to an address?"

"Not yet."

Jakus was leaning toward Jana, trying to hear the conversation over the noise in the plane's cabin. "I would like the number, Commander." His voice was raised to carry across the aisle to Jana. "May I have it?"

"Of course, Jakus."

Jana pulled a magazine from the seat-back pocket in front of her and began browsing through it without giving Jakus the number.

"The number?" Investigator Jakus asked again, his face reflecting growing irritation.

Jana continued leafing through the magazine. Jakus was

about to make his request again, angry now, leaning across the prosecutor. Truchanova pushed him gently but firmly back into his seat.

"You're crowding me," she warned him, then turned back to Jana. "You want to come along with us to the German police?"

"To the house as well," Jana said. "And I want to get whatever information the German police have gathered on their own about Bogan, or the crime."

"You're not the primary investigator," Jakus managed to get out before Truchanova squeezed his arm to shut him up.

"Investigator Jakus is very eager," she said by way of excusing his outburst. "I'm also eager. Just quieter. I can also get the information from you without making any promises. All I have to do is call Colonel Trokan."

"True. But I can then have Colonel Trokan talk to the attorney general, and he in turn will order you to . . ."

". . . give my information to you? He would, except you're not officially working on the case, Matinova. So he won't." Truchanova leaned back in her seat, believing the battle won.

Everybody always guarded their turf. The surprise generated by finding each other on the plane had triggered an involuntary threat response. The two of them were in a war over territorial rights.

Absurd, Jana realized, since they needed each other.

"Madam Prosecutor, we had agreed," Jana pointed out. "We keep out of each other's way. I stay out of the public sphere. We share information. I'm not challenging that agreement. I'm simply reasserting its terms. Both of us see the other stealing a march, and we think our territory is being invaded. Why don't we just put our emotions aside and stick to the original agreement?" Jana rattled off the phone number that she'd obtained from Kralik for Bogan's son in Berlin. "An offer of good faith and trust," Jana explained.

Jakus scribbled the number down on a piece of paper.

Jana played another card. "Think about it, Madam Truchanova. Would you rather have me investigating the case with you, or would you rather go your own way without me, leaving Investigator Jakus as your sole investigative support?"

Jakus nearly came out of his seat, ready to do battle, but Truchanova managed to stop him.

"Why didn't you give me the telephone number before this?" Truchanova demanded.

"Something came up."

"You had no intention of giving it to me."

"I was shot. Twice. Would you like to see the wounds?"

Truchanova gaped at her.

"It's true. After I got the number in Vienna."

"You were shot twice?"

"Twice," Jana affirmed. "We didn't broadcast it. It wouldn't have been helpful to tell the media that I was in Austria on business. They would have wanted to know what I was doing there. So, you see, I've honored our agreement that I stay out of the public eye. Now, do we go forward together?"

"You're not lying," Truchanova said to herself, her voice betraying her astonishment.

"Police commanders are not in the habit of lying to prosecutors. Prosecutors should be able to depend upon the police they work with to fulfill their promises. Any problems with that?"

"None." Truchanova was a very practical person. It was plainly in her best interest to continue the agreement with Jana. "The same terms and conditions, then."

"We see the German police together?"

"Yes."

"And share all our information?"

"As per the accord."

"Good." Jana gave Truchanova a smile. "When we get back to Bratislava, I'll write up the report on Vienna and several other items and get them to you. With that in mind, there is one other thing I want to ask you. I've read the murder book several times, and I can't escape the feeling that something's been left out."

"How so?" Truchanova asked, a slight hesitation in her voice that revealed to Jana that she was, in fact, deliberately holding something back.

"I don't quite know why I feel that way," Jana said, pretending not to suspect Truchanova of any duplicity. "Perhaps it's the things which haven't been done yet. Or the perceptible gaps in the reports." Jana waited for her observation to sink in with Truchanova. There was no response. "It's probably something else that's giving me that feeling. You know how it is when things are written up by someone else. We see spaces that shouldn't be there. I'm sure it's just my own sensitivity, my own observations, which are off the mark."

"Yes, that could be. We often misperceive." Again there was the faltering quality in the prosecutor's voice.

"Good to know how well we're cooperating." Jana inwardly cringed at her own blatant insincerity. "We should call ahead to the Berlin police from Prague. They can give us the exact location for the second address." She thought about the logistics of the situation. "Unfortunately, knowing how the courts operate, if the number I was given comes back to a second location, it's probably too late today for the police to get a second warrant."

"Tomorrow, then," Truchanova suggested.

"Good," Jana agreed.

Jana sat back in her seat absolutely convinced that the two were deliberately withholding something. She needed to know not only the information they were holding back, but why they were hiding it. The fact that they were keeping things from her would make it much harder for Jana to widen her investigation or to successfully put any case together. She shut her eyes, and woke up only when the plane landed in Prague. Both Jakus and Jana called their German police contacts from the airport, giving them both the new telephone number for Bogan's son. The three of them then boarded the Berlin flight.

They didn't talk to each other during the flight. When they reached Berlin airspace, the plane was put into a temporary holding pattern, circling the airport. Berlin unfolded below. It is not the prettiest city in the world, Jana thought. That honor belongs to Paris. Rome still has the glories of its ancient past and empire, Vienna its Hapsburg stateliness and kitsch, London its lurid history wound around Shakespearean legends. And Berlin?

Anger, violence, intrigue, and, most of all, fear.

A few minutes later, they landed.

Chapter 24

They met the German police officers outside the arrival area of Tegel. Following protocol, Jana and Truchanova had each separately phoned their own contacts in the German *Polizei*. Unfortunately, these contacts were from two separate departments of the police, and both had sent officers. Those officers had all met each other outside the terminal, and they were uneasily standing together to welcome their colleagues from Slovakia.

Jana immediately saw the police officer she was supposed to meet: Albrecht Konrad was a senior investigator with the *Kriminalpolizei*—or, as Albrecht himself called it, *Die Kripo*—the German state police charged with investigating serious crime. He and Jana served together on a regional interagency police task force dealing with central European crime suppression. The group met periodically in one or another capital, most often in Vienna, so they knew each other well.

Konrad was generally an aloof individual, but he and Jana had hit it off in their prior contacts, and the man broke out in a big smile when he saw her, still insisting on a formal handshake but clearly glad to see her.

"Welcome to Berlin, Commander Matinova."

"Jana," she corrected him, trying to be informal. Then

she introduced him to Truchanova and Investigator Jakus. "They're here to see you as well."

Konrad shrugged, looking slightly uncomfortable. "I believe they're meeting my friends from the *Bundeskriminalamt*." He gestured to the two other officers, neither of whom seemed pleased to see Jana. "Our FBI, only they're the BKA here."

Jana was surprised. Truchanova had taken the case up with an agency that was not usually involved in this sort of case. The prosecutor had a smug look on her face, appreciating the reference to the BKA being Germany's FBI. It put her a notch above Jana on the prestige ladder.

"Pleased to meet you," one of the BKA men said to Jana, without any real welcome in his voice. He nodded a greeting to Truchanova, the semblance of a smile on his face.

Truchanova and Jakus moved over to the two BKA men, Jana standing with Albrecht Konrad, the two groups facing each other as if they were on different sides in an athletic contest. The separation between them was more than just physical.

"We're here to talk to our friends from the BKA," Truchanova pointedly asserted. "Perhaps it would be best—to get the most out of this situation, you understand—if we separated at this stage of our inquiry."

"I see your point. You're probably right," Jana managed, although she didn't agree with the strategy at all. Separate meetings meant imperfectly shared information. Even worse, Jana felt that if the BKA was anything like the FBI was reputed to be, they would never get back to her with any information if she subsequently tried to contact them. All organizations like that had an unofficial policy of cooperating with other agencies only when they were forced to. On the bright side, Jana consoled herself with the thought that she'd have more freedom to operate without Truchanova around.

"What about the warrant on the second location? I should be there when it's served," Jana reminded Truchanova and the BKA people.

"The magistrate who authorized the first warrant won't be available until tomorrow morning," one of the BKA men reluctantly informed her. He had an air of superiority about him, which Jana instantly disliked. His attitude suggested a large gasbag, and she had the urge to put a pin in the man and deflate him.

He continued, as if to an inferior, explaining what those in the upper reaches of the universe were doing. "We felt it better to use the same magistrate who issued the warrant on the first location since he already has all the relevant information. We plan to serve both on the same day at the same time, with two teams. The magistrate will, naturally, want to deal with us on this issue, so, when he's ready, we'll see him; and I'm sure there will be no trouble in having you along while we serve them."

"Naturally. Very appropriate." Albrecht's voice had the tone of a man sucking on a sour lemon.

"Good," said the BKA agent.

"You can get in touch with Investigator Konrad when you're ready," Jana said. "He'll have my contact information."

"Certainly," assured one of the agents.

"Until then," Truchanova chimed in, pleased with events. She and Jakus moved off with the BKA officers.

"Blah, blah, blah, blah. Gas and more gas," Konrad murmured to Jana. "That's all they ever give you."

"Better for us that we keep distance between us and them," said Jana.

"No question."

They began to make their way out of the airport terminal.

"I want to see Zdenko Bogan's place of business," Jana said.

"As soon as I can set it up."

They walked out of the building to Konrad's car parked at the curb. Across the main terminal drive they could see Truchanova and her little coterie following the signs leading to one of the car-park areas.

Watching them, Konrad muttered something under his breath in German, a tinge of anger in his voice.

"What was that?" Jana asked, having the clear impression that it was not a compliment that had come out of Konrad's mouth.

"Pig fat."

"Very harsh; however, there's a germ of truth in it," Jana said.

They got in Konrad's car and drove off. They were headed north on Glinka Strasse, toward Unter den Linden, with Jana admiring the new shops and the bustle of the people going in and out of the stores, suggesting good economic times and the general lust for life that money in the pocket brings, when they ran into the demonstration.

The riot police were all over the place, dressed in heavy-duty crowd-control gear—large helmets, plastic faceplates, bulletproof vests—carrying shields and long riot batons. Traffic police had taken over an intersection and flagged down their car as it approached, trying to redirect them around the disturbance. Recognizing one of the cops, Konrad rolled down his window and called him by name.

"What the hell is happening?" Konrad asked.

"Gypsies."

"Roms? Here?"

The faint odor of tear gas wafted into the car.

"How far down the street?" Konrad wanted to know.

"Five hundred meters."

"The gypsies are creating a riot?" There was wonderment in Konrad's voice.

The traffic cop snorted in derision. "You couldn't get enough gypsies to fill up a Volkswagen if they knew it was for a riot. This is Berlin. Steal, yes; riot, no.

"They were having a corner demonstration," the cop continued. "Twenty of them parading around, and suddenly there were skinheads beating up on them; then people tried to stop it; more skinheads; then some Turks passed near enough to become targets, and now we've got half the Berlin bar population involved."

"*Scheisse*," said Konrad.

"What were the gypsies protesting?" Jana asked.

"War reparations," the cop said. "Half a century ago, and they're still pushing us for money."

"War reparations?" Konrad said. "Well, Adolf and his boys killed a few of them. The gypsies are entitled."

"He killed a lot of them," Jana corrected.

"Except everybody now wants a taste of money," the traffic cop grumbled.

"They lost everything," Jana reminded him.

"It was a long time ago."

The traffic officer looked down the street, then back to Konrad, and waved him ahead rather than into the detour.

"Go through. It's clear enough for you to cross."

Konrad put the car in gear, edging into the boulevard, preparing to make a left turn.

"A favorite spot for people kicking up a fuss," he told Jana. "Brandenburger Tor to our left, the Deutsche Staatsoper to our right; a little northwest we have the Reichstag so the legislators can take notice. The area is great for catching people's eyes."

Jana looked to the right where everyone seemed to be pointing. All she could see were police buses blocking the boulevard, with officers standing around them. The demonstrators and their enemies, the neo-Nazis, were all screened off. There was a wisp of gas hanging over the bus. Another group of riot police in formation went trotting past them toward the buses. Jana was tempted to get out of the car and follow the riot police behind the buses to see how they handled the event. She couldn't see at all from where they were.

Instead, she sat back in her seat, accepting that she was not going to get to see whether the police treated the gypsies any differently than the ones who had come to fight with them. She hoped they did. Picketing or demonstrating was not rioting. The police should see the difference and take the distinction into account. Unfortunately, nobody ever saw or did everything they were required to. And some people never saw anything. It was the human condition.

Chapter 25

It had been years since Jana had seen the student who had been an agent provocateur. One day after having moved out of her parents' home to see how it would be to live alone, she had gone home for a short visit. Her mother and father had been fighting when she arrived; for a few hours after that, things had not gone well between Jana and her mother. Her father had gone out, and Jana had rather innocently made a comment about her mother not giving her father a chance to explain his actions at a party the night before. Since her husband wasn't present at the moment, Jana's mother had settled on Jana as a substitute target for her rage.

The incident the night before had been minuscule. Jana's father had had one drink too many and had told a woman whom her mother loathed that he liked what she was wearing that evening. This had angered Jana's mother enough to make her stop talking to him; and then, when he'd gotten into a heated discussion damning the government for their policies regarding the minority communities in Slovakia, her mother had insisted on leaving, berating her father throughout the whole drive home.

Jana's father had been scheduled at the last minute to give a speech at a judges' conference in Kosice in eastern Slovakia, so he'd been forced to leave early that morning, with nothing resolved between him and his wife. Then, as she served lunch, Jana's mother had begun relating the events of the night before. When Jana gave the impression of taking her father's side, her mother had gone into a tirade. Facing a no-win situation, Jana had retreated to the backyard of the house and read a book until, after an hour of isolation and a twinge of hunger, she had gone into the kitchen for a quick snack.

As most parents do, when they've had time to reconsider their actions, Jana's mother had feelings of remorse for becoming so angry at her daughter and proceeded to serve Jana the meal of *kachna* and réd cabbage with a side of *knedliky* that she'd prepared, sneaking in a quick apology as she did so. Her mood improved even more as she watched her daughter relish the food, waiting until Jana had finished it to set out fresh strawberries and a small pitcher of fresh cream. Her mother's final wave of the olive branch was to suggest that the two of them go into town to see a lecture on a subject she was involved in. She knew the man who was lecturing and was interested in what he had to say. Rather than refuse and risk reopening the breach between them, Jana said she was happy to go along.

Her mother's mood switched to a pleasant excitement about getting out, and the two of them talked about the old days and her mother's enjoyment of going to party events, the wonderful conversations they'd had when Jana was younger about so many important matters, and the outings with Jana and all the other children. Her mother was still a devout Communist, still enthralled with being in what she thought was the advance guard of social change, always going to party events as if they were galas for the privileged.

It was her mother's belief that the world was better when governments had strong ideals; and that was exemplified, she thought, in the solidarity that the party brought to the people, uniting even the most disparate groups under the red banner. The lecture they were attending that day was called "Majority vs. Minority in the National Interest," a subject Jana was only mildly concerned with. But going to the lecture was a priority now, if not to serve the national interest, then to save the family unity.

The lecture was being held in a hall, one of the government buildings near Grassalkovich Palace. It was used on the weekends by a variety of Communist-approved organizations. It was not mandatory for anyone to attend these events, but the clean and pleasant surroundings near the palace gave the lectures and meetings at the hall an aura of respectability, so they were reasonably well attended. There were always a number of kids at them, whole families sometimes coming, depending upon the subject. Given the poor selection of entertainment and amusements under the regime, they were, at least, a type of diversion from humdrum ordinary life. The only demands for money were a plate placed prominently on a table at the entrance, by whatever group was presenting the event, on which you could drop the fewest number of *korona* that your conscience would tolerate; and, on another table holding various handouts, a slightly smaller plate.

Jana and her mother walked into the half-filled hall, her mother slipping a few coins into the plate at the door, a young woman who was standing guard over the plate welcoming them. The wall was not decorated with any Communist Party paraphernalia since it was not a party event, simply an event provided with a permit by the government. Jana's mother was saying hello to another woman when Jana saw the poster with the small photograph of the lecturer on it. It was Georg Repka, the one-time agent provocateur who had been beaten by the police, the one who had betrayed his fellow students. Jana turned, ready to leave without even telling her mother why she was going, when the urge to see Repka again, to see what kind of man the student had become, stopped her.

Jana's mother saw the change in her daughter's face and took her elbow. "You're not feeling well?"

"I'm fine. Mother," Jana said, indicating the poster, "you know Georg Repka?"

"He's always working on issues. A good thinker. You just know he'll go into politics. Georg stands out."

"I'm sure he does."

"He's not a party official, but he's respected by them."

"It's good when people respect you," Jana said without really meaning it. Internally, Jana could feel the turmoil of anticipation generated by the thought of seeing the man again. She had a dreadful feeling that she was going to be involved in an experience that she wished she could avoid, but which was rushing toward her with a momentum she couldn't stop.

"Let's get close before all the seats are taken," Jana's mother urged. They walked up to the first row and sat directly in front of the dais. "Why strain to hear when you can be right in front of the speaker?"

The room did not fill up, and only about half of the seats had been taken when the young woman who had been at the door came to the dais to introduce Repka. She went into the usual glowing praise, identifying him as a man who had become known as a clear-minded, respected social critic who had, even at a young age, caught the attention of the serious-minded people of Slovakia who were looking for future leaders, a man of high moral principles whom people could look up to. Her introduction went on much too long, but she finally wound down to let Repka take the podium.

There was a smattering of applause as Repka strode up the aisle to the dais, his face radiant as if he had been freshly anointed as a saint's representative and was now ready to explain heaven to them all. He still had the hitch in his stride caused by the police beating, though the limp was improved from when Jana had last seen him. Repka raised his hand to stop the applause and looked over the audience, immediately seeing Jana's mother and giving her a quick nod of acknowledgment. Jana's mother beamed back at him, happy to be recognized, nudging Jana just in case she had missed it. He had not recognized Jana.

Repka launched into his speech. The man was a natural crowd-pleaser. He began with a couple of jokes, comic stories that were harmless enough, then transitioned into the main portion of his talk, which began with an account of a hobo from another country begging for change from a woman after he had stolen a pie she had baked. Imagine, he said, the nerve of a person stealing from a woman, then trying to get money from her too. From there, he moved on to the subject of foreigners in general. Aliens had come into the country and were begging for handouts after they had already begun stealing the country's wealth. He then veered from this xenophobic call for distrust of foreigners because they didn't care about the needs of the Slovak people on to the Roma question.

The Roma question? Gypsies?

Jana was startled. She'd known there would be rhetoric, because her mother wouldn't have been interested in the lecture if that hadn't been expected. However, the excoriation of the gypsies that followed was beyond anything Jana could have imagined.

"We have been tainted by a foreign presence for many years. We've been strong enough to tolerate those who come into our country and take advantage of this land's people and their generosity. What we cannot and shall never tolerate is the alien, scabrous presence of those people who steal from us and then steal again, without ever contributing one iota to the common good. They demand, and demand, and demand more, never giving, always taking. The gypsy presence has to be dealt with. Let them go home. Let them be repatriated. Help them get out if it can be done quickly. No matter how they protest, help them, not too gently if necessary, to all get out. Wash our country clean."

Repka continued on and on, his speech broken only by applause, the man bathing in the glow of approval. He was calling for expelling the gypsies. He was preaching no tolerance. He seemed to be verging on calling for an extermination of the Roma, only pulling back at the last moment, implying to his audience that this might be the appropriate course if no other way of dealing with the alien Rom presence in their nation succeeded.

To Jana, it was as if the Nazis had come back into the country, only in another guise. She felt a new anger building on the anger she already felt for the man, now turning into rage. She wasn't sure she could contain it, but at the same time she didn't want to alienate her mother. But her mother sat beside her virtually eating out of the man's hand, applauding every time she got the chance. It finally became too much for Jana to endure, and she stood up, staring at Repka, swaying slightly, holding herself back from physically attacking the man, a man who had betrayed his own people before and was now calling for another betrayal.

Jana's mother grabbed her arm, trying to pull her down, the audience becoming aware that Jana was not standing in support, but in defiance. Repka began to dart glances at her, aware that things were not quite as he would like in his audience. The rest of the spectators had begun to focus so much on Jana that they were no longer hearing what he was saying. They had stopped applauding. The silence, combined with Jana standing indomitably in front of him, eventually wore Repka down, Jana impressing her will on his. The man's speech faltered, descending into silence, both he and Jana staring at each other.

"I think this lady is ill," Repka finally suggested. "Can one of us help the lady to get some air outside?"

"All of us need air in here," Jana responded.

Jana's mother forcefully yanked on her arm. Jana ignored her.

"You betrayed your friends; you want to betray your countrymen. You want them to beat the students again, only now they're gypsies. How long do you go on with this?" Jana asked.

"The lady is obviously sick," Repka announced. "Can we get on with this meeting? Will someone lead her out of here?"

The woman who had provided Repka's introduction came over to Jana. "You seem to be ailing," she whispered. "Why don't you come with me? I'll get you a glass of water and you can rest for a while." She tried to take Jana's arm, but Jana shook her off.

"You can't do it again, Repka. You'll be stopped." Jana turned to the audience. "Don't you see? He has to be stopped." There was no response. After several seconds of silence, Jana leaned over to her mother. "I'm going. You should come with me." Her mother didn't move. "I'll wait outside, Mother." Jana walked down the center aisle and out of the hall.

Jana's mother remained seated for a few moments,

uncertain what to do. Then she gave Repka an apologetic look, got up, and hurried after her daughter. She found Jana in the area just outside the lecture-hall entrance.

"Are you crazy?" Jana's mother snarled at her.

"No, Mother, I'm not crazy."

"Then why did you do this?"

Jana walked out of the building and onto the street, her mother following her.

"Why did you do this, Jana?" her mother repeated.

"Because someone has to stand up and stop him, Mother. You have to see what people like that are. You have to realize what they're doing. Then you have to stand up and say *enough*!"

"My friends will talk about this," Jana's mother complained. "The party will hear about what you said, and I'll have to answer for it."

"Does the party sponsor state action against the gypsies, Mother?"

"They're letting that flag fly to see which way it will blow. Then they'll decide. We've all talked about it. We have to do something about them. Don't you see?" Her mother's voice trailed off.

"Yes," said Jana, talking to herself rather than agreeing with her mother. "Except you can't see if you're looking through dirty glass."

They walked for a short distance together, awkwardly hugged, then went to their own separate homes.

Chapter 26

They drove west on Unter den Linden, which quickly became Strasse des 17 Juni, the car heading toward Charlottenburg. Jana thought about the events at the airport, deciding to explore the unease she'd experienced when they'd all come together.

"You don't get along with the BKA?" she asked Konrad.

"There's always rivalry. They accuse us of encroaching on them; we accuse them of being inept. They think they're the cavalry; and they think *Die Kripo* is the infantry. We think they don't really know how to work street crime; they think we hang out with thugs and can't be trusted. So, a small amount of friction."

"They've got something under a blanket they don't want us to know about."

"Naturally. They always do. So does your fellow Slovak, the prosecutor. Otherwise she wouldn't be hanging out with the BKA. That also means you won't be getting the whole truth from your people. Chances are you will get less than nothing. And so will I."

"Are we dealing with state secrets here? Earth-shaking events?"

Konrad winced. "I hope not. The last time I was involved in anything like that, the streets were littered with people who had been shot, stabbed, and generally maimed. The BKA were involved up to their asses in that one as well."

"What's going on, Albrecht?"

"All I know is that there's some kind of angst hanging in the air around the Ministry of the Interior and a few of the other parts of government."

"With all this hiding and concealment, it has to be big. The thing, whatever it is, has to affect a lot of people or there wouldn't be all this interest."

"I agree."

She thought about the murder of the Turk in Slovakia. "Have you had any mention of a man called Makine, also known as Koba?"

"Damn, is that bastard involved in this?"

"He may be."

"Maybe I should take my pension early?"

"You'd be bored."

"I like lying around. I'm just a simple person." He laughed at his description of himself. "Okay, I'm not so simple."

"Did you come up with anything on young Bogan?"

"He's not so young. And he's in the game."

"He's a criminal?"

"Not a good man, as we might say. He's playing with the Turks."

"Turks?"

"We've got a huge Turkish population here. They come into Germany for work. Considering the piss-poor wages they get in Turkey, it's not a bad idea. They've done pretty well, except for the usual fringe group that preys on them and everybody else. Lots of narcotics activity. They have the contacts in Turkey to bring it in. Some are hard-core thieves and enforcers. The German gangs like to use them for heavy-duty muscle because they're safe. It's hard to penetrate through the layers in the tight-knit Turkish community. Their 'capital' is Kreuzberg. Used to be primarily working-class German. The Turks have more or less taken the place over. The biggest Turkish population outside of Turkey. Tons of kebab shops and travel agents that want to send you back to Anatolia at cheap prices."

"Any informants who work the area?"

"One good one. I can nose around to see if any of my people have any others. Why?"

"I've got a Turk in Bratislava who was found with an ice pick in his eye."

"That's why you asked about Makine?"

"The ice pick sounds like Makine, doesn't it?"

"It's not a popular weapon for anyone else I can think of."

"There are two others possibly involved in the killing, one of them a German named Balder who worked with the Turk. I'll get you the workup we have on it."

She dialed Seges on her cell phone. He seemed preoccupied when he came on the line.

"What's wrong, Seges?" she asked.

"My life is being made miserable."

"What's Em doing?"

"It's my wife."

"Then what is she doing?"

"She's listening to that little monster and buying clothes and makeup and dishes, and now she's talking about buying furniture. It's just a matter of days before she throws me out."

"Why is she going to throw you out?"

"Because of *your* Em."

"She's not *my* Em," Jana interrupted.

"Because *this* Em has said that I haven't been nice enough to my wife, and now my wife is talking about divorcing me."

"Has she actually said she's divorcing you, Seges?"

"No, but I can see what's coming."

"No, you can't."

There was a long silence.

"She's talking about a boyfriend she had years ago," he said. "I know what that means."

"It means she wants you to pay more attention to her, that's all it means."

There was another silence. "How am I supposed to pay more attention to her?"

"Ask Em."

"Em will know?"

"That's what I said."

Seges was silent again. Jana took advantage of the moment to tell Seges to fax the information on the dead Turk and his friends to Albrecht Konrad. She asked Konrad for his fax number and passed it on to Seges. Then she hung up before Seges could complain any more.

She glanced out the window. The area was becoming less commercial and more residential.

"We're almost there," Konrad informed her.

They passed the large green area that housed the magnificent Schloss Charlottenburg, the palace surrounded by huge gardens that Frederick the First had built for his queen; then they swung onto a side street. It was lined with old but still-elegant houses, remnants of the aristocracy who used to live in these villas near the palace. Konrad pointed to a huge white wood-and-brick structure mostly concealed by large trees in its front yard. From what Jana could see of the lawn and the mansion, it was well kept up.

"Not a bad place to live, eh?" Konrad observed.

"I'll take it. I wonder exactly what the younger Bogan does to deserve all this."

Konrad gave her a knowing smile. "He knows how to stay out of the front lines. I've never seen the man, but from what I can gather he's provided the bankroll for a few criminal events. One was a wholesale jeweler who had too much gold on hand. The other was a bank. They tunneled from three doors down, under the intervening buildings. It was a hell of an engineering feat. We got most of the loot back from the first job and nothing back on the second. All in all, even though the first one went bad, he more than made up his costs for it with the second one. The man has walked away clean on everything, white as that house of his. He's banking outside of Germany; where, I don't know."

"His daddy has a bank in Vienna."

A long, satisfied "Ahhhh" came out of Konrad's mouth. "*That's* where it's coming and going. He gets his startup funds there, then deposits what he makes. I like it. Neat. Daddy is taking care of his son."

"Except we seem to have lost daddy and haven't quite found the son."

"You won't find him in there, either." He pointed a forefinger at the house. "There's nothing in the place." Konrad had a "cat who ate the canary" grin on his face. "Not one stick of furniture."

"You've already been inside?"

"You think I'm going to wait for the BKA to make a decision about whether I'm even going to be allowed to go in with them? I'd never even get a taste of what they found, if they ever could find anything. So, I didn't wait for a warrant."

Jana was not surprised that Konrad had already been in the villa. Thinking over the situation, she might have done the same thing.

"You have a key?"

"An easy lock pick. Except there's nothing to see inside."

"For my own satisfaction, I'd like to go in the house."

"Whatever you want."

They got out of the car and walked through the gate and up to the front door of the house. The surround of trees concealed them from the neighbors as Konrad picked the lock, and within seconds they slipped inside.

The rooms were spacious, light-filled, and, as Konrad had said, empty. Jana walked from room to room. Everything had been removed, even the light bulbs in the beautiful chandelier still hanging in the dance-floor–sized living room. Jana took one side of the double staircase leading to the second floor and went through every room upstairs. Not a stick of furniture anywhere. Even the floors had been scrubbed clean. Whoever had emptied the house had done a thorough job. There was nothing to find on the upper floor, Jana concluded. She went back downstairs.

As she came down, she noticed that there was a small square of paper just inside the front door, the dark color of the paper blending into the shadows so that it was almost invisible. Jana picked it up. It was a business card for the company that had done the moving.

"They were too proud of what they do to leave the place without their signature," she commented. Jana handed the card to Konrad.

He read it aloud: "Johan Krug and Sons. Quality in Moving. We are responsible for your belongings. Trust us to care for them. Foreign Moves Our Specialty." He rattled off their address and telephone number. "The name on the card is Kathe Krug. What happened to the 'and Sons'? I'd like to see the size of this lady Valkyrie who's moving furniture."

"How far away is the address?"

"It's on the Ku'damm, ten minutes away."

"That last line of the card caught my attention. 'Foreign Moves Our Specialty.'"

"Foreign."

"I think a quick visit to Kathe the Valkyrie is in order."

The Ku'damm is the primary shopping street in Berlin, a beehive of activity with the heaviest street traffic in the city. It took them slightly longer than the predicted ten minutes to get there, their car held up by the traffic clogging the road, and then they had trouble finding parking anywhere near the address on the card. They walked to the building, checked the listing in the lobby to assure themselves that the offices of Johan Krug and Sons were there, then went up to the third floor.

The Valkyrie was a surprise. Kathe Krug was petite to the point of being elfin, and very feminine, with an open smile for the two of them until Albrecht showed her his police credentials. Unlike most Germans, who instantly accede to any request by authorities, Krug became brusque and businesslike, refusing to give them any information on who had requested the move, when it had occurred, or where the contents of the house had gone.

"Our clients deserve privacy," Krug insisted.

"This is the first time I've run across a moving company concerned about people's rights to privacy," Konrad said as pleasantly as possible, flattered by her early smile, still trying to remain attractive to this very pretty woman. "Perhaps I can offer you a coffee, a snack, or dinner at the KaDeWe?" The KaDeWe was an upscale department store with the most extensive, and expensive, food and beverage section in the world.

Her lips stayed sealed, refusing to answer.

"If you don't want that, perhaps I can buy you a small hat? Or a cap, if you prefer? You could tilt it over one eye, and it would look charming on you. Or we can just go window-shopping down the street."

"Thank you. Not interested," she snapped.

"I'm sure your brothers will like me. A police officer knows how to look after a lady."

"I don't have any brothers."

"It says 'Krug and Sons' on the business card."

"We wouldn't get any business if the card said 'Krug and Daughter.'"

"I think if they knew how pretty the daughter was, everyone would use the firm no matter what was on the card."

Jana was getting tired of the flirting. It was evident that she had to play the "bad" cop. She put a hand on Konrad's arm to stop his blather, then focused on the woman. "Ms. Krug, you seem like a very reasonable person. I will be glad to recommend your company to anyone in this area. Unfortunately, I have a job to do in the interim.

"You have all these files." Jana indicated the file cabinets along the walls. "If my colleague and I are forced to get a warrant to search the premises, we'll have no alternative other than to take all of those files to our building to search them for the information we want. Regrettably, we're short-handed. And, being short-handed, we'll take a very long time to examine every cabinet and drawer, every piece of paper, down to the little memo notes you have posted on the walls. It might take months."

She paused for effect.

"And, when we put those files back, horrors! Police officers are sloppy and inefficient in placing items, particularly papers, where they should be filed." The woman was beginning to get the idea. "Everything will be mixed up. My apologies." There was no tone of apology in her voice.

She leaned closer to the woman. "Do you understand what kind of problems your company will have if we go through that procedure?" Jana looked at her watch, adding a touch of impatience to push the woman to make up her mind. "Now, your answer, please."

Kathe Krug's mouth had dropped open; now it closed with an audible click of her teeth. Within seconds, she was running around the office collecting pieces of paper. In less than five minutes, she placed a very full file in front of Jana.

"All here?" Jana asked, just to make sure. "The method of payment? And the duplicate on the payment check for the move?"

Ms. Krug nodded.

"Very good." Jana's voice conveyed a sense of admiration. "So much faster and more efficient than we would have been." She picked up the file. "We'll return it when we're finished." Jana began to turn away, then stopped. "My friend Mr. Konrad seems attracted to you. If I walk out to the hall and leave him here, he'll unquestionably ask you out again. Don't be afraid to say no. He won't do anything if you refuse. However, if you're thinking of saying yes, I would definitely find out if he's married."

Jana walked out of the office, looking at her watch. It was exactly thirty seconds before Albrecht Konrad came out, looking quite chagrined.

"She asked you if you were married," Jana hazarded, trying to keep a straight face.

"That wasn't very nice of you," he complained.

"Are we talking about how we obtained the files, or the suggestion that she ask if you were already committed to another lady?"

"Piss on you," he growled.

When they exited the building, Konrad was still sulking. Instead of the KaDeWe, which Albrecht now claimed was too expensive, they went to a nearby beer garden and ordered drinks, then began going through the files. The first thing they noticed was that there were two sets of invoices, indicating that there'd been two home moves: one for the house that they'd just come from, the other relating to the house the BKA were currently obtaining a warrant for. The first furniture move had been three days ago. The second house, with a telephone number correlating to the number Jana had obtained from the banker in Vienna, had been emptied and shipped a day and a half ago.

"The BKA is going to get a shock when they go inside both the homes and find out that they're empty," Konrad said, a pleased note in his voice.

"Call them. Tell them what we've found. They're a brother police agency. They have enough to do without going out on a dead lead."

"The bastards won't appreciate it if we tell them we went in the first house without a by-the-book search warrant."

"We never went in," Jana suggested to Konrad. She expanded on her suggestion, making up a cover story as she went along. "I understand an informant of yours told you that the Krug firm had become involved in transporting stolen merchandise. When you went to check it out, you asked for their customer list, and the Bogan name popped out at you. You then obtained the complete file, which told you that these houses had already been stripped."

"It won't hold up."

"Yes, it will. There won't be any reason for them to check with the Krug firm since we'll give them the file, and they'll be too grateful to think we've back-doored them."

He thought about the false story she'd suggested.

"Very devious." He nodded. "I like it."

"It comes from many years of dealing with bureaucracy."

He raised his beer in a toast to her. They clinked their glasses. "I like the way you do business, Matinova."

"One hand washes the other, Albrecht."

They sipped their beers, continuing to read through the file.

"The checks are both made out on Bogan's Vienna bank," Konrad said. "The man who signed them is named Radomir Kralik. You know the guy?"

"He's a vice president at the bank. He was close to Klara and Oto Bogan. Kralik's the man who gave me the telephone number of Bogan's son."

"A nice *kaffeeklatsch*. Except, where the hell have Bogan father and son gone to ground?"

"Add Radomir Kralik to that list. The Austrians are looking for him in connection with a shooting."

"Someone else killed?"

"A female Slovak police commander was shot."

Konrad stared at her. "He put a bullet in you?"

"Two, both flesh wounds. And we're not sure who did the shooting."

"The bandage under your chin?"

"Yes. Very noticeable?"

"It's there. You only notice it when you hold your head up."

"I have good posture. So I always hold my head up."

"I guess that means it's noticeable."

"Thank you, my good friend," she said, her tone anything but friendly, distressed about how badly she might look to anyone giving her a passing glance.

Albrecht ordered another beer for each of them. Jana checked the file to see where the furniture taken from both houses had been delivered. The location was a surprise.

"They sent the goods to France."

"France?"

"I get the idea that they're getting as far away from something or someone as they can. Two posh houses in Berlin, which they abandoned, forwarding their goods all the way to France and disappearing as quickly as possible themselves. It all says flight."

"Maybe they're frightened of you."

"I admit, I'm pretty frightening at times."

"My wife says that about me on occasion."

"Your wife? You mean the woman whom you had to tell pretty Kathe Krug about?"

Konrad winced at the jibe. "Enough, Matinova."

"You've been so helpful, I promise to take pity and stop for now." She went to the invoices again. "My, my. The owner listed on one house, the one in Charlottenburg, is Zdenko Bogan. The one listed on the other one is Radomir Kralik. Odd."

"Why so odd? He's tight with the family. He helped run the bank."

"Kralik told me he had little to do with the Bogans' son." She ruminated over the facts. "What are the odds that men who are both Slovaks, have close family ties, have homes in the same city, and then both ship their furniture to the Paris area, would have little to do with each other? Mr. Kralik lied to me."

"You think they were behind the attempt to kill you?"

"Maybe."

"And where does Makine, our friend Koba, the stuff of every cop's nightmare, fit in?"

Jana finished her second beer, thinking about the question. "Still too soon to come up with an answer to that question. Tomorrow we'll start working on the dead Turk and the others who were with him just before he had an ice pick put in his eye."

"Tomorrow," Konrad agreed, tossing the last of his beer down, then dropped a few euros on the table to pay the bill.

Just as they were about to get up, a man came in the front door, appeared to casually glance around the room, then walked to the bar and ordered a drink. Jana looked at him briefly. Hard to say why she fixed on the man. Police officers just develop cop's eyes, eyes that lock onto things that most people would never take a second look at. She looked away, then back to the man as he took a seat at the bar. He turned his head so half his face was revealed in the small bar mirror. There was a large chestnut birthmark on his cheek.

Jana felt a disquieting chill, remembering the account of the witness to the Bogan shooting whose husband had been knocked down by two men fleeing from the alley just after the killing of Klara Bogan. One of those men had a large chestnut birthmark on his cheek. Birthmarks are fairly common; birthmarks of that nature are not. Too much of a coincidence to have a man with the mark of Cain, as Jana thought of the birthmark, coming in to have a drink in the same bar they were in.

Jana touched Konrad on the arm. "The man at the bar."

Konrad turned to look at him just as he downed his drink.

The man glanced their way, left money on the counter to pay for his drink, then stood and quickly walked to the door, pausing to light a cigarette just before he walked out.

"One of the Bogan killers. I'm sure of it," was Jana's terse warning to Konrad.

Konrad stared as the door closed behind the man, rising in his seat.

"He came in here so I would see him. The man is trolling," Jana cautioned.

"Fishing?"

"Fishing," she affirmed. "For both of us. He wants us to come after him. If we do, bang-bang, we're dead."

"Police officers don't cower in bars." He pulled away from her, starting for the door.

She grabbed his arm and spoke louder and more forcefully. "The shootings in Bratislava were done with rifles with telescopic sights. You won't even see him if you go through the door. It's a snare. You're dead without getting a shot off."

Konrad stopped and gave her a penitent look, slowly sitting down again. "I guess this one policeman is going to cower in a bar."

Konrad called for police assistance, and the street was swarming with cops within minutes. The police went through the whole area, at Jana's direction particularly focusing on the buildings across the street.

They didn't find the man with the chestnut birthmark.

Or the other man who Jana was sure was with him.

The killers, whoever they were, wouldn't have stayed around the neighborhood. Successful murders are not committed in an area where police are flooding the streets. When it became clear that the search wouldn't find anyone, both Jana and Konrad decided it was safe for them to leave the bar and for Jana to find a hotel so she'd have a place to stay for the night.

Konrad was not in a good mood.

"My associates are going to think I'm a jackass for calling out the troops," he complained.

"A live jackass."

"Sometimes better to be a dead hero. I'll get nothing but grief from them over the next few days."

"I'm used to dealing with it. Refer them to me."

"If my wife divorces me when she hears I was hiding in

a bar with a policewoman, do you think Ms. Krug of Krug
and Sons will go out with me?"

They both laughed, a little too heartily for the joke, the
tension of the last hour beginning to seep away.

Konrad suggested a small, reasonably priced hotel a few
blocks away for Jana to stay in. She said she would walk,
but Konrad insisted that he drive her there. "They might
try and come after you if you pop out from under the
umbrella of protection we're providing."

"Whoever they are, they're too professional to take that
kind of a stupid chance."

"It always depends on the stakes."

"If only we knew what the stakes were," Jana complained. "Okay, chauffeur me over to the hotel."

Konrad dropped her off, telling her he'd come by to
pick her up in the morning as soon as he could get in
touch with his informant.

Jana decided to take a hot shower. She stripped, looking
at herself in the mirror. Not so good. She removed the
small bandage under her chin. The area around the scab
was slightly inflamed, and it looked ugly. She sent a silent
prayer to the gods of the universe to please not let it look
too bad when the healing was complete. The bandage
under her arm was too complex to remove. A little blood
had seeped through, but that was normal with all the
movement she'd gone through since it had been put on.
The throbbing soreness from the wound was constant,
aggravated as well by her moving around without concern
for the healing process. Fortunately, the pain was at a low
level, so she could continue to ignore the discomfort.

Jana was about to step into the shower when she
remembered that the doctors had told her to keep the
wound dry for the next few days. She stopped herself just

before turning the water on. Unlike in many of the low-end hotels in Europe, there was a bathtub. Jana turned on the water and the tub filled quickly. She eased into the tub, grateful for the heat seeping through her body. She didn't stay in the tub very long, afraid she might fall asleep in the warmth. After a few minutes, she climbed out and toweled herself off.

She was about to crawl under the covers, but on an impulse tried to call her granddaughter in the United States. Once more, she got an answering machine. Jana hung up, feeling a large pang of loneliness as she slipped into bed. She was alone in a foreign city in a strange hotel bed with no one to reach out to for comfort or love. As a last ritual, she called her department in Slovakia, giving them her location.

Jana had a final thought before she fell asleep. There were murderers out there who had absolutely no compunction about killing. They had tried to kill her once before. They hadn't given up.

It was not a pleasant thought to sleep on.

Chapter 27

Jana's father had died some time ago; her brother had become estranged from the family; and when her mother died, there was a quiet funeral at the graveyard with virtually no one who was close to either Jana or her mother attending, so it was bleak. Virtually all of Jana's mother's friends had suggested that, instead of friends coming to a cemetery service, a memorial be held for her. It was the party way. The event was held in the same small hall where her mother had participated in so many party meetings, in the government building near the Grassalkovich Palace.

Most of the people who attended had been her mother's comrades during her years of political involvement. There were also neighbors and a few low-level members of ministries who hadn't known Jana's mother but who had been sent to say a few words about her contributions to the state. One of them was the person who had organized the speakers at the event, not bothering to consult Jana about them. Trokan had come more as a friend to Jana than as a representative from the police, although he wore his full uniform as he always did when he felt it necessary to give weight to his presence. There was also a tired-looking reporter, overweight and sloppy in her ill-fitting dress, who had come determined to pester the mourners to get the human-interest element that would make her copy acceptable to her editor.

Jana gave her enough personal details to fill out her copy, then tried to shoo the woman away. The reporter gave her an annoyed look, but soon realized she was going to get nothing further and moved away toward a more receptive face in the crowd.

Jana didn't see the speakers' list until she and Trokan found their seats in the "family row" and the usher for the event handed her a small flyer that listed them. Underneath each listed speaker was a single line explaining what the speaker's position was in either the party or the government. The second speaker's name immediately caught Jana's eye. It was Georg Repka, the man who had betrayed his fellow students and whom Jana had had a confrontation with during his vitriolic speech against the Roms. Jana could not control the deep anger she felt at seeing him listed on the agenda.

Trokan heard the growl that came from her.

"A problem, Jana?"

"Repka, one of the speakers. He's a horror; a bad human being who shouldn't be here."

Jana got to her feet, looking around the room for Repka. Trokan got up with her, leaning in to her so he could talk without anyone else hearing. "Jana, are you saying this man was an enemy of your mother? That he did something to her that affected her badly? What was it?"

"He deceived his friends. His ideas about the world are repulsive. He's a betrayer. I want him off the speakers' list and out of here."

"Was he a friend of your mother's?"

"That doesn't matter."

"Of course it does. She selected her friends; you didn't. This isn't the time to create a stir. Let it rest for the moment."

"I loathe the man."

"Your mother didn't! Unsettling the people who have come to share their loss with each other is not the way to go."

A woman who lived down the street from Jana and her mother came over, her husband lagging slightly behind her.

"I'm so sorry about your mother's death, Jana," she whispered. Her husband said something in support of his wife's sentiments which Jana couldn't pick up, but for which she thanked them both. Several other neighbors offered their brief condolences. All the while, Jana was looking for Repka.

Jana saw the man who had made up the speakers' list and walked over to him. Trokan followed her.

"This isn't the thing to do, Jana," he appealed. "These people want comfort. This isn't a battlefield. It's a place for solace and remembrance. Let it go."

When they got to the man responsible for the speakers, Jana's voice was harsh. "Why wasn't I consulted about the speakers today?" she demanded.

He looked at her, taken aback by her aggressive posture and tone of voice. "I was told you were too busy with police work."

"What impelled you to put Georg Repka on the speakers' list?"

"He was a friend of hers, and they were party members together." The man looked to Trokan for support, since he seemed calm and appeared to have more rank than Jana did. "He came to me about this event and volunteered to give a little talk about your mother, so it seemed right."

"It was right, sir," Trokan interjected. "Thank you for the effort you've made in putting this event on."

"My thanks as well," Jana managed to get out, her rush to anger abating slightly. The colonel steered her back to their seats.

"This Repka will be coming in any time, Jana. What are you going to do when you see him?"

"I don't know."

"You had better decide before he comes in. This is no time, and no place, for sudden explosions and tumult."

"I want the man out of here, Colonel."

"What you want, at this moment, is to assuage your own feelings of anger at this Repka. What you have to ask yourself is how your mother would respond if she saw the man here. What would *she* think? What would *she* want you to do?"

Jana thought about Trokan's queries. They forced her to call into question what she thought about her mother.

"She had the same 'public concerns' he had," she finally allowed. "In ways, they sat in the same nest."

"You're saying, in a roundabout way, that she'd want him here?"

"Maybe."

"You haven't yet said what you'll do when you see Georg Repka."

"I'm thinking."

"Not much time to do that."

Jana heard a slight alteration in the hum of conversation at the rear of the room. Georg Repka had come in.

Trokan observed the change in Jana. "He's here?"

"Yes."

"Caution, Jana. He'll be presenting you with his condolences any moment now. Remember, when he does, that we're civilized people."

Jana forced herself to face forward, holding in what she was feeling. Within seconds, Repka was standing next to her.

"My sympathies on your loss, Madam Matinova."

He continued talking, Jana keeping her head down,

hiding her own emotions, managing to blot out most of his words of commiseration. What he was saying was all false. This was not a man who could empathize. She forced herself to concentrate on pretending he was a cipher, a blank, a negative space and, hence, nothing to respond to.

Repka went on and on; the longer he stayed, the more difficult it became to block him out completely. Jana's gorge began to rise. It was an internal war, Jana fighting to keep the anger inside herself. Finally, after an infinity of time had passed, he stopped and she somehow got out a "Thank you." Repka moved on and found a seat down the row.

Trokan patted her on the hand to show that he felt for her, aware of what she had gone through to control her anger and disgust with the man. "Congratulations."

She nodded.

"One more ordeal to go: he still has to give his eulogy. Remember that, while he's talking, you have to tolerate it."

Jana nodded again, remembering what she had done when she had heard him give his peroration on the gypsies. It would be just as difficult for her to listen today, perhaps even more so.

The ceremony began, the first speaker, not used to public speaking, providing a stuttering summary of her mother's life, including a mention of Jana and the brilliant police career her mother had been so proud of. After five minutes he trailed off, and Repka was summoned to the dais.

His presentation was engaging. The man was a consummate professional at what he was doing, a manipulator, his speech hitting all the right notes: her mother's belief in the family, her activity in the party, her encouragement of her daughter to join a profession that did not easily accept women but in which Jana, with her mother's aid and support, had became a champion of the public welfare.

And Jana's mother, he said, had never forgotten what being a Slovak meant, what defending the native traditions meant, what fighting foreign elements meant, what sacrifices were needed to save the Slavic bloodlines and keep them pure. Minorities and their views would not be tolerated. Yes, racial purity above all, expunging foreign influence and its corrupting practices by force if necessary. It was what she had preached and practiced.

By the time Repka was through, he had made Jana's mother a heroine, the quintessence of all the ideal qualities of femininity, motherhood, state virtue. The words had also damned her and himself as extremists and bigoted, narrow-minded racists.

Unfortunately, when he finished there was a murmur of approval from the assembled mourners, though it was quickly stifled for reasons of decorum.

Jana looked up at him. His eyes roved the audience as he took in their approbation, enjoying the brief moment of having them in his control. Then, for an instant, he glanced at Jana. There was a look of triumph in his eyes. He hadn't forgotten Jana and her challenge to him when he'd given the speech disparaging the Roms. He had remembered that he had a score to settle with her. In extolling her mother in this way, Georg Repka felt he had won the battle with Jana. The audience of mourners was there for him, for his greater glory, and not for Jana's mother.

Repka left the dais and slipped away from the proceedings.

The colonel leaned over to Jana. "I agree."

"With what?"

"There is ugliness about the man."

"You have a good nose, Colonel."

After the final speaker, everyone began to leave. The reporter came up to Jana gushing about the wonderful eulogy Repka had given, telling her she would be sure to include it in the article she was writing. Jana got away from her as quickly as possible.

Life goes on. Jana accepted the well-wishes of the people who had remained; then both she and Trokan left, driving to work.

Repka would surface again, Jana told herself. All creatures like that did. And then maybe the earth would open under him and he would receive what he had coming. Jana believed that was how things should happen.

That thought was her only consolation.

Chapter 28

Jana woke up the next morning before the sun rose over Berlin, wondering for a moment where she was, then remembering. Hotel rooms are generic. It always took her a moment after she woke up in a hotel room to realize that she was not lost.

She went through her morning ablutions and was preparing to go down to the room where the hotel was serving breakfast when Seges called.

"My wife has had a small breakdown. She had to be sedated."

"What happened?"

"She took the loss of Em very badly."

It sounded as if Seges was referring to someone who had died. A jolt of fear went through Jana. "What's happened to Em?" was all she could get out.

"The man came and took her, and my wife had become so attached to Em that she began to weep and wouldn't stop. It went on for hours, until I called the doctor and he gave her some medication. Except, this morning she's at it again, and I've called for the doctor again. So, I'm still at home now, and it's very hard here."

"Seges, what man came and took Em?"

"He said he was from social services."

"What social services?"

"Slovak social services."

"How did he know that Em was there and that he was to take her with him?"

"He just said he was told to take her. That was it."

Jana felt her alarm growing. "I didn't tell social services about Em. There was no order for them to take her. Did he show you his credentials?"

"No. But, the girl recognized him. As soon as she saw him, she began gathering her clothes together. My wife had bought them for her," he explained. "The girl liked the clothing. She liked my wife; my wife liked her. I even started to like her. It was hard when she left."

"Seges!" Jana shouted to stop him. "Did Em tell you the man was from social services?"

"Not exactly."

"What, *exactly*, did she say to the man? Seges, I want every word that you heard her say to the man and every word that he said to her. Do you understand? Every single word."

"Not much was said."

"Seges, tell me!"

"He came to the door. My wife answered. He told both of us he was from social services. That he'd been sent to take charge of Em. Em was in her bedroom. When she heard the man speaking, she came out. He nodded at her; she nodded back. Then she went back into the bedroom, packed, came out, hugged and kissed my wife, thanked her for her kindness, and the two of them walked out."

"He never said a word to Em; she never said a word to him?"

"Not a word."

"Did she appear frightened, anxious?"

"I didn't notice any fear. She was like herself. I thought you had sent social services to collect her."

"You had my number to call, Seges. Why didn't you call me?"

"It didn't seem necessary."

"Did you watch them when they left the house?"

"That was when my wife broke down. When she and Em went out yesterday, she had a street artist draw a picture of the two of them together. She began kissing the picture. Then she became hysterical. Crying, weeping as if her life was gone. I had to comfort my wife, you understand. It was bad. I had to care for her."

"Since she was taken from your home, have you talked to anyone from social services about who it was they sent after Em?"

There was a long pause on the line. Jana couldn't even hear the sound of breathing from Seges. Faulting the man now was useless. All Jana could hope for was information, and at the moment she was getting precious little of that.

"I haven't talked to anyone," Seges finally said. He paused again. "He seemed nice enough," was the excuse that eventually emerged.

"Seges, he was not *nice* enough. He may have not been *nice* at all!"

Jana considered the situation. Em might be in grave danger. They had to find her. The girl's life might depend upon it.

"The drawing of your wife and Em. Get that picture out everywhere. I want a general alert. Find her, Seges. Your career depends upon it. Do you understand the order I've given you?"

"Yes, Commander."

Jana pushed her anger at his incompetence away, making a last demand of her warrant officer. "Describe the man, Seges."

"Taller than me. Not very distinguished."

"Seges, you're a police officer. Eyes, hair, complexion?"

"He was, you know, just plain. With dark hair."

"His eyes, Seges. The color?"

"Sort of . . . muddy."

Muddy eyes. She had heard that before, from Em.

"Go forward with my instructions, Seges." Jana terminated the call.

She sat on the edge of the bed, trying to decide if there was any other course of action open to her. Seges had given her very few facts about the event. The only things Jana could be sure of were that the man had specifically come for Em and that Em and he had recognized each other. The girl had proved herself very resourceful. She knew Seges was a police officer. If she'd been afraid of the man, she would have shown it and asked for his help. She hadn't done that, so that was some small consolation.

Jana held herself responsible: she'd placed Em with Seges for safekeeping, and it had turned into a disaster. But there was nothing she could do about it from Berlin.

She didn't even know what the man looked like.

One thing nagged at her.

The eyes.

Em had told Jana that the fifth man who'd been at the meeting with the Turk and Sipo and the others had muddy eyes.

He had used Em as a courier before. Maybe that's what he wanted now.

Jana hoped that was all it was.

Please.

Chapter 29

Jana called Konrad and arranged for him to meet her in the hotel breakfast area on the second floor. As usual with breakfasts in European hotels, there were a few tables set up along one wall with the typical assortment of juices, dry cereals, a hot porridge pot, hard-boiled eggs, cold cuts, cheese, fresh fruit, breads, pastries, and what Jana was looking for: hot coffee. She poured herself a mug, and, as an afterthought, helped herself to a large piece of strudel. She sat at a corner table looking over her notes as she sipped coffee and ate an occasional bite of the pastry.

She had some of her rough notes from talks with her men. According to them, neighbors of the Turk's electronics store said he'd made occasional trips to Berlin. Balder, with his stolen-car enterprise involving BMWs and Mercedes, almost assuredly made similar trips. The third man in that equation was Akso, Balder's accomplice. That meant Akso probably had a nexus in Berlin as well. She took a deep, frustrated breath. There was not much there. Jana put the rough notes down and reflected on her own questions, trying to fill in the gaps.

Then there was the matter of the fifth man. He was the one Em worked with, the unidentified man at the meeting with Sipo prior to Klara Boganova and the Turk being murdered. Jana would have to keep him in the back of her mind while she was nosing around about the other four. He used Em as a courier. That meant slipping illegal items through whatever screens the police and other law enforcement agencies set up to intercept contraband. What was his connection with the other men? Worse, she had nothing to identify the man with except for a very vague description that was, for her purposes, practically worthless.

Jana finished her first cup of coffee and had just poured herself a second at the serving tables when Konrad came in. Trailing behind him was a toothpick of a man with dyed blond hair that contrasted with his very tawny skin. The combination of color might have been attractive, except for the red blotches of pimples, picked-over scabs, and pockmarks on his face. Jana's quick analysis was that the toothpick man had all the marks of a drug addict whose body chemistry had been out of balance for too long.

Jana directed the two to her table with a wave of her hand, decided against another piece of strudel, and walked to her seat, sitting across from both men.

"Good morning, Albrecht." She nodded at the food tables. "For a small charge you, too, can have the privilege of a healthy breakfast." Konrad shrugged the offer off. The toothpick sitting next to him continued to look at every other place in the room except at Jana.

"This is Zeki Erkin." Konrad flicked a thumb at the man. "He's a sometime colleague." This was Konrad's way of letting Jana know that this was the informant he'd told her about.

Jana ignored the fact that he was a drug addict and probably couldn't care less about the civilities of life. "Good morning, Mr. Erkin."

Jana always treated informants with courtesy when she first met them; and then later, when they became greedy or treacherous, which happened often, not so courteously. It was an art that all police officers had to learn. The informants were always criminals themselves. They had to be cultivated and catered to or praised and flattered—and bullied, when that time came.

"I like the blond hair. It goes well with your skin," Jana ventured.

"Thank you," he said, unenthusiastically, his voice so soft that Jana had to strain to hear it.

"Our mutual friend, Herr Konrad, has told me that you know a bit about the Turkish community, which I understand is quite large in Berlin."

"Kreuzberg section," he whispered. "Our town."

"Zeki was forced to move," Konrad alerted Jana, frowning slightly. "He got in a little trouble over a debt. I 'assisted' him in moving to another part of town. Not too far from Kreuzberg," he assured Jana. "Zeki still does his daylight hours in the area. He's just more careful. Right, Zeki?"

Zeki got out a self-conscious "Yes."

"You're in a hard business, Mr. Erkin," Jana sympathized.

"Sometimes," Erkin admitted.

"I assume Herr Konrad told you why I wanted to meet with you?"

"Yes."

Jana glanced at her notes, making sure she had the murdered Turk's name right.

"We had a Turkish man killed in Slovakia. We think he may have either come from Berlin or had 'business' contacts here. I understand you might have known about him. He was called 'The Turk' in our country, but his birth name was Murat Tabib. Did you know him, or know about him?"

Erkin gave an almost imperceptible nod.

"Good. Tell us about him."

There was silence from across the table.

"Tell her," Konrad growled, not appreciating the hesitation.

Erkin shifted in his seat, trying to make himself comfortable, unable to avoid the stares of both officers, his discomfort not abating no matter how he changed his position. It took a few more seconds for the words to come out. When they did, he spoke with a pronounced stutter, sudden intakes of breath leaving gaps between words. Again, an addict's symptoms indicating neurological damage. Between this and the ravages of metabolic distress reflected on his face, the man's body was signaling physical breakdown.

"He was into the drug business . . . then into home burglaries . . . then cars. He ran with a guy named Balder. Balder also did cars. Burglaries too. . . . He's supposed to be good with safes." Zeki managed a quick laugh, which seemed to have its own stutter. "Balder's German . . . but he speaks . . . better Turkish than me."

"Did you know a man named Akso? He ran with Balder."

"I think so. High voice. He . . . had a problem . . . with . . . with little boys. Liked . . . them too much. . . . Too much. The family of a boy . . . caught him. They cut off his balls." He began to laugh, laughing so long and loudly that he began to cough, the coughing lasting for a long minute. He only managed to stop himself by running over to the breakfast tables and grabbing one of the containers of fruit juice and drinking almost all of it down without breathing between gulps. Jana used the minute away from Erkin to question Konrad about him.

"This man is physically wasted. His speech patterns suggest brain damage. So how reliable is his information?"

"He's better than most. I know the Toothpick. Once in a while he's off, but he knows better than to fuck me over." He looked over at Erkin, who was still standing by the breakfast tables, panting from the exertion of his coughing, then turned back to Jana, satisfied that the man was going to recover. "I also think I know Akso, the eunuch. He's a halfer: his mother is a Turk, father German. The man was a child molester until the family of one of the boys chopped off the family jewels. Everybody working criminal in Berlin knows the story. After his testicles came off, he dropped his father's name, which was German, and now uses his mother's maiden name: Akso. I think he did the name change hoping the community wouldn't recognize him as the man who was no longer a man. I don't blame him. Who the hell wants to be known as a eunuch?"

He looked back at Erkin, who now seemed to be standing up, his breathing becoming easier. Yes, he would live. The German cop refocused on Jana. "A warning on Akso. Not having balls doesn't mean you can't be mean, and Akso is a mean man. People stay away from him."

Zeki Erkin came back to their table, still carrying the almost-empty juice container. He sat down, pallid from his coughing fit.

"The man from yesterday, at the bar. I think maybe you want to ask Zeki about him," Konrad suggested.

Jana nodded. "Just waiting for the right time." She gave Erkin a reassuring smile. "How are you feeling? Better, I hope."

"Yeah, better," he got out, pleased that she would ask after his welfare.

"Good. So, let's continue. Do you know a man with a large birthmark on his face? Red-brown." She held a clenched fist to the left side of her face. "A little bigger than this."

Erkin looked thoughtful, stoking the left side of his face as if testing to see if he had the birthmark. "I think so. Maybe."

"Why just 'maybe'?"

"I . . . saw it . . . him, I mean. . . ." He looked disoriented. "I can't remember so well sometimes."

Jana felt the sense of frustration that only a near miss can bring. "Give it time. It will come back to you."

"Yeah."

She decided to leave it for a moment, hoping he would remember later in the conversation. "Where can we find Balder?" she asked.

Erkin looked blank, a man without an answer.

"Assume Balder comes back to Berlin, right? He has to bed down somewhere. Do you know where he lives?" Erkin gave her the same blank look. She tried another tack.

"Balder's in the car business. He comes to Berlin to see his contacts, people he either works for or works with. Let's say he's done a safe or some other type of burglary. If he steals, he has to take the goods he's stolen to a receiver. So does Akso. Who does either one go to see?"

She could see the dawn of a notion on Erkin's face. "You have to . . . see Ayden Yunis for . . . that. He has a piece of the . . . car business. Stolen jewelry. . . . He . . . has a piece of everything," Erkin finished in a rush.

Jana checked with Konrad, who nodded. "Yunis owns a little chunk of this and a slice of that. On the surface, he owns a few restaurants in Kreuzberg. A bakery. Even owns a piece of a bank. But he's more than that. He's been around for a long time."

"A man who works the shady side?"

"He *is* the shady side in Kreuzberg."

"Just the kind of man I need. Will he see me?"

"I would think so. It makes for good will." Konrad laughed. "He always talks to the opposition. Tells stories. Likes a good joke."

"It sounds as if you're fond of him."

"He has a sense of humor."

"Ah, now I understand. He laughs before he takes people's money."

Konrad grimaced.

Jana turned back to Erkin. "Thank you, Mr. Erkin."

"You know . . . maybe I know . . . the man with . . . the mark on . . . his face from Yunis. I think maybe . . . I saw him there."

Jana felt hope rise, then told herself not to become excited over the information. The man was simply trying to please her.

"You suggested you saw the man with the mark on his face at Mr. Yunis's place. Can you remember when that was?"

His face got blank again. "I . . . I don't know."

"Thank you anyway, Mr. Erkin. In the future, if you remember, please tell Herr Konrad."

Zeki Erkin looked at Konrad, as if he had just realized he was sitting next to him. "Sure, I'll remember."

Jana had her doubts.

A few minutes later, they were on their way to Kreuzberg, dropping Erkin off before they actually entered the area. It wouldn't be too good for him if he was seen coming into the area accompanied by police officers. In fact, it would be very bad.

Chapter 30

After they let Erkin off, Konrad drove with more deliberation, keeping an eye on the sidewalks as well as the streets. Jana could see that he had become more wary.

"Trouble?"

"No. Just making sure that things are as they should be and not how they could be. This area used to have periodic disturbances that bordered on full-scale insurrections. Christ, there was war on Oranienstrasse every weekend. On May Day every year, the whole fucking place went into convulsions." He pointed to a small scar just above his right eyebrow. "No helmet, no faceplate. I was taking a cigarette break and some son of a bitch tossed a stone from a balcony. Boom, I was lying in an ambulance bleeding as bad as Akso must have been when they cut off his balls."

"Is the area still that bad?"

"Occasionally. Most of the action has become a little more discreet. Now the protests are more form than substance." He slowed down even more, pointing to a man standing on the corner.

"We are now officially entering Kreuzberg. The guy on the corner likes to greet people who wander into the section by taking them to places they can get laid, get dope, or get killed, depending on who they are and how much money they have." He shook his head in disgust. "In point of fact, it's not always the same guy. He's just the newest. When we take one down, as you'd expect, there's always another to take his place on the corner."

The difference between the area they'd just come from and the area they were now in was marked. Older areas are often more beautiful than other, newer locales. With Kreuzberg, that wasn't the case. It was rundown, dilapidated, decaying. The air had the cloying odor of garbage even when there was no actual garbage on the streets.

The one thing that made it seem like it wasn't the death spiral that so many older areas go through was the bustle on the sidewalks. They were alive with people. And the storefronts, rather than catering to the German public, seemed to belong to a separate population of Greeks, Eastern Europeans, counterculture proponents, and every other group that still hadn't assimilated into the native population of Berlin. However, judging from the storefronts, the clear preponderance of the population was Turkish.

"Look at the windows." Konrad pointed to something that resembled a Western supermarket, the sidewalk in front of the market crammed with burlap bags full of everything from dried fruit to a thousand and one spices. "They speak Turkindeutsche."

Konrad was right. The windows advertised the goods inside with a patois of German and Turkish that only a native Kreuzberger would be able to decipher.

"How much longer?" Jana asked.

"Sooner rather than later. You said you wanted to see Ayden Yunis, so I'm taking you to see him."

They crossed the Spree Kanal, the water below not looking very inviting, and within a few blocks were on Oranienstrasse. Two short blocks later, past the carts and the street vendors and even more foot traffic, they parked in front of a large bakery.

"This is where we find Yunis."

They got out of the car, Konrad checking out the building.

"Mr. Yunis and his palace. When he isn't doing something miserable to someone else, he's a cheerful guy who loves to be around baked goods. Nuts, eh? He works his non-baked-goods stuff out of the bakery just to the rear of the ovens."

They went in. The customers, like the people on the streets, were a mixture of cultures. The bakery products displayed in the cases were equally mixed, the bouquet of honey and nuts blending with rye seed and yeast, a fusion of baklava and Berliner *gebackene brot* enveloping everything.

Jana followed Konrad, who shouldered his way through the customers and around the counter, then walked down a small aisle, past the ovens and the racks of pastries and assorted breads in varied stages of baking. At the rear of the bakery was a curtained area in the corner. A number of people stood in front of the curtain, all of them men, several of them—younger and more belligerent-looking than the others—quickly forming a wall. They moved forward to intercept the two police officers.

"Kriminalpolizei," Konrad mouthed, showing them his police identification. As if following an order, the men dropped away, unblocking the way to the curtained area.

"You made it look easy," Jana complimented Konrad.

"The police aren't a threat to Yunis. It's his associates he's afraid of."

They reached the curtained entrance and Konrad, without hesitation, went inside, Jana following close behind. Ayden Yunis, an average-sized man with deep, sunken shadows under very dark eyes, sat at a small table working on papers spread in front of him. Jana had half expected him to be wearing a white baker's outfit. Instead, he was well dressed, in an expensive tailored suit, with a tiny, delicate flower in his lapel.

Yunis stood, giving them a half-bow.

"Please sit down, Investigator Konrad. And you as well, Commander Matinova."

They sat at the small table across from Yunis.

Yunis gave Jana a brief nod to go along with his prior bow. "Tea will be here in a minute."

"Thank you for seeing us, Herr Yunis." Konrad spoke with extraordinary deference to the man. "I know how full your day is."

"All this politeness from a police officer to a man he thinks is immoral." A sardonic smile flickered over Yunis's face. "I return your respect with my own." He looked at Jana, a glint of humor in his eye. "You're probably wondering how I know your name."

"No, Herr Yunis."

He examined her face to see if she was pretending to have knowledge she didn't have. He could see she wasn't feigning. It aroused his curiosity.

Jana saved him the embarrassment of asking about her reasoning. "We dropped Zeki Erkin off on the street. He depends on *your* good will to stay alive in Kreuzberg. Erkin took advantage of his opportunity by phoning to alert you that we were on our way. That gave him a stock of good will with you, or perhaps a favor of narcotics to feed his habit. He also told you I was not a German and gave you the name of the hotel where he met me. In turn, you had one of your subordinates call the hotel to verify Erkin's information. I registered under my name and title. Your man then informed you what he'd learned."

Yunis was pleased with her deductions, playfully applauding her reasoning. "Very good."

"Not hard if you know how informants operate."

"I'll have to remember not to trust that miserable little *scheisse*," Konrad grumbled, angry at himself for not anticipating what Erkin would do.

"You already knew that," Jana reminded him.

Konrad was irritated at himself. "I'm one of those people constantly required to relearn what I should know the first time around. And you, Herr Yunis. How do you deal with the Erkins of the world?"

"I have to be my own policeman. I get no other assistance," Yunis reminded him. "I'm required to know what's going on. Otherwise someone will soon be 'helping' me to forget. And that would be the end of your bringing me such charming and insightful guests as Commander Matinova." He regarded Jana for another few seconds. "I was wondering how I should pursue our relationship, Commander."

"Best to be direct with me. In turn I'll be direct with you," Jana suggested.

"Except one has to trust those whom one is direct with."

"Think of it as saving time. We both profit by not playing games. It's worth the risk."

One of Yunis's men came in with a tray of tulip-shaped glasses and a large carafe of tea. The man ceremoniously poured the tea into the glasses, handed one to each of them, placed the tea carafe on the table, and then immediately left.

They all sipped at their tea.

"Tea is wonderful. It eases one through troublesome times." Yunis took a deep sniff of the aroma wafting out of the glass. "There is a saying about why Turks drink tea at meetings. 'Conversations without tea are like the night sky without stars. The tea eases us over the bad spots, past the arguments.'" He took another sip, letting out an audible sigh.

"I truly hope we have no disagreements," Jana told him, taking another sip of her drink, following the ritual Yunis had laid out for them. She raised her glass in a small salute to the man. "Very good tea."

"Thank you."

Yunis studied her for another brief second.

"You know how to be silent at the right time."

"I appreciate your kind words, Herr Yunis."

He continued studying her, eventually smiling. "I don't think I'd want to gamble against you if you were on the other side." He nodded, as if agreeing with himself. "I have a marvelous idea. I'm playing cards this evening with several associates of mine. I had a fleeting thought that you might be able to assist me by joining in the process."

Jana shook her head. "I would think that the participants will all be men. They wouldn't be comfortable with me in the room."

"All of them appreciate an intelligent woman."

"Cards aren't my game. People are."

"They each have their unpredictability, and are both dangerous."

"There's a maxim in police work. You have to be able to at least see the danger to be able to avoid it. In this world, regrettably, I can't see or avoid it all the time. And I can't shun people if I'm going to do my job. However, I do know enough to stay away from games of chance."

Jana decided to end the preliminary bantering and get to the point of her being there.

"There were two murders in my country. They appear to be linked. Two men, both tied to the events, are originally from Berlin. We think they may have returned here.

One has Turkish blood. The other speaks Turkish. I've come here to ask if you can assist us in locating them."

"You're asking me to help you arrest these men?" His voice had taken on an inflection of surprise. "I would never do anything remotely like that. I protect my people. That's why I'm allowed to sit here drinking tea with police officers."

"I would never ask you to give up one of yours, Herr Yunis, particularly after enjoying your hospitality. I never repay kindness in that way." She held up the tea glass again, a toast to their shared attitude.

He held his up in return. "With that promise, I give you my word that Yunis listens to your every syllable."

Jana plunged ahead, relating the events that had occurred in Slovakia.

"One of the killings I've come to you about caused a national uproar in my country. It was a very public assassination, initially thought to be an attempt to kill a well-known person. Instead, his wife was killed. Later, in another location, a second man was killed. He was a Turk. We now believe the killings may have had wider implications. So I'm here as an emissary from my country, speaking to Herr Yunis, who has his own important place in the world. We feel Herr Yunis is the man who has the influence and command to help us determine why these events took place. We need your help."

Jana sat back, waiting for Yunis to absorb what she'd said. He tapped the side of his tea glass, thinking, studying the tawny liquid at its bottom, and then set it down on the table.

"What was the name of the Turk who was killed?"

"Murat Tabib."

"Murat Tabib, eh?" He repeated the name several times, rolling it around in his mouth as if savoring a morsel of food. "Yes, a Turk. I think I know that name. However, names are repeated often in our culture. It might or might not be the same man. There is also the possibility I may know his family. If I do, I will send them a condolence, a remembrance gift. When a family member dies, one must help fill the void that's left."

"That would be kind of you." Jana paused, finishing the last of her tea, studying the bottom of her glass. "Do you think you might aid us in another way? Perhaps set up a conversation for me with the men who were with Murat Tabib before he died?"

"They were with Tabib before he was killed? Or during the killing?"

"We don't know how much time elapsed between their meeting and when the murder took place. But we know they met before the event."

"And the killing that caused the national uproar is tied together with the killing of Tabib?"

"We think so. I would also point out that there were others at the meeting who were involved in the first of these killings, including a man whom we have yet to identify. The two men we think are here in Berlin may be able to help us with that as well."

Yunis poured himself a second glass of tea, then filled Jana's glass. He also noted that Konrad had merely sipped a small amount of his tea. When he set the carafe back down on the table, he somehow made the gesture of a rebuff to Konrad for outwardly rejecting the hospitality of the tea service.

"And how was Murat Tabib killed?" Yunis asked. "Perhaps his family will want to know."

"They most likely will."

"If they're here, and if I can find them," Yunis hastily added.

"Understood." Jana waited a moment to give her statement full effect. "Tabib had an ice pick driven through one of his eyes."

Yunis visibly jerked, spilling tea. He tried to recover, wiping ineffectually at the few drops that had fallen on his pants. He shouted something in Turkish, and the man who had served the tea came in with a small towel. Yunis grabbed it, wiped his hands, and threw it on the table. The tea server gathered the towel, the remaining glasses, and the tea carafe, waiting for a brief second for Jana to take a last sip and then recovering her glass as well before quickly exiting.

"My apology, Commander; my apology, Herr Konrad." Yunis gave them each a sad smile, his best attempt at an act of contrition. "The human condition is often defined by clumsiness. I try to keep those moments to a minimum."

Both of the police officers remained quiet, trying to minimize Yunis's perceptible embarrassment. The man was upset that he had lost his composure and control, both of which were very important to him. Eventually he settled back in his seat, able to slow his breathing, trying to pretend that he'd never been upset.

"The men you want to talk to: their names, please," he queried.

"One is named Akso; the other is a man named Balder," Jana told him.

A pen and a small pad had materialized in Yunis's hand, and he scrawled a few notes on the pad. "Yes, Ajda Akso and Balder." He put the notepad on the table, looking at Konrad. "You know Envers?"

"The hubbly-bubbly place?"

"The two will be there in one hour. There is to be no attempt to arrest these men. Understood?"

"Understood," Konrad agreed.

"They will answer all your questions about the murder of Murat Tabib, and the murder of the woman, at least all the questions they know the answers to. What was the woman's name? And her husband?" In a floral hand-writing, Yunis wrote down Klara and Oto Bogan's names, reciting them back to Jana to make sure he had them right. When he'd finished, Yunis stood, polite but now distant, shook hands with both police officers, wished them well, and called for the man who had brought their tea. The man led Jana and Konrad through the bakery and into the street without saying a word.

They walked to Konrad's car. All four tires on the vehicle had been slashed. Konrad spent a full minute cursing, enraged that this would happen.

"Kids. Maybe gang members. Some of the Yunis people, maybe. Juvenile stuff," Jana suggested. "They recognized it as a police vehicle."

There was no question in either of their minds that the people who lived in the area had no small amount of hatred for police.

"I hope every one of them dies tomorrow," Konrad snarled. "Tortured to death using a red-hot poker to liven it all up a bit."

Still fuming, he called headquarters for a tow truck. While they waited, the people on the street gave them a wide berth. The attention and avoidance of the locals gave the two police officers an even more intense feeling that they were in a very unfavorable environment.

The experience with Yunis had been odd for Jana. It was not her usual way of dealing. However, a number of things had come out of it. She began to mull over what she had deduced from the meeting. Yunis had immediately identified Akso and Balder. He also knew where they were staying; otherwise, he wouldn't have been comfortable declaring that they'd be ready for questioning within an hour. How could he know that with such certainty unless he'd had recent dealings with them?

Then there was his exaggerated care in making sure that he had the Bogan names right. Too much pretense. He knew about the murder of Klara and attempted murder of Oto Bogan. Even more telling was his response to the way Murat Tabib had been murdered. A man with his criminal background and wide experience with street ways shouldn't have reacted that strongly when Jana told him about the ice-pick murder. He had been shaken by the specific combination of the weapon and the way it had been used. Ayden Yunis believed that Makine's signature was on the killing. And Yunis had, through his response, revealed that he was afraid of the man. Why would Yunis be so deeply fearful unless he was himself involved in the events surrounding the ice-pick victim's death? There was also one other major issue that had to be determined: which side was Yunis on?

The police flatbed hauler arrived in thirty minutes, which was fairly quick; but by the time Konrad's car had been loaded aboard, the two officers only had a short time to get to Envers to meet the two men who might have information on the Bratislava murders. They squeezed into the cab of the truck, the driver slowly tooling the cumbersome vehicle through the streets.

Konrad passed the time by pointing out the businesses and people they passed on the road that were either fronts for one of the Yunis enterprises or allied with him in the criminal world: a man walking down the street who ran the Yunis loan-sharking operations, a secondhand clothing business used for narcotics importing, a building-supply store that was a front for cigarette smuggling. There was the bank that Yunis had an interest in, which was suspected of financing hundreds of other criminal enterprises. They passed a money-changing establishment that was, in fact, a currency-laundering operation. All of them put money in the Yunis coffers. Konrad ultimately finished with a flourish, waving his arm to encompass the entire neighborhood.

"All of these people, Greeks, Turks, Hansels and Gretels, all of them, whether they know it or not, are serfs in the service of their master, Mr. Yunis."

"Be thankful, Albrecht. Most captains of industry, especially his industry, are not that amenable to seeing police officers on short notice."

"I did him a big favor once, so he sees me." Konrad seemed discomfited. "Maybe I shouldn't have done it. I found out a young man was going to assassinate Yunis for using his sister as a prostitute. I made the mistake of telling Yunis. End of story for the young man, although, as a 'gift' to the family, Yunis took the girl out of the house where she was servicing the male population of Berlin and got her a job at a stationer's. That job lasted one month before she decided she liked it better out on the street."

"We all do idiotic things."

"Maybe I should have let Herr Yunis go to his god? Who knows what's right and what's wrong at times?" He thought about his blunder in getting the young man killed, looking a little disgusted with himself. "Mistakes are mistakes. You put them behind you. At least I got the trust of Yunis, and I go to him when I need him. Or he asks me to come. It's worked out."

"It never works out with these men. They always keep the balance on their side," Jana cautioned.

Konrad directed the driver to drop them in front of the place where Yunis had said he'd set up the meeting. "Envers," he announced to Jana.

The truck slowed to a stop in front of the building. Konrad shouted a *danke, vielen Danke* to the driver as he drove away while Jana checked out the area. Bookstores, junk shops, cafés, record shops, down the street what appeared to be a small cemetery, a few Prussian-façaded buildings with their straight rooflines on the other side.

The building they'd disembarked in front of had a modern façade, ugly in its concrete simplicity except for a portion of the lower floor of the building, which had a brick frontage which Jana thought might have been part of an older structure that the building had been constructed on top of. She hazarded a guess that the original building had been bombed in the Second World War and the property owners had erected the new building cheaply on the old foundations. The front of the structure had a sign that spelled out ENVERS in green neon. Stairs led up to a large door, which was propped open.

"What's a hubbly-bubbly place?" Jana asked, remembering what Konrad had said when Yunis directed them to come here.

"A coffeehouse, except it's mostly tea. They come here to smoke *nargilas*, water pipes, which most of the kids call hubbly-bubblies now. Eat a snack, talk to your friends, smoke a hubbly-bubbly, socialize. This place also deals a little hash on the side. Lots of Envers's customers think the pipe tastes better with dope than tobacco."

They walked up the steps and through the door into a smoky environment. More than half the tables were filled, most of the customers men over forty, a few younger ones sprinkled throughout, the majority of them smoking nargilas, a few eating or drinking tea, all of them talking as much as they were smoking.

Jana scanned the faces. None of the men looked back at her. She realized that she had very little idea of what the two men they were here to see looked like. She worried for a moment, then became conscious of the fact that she was the only woman in the place. It would be easier for the men who were coming to their rendezvous to identify her than for her to identify them.

"They'll have to find us," she mentioned.

"They will." Konrad pointed to a table in the rear of the café. "We just sit. A waiter will ask us to choose a flavor for the tobacco from the list on the table, then they'll bring each of us a hubbly-bubbly."

Konrad led the way. They eased into chairs, Jana not quite comfortable with being the only woman in the room, particularly in such a completely different culture. Both of them shifted their chairs slightly, Jana so that she had an unobstructed view of the front door, Konrad so he could see the entrance to the kitchen–restroom area. They read the tobacco menu on the table and Jana picked one with a fruity-sounding name. The waiter came over and Konrad ordered for both of them. A few minutes later the pipes were set on the floor next to them, the waiter placing a charcoal ember over the tobacco. With a touch of flair, he then handed them the hoses fitted with mouth-pieces so they could smoke.

To put an acceptable face on their presence, Jana decided she had to at least take a few puffs. She expected the smoldering tobacco to burn her throat. Instead, it was surprisingly cool. Jana even enjoyed the slightly euphoric feeling that it gave her. The minutes ticked by, passing quickly, until a full half hour had passed. Still no sign of Balder or the emasculated Akso. Yunis had said that the two men would be there. Their failure to appear made Jana progressively more uneasy. They wouldn't dare to disobey Yunis. Unless they were dancing to someone else's tune.

"I think we should pay up and get the hell out of here," a very nervous Konrad eventually suggested.

Jana didn't have to be convinced. She threw money on the table, and the two of them started for the front door. Before they stepped outside, Jana grabbed Konrad's arm.

"A wonderful setup: the two of us walk out of the door, which puts us at the top of the stairs, framed for a clear shot in the midday light."

The two turned as one, heading for the kitchen area and a hoped-for back exit. No one paid any attention to them as they hurried through the kitchen to the rear door. A large padlock on the door prevented them from opening it.

Jana had seen this kind of thing before. "They keep the door locked to prevent the kitchen help from stealing food out the back."

She pulled out her gun, which she'd tucked in a small holster hooked inside the back of her pants.

"You're not supposed to carry a gun in Germany," Konrad protested, at the same moment coming out with his weapon.

"I guess you'll have to report me." She stepped back toward the center of the kitchen, found the man who was giving the orders to the other help, put her gun to his head, and demanded the key to the door. Without the slightest hesitation, the man gave her the key, and she hurried to the door and unlocked the padlock. She and Konrad dashed outside and started down a metal staircase. They hadn't gone three steps when the first shot struck Konrad in the back.

Jana was unable to stop him from tumbling down the stairs. She took the short route to the ground by jumping over the railing and dropping the two and a half meters to the alley below. The next shot was fired while she was still in the air, the bullet passing so close to her head that she could feel the air being disturbed by the bullet's passage.

Jana grabbed Konrad's shirtfront and jacket and dragged him into the shadow of the wall opposite the stairs, crouching to make as small a target as possible. She quickly examined the German cop. He had been hit in a spot that should have been fatal, almost directly above where his heart would be. Seeing the entry wound, Jana was amazed that he was still breathing, although shallowly. There is no accounting for the ability of people to remain alive when they should be dead.

Jana looked up. A man was coming through the rear door of the hubbly-bubbly place, a gun in his hand. Jana didn't vacillate; she fired at him immediately. The shot hit the man, the force of the bullet driving him back into the café, discouraging anyone who was with him from chancing another attempt at coming out. Just to be sure, she fired two additional shots into the door, then frantically searched through Konrad's jacket until she found his cell phone. She hunted through his contacts, found the number for his office, and called it.

It took her a long minute to convince the German police that what she was telling them was true. She had to wait ten more agonizing minutes for them to arrive. Konrad was in an ambulance and on his way to the hospital five minutes after that.

There was no difficulty in identifying the man Jana had shot. Her bullet had hit him in the abdomen, the upward trajectory taking the slug through the aorta, killing him almost instantly. Even though he had several contradictory identifications on his person, the police were able to immediately identify him because, to the surprise of the ambulance attendants, his scrotum had been excised. In fact, there was not much of his sexual organs remaining. It was Akso.

All's well that ends well, reflected Jana. There would be no real loss to the world because of the death of this man.

Shortly after they arrived at the police building, the German police took Jana to their offices and began going over the events of the shooting in excruciating detail. The questioning was intense, continuing for three hours. At some point, the Kriminalpolizei contacted the BKA people, and several of them arrived to participate in the interrogation. Eventually Truchanova and Jakus showed up to throw in their own two cents. The end result was the police sending men out to Kreuzberg to bring Ayden Yunis in. But the attempt proved to be futile: Yunis had slipped into obscurity amidst the warren of buildings comprising the Kreuzberg area.

Jana's primary concern was Konrad. She insisted that

she be kept apprised of his medical condition. At last, word came in that Konrad was off the operating table. The bullet had missed his heart by less than a centimeter, exiting through his chest. Konrad would probably survive.

When the police ultimately told her that she could go, Jana asked where she could find Truchanova. The officers who had questioned her informed Jana that the prosecutor was in a meeting one floor down. With some reluctance, they also told her that the prosecutor was in conference with senior members of the Kriminalpolizei and the BKA people on the larger ramifications of events. As a courtesy, one of the interrogators escorted Jana to the room where the meeting was taking place, wished her well, and then left without going inside.

Jana entered just as the meeting was breaking up, the participants stuffing papers in their folders, a technician turning off a slide projector. Truchanova was one of the few people still sitting at the table, filling up her briefcase with her notes. She looked haggard, the grind of the meeting seeming to have affected her, sapping her energy. Jakus stood in a corner of the room, off to one side of Truchanova, a supernumerary merely taking up space.

Jana walked over to Truchanova, passing several of the BKA people who had been present at part of her interrogation. The men didn't bother to acknowledge her. Arrogance, all too often an unfortunate trait of law enforcement personnel. The nearsightedness created by self-importance would always get in the way of finding evidence, particularly in a case like this.

Jana sat down in an empty chair next to Truchanova.

"They're finished with you upstairs?" Truchanova was merely making conversation as she finished packing her papers away.

"For the moment." Jana watched the last of the participants going out the door. "Was it a good meeting? Is it all solved now?"

"Don't be a comedian." Truchanova snapped her briefcase shut to emphasize her irritation.

Jana felt her own surge of annoyance at the prosecutor. "Be civil, Madam Prosecutor."

"I'll be whatever I want," Truchanova barked back.

This late in the day, and as tired as she was, Jana wasn't about to let the challenge inherent in the prosecutor's tone go without a response. She matched Truchanova's truculence.

"Madam, today I've been shot at, and a police officer who I think of as a good man was nearly killed. Instead of being congratulated on killing one of the thugs who tried to murder both of us, I've been interrogated for hours by police who should instead have given me a medal. Then my pistol was taken away. The Germans told me that I was wrong to bring it into their country; that I may be prosecuted for that; and that it is evidence, so I may never get it back. This means I'm now defenseless against people who have tried to kill me on at least two occasions. Hence, I'm not feeling at all comic.

"However, I'm feeling no small amount of anger, and a large amount of frustration, at dealing with a prosecutor who is deliberately concealing information from me, which is preventing me from moving forward with this case."

"I don't like your attitude, Matinova. The reality is that I don't like you."

"Wonderful. We can now mutually dislike each other. Unfortunately, this doesn't help me in investigating my case. So, first things being first, what was this meeting about, Madam Truchanova?"

"I have other things on my plate besides the case you're

investigating, Matinova. You have no interest in what was discussed at the meeting."

"A lie, Truchanova. You came to Germany on one case and one case only. Then, here you are in conference with a room full of German police, including the BKA who generally handle cases of national importance, and you look me in the face and tell me it's none of my business."

"You're forgetting yourself, Matinova." The prosecutor's voice had gotten louder. "Your attitude is inappropriate. It's thuggish rather than professional. You're not being helpful."

Jana matched the woman's volume, her anger at all the troubles she'd experienced that day now compounded by the prosecutor's intransigence. "You've accepted my aid but won't aid me in return. You're busy concealing and dissembling rather than sharing. And, to top it all off, you think that I will cheerfully lap up the crap that you're laying out for me to eat. Well, think again!"

Jakus began to move forward, signaling to Jana that in case there was violence, he would support Truchanova. Jana swiveled in her chair to confront him.

"I've already killed one man today. I wouldn't think twice about killing another. Take another step toward me, and I will break your leg off and beat you to death with it."

Jakus stopped, not sure what he should do, looking to Truchanova for guidance. The woman slowly held up a hand for him to stop.

"I think we should discuss this on more convivial terms," Truchanova managed.

Jana shifted her attention back to the prosecutor, lowering her voice while still maintaining her intensity. "Let me tell you what the German police gave you on your case: nothing. Worse, you're all withholding evidence from me: the possible motive for these crimes. What I can see—whatever that motive is—is that it worries both our government and the German government. Which leads me to the question: why are both our government and the Germans so afraid or ashamed to let the motive become public?"

Truchanova's face told Jana that she was on point. There was an agreement between the two governments, tacit or explicit, that whatever was being concealed would stay under the covers, at least for the moment. Truchanova was operating under orders to keep her mouth shut. That had to be why the woman seemed so stressed. She was in a bind and was trying to find a way to deal with it, without much success.

Breathing heavily from the anger, Jana decided to try to moderate her own tone, realizing that her resentment was not going to pry any more information out of the prosecutor. At least Jana had laid her complaints on the table. Maybe some official back in Slovakia would listen. Maybe even Truchanova.

Jana went on, her voice more normal, although still edged.

"I'm being asked to go forward with my investigation without real assistance from either the Germans or the Slovaks. Not a good place for me to be in. My position is tenuous. There have been two attempts on my life. Am I being required to simply walk into danger without the slightest precautions? Where's my armor? My support systems? Just what are my government's officials asking me to do, Truchanova? Even more, what's the illustrious Truchanova asking me to do?"

Truchanova was now subdued rather than angry, slumped in her chair, her face slightly pale. She sat, not moving, as if the glue that held her together was, at the moment, not to be trusted. When she spoke, it was in a whisper.

"I can't give you any advice."

"None at all?"

"None." The prosecutor chose her words very carefully. "You've stirred things up, and that's good. And you're right: today, I didn't learn anything more of real substance than I knew before I came to Berlin." She appeared ready to say something else, then stopped. When she spoke again, her voice was slightly stronger. "I'm leaving Berlin, going back to Bratislava. I've been called back. After today, I'm glad to be returning home."

She got to her feet, picked up her briefcase, and walked toward the door, Jakus following her.

"I sincerely wish you luck," Truchanova called over her shoulder. She stopped at the door, looked back at Jana, then stared for a few seconds at Jakus, mulled something over in her mind, then decided.

"Jakus, leave her your gun."

The investigator stared at Truchanova as if he couldn't quite believe what she was ordering him to do.

"You heard me correctly. Leave her your gun!"

Very reluctantly, Jakus reached under his jacket, extracted his gun, and laid it on the table with a harsh thud. He then walked out, not happy with what he'd had to do. Truchanova nodded at Jana, and Jana nodded her thanks back. The prosecutor left, quietly closing the door behind her.

Jana walked to the gun, checked to make sure that it was loaded, then tucked it into her pants.

It wasn't much, but it was a small protection against whatever force was out there trying to prevent her from surviving. Thank God for small favors. Jana checked her purse for one other item that she'd secured earlier in the day. It was still there: Albrecht Konrad's badge and identification. She'd palmed it, slipping it into her purse just before the ambulance had carried him away from the scene of the shooting. A small increment of her own to add to Truchanova's largess. Besides, for some reason known only to God and her own scruples, she wanted to personally give it back to Konrad when he was awake.

Chapter 32

Jana hailed a cab, giving the business address of Bogan's son, Zdenko. Jana had no real information on the man except for the few lines in the murder book. He'd been conspicuously absent from all the events in Slovakia, including his mother's funeral, which pointed to a possible family breach. The business address was on Zimmerstrasse near Checkpoint Charlie, that vestige of the Cold War, the former entrance to East Berlin when it had been the capital of a Communist government.

The sky was bleak, washing out the color from the buildings, making even the most daring and novel of them shadowed and bleak-looking. The mostly steel-and-glass structure where Zdenko's office was housed looked more like a distorted skeleton than the light and airy construction it was supposed to be.

The cab dropped Jana off at the front of the building. Inside, her shoes were loud on the hard floor as she followed the signs and the red velvet chain that led to the reception desk. All incomers were stopped at the desk and required to produce identification and sign in before they were allowed into the building. Jana pulled out Albrecht Konrad's identification, the word *Polizei* written in big letters across the top of it, and held it in one hand so that Konrad's photograph was obscured by her fingers, then ducked under the chain, heading directly for the elevators. A guard near the desk immediately moved to intercept her. Jana flashed the ID at him without pausing, and he turned back to the desk area, not interested in stopping a police officer.

Jana took the elevator to the tenth floor and followed the suite direction arrows in the corridor until she came to a set of double doors with the words SHECKKARTE INTERNA-TIONALE across them in raised gold letters. Just below that caption, centered in smaller letters, was the word KREDIT-BANK. An international credit card bank, Jana translated to herself, wondering why the world needed a new credit card or another credit card system. She pulled the door open and walked in.

Inside, instead of the posh décor she had expected, there was an office that looked more like a dentist's waiting room: a few magazines on a side table, a couch covered with a plastic sheet, a pair of side chairs that still had their shipping covers on them. There were also two desks sharing a common credenza, the whole office being warmed by a pair of rotating floor heaters humming along at maximum capacity to ward off the noticeable chill.

One of the desks was empty. On the credenza was a small radio that was, incongruously for the setting, broadcasting a static-filled version of Carl Orff's *Carmina Burana*. Seated behind the other desk, working at a computer, was a woman Jana immediately recognized. It was Elke Rilke, the receptionist who had been working the front desk of the IEB in Vienna when Jana had met with Radomir Kralik.

"Good afternoon, Ms. Rilke." Jana realized her voice sounded as surprised as she felt. The woman stopped working and looked at Jana quizzically, not recognizing her.

She gave Jana a reproachful look. "People are supposed to stop at the desk in the lobby and call us. You didn't call."

"I was afraid whoever was here might not be here any more after I called from the lobby."

"Why wouldn't I stay here?" Rilke stared at Jana, still unable to place her; then, finally realizing who Jana was, her face lit up. "Ah, you're the police commander from Slovakia who came to visit Mr. Kralik." She looked puzzled. "What are you doing here?"

Jana moved further into the room, looking it over.

"This doesn't seem to be the IEB, and we're not in Vienna, are we?"

Rilke jumped up and turned off the radio. "I need company when I'm alone. I get a little uneasy." She appeared self-conscious at revealing a weakness. "Too many creaks and other strange noises. So I play the radio very loud."

There was a door that looked like it led to an inner office just to the rear of the desk next to Elke Rilke's. Without waiting for permission, Jana walked to the door, putting her hand on the door handle. "What's back here?"

"Nothing." Rilke shrugged. "You can go in if you want."

Jana opened the inner door and stepped through it. There were no offices there, just an unfinished suite where offices would be built, bare plaster walls, uncovered cement floors, electrical wires dangling, construction discards scattered around the floor, and absolutely no signs of habitation. It was very cold, the exposed heating ducts not yet functioning. Jana could see her own breath in the air. She quickly went back into Rilke's office, making sure the door leading to the frigid unfinished offices was completely closed.

Elke Rilke had moved to the couch, trying to relax. She was rubbing her hands together in unease.

"Not very hospitable, is it?" she said, a rueful expression

on her face. "That's the reason I get so uncomfortable here in the office. Nobody to talk to, and that thing with all that empty space like a haunted building behind me."

Jana stripped the cloth shipping cover off one of the incidental chairs, moved it near the couch, and sat in it. She rubbed her hands together in sympathy with Rilke. "I wouldn't like working here."

"It'll be good to be through and back in Vienna. I'm here just to close everything down."

"Who brought you up here?"

"Zdenko Bogan asked me to come."

"I thought you worked for Kralik at the Vienna bank."

"The two organizations are connected."

"What does Zdenko do?"

"Well, he runs this part."

"It can't be open for business yet, not in this condition."

"It isn't open to the general public. We service banks." Her face lit up. "It's a brilliant concept by Zdenko Bogan. He's incredibly bright."

"Please tell me about it, Ms. Rilke."

"'Elke,' please," Rilke suggested, trying to find a friend for herself in the cold, unappetizing environment she was working in.

"Thank you. And I'm Jana."

"Jana, then." She smiled at the establishment of the friendship. "Zdenko got the idea of offering individual banks credit cards. Not for use by the employees, but for the bank itself. They could use the cards when it came to making loans, or posting security for obtaining additional supplies of hard currency from governments, perhaps to finance buyouts of large corporations or underwrite huge stock issues. The subscribers to the credit card system that need an immediate influx of cash or credit merely use the credit card, and the money is immediately credited to that bank. In this way, small banks can compete with large banks that may already have that kind of cash, and larger banks can use their cash for other purposes, for example to bail themselves out if they've made a grand investment that's gone awry."

Jana considered the concept. "Your credit card employers are guaranteeing that they'll be able to hand out enormous sums if a credit card user bank calls for the increment of cash or credit it needs. It sounds wonderful, except where does this huge resource of ready cash come from?"

"Subscriber banks. Not just one or two, but a network of banks committed to the system and profiting from the huge credit grants. They earn interest on the money and share in the profit. Which is how most banks survive."

Elke Rilke positively glowed with pride as she continued to describe the project. She was now part of something momentous, and she loved it.

"Subscribers here eventually means banks all over the continent and into Asia and then North and South America and Africa. Competitors who can participate in each other's investments and profit, all the while knowing that their own investments are secure because of the little card that each bank has in its pocket. It's just like the individual who goes to the automated teller and uses it to get immediate cash, or the person who goes to the supermarket and pays with a plastic card instead of cash. You see how much can be done with this concept for the banks."

Rilke smiled at Jana, waiting for her admiration and approval, a little child delighted at being allowed to participate in a game for adults.

Jana gave Rilke the approval she needed. "It sounds like a great enterprise."

"All from the mind of Zdenko Bogan. Absolute genius. I'm so happy that they picked me to participate in the process. Naturally, I'm just doing the paperwork for the moment. I'm not a great industrial giant striding over the world like Zdenko." She tittered at the idea that she might be mistaken for a central figure in this grand plan. "It's wonderful enough for me just being on the edge of it."

Jana thought of the unfinished part of the office that she'd just been in. It was a mess of half-completed construction that looked like it was going to stay that way. That conclusion was backed up by the floor heaters that were sweeping back and forth in Elke Rilke's office. Their glow cast a pink smear of conflicting shadows around the room, giving the place an eerie look of impermanence, undermining Rilke's talk of financial empire. The space was not glowing with success.

"Why all this then? It rather looks like it's failing." Jana watched Rilke's face fall. "The rather modest furniture allowance and you having to fly here from Vienna don't quite give me the same sense of confidence that you have. Why are you up here? Why not another secretary? Why aren't the offices completed?"

"Why hire another secretary in Berlin, or finish the offices here when the whole back office is moving to France?" Elke explained. "Why complete these offices when they're being given up?"

"Why is the firm moving?"

"Mr. Bogan thought we would do much better in France. France has a number of smaller banks as well as a few larger ones. Zdenko thought they would be amenable to subscribing to the system. Not like London, which is old-line and clubby and will take some persuading to join. We'll go to them later. Remember, the more banks we have subscribed and using the bank's credit card, the more pressure there will be for the British to join us. And then we persuade the other banks around the world." She brightened up again. "In fact, I just had his and Mr. Kralik's belongings picked up from their Berlin residences and shipped to France."

"Do you have an address for them in France?"

"Only where the furniture and belongings are being stored until they take up permanent residence."

She rattled off an address on the outskirts of Paris. It was the same location Jana had found in the moving company's files, a storage warehouse.

"Do you know where they're staying?"

"Le Meurice on the rue de Rivoli." She gave Jana the full address, as well as the phone number, of the hotel.

"Wasn't the decision to make the move very sudden?" Jana asked, watching Elke Rilke's reaction. The woman's face flushed slightly.

"Yes, a surprise. Business always brings surprises. You understand," she hastily added, "I'm not in on these decisions. The original plan was for Berlin to be the center of the company." Her manner now seemed defensive. "Decisions have to be made and remade."

"Did it have anything to do with the killing of Mr. Bogan's wife, Klara?"

Rilke took a minute to answer the question, not liking the idea of the events surrounding the murder coming closer to her.

"Not that I know of." She considered the question again. "I hope not. I truly hope not."

Rilke's face and posture had changed. She was now unsure about her answer. The thought had entered her mind that there was at least the possibility that the killing of Zdenko Bogan's mother might be in some way responsible for the move to France.

"Is Radomir Kralik involved in the transfer to Paris?" Jana continued to watch Rilke closely. "Of course, I'm assuming he's part of the bank credit card program. Is he involved?"

"Well, he is and isn't."

"I'm not quite sure what you mean. Is he, or isn't he?"

"Well, when the shooting took place, not the one involving Klara Boganova but the shooting involving you, he became very frightened. With all that commotion on the street, he left the bank and then didn't come back. So I don't know if he's involved now, or not involved. I haven't heard from him since."

"Is he still living in Vienna?"

"I've called his landline. No answer. He hasn't responded to cell phone calls. I don't know where he is."

"Worried?"

"Of course. He's a nice man."

"When she was alive, did you have anything to do with Klara?"

"A little. She came to the bank, and I showed her around. Sometimes she would call Mr. Kralik."

"Is Mr. Kralik involved with the younger Bogan very much?"

Elke Rilke brightened up. "Certainly. After all, he's proud of his son."

"Proud of his son?"

"Zdenko Bogan."

"You mean Oto Bogan's son. Oto Bogan is Zdenko's father. Not Kralik."

"Oh no, I mean Zdenko Bogan is Radomir Kralik's son, not Oto Bogan's. Everybody at the bank knows it. All you have to do is to look at them together, and you can see the resemblance."

Jana remembered the strange marital arrangements of the Bogans and Kralik. The Bogans' marriage had completely been a marriage of convenience. But why? Why would they even have gotten married to begin with? Why the façade? Why carry on this fraudulent relationship? None of it quite made sense.

"And you, Elke, are you going to France with them?"

Elke Rilke's face fell. "I have to close down here. Then I go back to the Vienna bank. I'm hoping they will call on me to go to France after that." Her face lifted at the thought, then fell again. "Except I don't speak French. And if I were to go to Paris, I would be handicapped by not being able to speak the language."

"Perhaps you can learn," Jana suggested.

"Perhaps." There was a wistful sound to the word. "I would like that very much."

"Lots of luck with it."

"Thank you, Commander."

"Jana," Matinova reminded her.

"Yes. Jana," Elke Rilke corrected herself. "If you need anything at the bank, please call on me."

"I will."

They both stood. Jana gave Rilke a quick hug, then walked out of the office. A second later, Jana heard the faint sounds of *Carmina Burana* from inside.

Jana didn't envy Elke Rilke. It was cold and bleak in there.

Chapter 33

Jana left the building, suddenly aware of the feeling that she was being watched. She decided to walk for a block or so to check out the street. She soon spotted two men doing a tag-team surveillance of her, weaving in and out of the pedestrian traffic behind her on opposite sides of the street, first one man and then the other taking the lead. They were too coordinated not to be police. She kept walking, waiting for them to make a hostile move, perhaps an attempt to take her into custody, expecting them to be joined by others ahead of her—or in vehicles, if it was a high-priority surveillance.

After a few minutes, she was satisfied that there were just the two of them and another man who was lagging substantially behind them. He was watching them as well as her, and he was substantially better at the game than the police officers were. It also helped that the cops were so intent on watching Jana that they never saw the third man.

He was the one who intrigued her. He could be an assassin waiting for an opportunity to kill her, except that a professional assassin wouldn't be trailing after his intended victim in this fashion when there were police, however ineffective, standing between him and his target. The man was plainly aware of the cops, responding to their moves, consistently staying the same distance

behind them. Because he was so far back and because of
the intervening pedestrians and vehicles, Jana only caught
glimpses of him; they were enough to tell her that she
knew the man from somewhere, although she couldn't
place him. She recognized the manner in which he held
himself, the sure way he walked through the occasional
cluster of people, the tilt of his head. The man's identity
nagged at her.

Who are you? And what do you want from me? she
thought. Considering the events she had recently gone
through, the man's presence was much more worrisome
than that of the police. A name popped up, sending a
trickle of fear through her. Makine, also called Koba. Yes
or no? She couldn't quite be sure; he was too elusive, too
far back. She would just have to wait to get a closer view of
him. At the same time, she hoped he'd keep some distance
between them.

She checked her watch. It was getting late in the
day, and it was more important for her to pay a visit to
Albrecht Konrad at the hospital than to obsess about
either her police tail or the man behind them. She caught
a taxi to the Universitätsklinikum, the medical complex
near the Tiergarten, the huge cultural area and park that
is so central to Berlin. She checked behind the cab, wondering if the two police officers had managed to follow
her and whether the other shadow man was still tailing
all of them. The police had made no move to pick her
up. Unfortunately, if they were following her for her
protection, they were staying too far behind to offer any
real help if a threat emerged. As for the shadow taking
up the rear of this ensemble, following all of them made
no sense whatsoever. There had to be a reason, but it was
eluding her.

The taxi deposited Jana at the hospital complex, and

she hurried into the main building, not wanting to remain exposed in the open area fronting the hospital where she could present a clear target for passing cars. She quickly determined which room Albrecht Konrad was in from a desk clerk, then took an elevator up to his floor. She was encouraged that he was already out of intensive care and in a private room despite the fact that he'd just had major surgery.

When she got to the room, there was no guard posted. The German police hadn't followed sound practices. One of their own men had been shot. Given the circumstances surrounding the shooting, whoever had shot him might come after him again.

Jana stepped into the room. It was empty, the bed unoccupied, with no sign that anyone had recently been in it. As soon as she realized there was no patient in the room, she knew what to expect next. She reacted quickly. She snatched the German police identification she'd taken from Konrad as well as the pistol Jakus and Truchanova had given her from her purse, dropped them on the floor, and kicked them under the bed. A second later, the door to the room was thrown open and police charged inside, weapons out. One of them put a gun to her head, threw her against the wall, and patted her down. They spilled the contents of her purse onto the bed and checked her identification.

Anyone asking for Konrad was going to get a rather rough welcoming committee. The Berlin police had been taking care of their man after all.

They cleared Jana through their back office, apologizing for treating her so roughly. They were pleased when she complimented them on their protection of one of their own. She gathered her possessions from the bed, placing them beside her purse. Then, laughing and feigning embarrassment, she told the officers that she'd had a slight accident because of the shock of the gun being put to her head, and she needed to use the room's lavatory. The police officers, a little chagrined themselves at her confession, rapidly retreated from the room. Once they were outside, she heard them laughing loudly.

She recovered the gun and Konrad's police ID from under the bed, flushed the toilet several times with the bathroom door open so the police would hear it, then walked out of the room to the waiting officers. One of them escorted her up to Konrad's true hospital room, this one guarded by an officer who opened the door for her when he saw her police escort. Konrad was in bed, attached to a number of monitors, with an IV drip in his arm. His eyes were closed and he was softly snoring.

Jana decided she could no longer indulge herself with wanting to personally present Konrad with his ID since it had now become a liability rather than an aid, so she took it from her purse and slipped it under his pillow. As she straightened, she became aware that his eyes were now open and he was watching her.

"Was it any use?" he asked.

"A little."

"It wasn't in my things. I wasn't worried," he assured her. "You were the only one who could have it."

"A German police officer can open more doors in Berlin than a Slovak. I thought I needed it to become a little German." She sat in a chair near his head, noticing that he was running his tongue over his lips. "Water?"

"Yeah."

There was a glass of water with a flexible straw on the small table next to the bed. Jana held it near his mouth for him. He took a few sips, and then she eased the straw out of his mouth and took a very loud, exaggerated sip herself. Konrad smiled at her attempt at humor.

Jana set the glass down. "You're lucky to be alive, my friend."

"Both of us had the right shoes on." Konrad's speech still had an anesthetic slur. "Less than an inch more leather and you would be visiting my grave instead of my hospital bed, Slovak."

"Commander Slovak to you, Konrad!"

He managed a smile. "Are you a crap-head with your people too, Matinova?"

"Everyone is a crap-head on occasion, Albrecht."

"So my wife says." He shifted to a more comfortable position on the bed, grunting slightly with the effort and the pain. "It was Ayden Yunis who did us in."

"On the face of it. On the other hand, he could have had us killed, if he'd wanted, in a less conspicuous way. Yunis told us to go there to meet Balder and Akso. If he were the one who set this up, he would know it would be very evident, if we survived, that he was involved. I don't think he would take that risk. I think there might have been another scenario in play, one that Yunis didn't know about."

"What?" Konrad croaked.

"Maybe it was the two of them who wanted me dead? Maybe they were the ones who shot me in Austria? Maybe they wanted you dead because of what I'd brought to you: the killing in Bratislava and whatever evidence I'd found relating to it. Maybe they didn't want to answer any of our questions. So, bang-bang, and Herr Yunis and his orders be damned." She sat watching Konrad, not wanting to tire him out.

"I heard you got Mister No-Testicles."

"I had a clean shot."

"One man of theirs down won't stop them. They'll keep coming after you."

"I hope not."

"Optimism is nice, but misplaced in Berlin."

"On occasion, even in Berlin." She remembered the tails that she'd picked up. "Your guys have put a pair of watchers on me, maybe to look out for my safety. With some good Berlin police at my back, maybe I have nothing to worry about?"

He glanced at her, puzzled. "Tails?"

"Yes."

"I hadn't heard that they'd put anyone on you." His eyes started to close, but he forced them open. "I heard they took away your gun. You need one. I still don't like the feel out there on the street."

"You're living in a hospital room. You can't feel anything except strong anesthetic."

"I've got a great sense when it comes to smelling *scheisse*. You want my gun?"

"I have one."

"Good." Konrad's eyelids were getting heavier with the need to sleep. He was fighting to keep them open. "Slovakia, Austria, Germany, whatever it is, that's a big pile of *scheisse* you're in." He was almost asleep, making a last effort to stay awake. "The men who are following you— they're not my people. Maybe they're BKA. If they are, they're not as interested in protecting you as in finding out who's going to kill you, but not necessarily before you've been taken down. If they don't manage to save you, then they're rid of Jana Matinova, and maybe the bad guys fall into their lap for killing you. So, careful, Matinova."

Konrad's eyes closed and he began snoring.

Jana tiptoed out of the room.

It was dark outside. The wind had picked up. Hurrying,

hoping she wouldn't run into any problems, Jana walked to a nearby taxi stand. There was no sign of any of the people who had been following her. Jana gave the taxi driver the name of her hotel, feeling as tired as Albrecht Konrad, wishing she was already in bed. She decided to make an early night of it.

The taxi got her back to her hotel quickly. She took the stairs just to get some exercise, reached her floor and was ready to unlock her door when she noticed a thin line of light coming out from under the door.

Unless the cleaning personnel had left the light on, someone unwelcome was waiting for her in the room. Jana pulled out her gun, chambered a shell, and, as silently as possible, keyed herself into the room.

Em was sitting in a chair, waiting, a big smile on her face.

"Hello, Jana." She pointed at the gun. "Are you going to shoot me?"

Chapter 34

J ana put her gun away, sat on the bed, and stared at the
girl, more than a little astonished. Em was pleased with
Jana's surprise. She jumped up from the chair and gave
Jana a welcome hug and kiss on the cheek.

"I expected you earlier." Em walked back to the chair
and held up the murder book, which she'd had in her lap.
"I finished reading the book. There are all kinds of things
in there which I'd never imagined. I didn't know they cut
up the bodies of the victims afterward to find out things.
Ugh! I wouldn't want to do that." She sat back down and
opened the book to its index. "I looked through all the
reports, and there's no mention of me. How come?"

"Did you want to be mentioned in the book?"

"Sure." She shrugged as if everyone would want their
names mentioned in a murder book. "One day I might be
famous, and then you'll regret that you didn't even put a
single comment about me in the reports."

"Why do you think you should be mentioned in the
reports, Em?"

"Sipo, for one. I took you to him. And the meeting with
the Turk and the other men that were there. I was the
reason you found the Turk's body. So list me." She tapped
the book for emphasis. "It's only fair."

"Are those the only reasons?"

"For now. I'll think on it. Maybe I can come up with more things. If I come up with more things, what do I get?"

"You've already named your price: your name in the murder book."

"Who reads the book?"

"The police investigators, the judges, the defense counsel. Maybe others."

"That's good, except I think I want other stuff, more than just my name in the book, if I come up with information. How about cash?"

"You put a lot of trust in money."

"You can't eat money, but you can eat what it gets you."

"We'll talk about money if and when you have more information to give me."

Jana studied Em, still stunned by the girl's appearance in her hotel room. What part of the sky had Em dropped from and, even more puzzling, how had she gotten here? "You left the Seges family after you had agreed to stay until I came back from Germany. Why?"

"I had to. The man who came for me is my best customer. He had work. You can't turn down a job. You do, and your customer goes to somebody else. That means no money coming in. That happens, you have to sell cheap earrings in a snowstorm and freeze to death. You have to wear someone else's clothes." She gave Jana another one of her big smiles. "You like the outfit I have on? Mrs. Seges bought it for me."

"It's nice."

"I think so too."

"Your 'customer' is the fifth man at the meeting with the Turk, Sipo, Balder, and Akso?"

"If you say so."

"I'm asking you," Jana growled, irritated at Em's evasiveness.

"Yeah. Except I don't want to get him in trouble. He pays well."

"How did you come to Germany? Airplane?"

"Can't use airplanes any more. They make a big thing out of everyone who gets on a plane. I used the train. It was quick. No waiting at the stations. No searches."

"Why did you come to Berlin, Em? What did the man want you to do? Did you deliver a package? A message? What?"

"I told you, I can't say. It's against the rules."

"Em, I want you to tell me what he has you doing in Berlin."

Em's lips tightened, her chin jutting in defiance. "I can't say. Not even for you, Jana."

"Did the man tell you where I was staying?"

"'Course not. Mr. Seges did. I telephoned him when I got here, and he told me."

"And you told the hotel employees that you were my niece, just as you did with my officers? They let you in the room?"

"It worked once. So, you use it again. Find out what works. That's how you get through life."

"You're too young to be a philosopher."

"I think so too."

"What's the name of the man who asked you to come to Berlin?"

"He's never given me a name. Ever! He just gets in touch. I know who he is. That's it."

Jana didn't believe a word of it. It was all part of a continuing lie. It was imperative that she now confront Em about what was rapidly becoming a very uncomfortable, unworkable situation.

"Em, we've talked about this before. What you are doing is almost assuredly illegal. I can't be your friend if you're involved in unlawful conduct. And you can't stay here with me."

"I know. That's what I told the man. I made him promise me that this was the last time he would use me for this."

Jana was incredulous. Unfortunately, at the same time, she wanted to believe what Em said. The girl had found a chink, a weak spot in Jana's armor, a vulnerability that Jana wasn't quite able to protect. She kept asking herself why she was still hopefully standing on the edge of a cliff leading down to a big hurt when the girl had lied and manipulated her before and was doing it again. Her need to believe Em was so strong that only by main force was she able to compel herself to reject the girl's claims.

"We've been here before, Em. You're a proficient liar. You're so proficient at lying that I can't accept anything you say as genuine. You're here, sitting on that chair, except you're not. You're an impostor. And I can't—and won't—believe your hoax any more."

Tears began to flow down Em's face. There was no sound, no sobbing, just the tears, Em all the while staring at Jana as if she had been unexpectedly brutalized or given up to an enemy by a person whom she would never have expected to be disloyal. Em had been ravaged, and Jana was the one who had done it. It was a pitiful sight.

Jana was transfixed. Em's tears would have captured anyone. Jana found herself walking over to the girl, putting her arms around her, holding her tight.

When Jana pulled away from Em, she looked at the girl's face, hoping to see the pain gone. Em was still crying. "I have to tell you what I think. It's the way I am, Em. It doesn't mean the end of my concern about you," she murmured, trying to make the hurt fade for the girl— and for herself.

Em nodded, hesitated for a second, then took out a pouch that had been hanging around her neck, concealed by her dress. She held it out to Jana. "Take it."

"What is it, Em?"

"The money I was paid for coming to Berlin."

"Why are you giving it to me, Em?"

The tears had slowed and the girl was attempting to wipe them away. "So you know I'm telling the truth. I don't want you to think those things about me. I want you to like me. I want you to believe me." She gave Jana a faltering smile. "If I give up the money that I was paid to come up here, then you have to know I'm telling you what I feel. So there you are. You have to trust me now 'cause you know how important money is to me." The tears had completely stopped; Em was now hoping that Jana would give credence to what she'd said and believe that she would no longer involve herself with criminals.

Jana opened the pouch. There were U.S. dollars inside. She counted them. She counted fifteen hundred dollars in the pouch. Jana tucked the money back in.

"You get paid very well for what you do," she observed.

"For what I did," Em corrected. "U.S. dollars. I always insist on U.S. dollars. You can spend them anywhere." She puffed up with pride. "It shows you what the man who paid me that money thinks of what I do. Otherwise he wouldn't take the trouble to pay me like that."

Jana knew, in her heart of hearts, that she was being manipulated. But an inner voice kept urging her to accept what the girl told her, to believe that Em was finished with the business of being a courier for criminals, that she would be honest with Jana. One more time, bullied the voice. Just this last time.

"One more time, just this last time," Jana told Em, echoing the inner voice. "No more chances after this."

"We won't need any other chances," Em giggled, wiping a last tear that had clung to her chin. "So, what do we do next while we're both in Berlin?"

"Why do you think there's a 'next' thing?"

"There has to be a next thing. You're still working on the crime. I read the book. You're the detective. You have things to do."

"Nothing tonight. We eat; then we go to bed. Then I decide what I do tomorrow."

"I want to go to the zoo."

Jana couldn't quite believe that this was what Em wanted. She asked, just to make sure. "The zoo?"

"I've never been to a zoo," Em explained, shy now, a very little girl. "I want to see the animals."

"We'll see," Jana told her, realizing that she sounded like a harried mother with her small child. In a way, she was pleased with that picture in her mind.

They went downstairs, ate in the hotel restaurant, then went back up to the room. They shared the bed. Before she drifted off to sleep, Jana decided, whatever else came up tomorrow, she and Em were going to the zoo.

Chapter 35

They both woke up early, Em declaring loudly that she was hungry. Before they went downstairs to the hotel dining area, Em noticed a red neck scarf with Jana's clothing and decided to borrow it. She swung it around her neck, checking herself in the room's full-length mirror. Jana pointed out that it was too long for the girl's body. With a trace of hauteur, Em looped it around her neck one extra time, shortening it and, at the same time, giving it—and herself—the right touch of panache. Even her posture changed, Em's face now bearing a prouder look, a bit of a strut in her walk.

Em carried the look onto the elevator and into the dining room, modifying it only slightly when she went on a sampling expedition through most of the dishes on the food tables, piling items on her plate. Teenagers eat a lot, and Em was a living example of the species, eating far more than Jana thought could be humanly possible, especially considering the girl's size. Em chatted away between bites, telling Jana about what she wanted to see at the zoo.

Her highest priority was to see the tigers, then the hippos, then the poisonous snakes, with maybe the giraffes, lions, and elephants thrown in if there was time. She subsequently added the bears and the wolves to her list. Em also showed a remarkable knowledge of the

Zoologischer Garten, as if she had studied its layout. In scholarly detail, she went on about the zoo's architectural oddities, its 14,000-plus creatures, its magnificent aquarium, the Elephant Gate, blathering on until Jana felt like she was in the audience at a lecture. She began to eventually let the words go in one ear and out the other while she internally ran through the items that she needed to complete for the investigation after the zoo visit and before she left Berlin to return to Bratislava.

Tracking the financial movements of the Bogans was now becoming paramount. She decided to call her fraud investigator and see what progress he'd made. If the Bogans were changing their business location, they would shift their bank accounts to give them easy, quick access to a cash supply. The movement of the accounts might also tell Jana the Bogans' new residences. Banks require addresses and phone numbers for setting up new accounts. The Bogans wouldn't take the chance of listing false addresses. If they were discovered, that would suggest the possibility of money-laundering, and the authorities would be sure to investigate. Jana also had to talk to the German police to find out if they had had any luck in tracking Balder, the dead Akso's partner. Or in learning what Akso had been doing over the past weeks. Perhaps he and Balder had made ticket purchases, used credit cards, or written checks that might have been processed through a source usable for tracking.

Jana had now been targeted twice by shooters, once in Vienna and then in Berlin. She was also sure that when the man with the chestnut birthmark on his face had come into the bar where she'd been sitting with Albrecht Konrad, it had been for the purpose of setting up another assassination attempt, which would have been triggered if she and Konrad had followed him out of the bar. The facts pointed to Akso and Balder working together with the birthmarked man. Jana had to talk to the Germans about that connection and the connections between those three men and Ayden Yunis, the Turkish godfather. There was also one festering sore for Jana, the one source that she was currently precluded from talking to—the BKA. She made a small emendation to that thought: she was also closed off from getting information from some of her own people. Truchanova had made that very clear.

Em's patter began to run down. Jana waited for her to finish, and then the two of them got up from the table. Jana suggested that they take a cab, but Em objected, a little huffily. As far as she was concerned, they could get there without spending their money on a taxi. She knew "exactly" how to get to the zoo, and she wanted to experience the underground. Besides, Em pointed out, it wouldn't be traceable later if they took public transportation, and judging by what she'd divined from reading the murder book, it would be better for them not to leave too much of a trail.

"You see," Em said very proudly to Jana, "I'm helping. Maybe I'll even be able to save our lives."

"*I'm* the police officer," Jana reminded her.

"Even police officers need partners," Em retorted self-righteously.

"Only when the partners are grown up," said Jana, enjoying the irrational thought of the girl being her partner.

They took the U-Bahn from the station near the hotel. Em was excited, finding it almost impossible to stay in her seat. The girl had been on trains before; she said she'd come from Slovakia by train; so it seemed odd to Jana that she took so much pleasure from riding the underground rail.

"How come you wanted to go on the U-Bahn so badly?" Jana asked.

"I just enjoy wearing colors."

The answer didn't fit the question.

"Colors?"

"I'm not just on a train. I'm free today. I can do anything. I can wear bright clothes. I can talk and shout and scream if I want to. That's what I mean."

She gave an experimental shriek, everyone in the train car jumping at the sound. Most of them stared at Em as if she were some type of lunatic, wondering if they should get off at the next stop to escape her.

"See what I mean?" Em whispered. "Most times when I take trains or whatever, I have to watch how I act. Loud colors can't be worn. Today I can do it all." She flipped the ends of the bright red scarf on her neck to emphasize her point.

Em watched the tunnel walls go by, mesmerized by their flow past the window. Then she began to talk again as if she hadn't stopped, except the emotional tone in her voice was coming from another place, a place that was not happy.

"You stay in your seat. You never make eye contact with people. You pretend like you belong wherever you are, even though you've never been there before. You can't look like you're lost or worried about getting where you're going. You watch your hands. Keep them still. Act like you belong. You have to be like everyone else, except you're hiding the real you inside yourself. It's important to just be a continuation of them, one more gray person. If you're one of them, you're invisible."

"It must be hard."

"Some things are harder."

"Is this what you do when you're 'delivering' something?"

"Everyone has their own way to do jobs. Those are some of mine. Just tools." She quickly modified what she'd said. "Well, they *were* some of my tools until I gave up the job."

"Who taught you your job?"

"I'm not allowed to say." Em suddenly became fascinated with the way the train was going around a curve, the cars ahead a long serpentine shape weaving its way through the S-shaped tunnel. "Look at the train. What it's doing now is part of what you have to do all the time."

"What?"

"If you want to live and stay alive in the world, you have to curve around and slip your way through."

"More lessons from the man who taught you?"

"I never said it was a man."

"A woman? Your mother?"

"From the woman who *said* she was my mother."

"Your father came for you in Bratislava. He was late, but he came. Or was the man who came just your employer? Would you have liked him to be your father?"

Em was silent.

Jana decided not to press the girl. "I guess we'll have to figure out something else when we get back to Bratislava." She didn't want to articulate it, but it had to be understood. "You'll have to think about it."

"Yes."

Jana took another approach. "You knew all about the zoo, how to get there and everything. You must have read up on it before you came to Berlin."

"If you're a traveler, you have to know. So I found out."

"Gypsies often call themselves travelers. Are you a gypsy?"

"You asked me that before."

"I'm asking again."

"Gypsies don't belong. I belong."

"To whom?"

"To myself."

The train reached the station at the intersection of Budapester Strasse and Hardenbergplatz, near the hospital area where Jana had been the day before. It was at the rim of the zoo and its surrounding gardens, and a large number of passengers disembarked, jamming the station with foot traffic. The two of them walked up and out of the U-Bahn, Em twirling one of the ends of the red scarf as they made their way to the entrance of the zoo. Passersby smiled, amused at her joie de vivre and the pleasure she seemed to take in just being there. It was nice for them, as well as for her.

Jana scanned the passengers debarking from the U-Bahn, then checked the area around them. There seemed to be no threats, no one following them. Maybe it had been a good idea to come to the zoo today, she told herself. She deserved a pleasurable day off. She'd been shot and even then hadn't taken a day off. And, in Berlin, she had not allowed herself time to take a deep breath. It was time to breathe again, if just for a brief while, and this was a good place to do it. Everyone was here to have an enjoyable time. The sun was out and the cold abated to a degree, even the weather conspiring to make it a very agreeable outing. They reached the ticket booths and Jana paid their admission.

"We're going to have fun," Em informed her.

"Absolutely," Jana agreed.

They did have fun, taking in the hippos and the giraffes and the lions. Em was pleased that none of the caged animals gave them a mean look. The animals felt safe, away from people behind their bars; and Jana and Em, on their own side of the bars, were safe from the animals.

But not safe from the humans.

Jana saw the men watching them. It was the same two

who had followed her the day before. Although she had relaxed, Jana continued to frequently eye-check the surroundings. Even so, she'd been careless, caught up in the fun of the moment, and hadn't seen them. She immediately looked for escape routes, thinking she had to protect Em. Em would be at risk simply by being with her.

Jana tried to maintain her composure. Even though Konrad had not heard about police officers being assigned to follow her, he had been in the hospital; considering the events surrounding his shooting, one section or other of the German police, or even the BKA, might have assigned men to keep tabs on her. That would explain the presence of the shadows.

The two men were standing at a Y-juncture behind them, effectively blocking the way to the south and the Elephant Gate entrance, as well as the way to where they'd come in, the Lowenter entrance. Going east was their only option; then they'd have to go north past the zebra compound and make a circle back to where they'd entered. Once they got out of the enclosed zoo area, Jana would feel a lot better: there would be room to maneuver.

"Em, time to take a fast trip around the circle," Jana said.

She took Em's hand, forced to pull the reluctant girl away from her enjoyment of the pandas. Em protested that she wanted to stay longer.

"We have a problem, Em. There are some men behind us that I'm not sure about."

"Killers?"

"I don't know."

Em didn't show the slightest glimmer of fear. She glanced back. "The two ugly men?"

"Yes," Jana confirmed.

"I always wanted to know what a murderer looked like. Can you tell what they are just by looking at them?"

"No one can. If we could tell, we'd be able to stop people from killing one another."

Em appeared strangely excited that the men were following them, involved in a game that, as a child, she didn't quite understand. She seemed to see it as a sort of hide-and-seek, with both Jana and her needing to find a hiding place from the men who were trying to tag them. She became the leader, pulling Jana along.

"This is even better than I thought," Em crowed.

"Em, we may be in serious danger."

"Not yet. They're not close enough."

Jana took a brief look back. The two men were keeping pace with them, just as they had the day before. And farther behind them, keeping pace as well, was their shadow, the man who had been trailing after the two men when they had tracked her the previous day.

"There is someone else as well," Jana told Em.

Em sneaked a quick peek back. "I don't see him."

"Stop gawking back at them."

"I'm not gawking," she snapped, then realized she had been sharp to Jana, softening her tone. "What does he look like?"

"You can't make out features from this distance."

They crossed a small arched bridge over the seal pond, cutting to the left around the penguin house, approaching a refreshment area where there were food stands and a bathroom.

"I have to go to the bathroom," Em informed Jana.

"Try to hold it," Jana said.

"I have to go now," Em complained, quite emphatic in her demand.

Jana checked to see how close the two men were. As they had done yesterday, the two were keeping their distance. If they maintained that gap, there was no danger;

and since they were after Jana, there would be even less danger to Em if she were in the shelter of the WC.

"Quickly, then," Jana told her.

Em trotted over to the bathroom, Jana keeping a cautious eye on the men behind her. They had stopped, but the man keeping track of the other two watchers appeared to have moved closer, slipping through the crowd, using it as cover. The men he was closing in on still had no idea that they were themselves the subjects of surveillance.

Em came out of the WC smiling, unafraid, taking Jana's hand. "I'm hungry. Let's get a sausage."

"You ate a huge breakfast."

"I'm a growing person."

"Okay, but we walk to the gate while we're eating."

"Walk and eat?" Em complained.

"Walk and eat," Jana insisted.

"Actually, any time is a good time to eat sausage, walking or whatever."

They ambled to the other side of the building, where refreshments were served. Jana ordered a sausage and two sodas. Just as she was handed the sausage, she saw Ayden Yunis with one of his bodyguards from the bakery next to him. Both men were staring at her and Em from not more than six meters away. Jana dropped the sausage and, purely by reflex, swept a protesting Em behind her, reaching for her gun. Even as she was pulling out her weapon, Yunis shifted his attention from her. The two men who had been following Jana had come around the corner of the building with their guns out.

Yunis and his bodyguard darted for cover, drawing their own weapons. Jana pulled Em to the ground, covering her with her own body as gunfire began, the two watchers engaged in a firefight with Yunis and his bodyguard. The people in the refreshment area went wild, running, screaming, trying to drag their children to safety, even crossing the line of fire, not sure where the bullets were coming from, all of them desperate to get away. Jana held her fire, afraid she would hit bystanders, hoping that it would end with her police watchers winning the fight. A stray thought crossed her mind: if her apparent guardians kept up this kind of firefight, they might kill an innocent person. All police are trained not to shoot under circumstances like these. They were ignoring their police training.

In the flickering chaos of people running, shots going back and forth, and screams of panic, Jana thought she caught a glimpse of the man who had been tailing them all, looking very contained, almost aloof, slipping through the crowd with his own gun in his hand.

Then, as if an on-off switch had been thrown, the firing stopped.

Jana was still holding Em close, the two of them face to face. "Are you okay?"

"I'm fine," Em said, no fear in her eyes, just excitement. "Did you shoot anyone?"

"No."

"Too bad."

"Why too bad?"

"I could talk about it to people I know. It adds to the story."

"I'm glad I didn't shoot anyone." Jana was amazed at the girl's continued lack of fear. "You're not afraid?"

"I knew we'd be all right," she explained. "It's nothing to be panicked about. I have a guardian angel."

"I'm not a guardian angel," Jana told her.

"You're not a guardian angel," Em agreed, without the slightest change of affect.

"Stay down," Jana told her. "I'm going to see what's happened."

Jana got to her feet, tucking her gun away. Guards from the zoo began running into the square, coming to everyone's aid just a few minutes too late. Jana moved slowly, checking out the area. Yunis and his bodyguard were dead, both facedown on the ground. A short distance away from them were the two men who'd been tailing Jana. They had also both been shot, one of them dead, the other coughing up blood, suffering from multiple gunshot wounds. Jana bent closer to see if she could give him any aid, but he died before Jana could do anything for him.

Three bystanders had been shot, two women and a man, all of whom had been bringing their children to the zoo for the first times in their lives, each woman with a child, the man with his three sons. The two women had superficial wounds; the man, shot in the side, was bleeding badly. Jana took a scarf from a protesting bystander and shoved it under the injured man's shirt over the wound and used his belt to keep the scarf tight against him. As soon as she had finished tending to the man, she heard ambulance and police sirens approaching.

Jana looked around for the shadow man, but he was nowhere to be seen.

A moment later, the police began arriving en masse, the ambulances a few moments after that. Jana walked back to Em to wait for the police to get around to questioning her.

"Shouldn't we leave?" Em suggested. "If we stay, they'll only arrest us."

"They need to know what happened. I can tell them."

"It won't help them find the reason."

"How do you know?"

"Do you know the reason for the fight?"

"No . . ."

"Then how can you help them?"

"If I can't help them, maybe they can help me."

"Maybe." There was a strong sense of doubt in Em's voice. "If you talk to them, they'll find out you have a gun."

"So?"

"They'll take it away from you."

"Probably."

"Then you might want to give it to me to hold. They won't search me."

"I thought you had given up crime."

"Umm, I guess I forgot."

"Stop forgetting."

Ten minutes later, Jana talked to the police, and ten minutes after that the two of them were being transported to the main police station. Em was right: Jana's gun was taken away from her.

It did not make her happy.

Chapter 36

J ana and Em spent the first two hours with men from Die Kripo, the criminal police; the next two with the BKA; then they were questioned by both agencies together. The police separated Jana and Em, questioned each of them, then brought both of them into one room to confront them with "inconsistencies" in their separate statements. The differences in their statements turned out to be minuscule. The questioners of both agencies tried to make Jana out to be a party to the shootings, suggesting that perhaps she had lured Yunis to his death. But Jana's gun hadn't been fired recently, and there was also the undeniable fact that the two men who had shot it out with Yunis were German police officers, police officers who had *not* been detailed to follow Jana or the now dead Turks. The dead officers were from Munich. When the Munich police were called, no one in the department had known that they had been in Berlin for the past two days, nor did they have any idea what they were doing following Jana.

The Germans became more polite over the course of the day, particularly after Jana suggested some leads to follow up on. Even the BKA listened eagerly to what she had to say. There is nothing like a shootout in a public zoo, a place crowded with families, with parents shot and children being put at risk, to create an outcry and media frenzy. The media would focus on the police and their failure to protect the public. The fear of this imminent attack propelled the police into trying avenues they would ordinarily ignore, even if they were Slovak avenues.

Jana began talking about what needed to be done.

"Yunis had a bank and unquestionably accounts in the bank. Get the records on them. Track any financial connection between him, Balder, Akso, and Murat Tabib, the Turk who was killed in Bratislava. Also, see if there were any transactions between any of them and the Bogans or Radomir Kralik. Where have the dead Akso and the still at-large Balder been over the course of the past month?"

Jana continued in this vein, an investigation manual for the other officers. Did Akso or Balder have credit accounts? The accounts might give them a clue as to what the two men were involved in. Most particularly, Jana suggested, see if they had purchased any rifles. Also, the two Bogans had moved from Berlin. They either had accounts in France, or would be establishing accounts in France soon. The German police had to find them and track where all their payments and receipts went. Jana also strongly suggested that they connect with Lubos Papanek, her fraud investigator. He was working on the Viennese bank and might have found something.

Jana didn't wait for their agreement on this, immediately calling Papanek and informing him that he was to cooperate and exchange information with the Germans.

"Time to communicate with each other, gentlemen," she advised, all of them listening to the exchange with Papanek on a speakerphone. After the initial exchange of information, and the task allocations that ensued, Jana pointed out an issue that all the Germans were trying to ignore.

"Your two Munich cops who were killed at the zoo were dirty, gentlemen. Both of them bought and sold. They were there to kill either me or the Turkish godfather. Take your pick on the target. I'd opt for the Turkish godfather, since we have two dead Turks and one live Slovak police commander. But, examine both possibilities."

There was a general mix of foot-shuffling, downcast heads, and angry murmurs, all from the German police, all of them agreeing on the same conclusion: the dead German officers had probably come to the zoo knowing the Turk was going to be there, planning to kill him.

Jana felt a surge of anxiety. How had they known Ayden Yunis was going to be there? And, just as intriguing, why had Yunis even been at the zoo? Jana had no answers to either question. She hoped that the follow-up investigation the Germans were going to perform might fill some of the gaps left in her own investigation.

As the meeting wound down, Jana made one more attempt to get the piece of information that the German police and Truchanova had refused to give her before. She told the Kripo officers and the BKA that she had concluded that something was being withheld from her on the Bogan case. What had happened in Berlin was related to what had happened in Bratislava. Now that all the agencies involved had agreed to cooperate, wouldn't it be nice if they gave her the information they were withholding? She wanted to know what it was.

The criminal police looked blank; the BKA officers looked evasive. No question, the BKA was withholding information, and no amount of threatening, cajoling, or just plain pleading would get it out of them. Jana gave up. She would have to find the information on her own.

Besides the coordination between Jana's team and the German agencies, there was one other positive thing that came out of the long afternoon: the police returned the gun Jakus had loaned her. It had not been involved in a crime. They would close one eye to the fact that she should not have had a gun in her possession in their country. However, as to her own gun, they apologized profusely, informing her that it was still evidence in the assault on Albrecht Konrad, as well as in the death of one of the assailants, so they would continue to hold on to it. Jana was going to have to buy herself a new gun when she got back to Bratislava.

Jana and Em were released a short time after that.

They started back to the hotel, Em now hungrier than ever, complaining that all she'd had to eat while being held by the police was one stale pastry and a vending-machine chocolate bar. They stopped at a small restaurant near the hotel. It was a decent-looking café with thick wood furniture and chintz curtains on the window, somewhat better-looking than the plastic-on-plastic places nearby. The restaurant had a typically hearty mid-European menu posted next to the front door.

Em ordered a huge meal.

They were seated in a booth, Jana facing the entrance, the first course of the meal being placed on the table, when she caught a glimpse through the front-door window of a man just as he was turning away. He could have just been a potential customer who had decided not to eat at the restaurant after all; but he resembled the phantom shadow who had been trailing her for days. Given her state of mind, that was all Jana needed to propel her into action. She jumped to her feet, pulling out her gun at the same time, and ran to the door, losing precious seconds having to push her way past a couple who were just coming in.

Jana checked up and down the street, and even ran into traffic to get a longer, clearer view of the early evening crowd. There was no one even approximating the look of the man who had been following them, the last man standing in the shootout at the zoo. Jana quickly tucked her gun away, then walked back into the restaurant, taking her seat across from Em, who was very busy devouring her food.

"He wasn't there, was he?" Em said, her words barely audible through her mouthful of food.

"Who wasn't there?" Jana asked.

"The other man who was following them."

"No, he wasn't there," Jana acknowledged.

Em stuffed a large piece of veal into her mouth.

"You're going to choke on your food," Jana warned.

"No, I'm not," Em got out between chews. She swallowed most of the food in her mouth, easing it down with a few gulps of water.

"Are you going to shoot him when you see him?" Em eyed Jana over the rim of her glass. "The police won't like it if you do."

"I don't shoot anyone unless I have to."

"Like the man the police said you killed the other day."

"They told you about that?"

"They asked me if I knew anything about it. I told them I didn't."

"He was trying to kill me," Jana explained. "There was no other choice."

"Of course not." Em stuffed a large chunk of potato pancake into her mouth. "I just wanted to know if you would kill the man who followed us if he didn't have a gun and didn't try to kill you or me."

"It wouldn't be right to kill him under those circumstances," Jana told Em.

"I'm glad to hear that. I'll be sure to tell him the next time I see him."

Jana stared at Em, not quite sure if she was serious or not. The girl had an impish look on her face, enjoying Jana's reaction. She began to chuckle. Then she laughed louder, the strength of her laughter forcing some of the food out of her mouth.

"I was only joking," Em finally got out. "Just being funny." She cleaned her face off with a napkin, then wiped her plate with the last of her pancake and filled her mouth with it. "I lie great, don't I? I'm just a great pretender."

Jana nodded. "A great pretender."

Jana realized she wasn't very hungry. Days like today had a way of destroying appetites.

Em ordered a double serving of ice cream to finish off the meal.

Chapter 37

You can't do business unless someone wants to do business with you. So businesses advertise, or do other things to create product awareness. Customers have to know about what's being offered. It's the same with banks and their services.

Jana went to several German banks to determine if they had heard of any effort to set up a credit card system for banks. Everyone she talked to denigrated the concept, all the bank representatives informing her that they had never been approached by the Bogans' banking venture about their credit card system. None of them had any idea that the business even existed. One of the bank representatives suggested that Jana consult the Bankenverband, the Association of German Banks. Their main offices were located in Berlin just a short distance away. They would know everything that was going on in the German banking business.

Jana and Em enjoyed the walk between the last bank they'd visited and the bank association headquarters, window-shopping at the clothing stores along the way, chatting about the fashions and Em's particular interest in earrings. Jana was happy. She and Em seemed to be bonding, and Jana was thinking that she might even have a permanent presence in the girl's life, and Em in hers.

She was somewhat sorry to reach the headquarters of the Bankenverband on Bergstrasse. The walk and the closeness between herself and Em had given her a lot of pleasure.

The people at the association were even more cooperative than the people at the individual banks, sensitive to any issue involving criminality that might reflect on the association's members. They'd never heard of the credit card program. They even insisted on calling the European Banking Federation in Brussels to see if the central organization had ever been made aware of the concept. Again, they knew nothing.

"What have you learned?" Em optimistically inquired as they left Bankenverband. "Have you figured out why everyone is being shot?"

"No."

"Then what?"

"There are too many possibilities. The Bogans' company may not have its basic premise developed enough to be marketed. It may be in the process of being marketed to small institutions that aren't informing anyone else in the business about what they're doing. Then again, it just may be just some kind of cover for another practice."

They began walking along the street, window-shopping again.

"What kind of practice?" Em asked.

"Criminal practice."

"Like stealing money?"

"Criminals steal money," Jana affirmed.

"I know that's true," Em commented, sounding sage.

"Did you steal?"

"Once or twice. Except it was bad for my business, so I stopped. People, even thieves, need to trust someone. I couldn't be a traveler, running chores from one place or another, if they didn't trust me. Besides, if you cheat criminals, they get mad."

Jana did one of her visual checks of the street. Em recognized what she was doing.

"The man who was following us at the zoo isn't there," Em said. "I've been checking."

"I'm glad you're being cautious."

"I learned that lesson once."

"What happened?"

"A man followed me. I didn't check. He grabbed me and pulled me behind a building."

"What happened?"

"You know what happened. I don't have to say."

Jana looked at Em's face. There had been no change in her expression. She still appeared cheerful, happy with what she was doing, comfortable with herself. Not an appropriate emotional response for a child talking about being injured in the way Em obviously had been. The fact that she was remembering the event could have been reflected in her face, her posture, some physical change, even a small one. It wasn't there.

"What did you do afterward?" Jana asked.

"Watched while my client hid the body."

The answer to the question jolted Jana even more than what Em had said before that.

"Your client killed the man?" Jana asked, just to be sure.

Em nodded. "He apologized to me."

"Your client?"

"Yes. He lost sight of me for a minute. Then he had to go hunting for where I'd been taken. I couldn't blame him. It wasn't because of my job. I was just on the street when the person who did it to me was looking for a victim."

"A terrible thing. All of it must have been horrible for you. I'm sorry."

"He made up for it."

"Who?"

"My employer. He gave me a big bonus."

Jana stopped, putting her hand on Em's shoulder; then she hugged her.

"Why did you do that?" Em asked, looking puzzled. "I told you I was okay."

Jana tried to explain. "The attack, the murder, had to be frighteningly horrible for you, ugly beyond belief. I understand your attacker was killed. I don't blame you for being glad he was dead. But those are moments in life that had to scare you. Horrible events like that lodge in the corners of our minds. They don't get cleaned out very easily. We carry them with us. It hurts, and it may keep on hurting."

"I'm not hurt. I don't get hurt. I can't ever get hurt."

"Everybody gets hurt, Em."

"I can prove I can't get hurt."

"How?"

The girl whirled around and ran straight into the oncoming traffic of the busy street. It happened so quickly, Jana couldn't grab her. Em was suddenly in the middle of the street, running between and around the cars. They swerved to miss her, sliding sideways, some of them screeching to a halt, bumpers hitting bumpers. Vehicles drove onto the sidewalk to avoid collisions, pedestrians darting out of the way. The street became one massive jam of cars. Through the gaps between the cars, Jana could see Em reach the other side of the street and then turn to wave triumphantly at her.

Jana walked across the street after Em, in no danger herself from the stalled traffic, but very angry at what the girl had done. She warned herself to control her temper, although her anger was fueled by the blaring horns and the people coming out of their vehicles to yell at each other. Reaching the other side of the road, Jana found Em smiling as if nothing had happened.

"I told you I can't get hurt," she bragged.

Jana grabbed Em by her shoulders and shook her as hard as she could. She wanted to do more than shake her, but she was constrained by the thought that there was a serious problem with the girl. Her judgment was unsound. She needed help. Em had a personality disorder, some glitch that blocked her from realizing what was acceptable in human interaction.

Jana's anger began to diminish as she tried to put everything in perspective. The girl had been trying to show Jana how brave she was. She wanted attention, approval, admiration. Jana had to try to be tender and understanding. A stray thought crossed her mind: Em needed a leash. Jana pushed the thought away. At least she could see that the cheerful look had vanished from Em's face. There were even tears in the girl's eyes.

Em's voice had a touch of uncertainty when she spoke. "You didn't have to do that."

"Yes, I did."

"You were mean to me."

"A response to what you did. I'm sorry. I should have had better control."

Em wiped away the tears, her lips quivering. "I want to go home now."

"Slovakia?"

"Any place that's nicer to me." She thought about where she wanted to go. "Just back to the hotel room for now."

"That's fine with me."

They took the bus, avoiding each other's eyes, the ambiance of the afternoon gone. Jana forced herself to ask Em a few more questions, trying to bridge the gap between them and, at the same time, get a few needed answers.

"Your client followed you the day you were attacked. Is that usual in that business?"

There was a long silence, Jana forced to prompt Em by asking the question again. Grudgingly, Em answered. "Once in a while. They don't want to be caught, so they use me. Except, they want to make sure I do what I'm supposed to do. So they come along behind me and watch."

"The man who kept an eye on you when you were attacked—was he the man who's been following us?"

Em shrugged. "They're all the same. Who cares?"

Jana persisted. "Is he the same man, Em?"

"I can't talk about my clients."

"Em, our lives may depend upon your answer. Make an exception this time. I'm not asking for his name."

Em took so long to answer the question that Jana thought she was going to refuse. Then, very reluctantly, the word "no" rolled out of her mouth. They didn't talk for the rest of the ride back to the hotel.

In the lobby Jana went to the desk, checked for messages, and picked up her key. Em headed straight for the elevator, taking it up without waiting for Jana. When Jana went upstairs she expected to find Em waiting for her at the door. She wasn't there, or inside the room. Jana called the desk and asked if they had seen Em leave the hotel. When they told her they had not, Jana felt she had no choice but to search the hotel. She went through it floor by floor, checking the utility closets, the stair landings, working her way down to the main floor. The girl had vanished.

Jana went back to her room, wondering if she should report Em as missing. She decided that in this kind of a big city, there would be little hope of the police having much immediate success in finding Em. There was nothing to do but wait.

An hour later, Em knocked on the door. Jana let her in, neither of them saying anything until Em began talking, happy again.

"I know how to disappear, don't I?"

"You do."

"I'm a professional," she complimented herself. "You can hire me sometime, if you want."

Jana called the airlines and made a reservation for herself and Em. They would be flying back to Bratislava the next day.

Chapter 38

Mr. and Mrs. Seges met them when they landed. Jana thought of them as Mr. and Mrs. rather than as her warrant officer and his wife because of their attitude toward Em. They both greeted Jana formally, but Mrs. Seges was so affectionate with Em that an onlooker would have sworn that the girl was her child. Seges, although he hung back, made it clear by his body language that he was happy to see Em. He even gave her a peck on the cheek. The Segeses were more a couple with Em than without her. She was a bridge that allowed them to be comfortable with each other after so many years of bickering. For her part, Em was affectionate with the two of them also, particularly Mrs. Seges, she and Segesova going off hand in hand to drive home in the family car while Seges chauffeured Jana back to the police building.

Jana immediately went into meetings, first with Lubos Papanek to find out if anything further had developed in his cooperative venture with the German police. It had. The Berlin bank in which Ayden Yunis had owned the majority stock interest had made large transfers of money to the Bogan bank in Vienna and to a small, privately owned bank in Paris. There were also transfers from Oto and Zdenko Bogan from the Vienna bank to that same bank in Paris. The transfers, which had taken place over the last month, added up to nearly fifteen million euros.

"A large amount of money." Jana had a hard time imagining people who could blithely ship that kind of money from bank to bank, country to country. "I want you to keep on going as far as you can in tracking those funds."

"I'm on it. I didn't want to alert everyone that we were investigating the bank accounts. I'm trying a roundabout way of getting the information on them, using the bank's regular examiners as a screen for looking into the accounts instead of a police query. Give me some time and we'll have it."

"Anything on the directors or stockholders on the company the Bogans set up in Berlin?"

"Both of the live Bogans are on the papers, as well as the dead Klara. They own it all, except for a few shares owned by Radomir Kralik, the vice president at the Viennese bank."

"Check the ownership on the French bank that the money went to."

"We're doing that as well. Again, more time needed."

"I need it quickly, Papanek."

"When I get it, you get it."

"Good."

Jana called Colonel Trokan, and a half hour later she was in his office, briefing him on the events in Germany. Midway through the briefing, he stopped her.

"Four attempts to kill you over the last week, one in Vienna, three in Berlin. What the hell is going on?"

"Three attempts," Jana corrected. "One in Vienna and two in Berlin. I may have been the catalyst for the shooting in the zoo, but I don't think it was meant for me."

"The catalyst?"

"They may have been following me. Or someone else."

"You think they might have been after the little girl you're squiring around?"

Jana had left out any mention of Em in her reports of the Berlin events.

"The Germans called me," Trokan informed her by way of explanation. "They couldn't quite understand why she was trailing along in your wake." He leaned across his desk, a mocking look on his face. "Are we playing mother here? Police commanders have other responsibilities."

"I didn't take her to Berlin." Jana heard the defensive tone of her voice and consciously tried to change it. "I left her with Seges and his wife. The little lady found her own way to Berlin."

"You had nothing to do with it?"

"Absolutely nothing. She was on a business trip."

The colonel looked dubious.

"She has a commercial venture which took her to Berlin. She's a courier for criminal undertakings."

The colonel's face went from dubious to disbelieving. "She's how old? Thirteen?"

"We've both seen children used before. Thirteen-year-olds have babies. They fight in wars. They sell narcotics. She's a courier."

"We have an appropriate place for her, then: a cell."

"We have no proof, except what she's told me. And she's also told me that she has given the criminal business up."

The colonel eyed her skeptically.

"Once in that business, not very often out." He sighed. "Jana, you're not a social worker. You're not her favorite teacher. You're not a family member. What you are is a police officer." He tapped his chest several times with his right hand. "I, on the other hand, am your longtime friend and colleague; I have shared many problems with you, both yours and mine. I've pulled you out of difficulties, as you have me, and you and I work together as colleagues most of the days of the year. I'm also your colonel.

"Bearing that in mind, particularly the last part—you know, my being your colonel—I am giving you twenty-four hours to get rid of that girl."

"I don't think you should order me to do that, Colonel."

He stared at her, beginning to become angry, prepared to lose his temper.

Jana went on before he could show his displeasure in more obvious ways.

"If I 'get rid of her,' I'm convinced we will lose one of the best leads we have for solving this case."

For a second, Trokan wondered if Jana was lying to him. But just for a second. Jana Matinova might shy away from telling him about an event or tiptoe around a subject she didn't want to discuss, but she would never out-and-out lie to him. He relaxed, sitting back in his chair, waiting for her to explain.

Jana went into the details.

"Examine the shooting in the Berlin zoo. Why was Yunis in the zoo in the first place? The thought of the godfather of the Turkish community going to the zoo is ludicrous, unless he was there for a reason other than to see the penguins. He was there to further his criminal interests. He was standing, not walking and not eating, when the attack began. He wasn't sightseeing. Yunis was waiting. It seems clear that he wasn't waiting for those men, who had obviously come there to kill him. So he was waiting for someone else. Who?"

Trokan sat even further back in his chair. "I assume you're going to tell me in due time."

"It's more fun making you guess."

"I don't want to guess."

"Okay, don't guess. Just listen."

"Don't order me to do things."

"It wasn't an order."

"It sounded like one."

"Can I go on with my reasoning?"

"What do you think I'm waiting for?"

"The men who came to kill me in the hubbly-bubbly café were told that I'd be there by Yunis. He told them because he wanted them to talk to me, not murder me. If Yunis didn't tell the men to ambush me, then he would later know they'd disobeyed his order. He would never tolerate that sort of challenge. So they had to have been willing to confront his retaliation, to think they could do it and then get away with it. Why did they think so? Because they knew that there was someone else in this violent game of theirs who would save them. There was an individual or individuals who would take care of Yunis for them. Subsequently, Yunis is killed, not by his own people but by outside killers. My conclusion: I think we have multiple sides in what appears to be a continuing conflict."

"With one side represented by two rogue policemen who are brought in," Trokan muttered. "Yunis on the other. And someone else as well."

"Right."

"Fighting over land, or rackets, or . . . ?"

"Money. Lots of money."

"The bank money?"

"The bank money; maybe the banks themselves. We're still probing. The big question now is this: how could those two men, the two men who were following me in Berlin, have known Yunis was in the park to begin with? They had to have been guided there. What, or who, brought them to that spot?"

Trokan followed on with his own train of thought. "They were following you the day before; they picked up your trail again, trailing you to the zoo. You were careless when you thought they had given up their surveillance of you." Trokan was immediately concerned with how his words sounded, not wanting her to think he'd launched a criticism. "Not your fault. You were in a strange city. You had no support. It could happen to the best of us."

"I know, Colonel." She paused, satisfied that he had walked into the mousetrap she'd built. "Except I wasn't careless. I frequently checked for anyone following me, on the U-Bahn and off, all the way from the hotel to the zoo, and often in the zoo. They weren't there. Then, bang, they were. Someone else had told them we'd be there. They came because of information they'd received. And then they picked us up in the zoo, following us until we ran into Yunis, and then they began the attack."

"Who told them you'd be there? That Yunis would be there?"

"That's the big question of the day. There was another man who also followed me. I think that the two cops who had gone bad were killed by that man, after they killed Yunis. I think he arranged the whole business at the zoo. It will show up in the ballistics. I think the Germans will find that the two cops weren't killed by the Turks."

"When will the Germans have ballistics?"

Jana checked her watch. "They put a priority on it, so they should have at least a preliminary report by now."

He pushed his desk phone over to her side of the desk. "Call them."

Jana dialed the BKA's number in Germany and got one of the investigators she'd interacted with in Berlin. The ballistics preliminary was done. The two men who had been trailing Jana and Em hadn't been shot with the Turk's guns. There had been another shooter at the scene. Jana hung up and nodded to the colonel.

"The other man who had been shadowing you?" he asked.

"Yes."

"We need to know who that man is."

"I'll do my best to find out."

"And your best is always *the* best." Trokan sounded satisfied. "Always," he added, just to emphasize his feelings.

She got up and started to the door. "I have more work to do."

He waited until she put her hand on the doorknob.

"Have you ever heard of the Rostov Report?" he asked.

Jana paused, looking back at him. There was a tone to the question that indicated that if she hadn't heard about it, it would be a good thing if she found out what it was.

"Anything you might tell me about it, Colonel?"

He shrugged, as if he knew absolutely nothing about the report. "I heard someone in the ministry mention it, but it was unfamiliar to me, so I thought you might know about it."

"Why would I know, Colonel?"

"You generally know everything else that goes on in the government."

"Just some of it. I've never heard of a Rostov Report."

But now she had. The colonel had been doing his own homework. He had told her something that was connected to her investigation on the Bogan case.

"Hmm, I must be mistaken then," Trokan said, his look and tone of voice indicating that he wasn't mistaken. "Probably a report everyone is trying to keep secret. Secret reports have a way of sneaking out, don't you agree?"

"Yes, Colonel."

She started out of the office, the colonel's voice stopping her again.

"You didn't think I'd forgotten about the little girl, did you?"

"I was hoping."

"You said she was one of the best leads in the case and that you couldn't do it without her."

"I need more time to work on that, Colonel."

"You're telling me the absolute truth?"

"The absolute truth, Colonel."

"Careful with her, Jana."

"Thank you, Colonel." She paused, a wry smile on her face. "The Rostov Report. There are so many things that go on in even a small government that we need to know about but don't. I'll keep it in mind."

She walked back to her office, all the while thinking about the Rostov Report. Whatever it was, Colonel Trokan had told her it was a secret. Something very big. The colonel would have given it to her, even taken the chance of slipping it to her "under the table," if it hadn't been a major state secret that even he didn't have access to. Whatever he'd picked up about the report must have been minimal, but enough for him to know that she needed it. He couldn't tell her what it contained, but he'd given her enough to go on.

Rostov was a Russian name. If it was Russian and related to Slovakia, then it was probably linked to the Soviet occupation after the Second World War. The Russians had never been the great report writers that the Germans were, but winners like to bathe in their victory by rehashing, in print, their conquests and the spoils they get from them. They had written thousands of reports, examining every aspect of the dark era of the German occupation and the days that followed. Then, as with all government reports, they'd filed them, dossier after dossier, most of them never even opened for the public when Slovakia and the rest of the Eastern bloc had gone the way of the Berlin Wall. So if the Rostov Report was one of those files, it had been buried in the detritus of the years that followed, a mass of information that even the Russians had a hard time penetrating.

What would the report analyze or recount? What specific act would it storyboard? Who would be the players on the pages of the history it related?

If the report was connected in some way to the Bogan killings, then it was probably related to Jindrich Bogan, the man who had been killed in Paris. He and his parents had come from that period. Jana remembered the tattoo on Jindrich Bogan's arm. The Hlinka Guard. She had to find someone who could tell her more about that period of history.

The thought of the report and digging into the past made Jana think of another problem issue. She hadn't focused enough on Klara Boganova, or rather the young Klara Zuzulova who had married Kralik and then divorced him to marry Bogan. Why had she done that and then taken up with Kralik again? Why the bizarre charade? Whatever it was, obviously Klara and Oto Bogan had spent their life together cultivating it.

There was one person who might give her some of the information she needed. She called Comenius University. An hour later, she walked up the stairs into the half-rotunda of the front entrance.

Chapter 39

Comenius University was like a small baby that suddenly had become a giant: it just grew. With few other universities available, Comenius had thousands of students stuffed into one large building, several small ones nearby, and even smaller buildings scattered around the city. All of the buildings were old and crowded, and there was no funding available to ease the need for space. Anyone roving the halls had to be careful not to be crushed by the mass of humanity that filled them when the classrooms emptied.

This was one of those times, with the students cramming the halls. There was nothing Jana could do but force her way through, murmuring apologies if she pushed too hard. She got to Milan Denka's office by using her shoulders and elbows just like everyone else did, happy to finally slip through the outer door of the cramped suite. She made her way to Denka's cubbyhole office, pausing for a moment to fix her disheveled appearance before she went inside.

Denka was short, his clothes a little too big for his body, his features roseate, his once-thick red hair turning into thin pink wisps. His appearance belied the fact that he had one of the best legal minds in Bratislava. In addition to his duties as a professor of law at Comenius, he had a lively private practice that regularly placed him on the pages of the newspapers. He had also been Klara Boganova's lawyer and was now in charge of her estate. Denka took his glasses off, standing up to greet Jana, the barest hint of a smile on his face.

"It's been a year or two, Commander. Since I defended our mutual friend Kamzik, the multiple murderer."

Jana remembered. Denka had almost delivered a miracle acquittal. Almost.

"Professor-Doctor, thank you for seeing me."

He gestured her to a chair, sitting behind his desk again, pushing the books and papers that he'd been working on to one side to create a small open space between them.

"I'll write Kamzik and tell him you dropped by. He likes getting mail in prison. There's not much else for him to do there but read."

"Better than killing people."

"True." He looked her over. "I expected you to be running the police department by now, Commander."

Jana shook her head, pleased by the compliment but not entertained at the thought. "I have enough administrative duties as is, without having to take on more. I prefer what I do."

"I know what you mean." He sighed to emphasize how difficult administrative work was. "Nobody likes paperwork, particularly trial lawyers." He cleared his throat, becoming more businesslike. "I have a class soon, so I have a limited amount of time. How can I help you?"

"I came to talk to you about Klara Boganova."

Denka's eyes showed a flicker of interest. "I didn't know you were still involved in the case."

"Just in a small way."

"It was no tragedy. I didn't like the woman." Denka enjoyed the surprise he saw in Jana's face. "She's dead. In the privacy of this room, I can now tell the truth about Klara Boganova.

"She was extraordinarily mean-spirited, totally self-centered, determined to get her way, abusive to everyone around her. To know her was to loathe her. If she didn't like you, she would do anything and everything to hurt you. The lady was a destroyer. Klara was my client, and I worked for her. But I stayed away from her as much as I possibly could."

"You weren't there during the party when she was killed?"

"My choice. I worked with her; I didn't have to play with her."

"And her husband?"

"A big, handsome, photogenic man with a toothy smile and a glad hand who did what she told him to do."

"And her son?"

"I saw him a few times when he was young. I told you I stayed away from her as much as possible. In my profession, I mix with enough miserable people to know enough not to put myself through more of it in my off-hours by socializing with them."

"An aggressive woman who told her husband what to do. That suggests that she was also the business head in the family. Are you saying that?"

"A controlling person. She was the boss, in everything. Everything!"

"It would seem she was very successful at it."

"Yes."

"Where did she get her money from? Her family? Perhaps it was her husband's money?"

"You look at the basis of every great fortune and you'll find a crime." He smiled. "So I never ask that question. My clients might tell me something I don't want to hear."

"They were into the banking business. I'm aware of

the bank in Vienna. They also had a German operation. What else?"

"You think the shooting was wrapped up with the banking business? Bankers kill people with debt, not with bullets."

"I've always thought bankers got their money using any means that they could."

Denka went into a desk drawer, pulled out a thick folder, and began going through it.

"You have the Vienna bank. There is also an interest in a bank in Berlin." He read off the name. It was the bank that Yunis had owned the majority stock in. Denka closed his file. "I heard from another source that they were also negotiating for a bank in Moscow. It was not my brief, so I didn't inquire. I know there was opposition to the purchase, but there always is from some stockholder or another."

Jana thought about the last time she had seen Klara, just before she was killed. A driven woman with all kinds of secrets, her financial acumen hidden; her relationship with her lover Kralik also concealed. Indeed, a wily person. But all her deviousness had not helped her when she ended up on the cement floor of the soundstage, a lump of bloody flesh.

"Klara was a 'distinctive' woman," Denka concluded, a pejorative note in his voice.

"I would agree with that. Did you participate as their attorney in the purchase of the bank interests?"

"No. They used attorneys in the countries where the acquisitions took place. They would know the law of that country, so it was good business to use them instead of me."

"Did the money come from Slovakia?"

"Some of it, but not much."

"And the rest?"

"I don't know."

"There had to be a very large amount of capital involved."

"There had to be."

"Professor, I have evidence that Klara Boganova took part in the planning of the shootings the night she was killed. It was her orders that set up the place where the murder weapons were stored."

Denka eyed her, the skepticism apparent on his face. "That's hard to believe, particularly since she was the one who got killed."

"Bear with me on this for a moment. Assume she did what I've just told you. Assume, also, that there were two shooters. What would account for her being shot by the murderer when she had set it up?"

Denka considered it. Before he could answer, Jana responded to her own question.

"The murderer had his own agenda which Klara didn't know about, or the shooter changed his mind about the target at the last minute, or there was another person we haven't yet identified who was to be killed."

"Why do you think there was another person who was to be killed?"

"Two shooters."

He thought about it for a moment, eventually nodding his head. "I concur. If there were two shooters set up by Klara, then there were two targets. One was Oto Bogan, who was only saved when Colonel Trokan took the bullets meant for him. And since his wife participated in setting up the killing, the intended second target would not have been her. It would have been someone else."

Jana thought about the intended target. It would have been the person who tried to warn Oto Bogan. Not Sipo, but the man who controlled Sipo, the fifth man at the meeting with the Turk. Jana was sure she now knew who the target was: the man she had seen at the party who had left early. He'd left knowing he would be a probable target if he stayed. It was the man Jana had chased. The man she thought was Makine.

Klara believed she was going to dispose of her husband. She had also thought she would kill Makine.

Only Makine was a hard man to kill.

Moreover, there had also been an abrupt change of plans. The question was, who had changed the plans?

"Anything else, Commander?" Denka asked. He put his file back in its drawer, signaling the end of their meeting. "I have to prepare for my class."

"You've helped."

"Being on the other side as a defense counsel doesn't mean I'm a bad person and won't aid the police when I'm asked."

"Would you have helped me if your client had been alive?"

"Never."

They both knew where the other was coming from, each of them enjoying the knowledge of their difference.

"My last request, Professor. Have you ever heard of the Rostov Report?"

He ran the name through his mind. "I've never heard of it."

"Is there anyone at the school that you can think of who specializes in the history of the Soviet era? I'm looking for a professor who focuses, perhaps, on fairly recent history with particular focus on World War Two. Maybe with an emphasis on the factors that affected Slovakia's postwar recovery."

"A surprise request coming from a police officer."

"All kinds of things surprise us in murder cases. Death is just another one of our larger surprises."

Denka suddenly snapped his fingers in remembrance.

"There's one person. His name is Professor Pechy, first name Henrich." His face took on an annoyed look. "Sorry, he's not in town. He is, I think, in Germany doing research." He held a finger up indicating that she should wait, dialed a number on his desk phone, and almost immediately began speaking. "Where is Pechy doing his research?" He wrote the information down on a pad, hung up the phone, and handed the note to her.

"I was right: Germany. He's in Bad Arolsen. Doing research work at the International Tracing Archive. He won't be back for at least a month. His cell number is on there."

She thanked him and walked out into the hall, prepared to do battle with the students again. But the halls were almost completely empty. It was class time.

Chapter 40

Jana drove back to the office and called the number Denka had given her for Pechy. She got a recorded answer and left a message for him to call her.

She now had time to ease into a cup of coffee and catch up on the work she'd neglected while she was in Germany. On her desk were the Slovak newspapers she hadn't read while she'd been away. She quickly went through them, skimming until she came across a small article on the second page of one of the papers. Georg Repka, the man who'd betrayed his schoolmates, the man who had given the speech excoriating the gypsies, dehumanizing them, calling for their deportation and perhaps through that process their destruction, was being considered by the current government for appointment as the Minister of Minorities. Impossible, thought Jana. They had forgotten, or chosen to ignore, what the man was.

And what he was yesterday was exactly what he would be today: a man without scruples, a betrayer of ideals, a ruthless man who would go to any length to serve his self-interest without regard to the effect those actions would have on anyone else.

Jana sat thinking, trying to decide what to do. She had confronted Repka when he had first railed against the Roms. Her mother had been aghast, and the fallout from their arguments about Repka had almost sundered their relationship. At the time, that confrontation had been all she could do about Repka. In retrospect, it had not been enough. He might soon be the minister in a department where he could, and would, wreak havoc on the minorities he would be pledged to protect.

Jana had to take the responsibility to try and stop him.

There was a small opening. Small, but maybe enough.

There was a way to influence the other parties or people who might be concerned about his appointment, to call the problem to their attention in a way that would make them pay attention. Jiri Smid, the jailer's son, was the one who could help her with this. Jana called him and told him that she wanted to employ him for something that wasn't police work but was personal to Jana. His bill was to come directly to her.

Then she told him exactly what she wanted.

Jana continued with her other work and was on her second cup of coffee when she got the telephone call from France. Jobic Masson, the French detective, had found the Paris apartment where the man who had been killed by the hit-and-run driver had been living. He had been using the name Pascal Dionne. However, there was also additional identification in the man's Saint-Paul apartment that told Masson that the man was, indeed, Jindrich Bogan. Masson rattled on and on, telling her enough about the apartment and its contents for Jana to realize that she needed to go to Paris.

When she hung up, she called Colonel Trokan and told him what she had learned, and, after their usual skirmish about how Jana was being profligate with Slovak police funds, he authorized her trip. She made reservations on an Austrian Air flight leaving the next day out of Vienna International Airport, then booked herself into a small Paris hotel on rue de Rivoli halfway between rue Saint-Paul, where she had been told that Jindrich Bogan's apartment was, and Le Meurice, where his descendants were living. She was preparing to see three generations of Bogans, two living and one dead.

Jana made one additional phone call, to the father of the gypsy boy. His wife came on the line and told Jana that her husband was in the northeast and would not be back until the following day. When the woman started to carry on again about her son, Jana quietly informed her that she hoped to have additional information on the case soon; but, in the meantime, she would be out of town herself and would call again when she got back to Bratislava.

After she had hung up, she told Jonas and Grzner to find the two Roms who had been with the youth when he was shot in the throat, and to bring them in. The young men were in her office within two hours.

The two sat in the small interrogation room for thirty minutes while Grzner and Jonas listened and recorded their conversations, waiting for them to talk about the death of the gypsy youth. It was an exercise in futility, the two of them not saying anything except when one sponged a cigarette off of the other, and to briefly complain about the room being cold.

Jana reviewed the reports, including the toxicology on the dead youth. No question about it in Jana's mind now. She went into the interrogation room, Grzner and Jonas taking up positions behind the youths, Jana sitting at the table in front of them.

She laid the toxicology report down on the table and told them to read it. One of them picked up the report, glanced at it, a blank look on his face, then quickly put it down. The other made no attempt to even pick it up. Both of them stared at her, not even trying. It was obvious: they couldn't read.

It was not unusual for Jana to run into this with gypsies. The two young men sitting in front of her were the product of gypsy poverty and distrust of the *gaje*. They wouldn't mix with the surrounding Slovak community. They had probably never been to public school because of that distrust. Jana didn't blame them for this distrust. The Roms had been betrayed too many times before not to have had it deeply ingrained in their belief system. Jana sat back and told them what the report said. They looked at her blankly.

Jana decided to be blunt. "Your friend was murdered."

That got a response, both of them gaping at her.

"Your statements said that he was active, talking to you, very aware of what was going on when he tried to climb through the fence." Jana was hard-edged when she talked. "You said his shotgun went off accidentally. This new analysis says that you lied. It indicates that he was unconscious at the time of his death. He could no more have talked and walked than if his head had been cut off. And it nearly was, considering that the shot that killed him almost decapitated the poor fellow.

"So, we're here not to decide whether or not you killed him, but why you killed him."

When suspects are confronted with a police accusation, they often break out into what officers call the "fear disease." Within seconds, the sweat stands out on their faces, tremors are visible on one portion of the body or another, and their eyes show symptoms of nystagmus: flickering from side to side, not focusing well, blinking. Both of the men began showing symptoms of the "disease."

Jana had pushed them to where she wanted them to be. They were afraid of her. Even more, they were afraid of what was on the paper.

"The wound caused by the shell showed virtually no spread in the shot, which means it was fired from close up. That means it could not have been fired from more than a foot or two away. Close-up powder burns as well. Since he was not conscious at the time, the dead man could only have been shot by someone who intended to kill him with a shot fired at close range. Therefore, what we have is a planned and deliberate murder. I want to know which of you fired the shot."

The one on Jana's left immediately looked to the one on her right, the one on her right cringing back and deflating. Jana now knew who the actual killer was. She looked to the one on her left first. The next steps were clear: ease the fear; separate him from the man sitting next to him; make him her friend; give him the hope that if he cooperated, he might save himself.

"I thought you were the innocent one. Thank you for showing us who did the killing. That means we probably won't be bothering you too much more. He did do the actual killing, didn't he?"

The man gulped, his Adam's apple going up and down. He got out a weak "Yes."

"He's lying," the other one gasped.

Jana continued to address the one on her left. "One of my officers will be taking you outside to sign a statement before you're released. Of course, it depends upon your telling him the complete truth about how the events occurred."

She nodded at Jonas, who took the man's arm and propelled him out of the room. He would finish the job with that one; Jana now focused on the other one.

"We know that you killed him. Investigator Jonas is with your friend. They'll be through soon. As I think you know, your friend will give Investigator Jonas a complete statement before they're though. We could prosecute you without the testimony of your friend. The scientific evidence is all in this report. There's no question. It's incontrovertible. However, this is an opportunity for you to tell your side of the story."

She checked her reports again.

"Ah, yes, the knees. You or your friend or someone else broke his knees some time before the 'hunting' trip. The man you killed was crippled by that attack and had to have surgery. Obviously, you had a reason then for being angry and punishing him. Then, later, after he had received medical treatment and his knees had mostly healed, you decided to kill him. Or, perhaps you were made to kill him. Was that it? Were you forced to kill him? Something or someone made you kill him, right?"

She tried to look as if she were sympathetic to the man.

He didn't reply.

"It's important that we have your side of the story," she said. "Everything you say to us will go before the judge. Everything your friend says as well. All the reports that have been made, including the coroner's report, will be read. Do you understand that?"

The man managed a nod.

"Before we get to the shooting, let's talk about your breaking the man's knees. Why did you do it?"

"He got the *vitsa* leader's daughter pregnant. His father was asked to pay for the damage to the family honor. His father refused to pay the money. He called her things. Honor had to be satisfied."

"So you broke his knees?"

The man shook his head. "He was a friend of mine. I couldn't break his knees. Not for that. Other men in the village did it."

"You didn't take part?"

"I didn't do any of it."

Jana made a show of writing it all down, getting the names of the men who had done the crushing of the youth's knees and the name of the village head who had ordered it.

"I'm glad you didn't do something that horrible to your friend." Jana's voice had a necessary compassion she didn't feel. It was all part of the questioning process, and not a part she liked. "You showed humanity."

"Thank you."

"Then your friend committed another foolish act, didn't he?"

The man hesitated. "Yes."

"He saw the girl again?"

The man nodded.

"They were seen?"

He nodded again.

"And you were ordered to kill him?"

He sat, immobile. Jana went on as if he had answered. "Did your friend help you do the killing?"

The man stiffened. "I didn't need his help."

"Didn't your friend help you get him drunk? And give him additional pain pills? Hold him down, perhaps?"

He shook his head no.

"Your friend must have helped you carry him over to the fence so you could set up your story?"

The man brightened slightly. "He was too heavy for me to carry by myself."

"I would think so, even for a strong man like you."

"Yes."

"Tell me, if you refused to have anything to do with breaking your friend's kneecaps, why did you agree to kill him?"

For the first time there was the sound of anger in the young man's voice. "He didn't stop. Even after he had been told to stay away. Even after his knees were broken. He didn't care about our honor. He didn't care about the fact that I pleaded with him to stop. He spit in our faces. After a while I couldn't even look at him. He was no longer my friend." He smiled. "When I was told that I had to protect our honor, I was ready to do it." He looked at Jana with concern in his eyes. "You can see, I had to do it."

"Yes, I can see." She picked up the reports she'd brought in. "Investigator Grzner will write up what you said. Then he'll read it to you. If you have anything to add, just tell him. He'll put it in the report. After that, you can put your mark on the paper. That way we'll be able to get your side of the story to the judges. Okay?"

"Yes."

"One more thing. The girl. Was she related to you?"

He nodded. "My sister."

Jana had half expected the answer. "How has she reacted to her boyfriend's death?"

"Fine."

"Fine?"

"She knew what had to be done. It's not as if he was her husband." The anger came back into his voice. "He wouldn't marry her."

"I see."

Jana left Grzner with the Rom. She walked past the room where Jonas was questioning the other young man. Jonas gave her a quick sign to indicate everything was going all right, so she went on to her office, calling for Seges to come in.

"We have the two men in custody who did the shotgun killing of the young gypsy. We may have others to take into custody when I get back from Paris. I'll review the evidence on them, then decide."

"You're going to Paris?" Seges looked impressed.

"Business, not pleasure. The man who was killed in Paris by the truck, the one the French wanted us to identify. He's related to the Bogan case. I think I'll find additional evidence in Paris."

Seges rocked back and forth, not really interested in the reasons for the trip. "I've been told that Paris is nice even to do business in. There are also other things to become involved with." He gave her his equivalent of a leer.

"Wipe the smirk off your face, Seges."

He quickly dropped the leer.

Jana began pulling together things that she would need for her trip. "I need to see Em as soon as possible. I'd like to speak to her alone. Do you think you might leave work early, perhaps take your wife out to a movie or for a hot chocolate and a pastry, so we can have the time I need?"

"Are you planning to take her out of our house?"

"I'm not planning anything except a talk with her."

"My wife and I get along much better with her around. So we thought she could possibly continue to stay on with us—if you approve, of course."

"It's not for me to say. There are rules. You know them. You will have to apply to get approval for child custody."

"Certainly, Commander."

"I'm glad you are hitting if off with her, Seges. Did it surprise you?"

"Yes, Commander. A pleasant surprise. I guess we often just don't know what we really need in life."

"I'm glad for you both."

"It was your suggestion that we take her in for a few days. It grew from there, particularly with my wife."

"You want to take her in permanently?"

"I guess so."

He resembled a very large doll with a proportionately large smile on his face, his hands behind his back, shifting from one leg to the other, happy to be feeling the emotions that his almost-family had brought him. Jana reached into her top drawer and pulled out the little bag with the money that Em had given her in Germany. She tossed it to Seges.

"This is Em's. There's money inside. Give it to her when you get home."

"Money?"

"American dollars. Remember, I've counted it, Seges."

He looked hurt by the insinuation that he might take any of Em's money.

"Make the call to your wife, Seges. You can leave any time to pick her up."

"Yes, Commander." He did his approximation of a snappy about-face and walked out, trailing good will.

Jana wrote a small memo for both Jonas and Grzner, outlining the charges that she thought should be written up on the two who had killed the young man, at the same time thinking about the craziness of the whole incident and the lives now damaged beyond repair. Whether Rom law or Slovak law, the results of enforcement are invariably traumatic. Whatever the violation and whatever law is enforced, the waves that were made by the crime and then by its penalty spread out in concentric circles, eventually affecting everyone: the families, the police who became immersed in the horror, the prosecutors, the judges, all of them suffocating in the mess.

Jana picked up the material she was taking to Paris and left the building. She sat at a roadside coffeeshop watching the wind pick up the snow from the ground and swirl it in the air, thinking about what she had to talk to Em about, the things she had to confront her with, the answers that she already knew. She hoped she would soon be able to give the colonel the answers to his questions about why she needed Em to solve the case.

She arrived at the Seges house after waiting for an hour to give Seges and his wife time to leave. Unhappily, they were still there when Jana arrived, Seges's wife frightened and stunned, Seges looking very unsure of himself. Em was gone again.

Jana waited a few minutes for things to settle down, hugging Mrs. Seges to calm her and assuring her that everything would be all right, even though she knew it wouldn't. Their dream of permanently taking the girl in would never be a reality.

"What happened?" Jana eventually asked.

"She just picked up her things and left," Mrs. Seges said. "Just like that. Not even a kiss on the cheek."

Jana glanced at Seges, reasonably certain she knew why the girl had gone. "She was here when you arrived?"

He nodded unhappily, trying to keep himself from breaking down.

"What did you say to Em when you came home?"

"Nothing much. I asked my wife to go out with me, that's all. The next thing I knew, Em was gone."

"Did you tell your wife that I was coming over to talk to Em?"

"Of course. And my wife told her that you wanted to talk with her."

"Which of you told Em that I was going to Paris on the Bogan case?"

Mrs. Seges's voice was weak when she spoke. "I said you were going to Paris. I didn't know why."

Seges looked progressively more uncomfortable. "You didn't prohibit me from telling Em that you were going to Paris."

"No, I didn't," Jana agreed.

He seemed slightly relieved, brightening even more a second later. "I gave her the money you told me was hers."

"And?"

"She was surprised."

"Happy?"

"Not particularly. She just hung the bag around her neck."

"Then you told her about what I was going to do in Paris?"

"She kind of asked me why you were going."

"Kind of?"

"She was saying this and that, and then she said she'd never been to Paris and wanted to see it. She asked me if you were going to see the Eiffel Tower and Napoleon's tomb and all those places. And when I said it was business, she looked at me as if she expected me to tell her what the business was."

"So you did."

"Yes . . ."

"And then?"

"She borrowed my wife's cell phone, went into the kitchen to use it, then came running out and grabbed her things."

"She just ran off." Mrs. Seges began to cry.

"She'll come back," Seges reassured her.

"Only after she's been to Paris," Jana said.

They both stared at Jana, not quite believing what they'd just heard.

"Paris," Jana repeated.

She was sure of it.

Chapter 41

A s the plane descended into Paris, Jana felt the slight
sense of foreboding that she always had when she was
a passenger on an aircraft nosing down into an overcast
sky, the worry that the pilot might misjudge the landing
in the dreary gloom.

The landing was perfect. The plane taxied to its terminal berth without a wait, the passengers disembarking
almost immediately. Jana walked through the discharge
ramp into the passenger waiting area expecting to see
Masson waiting for her, since cops are allowed into the
secure areas. He was not there, though, so she found her
own way through the airport maze to the baggage area,
picked up her bag from the carousel, then walked to the
Metro station, taking the Metro to a stop that was supposed to be near enough to her hotel to walk the rest of
the distance.

It was cold in Paris, below freezing, people bundled
up, all the women and most of the men wearing heavy
coats and jackets, collars up, scarves around their necks.
The pedestrians all seemed to be hurrying to get back to
indoor warmth as quickly as possible. They brooked no
interference with their determination to get out of the
cold, which worked against Jana. Her requests for directions met abrupt, shrug-off answers and half-thought-out

gestures in the general direction of where people thought Jana's hotel was. The vagueness of the directions resulted in her missing the hotel by several blocks, a friendly optometrist at a small shop at last taking the time to tell her exactly how to get there. When she arrived, she was happy to step out of the frosty street.

Jana's question to the hotel clerk who checked her in about whether a young girl had been there asking about her was met with a vacant look. Based on prior experience, she had expected Em to be waiting for her when she got there. She was convinced that if Em wasn't there yet, she would be soon. Jana's room was clean and neat, a little too noisy because of the heavy traffic on the rue de Rivoli, but the noise was muted enough by the double-glazed window for her to know she would be able to sleep at night when the traffic eased off. She called Investigator Masson and was informed that he was out for the day on an investigation. She left a message, unpacked, and then decided she would use this window of opportunity to see a little of Paris while she had the chance.

The desk clerk provided Jana with a pocket-size map of the city and explicit directions on how to use the Metro to get around. Twenty minutes later, Jana was on the Champs-Elysées, on the top of the Arc de Triomphe, looking over the city. It was windy, which made it even colder at the top of the monument, but she ignored the windchill to enjoy the view of the city from the top of the 164-foot structure.

Paris, at this late-afternoon hour, was gorgeous, the overcast lifting just for Jana, the boulevards radiating out from the axis of the Arc like the straight lines of a *haut* designer gown, the Eiffel Tower in the distance a jewel on the hem of the flowing dress. Jana walked around the edge of the monument, watching the people parade below, ticking off the sights from her map. She had just decided to leave, wanting to walk down the Champs, and was looking around for the *ascenseur* when she saw Em standing by the parapet on the opposite side of the monument. The girl gaily waved at her as if they were together on a gala holiday enjoying the sights.

Even though Jana had expected to see Em, she still felt a slight quiver of shock at her appearance. Jana stared at her, not quite sure how to act. Then, forcing herself to abandon the emotions she still felt for the girl, she walked to the *ascenseur* without waiting for Em and took it down to the street.

The clouds moved to hide the sun, and the temperature dropped. Jana walked east on the Champs, crossing the street that circled the monument, then was taken aback to realize that it was named the rue de Presbourg. Presbourg had been the old Austrian name for Bratislava. In the back of her mind, the remnant from some half-forgotten history class surfaced. Napoleon was victorious against the Austrians at Presbourg when Slovakia had been a vassal in the Austro-Hungarian Empire. An omen for Jana. She had come to Paris to fight a battle, and she was being given fair warning that it was about to begin.

She walked several blocks, no longer interested in fashions or fads, passing the storefronts without seeing them. A stomach pang made her realize that she was hungry, so she checked the prices on a board in front of a French restaurant, decided it was much too expensive, then settled for an Italian restaurant that boasted twenty different types of pizza. The restaurant had set up heating lamps in the enclosed glass veranda that fronted it, an added inducement for Jana to sit there. She ordered a plain pizza, all the while waiting for Em to make her appearance. The pizza arrived just as Em walked into the restaurant.

The girl headed straight for Jana's table, taking off the new winter jacket she was wearing.

"Prices are very high in Paris. I had to pay a fortune for this, except I couldn't leave Paris without buying clothing of some sort." Em held the jacket to show it off. "Fully lined, darts on the side."

"Very nice," Jana muttered between her first bites of pizza.

Em sat across from her, not saying a word about Jana ignoring her on the top of the monument.

"I'd love a slice of pizza." She stared at the pizza hungrily. Without waiting for permission, she took a slice and took such a huge bite out of it that she was forced to stuff some of it into her mouth with her fingers. "Pizza is good when it's cold outside."

Jana kept eating, not paying attention to Em, the girl chattering on as if there were nothing unusual about them being in a Paris restaurant on the Champs-Elysées eating pizza.

"I came in last night, so I've had more time than you to wander around and take in the sights. A funny story: I went to the top of the Eiffel Tower. There are signs in the elevators that say 'Beware of Pickpockets.' Well, we got to the top, and these people come rushing on just as I'm getting off, and I feel a man grabbing at me. So I start to fight him off, thinking he's a pickpocket or worse, and it turns out he's just an usher for people when they get out of the elevator to direct them in the right direction. Can you believe I almost bit the man or worse?"

Jana kept eating. Em went on as if they were having an exchange of pleasantries.

"I've been all over the place, to Saint-Honoré where all the fashionable shops are, then over to the island in the middle of the river." She tried to recall the name of the island and couldn't. "The one with Notre Dame Cathedral. The cathedral here is better than the one in Vienna, but I like the one in Prague the best."

She continued to talk between bites. She finished her slice and looked with longing at the last piece remaining on the serving plate. Very carefully Jana cut it in half. She took one of the pieces for herself, and pushed the remaining slice over to Em. The girl began stuffing it in her mouth, again talking and chewing at the same time. "I think the Danube is bigger than the Seine. Maybe not as clean, though. They keep this city pretty fresh, which is nice. I thought your hotel was nice, but mine is newer."

"You checked out my hotel?"

"I wanted to make sure you had a pleasant place to stay."

"Where are you staying?" Jana asked her.

"Down the street." Em made a vague gesture to the east. "Kind of like yours, only on a side street." She finished the last of her pizza. "I bet you were surprised when you saw me at the top of the monument."

"No."

"Not even a little bit?"

Jana nibbled at the sliver of pizza she'd cut. "I knew you'd be here."

"That's because you're a detective." Em brightened, turning up her personality. "Since I've met you, I've thought I might like to be a detective when I grow up. It would be great to work together."

"I don't think so." Jana signaled the waiter and ordered an espresso.

"Why not?"

"Because you're involved in criminal activities, and the police don't hire criminals to be detectives."

"I've never been caught. How would they know I'm a criminal?"

"Because I'd tell them."

Em nodded, looking wise. "Yes, I suppose you would. It's your job."

"It's my job," Jana agreed.

"I haven't stolen anything of yours."

"I'm not sure that's true."

"Why would I steal from you?"

"For the same reason you lie. I thought you were just a very young girl when we met, but then you told me you did criminal things."

"I don't remember that." Her features skewed as she tried to remember telling Jana she was a criminal. "I would never say that."

"How old are you, Em?"

"As old or as young as you want." She nodded. "I can look older, if you want me to."

"Or younger than you are, when you want to."

"All people change their looks when they need to."

"People don't like it when they're manipulated, Em."

The girl suddenly looked older. "I gave you what you wanted, Jana. I gave Mrs. Seges what she needed. I pay back for what I get."

"Only a small portion of what you take."

Em frowned. "You said I was a criminal. Why?"

The waiter brought the espresso Jana had ordered. She sipped silently.

Em grew impatient. "Can you answer the question?"

"Em, I was flattered enough by the connection I thought we had, naïve and stupid enough to ignore your travel between countries, your always showing up no matter where I was, as if you were a pop-up doll made to bring laughter to my life. You told me you ran errands for criminals, that you often delivered things for them. But when you attached yourself to me, it was more than that."

Em signaled the waiter and pointed at Jana's espresso, indicating she wanted one. Even though Jana knew what Em was, and how self-sufficient she had shown herself to be, the girl's composure continued to surprise her. They were both silent until Em's espresso was served.

"What was it that I did to you?" There was a flat, metallic quality to Em's voice. "I took nothing. I even made useful suggestions."

"Em, you told me that you went on trips for 'clients,' and they would often follow you, at a distance, just to make sure that nothing went wrong and to see to it that whatever you had to do, you did, without interference from others."

"Okay, so?"

"It was the Berlin trip. Everything became clearer there. You appeared in my room, insisting on going to the zoo."

"It wasn't my fault that the trip got spoiled by those men later."

"Of course it was."

For the first time Em looked taken aback.

"Ayden Yunis was at the zoo because he was expecting someone. He was expecting you. That's why you wanted to go there. And I was naïve enough to believe that I was just taking a girl on her first visit to the zoo. But your employer was there too, behind us, trailing along to make sure that you got to the meeting. He was doing the same thing when the man attacked you, the time you were on one of those trips for him. He killed the man who attacked you. Before we went to the zoo, you put on my red scarf so the man following us wouldn't lose you in the crowd. I don't blame you for using the scarf. After all, you had been through a terrible ordeal once before, and you didn't want it to happen again."

Em sipped at her coffee, her face showing no emotion as she listened to Jana's narrative.

"What were you bringing to Yunis? Details of a criminal process? Sums of money that were due or owing? Information about shipments that were to arrive? Plans for expansion of their mutual activities? There were things that your employer, or Yunis, was not comfortable putting on paper or talking about on the telephone. So they used a personal voicemail system: you."

Em gave Jana an empty smile, then stood up, putting on her jacket.

"Sit down, Em," Jana ordered. "We've not finished yet."

"I have to go, Jana. People are waiting for me."

"If you try to go just now, I'll physically restrain you until the French police arrive. You're a material witness on a murder, if not two of them. I assure you that if I request it, the French will hold you for the German police. And for the Slovak police. And for the Austrian police. Chances are you'll be in one juvenile facility or another, and then another, for weeks, or longer, if I have my way. So, sit down!"

The girl sat. "I won't say anything, so there's no use in holding me."

"Of course you'll answer me, and quickly. Here. Now."

The girl stared at her, her eyes blank. It was time to go forward, for Jana to get the questions resolved.

"What I'm going to ask you for are small details, details which you won't ever be asked to repeat again, and which I'll keep silent. I'll act on them without naming you as a source, if I take any action on them at all. Do you understand what I'm saying?"

Em considered what Jana had just told her, then nodded a yes.

"Good. The first question concerns the men who killed Yunis. Did you know that they were going to come after Yunis?"

"No."

The answer had been quick and direct with no evasion. Jana had come to the same conclusion herself. The girl wouldn't have gone with Jana to the zoo if she had known that.

"You had come to the zoo to meet with Yunis and deliver a message. Did the subject of your message have anything to do with Yunis and his bank? That he was in danger?"

There was a split second of indecision, but the answer was still direct and without any of the facial characteristics that would have indicated a lie.

"Yes."

"Did you talk to your employer about someone in the Yunis organization betraying Yunis?"

"My employer told me to tell Yunis that."

"Was it the man named Balder?"

There was a long silence.

"I'll repeat what I said before. I promise you I will not call on you to testify on any of the killings. Your name will not go down on any piece of paper. I will tell no one that you gave me the name. And it will never get back to your employer. All you need to do is say the name of the man your employer told you to give to Yunis."

Em looked at Jana, trying to make up her mind. "You swear?"

"I swear I will fulfill all my promises."

Em nodded. "Balder."

"I have just a few more questions before you go."

The girl sat silent, waiting.

"When you first met me, when you knocked on my door, frozen, selling your earrings, you knew that it was my house, didn't you?"

There was no hesitation. "Yes."

"Your employer told you?"

"Yes."

"Why?"

"I was to stay with you."

"To use me?"

"That came later."

"If not to use me, then why would he send you to me? To a police commander?"

"To protect me."

Jana felt a jolt at the answer. She had never even considered this possibility. There had been absolutely nothing to point to it. But she could understand the motivation on the part of the girl's employer. There was a war on, people were being killed, and he was protecting an asset. What better place to put his asset than under the protecting arm of a police officer? So he'd sent her out in the storm to knock on Jana's door. What human being could refuse to give sanctuary to a little girl who would freeze to death if she were left out in the storm?

Em decided that the pause in the conversation was her cue to stand. She quickly fastened the buttons on her jacket. "Thank you for the pizza."

The girl was going, and Jana didn't know if she would ever see her again. She tried to get close one last time. "The relationship meant something to me. Perhaps, some time or another, we can . . . have pizza again, or whatever?"

"Sure."

Em left the restaurant. The girl would never trust anyone. The door to her emotions was closed. It was why she was what she was.

Jana watched her through the veranda windows until she disappeared in the crowd.

Chapter 42

Masson called her at the hotel, and Jana arranged to meet him near the address he had given her for Jindrich Bogan's apartment on rue Saint-Paul, confident that she could get there after her hotel desk clerk gave her directions. She also had the map if she needed it, and the crisp, sunny morning was an open invitation to walk. Jana was assured by the desk clerk that she would be able to reach the address within fifteen minutes.

With an hour to kill, Jana took a circuitous stroll through the Marais, the arrondissement where the hotel was located, one of the older districts in the center of Paris, made new again by the art crowd, the gay crowd, and all the artisans in between who were busy making a living off the tourist trade. She made one stop, at a small bakery, one of the many scattered everywhere in Paris, to buy herself a small *chocolat fondant*, which she savored as she walked. As the time approached, Jana made her way back to the rue de Rivoli and headed toward rue Saint-Paul. Just as the desk clerk had told her, she was at the address within fifteen minutes. Masson was waiting for her in front of a red-façaded bookshop reading a small paperback.

They recognized each other without even having arranged a signal, police officer recognizing police officer, both shaking hands. Masson was younger than Jana had thought he would be, with a full head of wavy black hair, one of those boyish-faced people who always seem to be in a good humor. He waved the book at her.

"I stop in here for English books. I get points for my promotional if I can understand the tourists. And we get lots of miserable tourists," he explained, giving her the head inclination and lip pout that the French are so famous for when things are a bit much. "Welcome to my city." He laughed. "I claim it once in a while, thinking I might impress an important person like you."

"You think I might borrow it on occasion?"

"Sorry, my wife won't let me make even a loan." He laughed again. "I promised her the moon once, and when I couldn't deliver she said I should stop making promises I couldn't keep. She married me despite my bragging."

"That means you've married the right person."

They moved down the street, Masson giving Jana a running commentary on the weather, Paris at this time of the year, her hotel, his wife, and, eventually, the murdered Pascal as they walked to the address where the dead man's apartment was located.

The building was typical for the area, scrolled iron railings in front of French-door windows, small balconies on the top level, towels laid out to dry on the ironwork, and flower pots in the corners. A very large wooden door faced the street, a digicode keypad beside it. Masson punched in a four-character code that opened the door and led Jana into the cobblestoned courtyard.

A lone one-story building cut across the middle of the courtyard, the smaller construction surrounded by the higher six-story apartment building. The structure was a residence constructed in a different style than the main building, the dissimilarities indicating that it postdated the nineteenth-century structure above and around it.

"That's where he lived." Masson gestured toward the one-story structure, pulling out a key. "He paid all the tenants in the building to give him the privilege of erecting the thing in the middle of the courtyard. Crazy, eh? People willing to screw up the look of their space for a few extra coins."

"Odd to want to build here."

"It terminates on two sides at the surrounding walls, and on the other side of the building there's a gate leading out of the courtyard. If he didn't want to see the bill collectors, or anyone else who might be bringing him trouble from any one side, he could go out the other."

They walked to the door of the house.

"Metal," Masson pointed out. "You'd need a stick of dynamite if you didn't have the key. It has rods that slip into the four sides of the metal frame, making it virtually entry-proof. He had the key on him when he was killed. Otherwise we'd have had to get in by taking a day to drill our way through."

Masson keyed their way in, giving Jana a quick tour of the house just to show her the layout. The main room was large, high-ceilinged, and sparsely furnished in black and white furniture that accentuated the space. Jindrich had liked breathing room, maybe a residual need from having spent time in the confinement of a prison cell when he was younger. Perhaps this was even one of the reasons he wanted a separate structure from everyone else. Bars in prison cells don't make for much privacy. A small kitchen occupied one corner of the room, and at the other end of the structure there was a large, raised open platform with a huge master bed sitting on top of it. To the rear of the bed was a spacious, fully tiled bathroom, and on the other side of it a wardrobe room containing an extensive selection of clothes.

There were two features that intrigued Jana. The first was a raised platform that came up to her knees running along the bottom of both of the main walls, from one end to the other, of the large living room. The second feature was the windows along those walls. They were long slits running up and down. It reminded her of the old castles that dotted most of Europe, their walls built with slit openings that archers could fire through at anyone attacking the castle while the slit minimally exposed their bodies to return fire. The raised platform would make it easy to reach the entire slit from top to bottom, increasing the firing perimeter from inside.

"Did you find any weapons in the place when you came in?" Jana asked.

"Two assault rifles, one shotgun, two handguns, a store of ammunition, and a gas mask. They're at the station if you want to examine them."

"Why would he want a gas mask?" Jana proceeded to answer her own question. "The man had his fortress and was prepared for any eventuality."

"Over here." Masson walked over to a corner of the room where there were a number of electronic control panels. "Three types of burglar alarms, motion detectors on the walls, and a connection to an immediate-response guard company that sends both armed guards and dogs if it's triggered. The man was making sure he wasn't surprised."

Jana stared at the material piled in the center of the room. There were a file cabinet, several small cardboard boxes, and papers with folders stacked around them gathered on top of a rug. And laid out on the rug in a large, tiered series of arcs were what looked like bank documents.

"What you talked to me about?" Jana asked.

Masson nodded. Both of them sat at the base of the area of documents and Jana began to go through them. They were from different banks all over Europe. All appeared to be versions of bankbooks, in one certificate form or another, listing withdrawals, deposits, transfers, charges, interest payments, and items Jana had no idea about because they were in languages she could not understand. There were some groups of documents that, although differently dated, all came from the same bank. These documents had been piled on top of each other, some canceled, some out of date. There were more than a hundred "books" in total. None of the names on the papers were familiar to Jana except Pascal Dionne, the false name of the man she now knew was really Jindrich Bogan from Slovakia.

Jana took a scrap of paper and, using the books with the latest dates, tried to do a rough estimate of how much money was currently indicated as deposited in the bank accounts. It took her three hours to make her computations. When she came up with a final figure, it left her stunned. The total was approximately 675 million euros. She showed Masson the figure. He nodded.

"Mine was slightly under the figure you came up with, but it's close enough."

"Ever see accounts with sums like these before?"

"Never."

"My guess is we'll never see it again in our lifetime."

Jana checked the names of the banks that had extant accounts. Of all the banks Jindrich had used over the course of the years, there were ten banks that now had the majority of the funds. One of those banks was the bank that Yunis had owned in Berlin. The Viennese bank where Radomir Kralik was a vice president was another. The two small French banks that the Bogans were sending their money to were there as well. Jana added them to the list she was making. There was also a bank in Moscow and two banks in the U.S., one in Chicago and the other in Los Angeles. There were three banks in Asia, one in Bangkok, another in Manila, and one in Hong Kong. None of them were well-known banks, but a bank doesn't have to be a household name to keep funds, or to do whatever it wants to make itself even more money.

There were large printed notices on the covers or on the first pages of all the bank documents. From the languages she could translate, or guess at, Jana gathered that the documents were non-withdrawal credentials. You couldn't simply present the passbook or certification to withdraw funds: a special credential was required.

"Did you find the document that authorizes withdrawal of these funds?"

Masson leaned back on the couch where he was sitting and threw up his hands in frustration.

"I went through all the files with three other officers and two accountants. The examination was not as precise as I would have liked, but I'm sure that there was no single, or even multiple, withdrawal authorization or identification contained in the material."

"There has to be a bearer document, one that would allow the account holder to go into the bank to withdraw or transfer money," Jana told Masson.

"We went through it all, piece by piece. We kept the place looking pretty neat, but we went into every nook and cranny, the clothes in the dressing room, the cereal boxes in the kitchen, the toilet tank, the bedding, even the springs. If there was a hole or a crevice, we went into it. We brought in special equipment to examine the walls and the floors. Nothing! We even looked under the house. Everything was negative."

"If it's not here, it's out there somewhere."

"Where?"

"Maybe the Bogans know." She thought about their next step, not wanting to rush into a meeting with the Bogans until she was absolutely sure of her ground. "I want to walk the apartment myself. Just a quick look, then I think we have to visit Le Meurice and talk to the Bogans."

"*D'accord*," Masson approved, settling back on the couch, waiting for Jana to finish her examination of the apartment. Jana navigated by instinct, going from the living room into the bathroom, then to the dressing room. She realized that she hadn't seen anything that was truly personal that could tell her anything of substance about the man. She left the dressing area and went to the bed. The bedclothes were all piled up in the middle of the mattress, parts of the mattress visibly slashed, undoubtedly by the police during their search. She took one step back to survey the whole room.

Instead of end tables, there were several small built-in shelves at each side of the bed. On one of the shelves was an envelope, and one sheet of paper lay on the floor. The sheet of paper looked like a discard, tossed there after a superficial examination by one of the police officers during the search. To the cop, it had been unimportant. Maybe he hadn't known enough about the case to make the appropriate decision as to its significance. Jana picked it up and read:

Grandfather, it's time for a reckoning on the accounts. Immediately. I will not tolerate the status quo. The banks are also in the mix. It's over. Now! This has to be at once. Anything less is unacceptable. The present situation is finished. Zdenko.

Jana tucked the letter into the envelope, then the envelope into her purse. It's invariably true: the devil is in the details. She now had a course of questioning to pursue when she met Zdenko.

Within minutes, they were on their way to Le Meurice.

Chapter 43

Le Meurice is one of the so-called palace hotels, overlooking the Tuileries Garden, almost touching the Louvre across the street and just down the block. It is opulent without being lurid, making no bones about catering to the rich. Any guest coming through the front doors for the first time is immediately informed by the marble and terrazzo floors, the crystal chandeliers, the multiplicity of sumptuous fabrics on the lobby furniture, and the huge gilded mirrors on the walls that no expense is going to be spared in making him feel that he is as royal as any one of the monarchs who, in another epoch, lived in the area. The Nazis liked the hotel so much that when they occupied Paris during the Second World War, they requisitioned it for their high command. Of course, when the Allies retook Paris, the liberated French scoured the walls with disinfectant and then made the hotel even more luxurious.

As they went inside, Masson confessed that this was the first time he'd ever been inside the hotel. Both of them were impressed: the hotel's display of wealth and cultivated abundance had been tailored to make an impact. The decorator's final touch was wall-mounted gold-framed mirrors that reflected the guest walking through the lobby, the mirrors artfully placed to bring the guest into the framed display. The management of Le Meurice knew that the affluent loved to display themselves in their privileged circumstances.

"My mother once came here with a boyfriend who wanted to impress her," Masson confided to Matinova. "They got married just before I was born. So, by proxy, the hotel is responsible for my existence."

"Was it a good marriage?"

"Better than most. Later they had three daughters, so they obviously didn't really need the hotel to encourage them." He thought about it for a moment. "Still, it was their first time, so maybe they did."

"Perhaps you should approach the management and offer them your endorsement," Jana suggested.

They moved farther into the hotel, trying to look like they belonged.

Masson had called ahead to get the numbers of the rooms that the Bogans were occupying. In fact, they were in two adjoining presidential suites. He checked with one of the roving hotel floor employees for directions, the man pointing them to the twin suites located on the first floor. Jana and Masson then walked up the stairs to the suites.

Masson knocked on the first suite's door and it was opened almost immediately by a man dressed in the livery of a butler: white gloves, checkered vest, and slightly bored look.

"Yes?" the man said.

"Is Mr. Bogan in?" Masson requested.

"If I may, who is asking?"

Masson held his police credentials up to the man's eye level, almost pressed against his face.

"Tell your master that Police Investigator Masson is here."

Masson walked past the butler into the suite. Jana stepped in behind him, the butler still standing at the door, unsure as to what to do. He eventually decided to close the door behind them; then he stalked off to get Bogan.

"I'm already angry at the Bogans," Masson announced.

"You haven't heard enough about them to be angry."

"I'm angry that they can afford rooms like these when I can't even afford to have breakfast or lunch here."

Jana half agreed with Masson's anger. The room was enormous, with inlaid wood floors, furniture in silk damask, everything reeking of comfort and cosseting.

"We know that the father and son have enough money not to mind spending it in big chunks," Jana observed. "On the other hand, it's my guess that they are expecting even more money."

"We have most of the bank documents," Masson reminded Jana.

"Not the most important one," Jana responded.

The butler reentered the room. "Mr. Bogan has just finished his morning ablutions. He'll be in shortly." He lifted a silver tray of used breakfast dishes that was resting on a delicate white-and-gold French provincial table and carried them out of the suite, silently closing the door behind him. Oto Bogan came into the room almost immediately after the butler had left.

Bogan was in a silk dressing robe, a towel around his neck, hair slightly tousled, displaying the same big politician's personality that Jana had witnessed on the night his wife was shot. He immediately apologized for keeping them waiting and urged them to sit down, offering to call for coffee for them. Both Jana and Masson refused the coffee offer, and Bogan beckoned them again to sit.

Oto Bogan rambled on about his late rise from sleep

due to the bankers' dinner he'd attended the night before where he'd had too much coffee and alcohol, resulting in too many trips to the bathroom during the night. His chatter ultimately ran down. He turned to Jana, pasting an artificial smile on his face.

"You're the commander from Slovakia," he said. "You look better out of uniform."

"Uniforms are a necessary item in my business."

"Right." He suddenly looked as if he'd eaten food that wasn't as fresh as he'd thought it was. "You did me a service."

"Colonel Trokan saved your life."

"He did get shot, didn't he?" Bogan said. "How is the colonel?"

There was no real concern for Trokan in the man's voice. He was merely going through the social artifice of being polite. He went on without waiting for Jana to answer the question.

"I think that the general public never realizes what the police do for them. It took an event like the death of my wife to convince me that your services are absolutely invaluable."

"We didn't seem to help much that night."

"That's because I wouldn't listen to you. If I'd heeded your warnings, I would never have walked out into the spotlight, and my dear wife Klara would still be with us."

"Your wife urged you to go on with the celebration, Mr. Bogan. If anyone was responsible, it would be her."

Bogan began looking even more agitated. "She just wanted me to have my party. She didn't have the slightest thought that those crazy things were going to happen."

Jana just smiled at the man. Her silence affected Bogan. He looked from Jana to Masson, then back to Jana again.

"There must be a reason that you've looked me up," he finally said. "Can I help you with anything?"

"Your wife was involved in the shooting, Mr. Bogan," Jana told him. "She helped set it up."

Bogan stared at her, not in disbelief, but in fear tinged with dismay. His forehead began to sweat, and he mopped at it with the towel around his neck. "Impossible."

Bogan's inflection sounded tinny, off-kilter. He believed in the possibility of his wife's being involved in a plot to kill him.

"There's no question that she arranged things at the soundstage to facilitate the shooting." Jana watched Bogan very carefully, checking for the telltale signs that he knew what she was talking about and believed it. "We found the weapons. We have people who will attest to the fact that she created the hiding place for the guns."

Bogan's face had drained of color, looking as if he had ingested poison and was feeling its first terrible effects.

"Would you like a glass of water, Mr. Bogan?"

"I'm fine," he said falteringly.

"You don't look fine."

"I told you . . . I . . . had a bad night."

"So, we can go on?"

"Yes."

"Were you on good terms with your wife, Mr. Bogan?"

"The best of terms. I loved her; she loved me. The party she put on is clear evidence of that."

"Then why was she living with Radomir Kralik? They were married before she married you. Afterward, they stayed lovers. You knew they continued to be lovers, yet you remained in the marriage. I would hazard a guess that you were always married in name only. I think that was the way your marriage was set up from the very beginning, wasn't it, Mr. Bogan? You'd both agreed to a marriage of convenience, Mr. Bogan. What was the convenience, the reason for the marriage?"

Bogan's eyes had become unfocused, his attention on some inner turmoil. Jana raised her voice, leaning closer, trying to bring the man back to the issue at hand.

"She wanted you dead, Mr. Bogan. She had decided that you were disposable. An item she was ready to discard. I wonder if the planned shooting had anything to do with the death of your father, Mr. Bogan. Jindrich Bogan was your father, wasn't he, Mr. Bogan?"

The mention of Jindrich Bogan snapped Oto's head up, bringing him back to the moment, his eyes now clear.

"I didn't know my father very well," he said.

"Hard to know a father who spent so much time away from home, Mr. Bogan."

Masson stirred in his chair. "We have a number of passports that belonged to your father. They were under different names. They had many, many entry visas from all over the world. He was constantly on the move."

Jana picked up the drumbeat. "We've been to his Paris residence. It was a little like a fortress. What was he a part of that made him so afraid?"

"You would have to ask my father," Bogan whispered.

"He's dead, Mr. Bogan. He was run down by a truck. It's hard for him to answer under those circumstances."

Bogan's voice stayed at the whisper level. "Then, perhaps, you should talk to my son about all this."

"I think your son may have been involved in your father's murder, Mr. Bogan. That's why we're talking to you first. The man you claim as your son seems to be a very dangerous person. You know that, don't you?"

Bogan bent forward as if he were suffering from a

terrible bellyache, then slowly straightened up, his face haunted.

"Is he in his suite, Mr. Bogan?"

Bogan's eyes said he was. "The last few weeks have been very hard for me," he whispered. "I've been afraid."

"I know." Jana could see the upheaval going on inside the man. All Jana could do for him, at the moment, was to give him a smile of understanding. "You offered to call your son Zdenko. I think that's a good idea. Call and ask him to come over."

The phone was at his elbow. After a few seconds of ambivalence, Bogan reached for the receiver. Jana held out her hand to momentarily stop him from making the call.

"If Zdenko was involved in Klara's murder, you may be setting in motion another attempt, this time against you, if you ask him to come here." She watched his reaction. He stared at her without surprise. He believed his son was involved in the murder of his wife.

"Knowing that," she continued, "why are you here, Mr. Bogan? With your son."

He hesitated, a lost look on his face. His words came slowly. "You stay close to your enemy. If I didn't stay where he could keep an eye on me, he would have killed me long ago. So where else, for me? The police? The banks would come under scrutiny. I go to the police, and everything I have, everything I own, comes tumbling down. Too much in my past; too much now. So, where else for me but here?" He was silent for a moment. "Either way, I'm gone."

"Mr. Bogan, if you don't make the telephone call, he will come for you anyway. Today, tomorrow. Soon."

Bogan gave a resigned nod.

"You have to act, Mr. Bogan. It's the only way we can do anything to protect you. You understand that?"

Another nod.

"What do I say to him?" The words came out of Bogan's mouth as if they were being filtered over sandpaper. "He doesn't listen much to me."

"Tell him that a serious issue has arisen, and that you need to speak to him. If he tells you to come to his suite, indicate that you have papers and other items here that you've set up for him to review. That way he has to come to us. Understand?"

Bogan nodded again. Jana gestured for him to dial, moving the receiver so that she could listen in as Bogan talked. Zdenko Bogan answered the phone after the first ring. He argued for a moment about coming over, telling his putative father that he was busy, reluctantly agreeing to come over only when Oto went through his ruse of having papers for Zdenko to review.

As soon as Zdenko hung up, Bogan began to cry. "I'm sure he didn't believe me. He's the one who handles the paperwork, not me. He'll know I betrayed him; he'll know you're here."

Not good. Zdenko would be coming, but now he would come prepared. Jana pulled out her gun, jacking a shell into the chamber.

"You'll need your gun," she warned Masson.

He took out his gun, cocked the weapon, and the two of them stood on opposite sides of the door, ready for Zdenko to come in. They realized they had made a terrible mistake only when the firing started.

The first two shots hit the older Bogan, driving him back into his chair. The third shot hit Masson, the French detective going down, clutching at his leg. Jana dropped to the floor, rolling and firing back at the gunman, catching a glimpse of him as she rolled. It had to be Zdenko Bogan: he had a large chestnut birthmark on his face.

Jana managed to take refuge behind the end of a large mirrored bureau, waiting out the next few bullets, which shattered the glass of the mirror, all the while hoping she'd get a clean shot at the man. Then there was silence.

The hush was like a silent drum in her ears, driving her to take the next step. She began a whispered ten count just to steady herself, then rolled behind a couch, coming up almost immediately with her gun at the ready.

Zdenko Bogan was gone.

Jana took a zigzag path through the suite in the direction he would have had to retreat, using the shelter of the occasional piece of furniture. Then she saw the open door. It led to the other suite. Zdenko was not in the suite. He would be out of the hotel by now.

Jana hurriedly retraced her steps, angry at herself. They had made a gross oversight. And the older Bogan had failed to correct them. The two presidential suites were connected. Zdenko had simply come in through the joining door instead of the hall entrance, surprising them all.

Masson staggered erect, clutching his thigh, obviously in pain. Jana glanced at him, then checked Oto Bogan. He was dead. As she was checking him, Masson hobbled over.

"I'm your partner. You're supposed to check my health first, not some banker. Or is it because you don't like Frenchmen?"

"Unlike some others, I like the French," she assured him, then rang the front desk and told them to call for an ambulance and the police, giving them as complete a description as she could of Zdenko Bogan, focusing on the chestnut-colored birthmark on his face. All the time she was on the phone, she watched Masson as he stared down at the body of Oto Bogan. The dead man had bled all over the suite's beautiful white carpet.

"Be grateful Zdenko shot Mr. Bogan first," Jana advised.

"His choice of Bogan as the first target gave us the extra second to react. It saved you from a better-aimed bullet."

Masson picked up a napkin that had been left over from the coffee set that had been removed and pressed it over his wound. "That was one hell of a bad relationship. It's not every man who can put a few bullets in his father."

"Oto Bogan wasn't Zdenko's father. He pretended to be his father. My belief is that Zdenko hated Oto Bogan. That has to be why he shot him before trying to kill us."

Masson swayed slightly, catching himself before going down.

"Lie down before you fall down," Jana advised him.

"Never lie down after you've been shot. You may never get up again. I learned that from my first partner."

Masson was true to his word.

When the ambulance came, he was still on his feet, and he insisted on hobbling to it.

Chapter 44

Zdenko Bogan was nowhere to be found in Paris. The French police were all over the city searching for him, but he had gone to ground. All large cities are good places to hide, if you know the right places. And Paris is better than most, with the *banlieues* that daily give sanctuary to thousands of illegal immigrants. But Jana had a hunch that Zdenko wouldn't be hiding in Paris for very long. She thought she might even know where he would run to.

Jana consulted with Masson's supervisors, giving them her conclusions about the evidence that she and Masson had gone over at Jindrich Bogan's Paris apartment; then she put them in touch with the BKA people in Berlin, as well as her own fraud expert. She urged them all to get in touch with the authorities in the countries where the bank accounts containing the enormous hoards of money were. They needed to freeze the accounts until the sources of the caches were determined and legitimate ownership established. The operative word was legitimate, and Jana had absolutely no doubt in her mind that they would find that every cent in those accounts was illegitimate.

Jana called the number she had been given for Henrich Pechy, the man recommended to her by Milan Denka as an expert on the aftermath of World War II in Slovakia.

The man answered the phone without any preliminary civility, an angry tone in his voice: "What do you want?"

Jana introduced herself, indicating that she needed to talk to him about an investigation she was conducting in Slovakia.

"What about?" His voice was even brusquer.

"Have you ever heard of the Rostov Report, Professor?"

Pechy hung up on her.

Jana was not unhappy with the response. It made it clear that she was on the right track. It also made it imperative that she talk to Pechy.

Jana called the airline to arrange for a change in her return ticket. She would now make an interim stop in Frankfurt, rent a car, and drive the two hundred kilometers to the town of Bad Arolsen. The next morning, Jana left Paris and six hours later was parking in the lot of the International Tracing Service in Bad Arolsen.

The ITC was easy to find. It was in a pleasant location, a four-story main building resting among grass and trees, a walk leading to its front entrance lined with hedges, everything well trimmed, the serenity belying the contents of the main building and the four nearby smaller structures. Jana had done a little homework. The buildings housed over fifty million references and documents containing information relating to over seventeen and a half million people who had been victims of the Nazi holocaust—not only Jews, but Poles and Russians and Slovaks and gypsies and Sinti and all of the target populations that had been the casualties of what the gypsies called the *Porrajmos*, the Great Devouring. Its story was packed inside these buildings. If you wanted something from that black era, this was as good a place as any to do the research.

It was also the era that Henrich Pechy was interested in. It didn't take Jana long to track Pechy down. He was in the record stacks in the main building, ensconced in a stall that the ITC had assigned to him for his work. Pechy didn't like being disturbed. He was as abrupt and angry as he had previously been to Jana when she had tried to talk to him by telephone, only agreeing to speak with her when she reminded him that she was a commander of the Slovak Police and told him she would make his life miserable if he didn't talk to her now.

Reluctantly, Pechy showed her to a small glass-walled meeting room that was set aside for visitors. He sat down grumpily, arms folded across his chest, and told her to be quick about what she wanted.

"You're here doing research, Professor Pechy."

"That should be obvious, Commander."

"I've been informed that you're an expert on the end of World War Two and its immediate aftermath in Slovakia, correct?"

"You know that already, or you wouldn't be contacting me. So get on with it."

The man wasn't just angry about being interrupted, Jana concluded: he was truly ungiving and bad-tempered. She didn't envy his students.

"In your research, have you ever run into the names Bogan or Zuzulova?"

He mulled the question over. "Why do you want to know?"

The question was a giveaway. It was now plain that he had information on the families and their history in Slovakia.

"Are they in the Rostov Report?"

"I would like to go back to my work," Pechy growled.

"This is your work, Professor."

"You're wrong. And I can't talk about my work, Commander."

"Has the government told you not to talk about your work, Professor?"

"If I affirm or deny that fact, then I'm talking about my work; so I can't say yes or no without, in fact, talking about it." He had a smirk on his face. "Now may I go back to my work?"

"I have something important to tell you, Professor."

"Oh, yes?" His voice was skeptical, and sarcastic. "The police are now telling me what's important in my field? Have you had any experience or training in what I do?"

The man had a large sense of his own importance. It did not make for an easy interaction. Jana decided to see if Pechy had any information on Jindrich, Zdenko's grandfather.

"What did Jindrich Bogan have to do with events in the Second World War?" Jana asked.

He looked at her without comprehension. The man knew nothing about Jindrich. It would have been Jindrich's father then, as the adult in Slovakia during World War II, whom he had information on.

"Jindrich's father then. As a researcher, what did he do to make you interested in him?" Jana remembered the Hlinka Guard tattoo on Jindrich's arm. "There was a Bogan in the Hlinka Guard, wasn't there?"

Professor Pechy's eyes widened. "There may have been." His voice was uneasy. "Why do you ask?"

"I got on to this topic by investigating a murder case, Professor. Now I'm investigating a *multiple* murder case. One of the victims was Klara Boganova, born Zuzulova. Her husband has also been killed. And a few months ago, Jindrich Bogan. Jindrich had a Hlinka Guard tattoo on his arm."

There was a dawning awareness on Pechy's face.

"Professor, who was the head of the Hlinka Guard?"

"A man named Alexander Mach. A butcher, a fascist, and a thief. Long dead."

The name had not come up in the investigation.

"Who was the number two man in the Guard, Professor?" Jana asked.

"Bogan." The name came out reluctantly. "Tomas Bogan."

"Thank you, Professor. Do you know if he had a son, and if the son's name was Jindrich Bogan?"

"I don't know."

"Easy enough for me to find out later, Professor Pechy." There was probably no reason for Pechy to even consider focusing on Jindrich in his research. She would research the records in Slovakia herself. Jana was sure the records would reveal that Jindrich's father was Tomas Bogan. "And the grandfather of Klara Zuzulova? In the Hlinka Guard as well?"

"Yes. Bogan's chief aide."

Jana had the connection she was looking for. Zuzulova and Bogan had married to maintain the tie between their families. But why was it so important?

"The Rostov Report, Professor," Jana said. "It's the reason I'm here to talk to you. What's the subject of the report?"

"I can't say. The government has tied my hands."

"It's amazing how governments do these things. I think, under the circumstances, that's an improper order by the government. Sometimes good men see that they have to band together, agree to disagree with the government, and risk its wrath by doing the right thing. We have to disobey when we know that to obey them is wrong."

Pechy's face told Jana that he was still set against giving her the information. She would have to bait a hook and dangle it in front of his face.

"I have information that any academic in the world

who was in your position would give half of his teeth
to get. I think it will give your research an impact like
nothing else anyone could offer you. That's your reward
if you talk to me."

Pechy looked interested.

"I guarantee you won't be disappointed, Professor. You
have had a good career so far. The information I give you
will make it a great career."

A flash of avarice on his face. "How do I know you're
not just on a fishing expedition and have absolutely no
information that would be of interest?" he asked.

Jana showed the bait.

"Bank contents, Professor. Accounts dating back to the
end of the Second World War."

The professor's breathing accelerated. He wanted what
Jana had.

"And now, Professor: the Rostov Report."

"I'm uncomfortable with disobeying the government." The man's voice had softened, his distemper
completely gone.

"This stays between us, Professor."

That last assurance worked. The professor started
slowly; then his narrative began to speed up.

"When Communism fell in Russia, the Soviet National
Archives were opened up for research. There were some
limitations, but they were minor in most areas. Unfortunately, the National Archives were vast; they included documents from the entire Soviet empire, and they were badly
indexed. So it has taken years for items to surface. One very
long document, a study, surfaced five months ago."

"The Rostov Report?"

"Yes. Rostov was a colonel in the USSR. He had been
ordered to make an assessment of the paramilitary organizations that had sprung up under the fascist regimes."

"The Hlinka Guard?"

"One of them. All of the pro-fascist regimes developed them. The Ustashi in Croatia, the Arrow Cross in Hungary, Chetniks in Serbia, and on and on. They were violent, brutish fanatics who assisted in the death roundups, confiscating property, lining their own pockets, and lusting after more. But what could they do with what they stole? They needed an approach. Common interests drove them into developing a liaison between the different organizations. And your Bogan was the designated agent who went from country to country, establishing and strengthening the ties between them all. Tomas Bogan had been a banker before he became a member of the Hlinka Guard, so he knew money. And the strongest mutual tie between these organizations was money.

"One day, after the war, the Russians caught up with him. They beat him to death. The question remained: what had Tomas Bogan done when he acted as liaison between the other groups involved in the same crimes the Hlinka Guard was involved with? That was what the Rostov Report explored."

Pechy spent an hour briefing Jana on what was in the Rostov Report.

When he was through, Jana filled him in on what she had learned in Paris. He was ecstatic. He even became polite.

Jana didn't stay long after that. She drove back to Frankfurt and caught a flight to Vienna's Schwechat Airport. Once she had found the letter on the floor of the dead Jindrich Bogan's apartment in Paris, everything else had fallen into place.

Chapter 45

O n the plane to Austria, Jana reviewed Zdenko's letter. "Grandfather, it's time for a reckoning on the accounts. Immediately. I will not tolerate the status quo. The banks are also in the mix. It's over. Now! This has to be at once. Anything less is unacceptable. The present situation is finished. Zdenko."

There was no doubting the urgency in the communication. Or the implied threat. Considering that Zdenko had killed Oto Bogan at the hotel, the threat was a real one. The old man had to have known he was in danger, and he had taken the only precautions he could: he had built himself a small fortress and had armed himself as best he could.

It had not been enough.

". . . a reckoning on the accounts." "The banks are also in the mix." "The present situation is finished." It was all there, if you knew the events surrounding the assertions in the letter.

The only accounts Zdenko could have been talking about were the accounts found in the apartment, the bank accounts with the incredibly large sums of money in them. Jindrich had controlled the accounts. He had been the keeper. And now Zdenko wanted an accounting. And that was not all the grandson was asking for. He surely wanted money, perhaps all of it. The banks were part of the demand. Family quarrels over money and the family business were always the worst of all quarrels. They generally became wars.

Without knowing it, Jana had stumbled into the middle of a battle. Mother dead, putative father dead, putative grandfather dead, all probably by Zdenko's hand or at his order. Klara had, as described by her lawyer, been absolutely ruthless. Like mother, like son. Zdenko had learned at her knee. The empire awaited him. All he had to do was take it. He had not given up trying.

Unfortunately for Zdenko, he needed the accounts' identification credential from his grandfather to get to the sums in the accounts. The question paramount in Jana's mind was: did Zdenko now have the credential in his possession? Jana's instincts told her that he didn't. Its location and the identity of the person in possession of it were probably the keys to the ongoing series of murders.

There was a secondary question: why was Makine involved in this? Surely because of some type of interest in the money. Money was one of the things that drove men like Makine. And, like Zdenko, part of his quest for control had to be over the banks themselves. Yunis had been Makine's ally, and Yunis had run the bank in Berlin. Makine had tried to warn him, as he had tried to warn Bogan on the night of the first attempt to kill him. Which meant Bogan was also Makine's ally, and Yunis's ally. The common thread was the bank.

Which brought Jana to her last question: why had Mrs. Bogan tried to set up the killing of Oto Bogan that evening? For the same reason that Makine had tried to warn him. She was on the other side, perhaps leading the charge. Jana thought of the dead Turk in Bratislava, killed with an ice pick. That was done after Makine learned of the upcoming assassination attempt on Bogan. Makine had killed him in retribution. It was all a mass of murder porridge that was still simmering on the stove.

When Jana landed in Vienna, she immediately went to meet with the Austrian police. The meeting lasted just long enough for her to brief them. The basic plan they developed was quickly agreed on, and everything needed to carry it out was in place slightly less than two hours after that. Surveillance was instituted on the IEB, the bank the Bogans owned, and on the Gumpendorfer address where Radomir Kralik lived. The Gumpendorfer address was supposedly unoccupied, but on the second night one of the surveillance officers saw a light pop on in the window, then pop off again a minute later.

Nobody was supposed to be there.

Someone obviously was.

They called for Jana and the *Einsatzgruppe*, the WEGA special action unit arriving just before Jana did, effectively sealing off the location. It was a very swift, practiced operation, made easier by the fact that its focus was a single apartment floor, which helped the police minimize any threat to the operation or to the building's other tenants.

It was morning. Vienna was waking up. Night is always the best time to storm a location, because everyone is asleep and surprise is a strong factor. But that was not to be. They couldn't wait; they had to go now. Jana shunned the elevator, taking the stairs to the top floor just a moment after the members of the WEGA unit had taken up their positions.

The Austrians welcomed Jana's presence. They were not Slovak speakers, while Jana, as a Slovak native, shared the language with Kralik and Zdenko Bogan. Equally important, she knew the players who they thought could be in the suite. She knew their mindsets and the way they might react. So the Austrians stepped back and let her step forward. Now Jana wanted time to reason out her approach in dealing with the man or men inside Kralik's apartment.

Jana reached the top floor, coming out on the side of the foyer. The police were stationed around the one door leading into the apartment. The setup was both good and bad. There was no back door for the people inside to try to escape through. Unfortunately, there was no other entrance through which the police could come in either; so, if they made a mistake, they would be easy targets. One of the officers had a battering ram. Jana had described the interior of the apartment behind the door in fairly exten-sive detail to the WEGA men, so they knew where to go and what to anticipate in the way of inanimate obstacles when they broke in. Unfortunately, knowing how Zdenko Bogan had responded when Jana and Masson had tried to deal with him in Paris, there was no doubt in anyone's mind that the apartment could dissolve into a free-fire zone at any point in the attempted arrest.

They had the phone number of the apartment, and when Jana was given the signal that they were ready, she dialed it. She let it ring for a long minute, then dialed once more. Again, there was no answer. Jana rang the doorbell, and followed it up by pounding on the door and calling out in both Slovak and German that they were police, telling the occupants to open the door. Again, no response. Jana moved to the next level, signaling to the head of the WEGA unit. With no response, the only option was a direct assault, and within seconds they'd pounded their way through the door, had tossed stun gre-nades into the apartment, and were flooding inside.

No one was there.

Except someone had to be. The officer who had seen

the light come on was adamant, swearing that he'd seen the illumination, pointing to the window he'd observed it in. If the officer had, indeed, seen a light, perhaps there was a logical explanation. If, as Jana assumed, there was someone still in the apartment, the person was hidden, and that meant there was a hideaway room in the suite. That would also explain the light. If someone was occupying a hideaway room at night, he might want to come out to use the bathroom or perhaps the kitchen to get water. All it took to betray his presence was a brief moment, a quick light while the man navigated from one spot to the other.

The window that had shown the light was in the master bedroom suite. Jana lightly tapped on the side wall facing the window, working her way to the wall against which the bed's headboard rested. Immediately next to the headboard she heard the hollow sound she'd expected. Jana then checked along the angle of the wall and along the baseboard. No question. There was a space behind the wall.

The special services men stationed themselves near the hideaway. When they were ready, Jana stood off to the side of the space behind the wall, reached over and knocked loudly to alert whoever was inside. After a pause she called to the man in the room.

"Police! We're here in force. Come out now. If you have a weapon, leave it inside."

Firing began from inside the hidden room, bullets patterning the wall as they came though. Jana was just out of the line of fire. She threw herself farther back so she wouldn't be hit as the police opened up on that section of the wall, their weapons on full automatic.

There is nothing better than automatic weapons for tearing through lath and plaster. Within a minute, the wall was completely shredded, just a few shards of plaster clinging to the edges of the hidden area's entryway. An *Einsatzgruppe* man tossed a stun grenade into the hole just to make sure that the occupant would be momentarily incapacitated if he was still alive. That way, he wouldn't be able to fire at them when they entered. Several of the officers barreled into the hideaway, dragging out the body of a man a few moments later. One of the officers carried out the assault rifle the man had been armed with.

Jana went over the body, searching for identification.

It was Kabil Balder. In a way, Jana was relieved. He was one of the thugs who had been at the meeting with Makine in Bratislava. He had also been Akso's partner in trying to kill her, and, she believed, he had been half of the two-man assassination team, along with Zdenko Bogan, that had killed Klara Boganova. He'd been described by the Turkish informer and Konrad in Berlin as a "safe man." So he was probably one of the men who had broken into the Bogan houses in Bratislava and Hungary. Another man the world would not miss.

The Austrians went through the few items in the hideaway. It was fairly large for a construction of this sort, big enough to have been occupied by another person or perhaps two, but there was no evidence to suggest that there had been more than one person inside it.

Jana questioned the officers who had been on the surveillance watch at the apartment. The light had come from the apartment just before dawn, and they had also seen two men exit the building just before that. Both men had been dressed in suits, both carrying briefcases. The men had looked like professionals, managers of some business or other who were getting an early jump on going to work. The officers had logged the event in their notes, but both thought the two men looked so commonplace, as they phrased it, that they hadn't thought to call it to anyone's attention.

If Balder was in Vienna, Jana was confident that his master, Zdenko, was also in the city. And Radomir Kralik. In Jana's mind, they were the two "businessmen" who had left the apartment together. Father and son had come to pick up the withdrawal authorization document for the money in the bank accounts. Jana checked her watch. Just one hour to wait for the bank to open. Perhaps there was enough time for them to get there and set up their apprehension net before the men could enter the bank.

She quickly discussed it with the Criminal Investigation Department captain and the WEGA commander. If the fugitives were going to the bank, all of them decided that it would be better to try to confront them in the street before they got inside the bank. The Austrians got their officers organized, and they were at the bank in twenty minutes.

The bank was still not open. Jana checked her watch against the hours posted on the door. They had just enough time to deploy a number of officers dressed in civilian clothes around the street. A few minutes after they finished doing that, Zdenko Bogan, the large chestnut birthmark apparent on his face, Radomir Kralik, and Elke Rilke, Kralik's secretary, came walking down the street toward the bank. The only one who looked like she was enjoying herself was Rilke.

Jana signaled the Austrian operations officer, he said a few words into his call module, and the police closed in.

Fortune was not on their side.

Zdenko saw them almost at once, and immediately came out with a gun. The Austrians wasted no time in firing at him. He got off one shot before he was driven to the ground by the force of the bullets. Kralik made the mistake of going down on his knees beside Zdenko, perhaps trying to comfort his son. His intention was ambiguous. And it was his bad luck to be too close to Zdenko's gun for the uneasy officers to take any chances. Kralik was the recipient of a volley of bullets from several of the officers. All the while, Elke Rilke was holding her hands over her ears trying to blot out the sound, adding to it at the same time by screaming over and over again.

They covered the bodies as the bank employees began arriving. As Elke's screams devolved into sobs and tears, Jana tried to comfort her, taking her into the bank accompanied by the Austrian captain in charge of the operation. They informed the bank officials that the bank would have to stay closed until the bodies were removed and their on-scene investigation was complete. The captain, Jana, and Elke sat at Kralik's old desk.

"I know this is a terrible time for you," Jana sympathized with Elke. "You had no reason to think this would happen."

Elke nodded, the shock still evident on her face.

"Zdenko was dangerous. He'd already killed Klara Bogan and his grandfather, Jindrich."

Elke stared at Jana. "He couldn't have."

"We know he did," Jana assured her. "When Zdenko drew a gun and fired at the officers, they had no choice."

Elke shook her head, either trying to deny events or to clear her mind.

"They shot Mr. Kralik," she moaned. "There was no reason to shoot Mr. Kralik. He didn't have a gun."

Jana glanced at the Austrian captain, who looked abashed at the truth of what Elke was saying. Jana tried to smooth over the problem.

"In a gun battle, things often don't go as planned. He looked like he might be reaching for Zdenko's gun. There will be an inquiry, as there is in all shootings. A magistrate will decide."

The Austrian captain looked even more uncomfortable. Jana glanced at him, then went back to Elke.

"When did Zdenko and Kralik get in touch with you?" Jana asked.

"They called me at home this morning. They wanted to take me to an early breakfast. They were very nice to me, both of them. And then, just like three friends, we came to the bank."

"Elke, Mr. Kralik trusted you. Do you have an item in your possession that he asked you to hold for him or for Zdenko? Were you all going to the bank to pick it up?"

Elke was expressionless for a moment, then connected with the question. "Do you mean the package that came yesterday?"

"From Paris?"

"Yes, from Paris."

A few minutes later Elke recovered a large package from one of the bank safe-deposit boxes and gave it to Jana. There was a cover letter with the package, from the syndic, the managing agent for the property that Jindrich Bogan had owned in Paris. The letter was brief, merely stating that they had been informed by the French police that Pascal Dionne was dead and, pursuant to his instructions, they were forwarding the ownership documents for his residence, as well as other documents in their possession, to his next of kin, care of the IEB bank. Jindrich Bogan had provided for his succession.

Jana opened the package. There were two separate parcels inside. The first held the deed for the Saint-Paul property in Paris. The second package was the more interesting. It held an old leather-covered album. In the album were wartime photos of members of the Hlinka Guard in all their glory, parading, herding prisoners, partying, a self-proclaimed elite that was, despite all their pictured grandeur, soon to be consigned to the fires of war.

There was also a list of names of wartime contributors, enumerating the percentages of money and gold they had contributed to their paramilitary organizations' mutual fund. And, the prize in the cake, the authorizing identification document for withdrawals from the accounts listed in the documents found in the Paris apartment. The items of trust in his possession had been delivered to his successors. Unfortunately, his successors had also arranged for his death.

Unknowingly, they had arranged for their own deaths as well.

Chapter 46

Jana arrived in Bratislava on the first train from Austria. She was tired. The wound under her arm was itchy and the scab from the bullet graze under her chin still unsightly, and she found it hard to look in a mirror. Seges met her at the depot in Petržalka. He initially avoided any mention of Em. Then, as if the pressure was too much for him, he launched into a sudden tirade about Em deserting them, not caring that they cared about her, the girl just running off, doing a "gypsy" on them. It went on for some time, Jana initially telling him to shut up, then relenting and trying to be kind to the man by telling him a few white lies.

"Her father called for her to come, and she ran to him because he needed her. Em didn't have time to talk about it with you or to express her feelings. She did what every good daughter would do under the circumstances." It was a bent reality, but there was enough authenticity to it for Jana to sound like she was telling the truth. "Little girls have to go when their fathers call, no matter what else is going on around them."

Seges reflected on what Jana had said, slightly placated. "Yes, that's true." He ruminated for a moment. "I didn't know you met with her after she left us."

"Her father was in Paris. She looked me up."

"Paris? She found you in Paris?"

"Seges, I don't have to tell you how resourceful that girl is. You saw it yourself, over and over again."

"That's true. Em is amazing. Amazing! Did she say anything that I can tell my wife? She's still very broken up about Em leaving. She cries every night. I'd like to go back to her this evening with a few words."

"Em said she loved you both and was sorry that things had turned out like they had. It was sudden, and the way she left bothered her badly. She had hoped it would be different." It was now a bald-faced lie, but Jana had to say something to alleviate the sadness in her warrant officer's face.

Seges lit up instantly, a thankful note in his voice. "So she cared after all?"

"Of course she cared."

"My wife will be very happy."

"Then I'm happy too."

Jana felt the ache inside herself. It was deep. There was no lie someone could tell her to ease the loss. Em had left a scar.

Now that some of his grief had been eased, Seges prattled on about this and that, personnel matters, cases. They were approaching the police building when Seges told her about the father of the young man who had been killed because of the "business" over the woman he'd made pregnant.

The young man's father had sought out the village chief who had ordered the boy killed. They had gotten into a shootout, and the village chief had been killed. The police were currently holding the father.

The news jolted Jana. "And the rest of the family? Have you or anyone else talked to them?"

She remembered them all in her office, crying, desperate

to make some sense out of their loss, and their now-imprisoned father, sweet and caring, trying to ease his family's pain, to find logic in the events, to make logic out of them. He had sought justice and killed a man. Now he was in jail. The latest killing had not helped his son; the son was still dead. And now the family had no father. The world was crazy.

"No loss," said Seges. "Just gypsies fighting it out."

"Seges, a human being has died," was all she could say.

"Yes, Commander."

They reached the police building. Seges thankfully stayed silent while they went up to their offices. Jana immediately called Trokan to brief him on what had happened over the last few days. He asked her to come over to his office, and they spent the next two hours going over the events, Jana taking him through a chronological, step-by-step accounting, spending much of the time tracing the history of the bank accounts. Millions stolen during the war, then banked; with interest over the years, they had become tens of millions, then hundreds of millions.

Jindrich had invested in banks as well, leading to more growth in the funds. And with control of the banks, it was easy for the family to move the money around, to build up their own criminal business outside the purview of the banks, laundering the funds through the banks and reinvesting, facilitating more funds. Money makes money. Banks keep it safe and make more money themselves because of the money banked with them. A simple formula that can't go wrong. Except it had.

When she was through, Trokan had a few questions.

"Why the marriage between Bogan the father and Zuzulova?"

"The son of the number one guy and the number two guy arranged a royal marriage. Royal marriages are to safeguard the kingdom by making sure the heirs don't fight over it."

"It didn't work," Trokan pointed out. "They fought."

"I guess that's why kingdoms keep falling," Jana reflected.

"Why did Zuzulova arrange to kill Oto Bogan at his party?"

"She never loved the man. I think she wanted him out of her way. She had Kralik, and her son. So, no Oto Bogan."

"If she planned it, why was she killed?"

"Zdenko Bogan didn't like his mother. Not many people did. If she was gone, it would all be his. He probably planned it. On the other hand, sitting up there on the catwalk, I don't think he could have resisted it even if he'd planned to kill someone else. The gentleman had a personality disorder."

"A personality disorder?" Trokan asked, not quite believing she had said that.

Jana corrected herself. "A crazy man."

"Very crazy." Trokan reflected. "The family that kills together kills each other, eh?" Trokan laughed at his aphorism, then got serious again. "And where is Makine? Or is he using the name Koba today?"

"I don't know."

"In Paris? Austria? Where?"

"Around."

"And the girl?"

"Around. With him."

"I told you to stay away from her." Trokan preened at the thought of having one up on Jana. "Next time, listen to the wise Colonel Trokan."

"If I'd listened, we wouldn't have solved the case."

He made a rude noise to show that he disagreed, then thought about the latest events.

"The material you found on the accounts? The withdrawal identification document?" Trokan's voice was eager. "That thing is worth a lot of money. What did you do with it?"

"The Austrians have it. They're going to share it with the Germans, and us, and anyone else who needs a peek." She prodded Trokan. "Planning to make a large withdrawal, Colonel?"

"I'd be afraid you might come after me, Jana."

"One of the few things I'm good at."

"You're good at lots of things."

"Thank you." She thought about the accumulation of money over the years. "What a waste. It could have been put to better use."

"A waste," Trokan agreed. "Have you talked to Truchanova yet?"

"That's where I'm going next."

She got up to leave.

"Thank you for the tip on the Rostov Report," she said. "It made sense of everything."

"I'm just a humble civil servant doing my duty. And since I was ordered not to tell anyone about the report, I still haven't told anyone, not even you."

"Naturally, Colonel."

"Have fun with Truchanova."

Jana went back to her office and picked up the smaller package, which the Austrians had let her keep, then drove to the prosecutor's office. Jana walked into Truchanova's outer office and waited while the prosecutor's secretary scurried down the corridor to find her. Truchanova was there a moment later, leading Jana into her inner office and closing the door behind them. They were still wary of each other. Jana laid the package she'd brought from Austria on Truchanova's desk.

"The Austrians thought this had more to do with Slovakia than with them," Jana said.

"They called me."

"Then you know it all."

"If there's anything they missed telling me, I can get it from your paperwork when you write it up."

"I'd like to see a copy of the Rostov Report. I've only been told what it's about."

Truchanova's lips twisted in a moue of refusal. "I can't give it to you until the government authorizes me to let you read it."

"Still ashamed, are they?"

"There's a lot of money at stake. The Germans, the Austrians, the Ukrainians, the Slovaks—they're all being asked to indemnify the victims."

"Still a hush-hush secret, eh? Why? The governments have the money now."

Truchanova stared at Jana, still stone-faced.

Jana opened the package. The album containing the pictures of the uniformed Hlinka Guard was inside. Jana pointed to the photograph on the top. One of the guards was holding a small boy in his arms.

"From what I can make out, the baby is Jindrich Bogan in his father's arms," Jana explained. "You can see the edge of the tattoo on the baby."

Truchanova looked at it. "I can see," she snapped. "Not a very fatherly thing to do to a baby."

"He wasn't a very fatherly type."

Jana was ready to go.

"There's something I'd like you to chew over," she said. "All the things they stole: money, goods sucked up, lives destroyed, the whole lot taken from people who had spent lifetimes just trying to live, protect their families and see their sons and daughters and grandchildren prospering. Now that we have it all, years and years later, we're still ashamed and unwilling to confess what happened."

She walked to the door.

"Thank you for the good work," Truchanova managed to get out.

Jana paused, needing to get the rest of what she was thinking off her chest. She decided to spit it out. She had to make the woman understand.

"When the Nazis still occupied our country, there was a national uprising against them. We lost thousands of men in that fight against fascism. We have no reason to be ashamed because the men in those pictures committed crimes against our people. They stole; we didn't! Tell the world! We still come out ahead. Everyone comes out ahead. Truchanova, don't let the government commit an injustice because they're still ashamed. Stand up. Do your job!"

She left the office.

She drove to Jiri's stamp shop, hoping he had finished his research on the material she had asked him to gather for her. When she walked in, Smid was sitting at the counter waiting on one of his son's clients. Jiri was behind his half-desk, working at the end of the counter. His father called Jiri's attention to Jana's arrival.

Jiri got up, smiling at Jana, and set a paper-wrapped package on the countertop.

"I found tons of material for you, Commander. Reports on speeches Repka gave, articles he wrote. I even found a small movie he made."

"Wonderful."

"This Repka is not a nice man. He doesn't like a lot of people. And the ones he doesn't like, he thinks should get put in a hole somewhere. I think if he had his way, he'd kill all the gypsies."

"That's my impression."

"Isn't he being considered for some type of appointment with the government?"

"Yes."

"What are you going to do with the material, Commander?"

"Make copies of it. Then send it to the powers that be."

She paid Jiri for his work.

"Thank you." Jiri thought about the research he'd done. "What are you going to do if they don't listen?"

"Then I'll send it out to everyone else in the world, the newspapers, television, radio stations. Everyone!"

He stared at her. "I hope it works."

"So do I."

We have to stand up, Jana thought. There are risks, but you have to stand up.

Jana waved a good-bye to Smid, who was still behind the counter, then walked out of the store. She was heading toward her car when someone called from behind her. Jana started to turn around.

"Don't turn around, Commander," said the voice. It was a man, the tone of his voice not threatening, but steely, a dangerous edge to it. She had heard it before. It had been years ago. Only on one occasion, but the memory came flooding back. It was Makine, the man they called Koba. She felt that surge of fear that only a near-death experience can generate. Incongruously, the only thing she could think of doing was to ask a question.

"Which of them were your banks, Makine? Was there more than one?"

"That's not a question that has an answer for you, Commander."

"What does Koba want with me, then?"

"Nothing any more. An associate of mine wanted to say a word."

"Hello, Jana." It was Em's voice. "I want to thank you. You were very nice to me when I was cold and hungry."

"You're welcome, Em."

"Tell Mr. and Mrs. Seges that I won't forget them either."

"I've already thanked them for you, Em."

"If I can, I'll visit."

"I'm sure they'd like that."

Jana waited, expecting further conversation. There was none.

"Good-bye again, Em," she said.

There was no response. They were gone.

Jana walked to her car without looking back. She had work to do. Then she'd call her granddaughter. At least that love was real.

About the Author

Michael Genelin came to writing crime stories quite naturally: He spent many years in the Los Angeles District Attorney's Office. While attending law school at UCLA, he had decided that becoming a trial lawyer, preferably in a criminal law practice, was the direction he wanted to take. He clerked for various civil firms while he was at UCLA, but that merely whetted his appetite for criminal law. Civil law was dull. So, it was natural for him, after graduating and passing the bar, to join an office where he could learn his craft by trying lots of cases. That meant becoming a deputy district attorney.

From a trial lawyer to Head of Trials was a process that taught him about criminal forensics, the art of cross examination, the art of picking juries and criminal investigation and all the small nuances that make a successful practitioner. It also taught him about people. As Head of Trials he not only tried cases, but supervised the successful investigation and charging of thousands of defendants by other deputies. After supervising the Trials Division he was asked to develop the Career Criminal division, while continuing to try many large cases (example: The Sal Mineo Murder case). They prosecuted those cases that involved defendants who had long histories of violent crime and were lifetime criminals. Then, during the height of the gang problem in Los Angeles, he became the Head of the Hard Core Gang Division. As such, during that period, the lawyers in his division investigated, charged and tried 85% of all the murders committed in Los Angeles. To aid in those prosecutions he helped write the Street Terrorism Act, a primary weapon against street crime in California. Thereafter, this legislation was adopted in other states. Because of his contributions to the criminal justice system, he received a number of awards, including The Governor's Criminal Justice Award for Service to California's Citizens. All in all, not bad schooling for writing crime novels.

After leaving the DA's office, he went to work as an international consultant in government reform on a number of projects for the US Agency for International Development, the American Bar Association, the Department of Justice, and the State Department. As such, he worked for substantial periods of time in a number of countries, including Slovakia, Palestine, Nepal, Indonesia, South Sudan, Tanzania, and others. He helped create and rewrite penal codes, codes of evidence, freedom of Information acts, civil service rules, taught trial tactics, homicide investigation and trial prosecution, fraud investigation, and most of all, anti-corruption investigation and trial processes.

As for writing, he sold his first TV shows when he was still in the L.A. District Attorney's office. They were, of course, crime based. He also had a number of plays staged, one of which was produced at the Mark Taper Forum, the premier stage in Los Angeles. As well, he developed a number of motion picture projects which were optioned by major production companies. Later, while serving in Palestine, he turned his attention to writing novels. And, when he moved to Paris, he finished the first of his books, which was published by Soho Press. A number of books later, he finds that he's enjoying the process of writing more than ever.

OTHER TITLES IN THE SOHO CRIME SERIES